THE RIGHT
TIME

By Danielle Steel

The Right Time • The Duchess • Against All Odds
Dangerous Games • The Mistress • The Award • Rushing Waters
Magic • The Apartment • Property Of A Noblewoman • Blue
Precious Gifts • Undercover • Country • Prodigal Son • Pegasus
A Perfect Life • Power Play • Winners • First Sight • Until The End Of Time
The Sins Of The Mother • Friends Forever • Betrayal • Hotel Vendôme
Happy Birthday • 44 Charles Street • Legacy • Family Ties • Big Girl
Southern Lights • Matters Of The Heart • One Day At A Time
A Good Woman • Rogue • Honor Thyself • Amazing Grace • Bungalow 2
Sisters • H.R.H. • Coming Out • The House • Toxic Bachelors • Miracle
Impossible • Echoes • Second Chance • Ransom • Safe Harbour
Johnny Angel • Dating Game • Answered Prayers • Sunset In St. Tropez
The Cottage • The Kiss • Leap Of Faith • Lone Eagle • Journey
The House On Hope Street • The Wedding • Irresistible Forces
Granny Dan • Bittersweet • Mirror Image • The Klone And I
The Long Road Home • The Ghost • Special Delivery • The Ranch
Silent Honor • Malice • Five Days In Paris • Lightning • Wings • The Gift
Accident • Vanished • Mixed Blessings • Jewels • No Greater Love
Heartbeat • Message From Nam • Daddy • Star • Zoya • Kaleidoscope
Fine Things • Wanderlust • Secrets • Family Album • Full Circle • Changes
Thurston House • Crossings • Once In A Lifetime • A Perfect Stranger
Remembrance • Palomino • Love: *Poems* • The Ring • Loving
To Love Again • Summer's End • Season Of Passion • The Promise
Now And Forever • Passion's Promise • Going Home

Nonfiction
Pure Joy: *The Dogs We Love*
A Gift Of Hope: *Helping the Homeless*
His Bright Light: *The Story of Nick Traina*

For Children
Pretty Minnie In Paris
Pretty Minnie In Hollywood

Danielle Steel

THE RIGHT TIME

MACMILLAN

First published 2017 by Delacorte Press,
an imprint of Random House,
a division of Penguin Random House LLC, New York.

First published in the UK 2017 by Macmillan
an imprint of Pan Macmillan
20 New Wharf Road, London N1 9RR
Associated companies throughout the world
www.panmacmillan.com

ISBN 978-1-5098-0030-8

A CIP catalogue record for this book is available from the British Library.

Printed and bound by CPI Group (UK) Ltd, Croydon, CR0 4YY

Visit **www.panmacmillan.com** to read more about all our books
and to buy them. You will also find features, author interviews and
news of any author events, and you can sign up for e-newsletters
so that you're always first to hear about our new releases.

To my very special, much loved children,
Beatrix, Trevor, Todd, Samantha, Nick,
Victoria, Vanessa, Maxx, and Zara,

May you work hard, love well, and be greatly loved,
and may all your victories and accomplishments
be celebrated and appreciated.

Anything and everything you wish is possible,
and good things happen at the right time.
I love you with all my heart and soul,

Mom/DS

Foreword

Dear Friends,

I hope you enjoy *The Right Time*. It touches on a number of subjects I love and care about with the twists and turns in the plot. I always love celebrating the strength of the human spirit, and what people do when faced with seemingly insurmountable challenges in their lives, and how unexpected events can turn disaster or tragedy around. Life presents an unexpected solution for Alex, orphaned and alone in the world at fourteen, by placing her in a convent with a group of very lively, enterprising nuns. Instead of sequestered, she is gently sheltered and then encouraged to step into the world to follow the path she was meant to be on, with courage and a sense of discovery about herself and what the world has to offer her.

I love the fact that Alex follows an unusual path as a mystery writer. I love how hard she works at it. I always enjoy exploring how each of us expresses our particular talents. And I felt a bond with her, because I too began writing when I was very young, and wrote my first book at nineteen. What happens after that can be very challenging, cast into a very adult world at a young age— and beyond that, if fame happens, it presents years and years of challenges and decisions about how one lives with it. It's not an easy life to lead, and no matter how hard you try, you can't hide from it forever. Watching Alex struggle with fame and success, and the price you pay for them, was familiar to me too. Each person lives success differently, and her adventures along the way help her become the person she is destined to be.

Whatever your path in life, you have a talent, whatever it is. How you express it, how you live it, and how you share it with others are unique to you. You have your own special way of dealing with life and the gifts you've been given, whether you hide those gifts or share them openly. I hope you enjoy reading about this talented young mystery writer, and following her story as it unfolds. Victory and success come in many forms and guises, her path is an exciting, fascinating, and rewarding one, and I'm sure yours will be too!

With much love,
Danielle

THE RIGHT
TIME

Chapter 1

Alexandra Cortez Winslow was seven years old, with long straight black hair, creamy white skin, and big green eyes, which she had squeezed shut as she lay facedown on her bed, trying not to listen to her parents argue. Sometimes their fights lasted for hours. They always ended with a door slamming, and then her father would come up to see her in her bedroom and tell her everything was fine.

They had been arguing for an hour this time, and Alex could hear her mother screaming. She had a hot Latin temper, and Alex could remember her parents' arguments for as long as she'd been alive. They had gotten worse in the last year or two, and afterward her mother would be gone for a few days, or a few weeks sometimes, and everything would be quiet for a while when she came back. And then it would start again, like tonight. Her mother had said at dinner that she wanted to go to Miami for a few days to see friends, her father had reminded her unhappily that she'd just been there, and then they sent Alex upstairs. Her mother didn't care who heard them fight, but her father always sent Alex to her room. She put her pillows over her head as she tried not to listen, but you could hear them all over the house. They lived in a residential neighborhood of Boston, and sometimes Alex's friends next door said they could hear them too. Her mother did most of the shouting, and threw things sometimes, while Alex's father tried to calm her down before she broke something or one of the neighbors called the police. That hadn't happened yet, but he was afraid that one day it might.

Carmen Cortez and Eric Winslow had met in Miami when he was there on a business trip. He was the head of a construction firm that built office buildings and specialized in banks. He was there for a job they were bidding on, and had gone to dinner alone at a lively restaurant on the first night of his trip. He had seen a group of attractive young people walk in, and heard them speaking Spanish when they sat down at a table next to his, and a spectacular-looking young woman had instantly caught his eye. Sensing him watching her, she had glanced over and smiled at him. He was a goner after that.

Eric was a sensible man with a quiet life. He had been married to a college professor who had died of breast cancer two years before, after putting up a noble fight. They had no children, and had made a conscious decision not to have any, due to health problems his wife had had all her life. They had never been unhappy about their decision, and accepted it as a reasonable choice for them.

He had done well at his job over the years, Barbara enjoyed her work teaching American history at Boston University, and they loved their home, which felt too large for him without her. He had expected them to spend their golden years together and hadn't anticipated being widowed at forty-eight. That hadn't been in their plan, and once she was gone, he felt like a marble in a shoebox, rolling around, lost at home, as he sat alone reading in his den every night. Everything seemed so meaningless without her. He traveled for business frequently, but there was no one to come home to, no one to tell about the projects he was working on, and he had thought this trip to Miami would be no different. The silence in the house would be deafening when he got back. Their housekeeper, Elena, still came in several times a week and prepared meals she left for him in the freezer, and he put them in the microwave when he got home from work. He had no family, no siblings, no children, and he felt like a fifth wheel now with their friends, and spent most of his nights and weekends alone. His only pleasure and distraction were the crime thrillers he loved to read. He had a bookcase full of them.

He was surprised when a live salsa band started playing at the restaurant during dinner the night he met Carmen, and even more so when she got up and invited him to dance. She was wearing a short, low-cut red dress that clung to her perfect body, and she told him that she was a model and occasional actress. She had come from Cuba at eighteen four years before. They danced for a few minutes, and then with a warm smile she went back to her friends. He had no idea what had gotten into him when he agreed to dance with her, it was unlike him, but she was so dazzling that when she walked over to him, he couldn't decline. She concentrated on her friends after that, and he noticed that they laughed a lot, and he felt faintly ridiculous, but he gave her his business card when he left the restaurant, and told her where he was staying in Miami. He was certain that a woman as vivacious and young as Carmen would never call him.

"If you ever come to Boston . . ." he said, thinking of how foolish he sounded. He was twenty-eight years older than she was, more than twice her age. He realized full well how old he must seem to her and her friends, but he had never met another woman as exciting in his life. She had black hair and green eyes, light olive skin, a tan, and a flawless body. He thought of her all night, and was stunned when she called him at the hotel the next morning, before he left for a meeting. He invited her to dinner, and she told him where to meet her, and he was obsessed with images of her all day.

She looked fabulous when he saw her at the restaurant, wearing a short black dress and high heels. They went dancing after dinner, and then to a bar she suggested, and they talked until four A.M. He was fascinated by her. She explained to him that she was a trade show model, and had dreams of going to L.A. or New York for a big acting career. And in the meantime, since arriving from Havana, she had worked as a waitress, a model, a bartender, and a disco dancer to make ends meet. She spoke excellent English, with an accent, and he thought she was the most beautiful girl he'd ever seen. He was leaving for Boston the next day, but he said if his firm got the Miami project, he'd be back in town frequently. In the end, he returned to Miami two weeks later, just to see her. They had a fantastic weekend, and within a month, he was head over heels in love, and totally besotted with her. It seemed foolish at his age, but he didn't care.

Eric took Carmen to restaurants she had heard of but never been to, and they went for long walks on the beach. And on the second weekend he came to visit her, she stayed at his hotel with him. Eric was a handsome man, with a trim, athletic physique, and she said she wasn't bothered by his age. He was aware of her financial struggles and offered to help her, but she always thanked him and declined. His firm didn't get the project that they'd bid on in Miami, but three months after they started dating, in a moment of impulsive madness totally uncharacteristic of him, Eric asked Carmen to marry him. And she accepted.

They were married by a justice of the peace in Miami. Although her mother couldn't leave Havana, a handful of Carmen's friends were present, and he had arranged for a wedding dinner at the Fontainebleau Hotel, which Carmen loved. At the end of the weekend, Carmen took her three suitcases full of everything she owned and flew to Boston with him for the first time. When they arrived, he carried his exotic bride over the threshold into a world that was totally unfamiliar to her. Her first months were acute culture shock. The weather was cold and gray, and it snowed frequently, which she hated. She was cold all the time, bored while he was at work, and missed her friends. He took her to Miami after a few months to see her pals. They were all envious of her comfortable new life, although dubious about his age. And six months after they were married, Eric and Carmen were both surprised when they discovered she was pregnant. It was an accident, but after careful thought, Eric felt it was a fortuitous one. Having children had never been an option with Barbara's health, but now the idea of a baby delighted him, and he hoped it would be a son to carry on his name. He would teach him to play baseball since he was an avid sports fan, and take him to games. He might even coach him in Little League. He thought a baby would help to bond Carmen to him, since she still felt out of place in his conservative Boston world and had no friends of her own there. She didn't like his friends and found them boring, so they spent their time with each other.

Carmen was considerably less excited about the baby than he was, and didn't feel ready for motherhood at twenty-two. It would shelve her modeling career for a year, although she hadn't been able to get work in Boston, and she had nothing to do all day. Eventually she watched Spanish soap operas on TV until Eric got home from work, and waited for the baby to arrive. It was due in February. And having convinced each other it was a boy, they decorated the nursery in blue. Eric could hardly contain himself he was so excited, and bought a box of cigars to hand out on the big day.

Alexandra was born on the night of a blizzard in Boston. The delivery was worse than anything Carmen had imagined, and than he had feared. The doctor said it was normal for a first labor to be lengthy, and for the delivery to be as rough as it was. Carmen didn't even want to see the baby once it was born. Eric had been in the delivery room with her, and there was a shocked silence when the doctor announced that it was a girl. It took Eric several hours to get over his disappointment, but once he held her, he fell in love with his daughter. Carmen was heavily sedated and asleep by then, and she didn't adjust to the baby as easily as he did. Their housekeeper, Elena, took care of Alexandra when they got home, and all Carmen could talk about was getting her figure back and going to Miami to see her friends. She hadn't been in months, since Eric didn't want her traveling in the last stages of the pregnancy.

Going to a local gym every day and dieting, and as young as she was, Carmen got her figure back quickly, and when Alexandra was three months old, Carmen went to Miami for three days and stayed two weeks, partying with her friends. But she was in much better spirits when she got back. Eric and Elena took care of the baby while she was away.

She made regular trips to Florida every month after that, even worked a couple of trade shows while she was there, and left the baby with Eric. She still had no friends in Boston, and their life was too boring and traditional for her. It became rapidly obvious to him that motherhood wasn't Carmen's strong suit. All she wanted was to be in Miami with her friends. And when Alex was a year old, Eric discovered that Carmen was having an affair with a male dancer in

Miami. He was from Puerto Rico, and she was tearful about it when she confessed and promised it wouldn't happen again.

She had several slips in spite of that and committed numerous indiscretions over the years. She was lonely in Boston, she thought Eric's life was tedious and dull, and so was he. Despite Carmen's behavior, he did everything possible to keep the marriage together, for the child's sake as well as his. He was still very taken with his wife in the early years, until it finally dawned on him when Alex was three years old that Carmen was never going to settle down and didn't love him. She might stay with him for practical reasons, and the perks of his lifestyle, but she wasn't in love with him. Eric's worst fear was that she would take the child and leave him, and he didn't want to lose Alex, or even share custody. He knew that if Carmen left him and took Alex to Miami, it would be an unsavory life for a little girl, among Carmen's loosely behaved friends. Alex was his daughter and he wanted her to live a wholesome, traditional life, not the haphazard, dubious one her mother engaged in as soon as she went back to her old familiar world.

The only way Eric managed to keep the marriage together was by letting Carmen do what she wanted, come and go as she pleased, and he turned a blind eye to her affairs, although he could always tell when there was a new man in her life. She spent all her time on the phone, smiling happily when she got calls from him.

Their fights were fierce and legendary when she was back in town. She drank too much when he took her to business parties, and flirted with every man in sight. She was a very badly behaved young woman, but strikingly beautiful, and every head turned when she walked into a room with him. There was a certain pride for Eric in being with her, but she was a wild free spirit he knew he would never tame, and could barely keep. She flew off at will and returned when it suited her, and neglected their child. She never asked to take Alex with her on her trips to Miami. Carmen was happy to leave her with her father, and he was relieved.

Alex was growing up listening to them fighting, or alone with her father when her mother was away. Eric took wonderful care of her, with Elena's help. The housekeeper was like a loving grandmother to the child. She strongly disapproved of Carmen, and spoke to her harshly in Spanish. She spoke Spanish to Alex as well, as did Carmen. Alex was fully bilingual by the time she was three, and an adorable, loving child. She adored her father and loved her mother, but she also knew that she couldn't rely on her mother. She could always count on him.

Eric took Alex to school in the morning, and Elena picked her up after school, even when Carmen was in town, while she went shopping, got her nails done, or spent hours on the phone with her friends in Florida. It was as though she wasn't really there when she was in Boston with them. Alex tried to do little things for her mother, to make her happy, so they wouldn't fight as much, but it never changed anything. Sometimes Alex thought that if she tried to be really, really good, her mother wouldn't get so mad at them, but she did anyway. It was obvious even to Alex that her mother hated being there.

The fight that had driven Alex to hide under her pillows was no different from all the others, but it took a long time for the arguing to stop, and finally she heard the familiar door slam that meant it was over for now. She had seen her mother pack a suitcase that afternoon, and could guess where she was going. And a few minutes later, her father came up the stairs and opened the door to her room. It was still painted pale blue, and she knew why. Her father had told her that he had been foolish enough to want a little boy before she was born, and had no idea then how lucky he was to have a little girl instead.

He had started taking her to baseball games with him when she was five, and taught her about the players and the rules of the game. She knew more about baseball than most boys did, and he had been pitching balls to her in the backyard for years. He bragged to his friends that she was a good little hitter, had great hand-eye coordination, could hit a ball harder than any kid, and had an amazing pitching arm.

Eric always read to her at night before she went to sleep. He was addicted to spy stories and crime thrillers, and he encouraged Alex to read in her spare time. They'd been through all the classic stories for children her age, *Charlotte's Web, Stuart Little,* the Winnie-the-Pooh books when she was younger, and *Anne of Green Gables.* He had recently started her on Nancy Drew books, although she was a little young for them, but she loved them. Reading was her escape from the tension between her parents and her mother's bad moods. Books were her friends.

She was already on her second Nancy Drew book, and her father read her a chapter every night. She loved the mysteries Nancy solved, and how keenly observant she was.

"Ready for some Nancy Drew?" he asked with a smile as he walked into the room and Alex emerged from under her pillows with tousled hair and wide eyes, and nodded.

"Did she go away?" Alex asked in a constricted voice.

"She'll be back in a few days," he said reassuringly. Alex knew that was true, although she always worried that one day she might not come home. Her mother was a difficult person, she got angry a lot, and she didn't like reading stories or playing games, but she was still her mother, and sometimes she put nail polish on Alex's toes, which she liked a lot. Once her mother had put gold polish on her, and she had taken off her socks and showed her friends at school.

Eric took out the book from the bookcase in Alex's room, and they settled onto her bed next to each other, against the pillows. They had started with *The Hidden Staircase,* and he told Alex they were written a long time ago, but were still very good. They were reading *The Secret at Shadow Ranch* now, which Alex was really enjoying. She loved the way her father read them to her, with lots of drama in his voice. He made the story sound really exciting.

He put an arm around her as they sat on the bed, and they read two chapters before she had to go to sleep. She had school the next day. As he finished reading, Alex looked up at him with her big green eyes.

"Do you think she'll call from Miami?"

"I'm not sure," he said honestly. Carmen was hard to predict, and sometimes she seemed to forget them entirely. Most often she did.

"Was she really mad when she left?" Alex asked softly, worried. He nodded, trying not to look upset about it, but she knew he was. It was like living on the side of a volcano, and hard on them both.

"Do you want to go to spring training with me?" he asked, to distract her. It was fun going on trips with him, and he had taken her to the Red Sox's spring training once before. She nodded and smiled at him.

She changed into her pajamas, brushed her teeth, got into bed, and he tucked her in, kissed her, turned off the light, and then stood in the doorway for a minute.

"Everything's going to be all right, Alex. It always is. Mommy will be happy when she comes home." But not for long, Alex knew only too well. "Sleep tight, I love you," he said, as he did every night.

"I love you too, Daddy," she said, and closed her eyes, thinking of

Nancy Drew and the mystery she was trying to solve in the book they'd read that night. Nancy Drew was so smart, and always figured everything out, as if she had magical powers. Alex wished she had those same powers to know when her mother would come back. Maybe by the time they finished reading the book.

Chapter 2

Eric and Alex followed their usual routine the next day. Carmen's departure for Miami the night before didn't change much for them. She never got up in the morning, and Eric always let her sleep late. He cooked Alex's breakfast of oatmeal, toast, and bacon, and on the weekends he made pancakes or eggs. Elena left dinner for them when she went home at night. Carmen had never tried to learn to cook. Her repertoire included a few Cuban dishes that were too spicy for Alex, and Eric didn't like them either.

He made Alex's lunch and put it in her Wonder Woman lunch box with a snack. Pattie, their neighbor, was picking her up after school, and Alex was going to their house to play. They had four children, two older and two younger than Alex, and Pattie often brought Alex home with them. Alex liked going to their house, there was always something to do. Her own house was so quiet until her dad got home. He picked her up at Pattie's on the way, and then they went back to their house to eat the dinner Elena had left for them. They had a whole system worked out, and Carmen's absences didn't alter anything, except that Alex was subdued when her mother was away. She was always worried about when she would come back.

"How is she?" Eric asked Pattie in an undertone, when he got to their house to pick her up that night. The two boys were chasing each other, and he could hear the TV blaring in the playroom downstairs while Pattie cooked dinner. Her husband was a lawyer and worked late a lot of nights. She was a nice woman and Eric was grateful for her help.

"She seems okay, a little quiet." But they both knew that wasn't unusual for Alex, who was an introverted child. She liked being with other children, but as an only child who spent a lot of time with her father, she was more accustomed to the company of adults. "But she always is when Carmen's gone."

Pattie guessed correctly that it had to be stressful for Alex, even though she didn't say much about it. But Pattie and her husband had heard Carmen and Eric's fights on warm nights when the windows were open. It wasn't a happy atmosphere for a child. Pattie had never hit it off with Carmen, who had no interest in getting to know other mothers, organizing playdates, or inviting Alex's friends to their house. She seemed more interested in herself than anyone else, including her daughter. And she didn't look or act like anyone's mother. Pattie was considerably older. Carmen was only thirty then but didn't look it. She acted and dressed more like twenty, and was a pretty girl. Pattie couldn't help thinking Carmen and Eric were an odd couple, and it was easy to see that he had been dazzled by her looks, married her in haste, and lived to regret it. Their eight-year marriage had been turbulent and troubled from the first, which was no secret in the neighborhood. And Elena gave Pattie an earful, whenever she was willing to listen, which she tried not to do often.

She didn't want to intrude, but she was happy to help with Alex whenever she could. She felt sorry for the little girl.

Eric and Alex went home then, and he warmed up dinner while she did her homework at the kitchen table. She took a bath on her own after dinner, and her father helped her wash her hair. He told her he had gone to the bookstore that day and picked up some new books by his favorite writers, and they were going to read her Nancy Drew book again that night.

They spent two weeks following all their usual routines, waiting for Carmen to come home. She didn't call at all this time, but she'd done that before, usually when she was involved with a new man. But to Alex, Eric pretended not to be concerned. Finally Carmen called him at the office, because she knew it was hard for him to talk around their daughter, and she had something important to tell him and didn't want to be the one to tell Alex.

He was distracted when he picked up the phone.

"I'm not coming back," Carmen said in a flat voice.

"This week?" He assumed that was what she meant.

"Never," she said simply. "I can't do it anymore. I wasted my best years in Boston. I don't know how you stand it. It's the most boring city in the world." Or maybe it was just his life, or him, but she had grown up with the music and lively Caribbean atmosphere of Cuba, where people talked and laughed and danced and drank rum. It was a sensual world. When she was with Eric in Boston, she felt dead. Miami felt like the center of the universe to her.

"You're staying in Miami?" He was worried and sad about it, but not surprised. He had feared this happening for years. In some ways it would be a relief to him from the constant fighting, but an agony for their little girl.

"For a while. I got booked for two trade shows, and I met someone who said he can set me up with an agency in Vegas, and I can find modeling work there all the time." Probably topless, but she didn't mind.

"That's not a wholesome place for a child," he told her seriously. He didn't want his daughter growing up in Las Vegas, not with the kind of people Carmen hung out with. Her plan was worse than he had envisioned in all the years he had worried about her leaving. He wasn't in love with her anymore. Living with her was just too difficult, but he didn't want to lose Alex, even half the time, if they shared custody. This was his worst nightmare come true. His heart had skipped a beat when she told him what she wanted to do, and he didn't think he could stop her.

"I'm not taking her with me," Carmen said, without any sign of regret. "She's better off in Boston with you. She can come to visit me when I get settled. I'll see how I like Vegas, or I might go to L.A. You're right, it's no life for a kid. And I need to be free."

She knew herself well, and as far as Eric was concerned, she had been as good as free for years. She had never really acted like a wife to him. Their sex life had been fabulous at first, but once that cooled down after the baby, she acted like a stranger. She couldn't wait to leave at every opportunity, and they hadn't had sex with each other in almost five years. She had made it seem like an obligation for two years before that. The fire had gone out of their marriage within a year. It had been a colossal mistake. He had been a fool to marry her and he knew it. She was almost thirty years younger, hated everything about his life, and their marriage was a farce.

"Maybe I'll come to visit her sometime," Carmen said vaguely, as his heart ached for his child. However irresponsible a mother Carmen was, Alex still had some illusions about her. She was the only mother Alex had, and the child loved her.

"You're welcome to visit whenever you want. She's going to miss you," he said sadly. "Having just a father is not the same."

"You're better with her than I am," Carmen said honestly. "I felt like I was in prison when I was at home with the two of you."

"I know, but that's not going to be easy for her to understand." And then he asked her the question on his mind. Although it no longer made any difference, he was curious why she was leaving now. "Is there someone else?"

She hesitated for a long time, and then answered, "Yes, I guess there is. It's probably not serious, but we have a good time together. He's got connections in Vegas and L.A.," which was something Eric couldn't offer her with his quiet, mundane existence. He had hoped to give her stability and provide a good life for her, but nothing about his life was appealing to her, not even their child. She just didn't seem to have it in her to be a mother. She was too selfish and immature and wanted to be part of a flashy world, and there was no place in it for Eric or Alex. "I want a divorce," she said, adding the icing on the cake. "I'm done." He didn't expect her to come back, but he'd thought she'd wait a while before asking for a divorce. It was a lot to tell Alex all at once, and he wondered if he should, or tell her that part later. "You can have full custody," she added. That much was good news to him, it was what he had always wanted if she left for good.

"Thank you. Do you want any kind of regular visitation?" He hoped not, but thought it only fair to ask. She was definitely off and running with her own life, with no regard for him or their daughter. She wasn't evil, just a totally irresponsible person, which he couldn't explain to a child of seven, although in her own way, Alex knew it.

"No, let's just see how it goes until I get settled. I'll let you know where I am." And then she broached a delicate subject, not sure how he'd react, although he'd always been generous while she lived with him. "Could I have some kind of support, like for a year or two, until I get a good job?" He hesitated, but she was his child's mother. He respected that even if she didn't.

"Yes. We'll figure it out, as long as it's a reasonable amount."

"Are you going to call her?" he asked, sounding worried. He thought she should. She couldn't just disappear out of their daughter's life, and he was afraid now that she would.

"Thank you for the support money. I'm not going to call her for a while. Why don't you explain things to her for now?" Carmen said, knowing she could count on him and escape her responsibilities entirely. He hadn't expected her to be this extreme, and to sever her ties with them almost completely, and he knew he was right to assume it was about a man. "I'll let you know where to send the check," she said blithely.

"You should call her from time to time," he urged the woman who no longer wanted to be his wife, or even Alex's mother.

"Yeah," she said vaguely, "I'll try . . . and Eric . . . I'm sorry . . . I just couldn't do it. It was killing me." He almost felt sorry for her when she said it, because he knew it was true. It was killing him too. After eight years of torture, he felt dead inside.

"I know," he said in a low tone. And now their daughter was the one who would be hurt, essentially losing her mother at seven. She wouldn't understand that it had to do with her mother and what she was incapable of doing, and not with anything Alex had done wrong. Those were complicated, subtle concepts for a child her age.

After he hung up, he sat staring out the window, thinking about the conversation. He knew he shouldn't have been surprised, but he was in a way. It had gone badly for so long that he was used to it, and hadn't really expected it to change for better or worse, although he had known in his heart of hearts that she might leave one day. And now she had. At least he no longer had to dread it, or fear he would lose Alex.

He left work early that day and picked Alex up at school himself. He called Pattie to let her know, and she heard an odd tone in his voice immediately.

"Is something wrong?" She liked him and thought he was a good father and compensated well for Carmen's failings with the child.

"No . . . yes . . ." He took a breath. "Carmen wants a divorce."

"Is she back?"

"No, she's in Miami. She's thinking about moving to Vegas or L.A. I guess she has a new man in her life. But it was only a matter of time before she did this anyway. I hoped she'd wait till Alex was older, but she's made up her mind. She's not coming back."

It dawned on him that she hadn't asked him to send her clothes. Maybe she didn't want the respectable things she wore in Boston. Maybe she wanted to throw away everything about that life, including him and their daughter.

Pattie had expected it for years, but she sounded worried. "Does she want custody?"

"No, she's giving me full custody." Pattie was relieved as soon as he said it. "I'm glad, but it's going to be tough on Alex. Being abandoned by your mother at her age is a lot to try to understand."

"Let me know if there's anything I can do," Pattie said kindly.

"We'll be okay," he said as much to reassure himself.

"I know you will. But Alex may react to it for a while." She was young for such a major blow, even though Pattie had always felt that Carmen was an inadequate mother, and she had proven it to all of them now, without a backward glance.

Eric was waiting outside school in his Volvo station wagon when

Alex got out with the others. She didn't see him at first, and then he called out to her and waved and she ran toward him and got into the car. She looked at him solemnly for a moment, and a sixth sense told her what he hadn't said yet. He was still searching for the right words to break the news.

"Mom's not coming back, is she?" she said immediately. She could read it in his eyes. He hesitated, and then he nodded. There was no escaping the truth, and he didn't want to lie to her. In some ways it was like a death, except she'd said she would come back for a visit one day, but he didn't want to promise that either, knowing Carmen as he did. She was unreliable and flighty and might not even miss Alex. Out of sight, out of mind. "Will I ever see her again?" Alex said, white-faced with a look of panic.

"Yes," he said clearly, "but I don't know when. She doesn't know where she's going to live, but she said you could come to visit when she settles down, or maybe she'll come to visit here."

"Will I live with you?" Alex asked, as tears filled her eyes for a woman who had never been a mother to her, but she loved anyway.

"Of course. You're stuck with me forever," he said as he leaned over and put his arms around her. "I love you. Mom just needs her own life, that's the way she is. It's not about you or anything you did wrong or could have done differently." He wanted desperately to get the point across to Alex, and hoped he was.

"I know," Alex said bravely, wiping the tears off her cheeks as he started the car. "Maybe she wasn't ready to be a mom." She was trying to find a reason why it hadn't worked out, for either of them.

"Maybe. But we have each other, Al. We're going to do fun things together, read lots of books, go to baseball games, we can take some trips."

"Can we go to visit Mom, wherever she is?"

"Sure," he said as he drove home. "And for now, let's read all the Nancy Drews, the whole series. How about that?" Even at her age, she knew what he was doing, he was trying to make the best of it and cheer her up. She smiled at her father and nodded.

"I'd like that. And then can I read some of your mystery books?" She knew how much he enjoyed them, and he told her about them sometimes.

"Maybe when you're a little older." He listed all the things they were going to do together in the immediate future and the coming months, and tried to make her mother's defection sound like an opportunity and a blessing.

"Are you getting divorced?" She startled him with the question. "Sally Portman's parents got divorced last year. Now she spends weekends and Wednesday nights at her dad's."

"I think that could happen, not the weekends and Wednesdays, but maybe Mom and I will get divorced since she doesn't want to live here with us anymore."

Alex nodded sagely, trying to absorb it. "Do you think she'll get married again?"

"I don't know," he said honestly.

"Will you?"

He laughed at the question. "I don't think so, Miss Alex. Let's just concentrate on each other for now. We can't solve all the mysteries at once." She had taken the news well, even though he knew she was very sad about it. They finished *The Secret at Shadow Ranch* that night. Alex loved the way it turned out, and the book suddenly had new meaning to her. As she listened to her father's voice tell the story, she realized now that she lived alone with her father, just like Nancy. Nancy Drew didn't have a mother either. Maybe one day she and her father could solve mysteries too. She wondered what had happened to Nancy Drew's mom.

"You never know how a mystery is going to end," she said thoughtfully when they finished the last page, but she had guessed the ending, or almost. She liked trying to figure it out along the way, and she was good at it.

"Life is a little bit like that too. Always full of surprises, sometimes good, sometimes not so good," her father said quietly.

"I like the guessing part," she commented.

"So do I," he said, as he kissed her good night and tucked her into bed. "That's why I like mystery books so much."

She nodded, and he left the room after he turned off the light. She lay in bed, not knowing where her mother was and if she missed her at all, and if she was thinking about her. Two tears slid down her cheeks and into her pillow. Wondering when she would see her mother again, she said a little prayer for her and then drifted off to sleep, and dreamed of Carmen. She looked beautiful in the dream, and she had come back to live with them. She hoped her mother would too one day.

Chapter 3

Carmen filed for divorce a month after she called Eric, and he didn't tell Alex. She didn't need to know the technical details of the end of their marriage. She asked for a small amount of support for two years, and he agreed to give it to her, as he had on the phone. She wasn't after money. Her freedom meant more to her. She was still in Miami when she wrote to him, she still hadn't called Alex, and she said she was leaving for Las Vegas soon. Eric knew that if he was sending her money, he could keep track of where she was. For Alex's sake, he didn't want her disappearing, in case they needed or wanted to get in touch.

Two months later, she wrote to him from Las Vegas to give him her new address.

Alex was doing well, and had gotten over the initial shock of her mother not coming back. He wondered if she had expected it too. Both her teacher and Pattie reported that she was a little less chatty than before but seemed okay, which was his impression at home too.

They went to a dude ranch in Wyoming that summer, and Alex loved riding the horses and going to the rodeo. Once in a while, he remembered how much he had wanted a son before she was born, but she was loving and affectionate and there was nothing she couldn't do. She loved baseball, she loved the books he selected for her, and she was good at sports. Her teacher said she had a gift for writing, and when they got back from Wyoming, Alex told him that she thought she might like to write books one day. She was eight and going into third grade, and they had heard nothing from Carmen since she wrote from Las Vegas.

"Do you think I could write mystery books when I'm grown up, Daddy?" She looked very intent when she asked him.

"You could," he said thoughtfully, "but most of the big mystery writers are men. It's a kind of book that men usually write. And in the case of the tougher thrillers and spy stories I like to read, it's a style that men are naturally good at. Personally I don't like to read mysteries written by women. I never do. So if you're going to write mystery books, you'll either have to write 'cozy' mysteries, like a woman called Agatha Christie, or if you write crime stories like I and a lot of men read, you should probably do it under a man's name." He sounded serious about it, and she was sure that he knew everything about mysteries because he read so many of them. It was all she ever saw him read.

"You mean I'd have to pretend to be a man?" She was startled by that idea, and he nodded. "Like wear a fake mustache and men's clothes?" He laughed at her interpretation of it.

"You might look cute in a fake mustache," he teased her. "No, I meant you could write them using a man's name, so people think a man wrote them. There are some very good female mystery and crime writers, but I like male crime writers better myself. But you don't have to wear boys' clothes," he said, and she seemed relieved.

"Why wouldn't they read them if they knew I was a woman?" It made no sense to her, although she trusted whatever her father told her.

"Because in most cases, men write thrillers and women don't." He spoke with conviction on the subject.

"That's silly, Daddy. I bet women could write them too."

He shook his head and seemed convinced.

"Then I'll use your name if I write when I'm older, and people will think it's you." She laughed at the idea, but she was impressed by what he'd said, and wondered if it was true. Her father was usually right about most things. And she liked the idea of writing books in his name. It sounded like fun to her, especially if it would make women and men want to read her books.

It was many months later when they finally heard from her mother again. She had been gone almost a year by then. Eric got a postcard from her saying that her boyfriend had some work to do in New York, and they were driving from Las Vegas, and would stop in Boston to see Alex. The divorce wasn't final yet, and Eric didn't tell Alex about her mother's visit. He didn't want to raise her hopes and disappoint her if in the end, she changed plans and didn't show up.

Carmen called the house late one night, and Eric answered. Alex was sound asleep.

"We just got to town," she said in her familiar voice.

"Where are you staying?"

She mentioned a cheap motel outside the city. "Can I see her tomorrow?"

It was Friday night, so Alex didn't have school the next day. But even if she did, Eric would have kept her home to see her mother. It was too important not to. And he was sorry now that he hadn't warned Alex that her mother was coming to town.

"Of course. She's going to be thrilled to see you. How long are you staying?" He wondered whether seeing her mother would disrupt or upset her, but either way, he thought Alex should have a chance to visit with Carmen. It had been too long. And Alex talked about her from time to time, and said she missed her, hoped she was okay, and that she'd call. And now she was here. He hoped it wouldn't be a shock.

"We're going to New York tomorrow. I'm just here for the day," Carmen said blithely.

"Do you want to pick her up after breakfast?" he offered, and Carmen hesitated for what seemed like a long time.

"Why don't I just come to the house?"

He wasn't anxious to see her, but he thought it might be easier for Alex that way. After nearly a year of total silence, her mother would feel like a stranger.

"Whatever you like," he said politely, and she said she would be there at ten o'clock and they hung up.

He woke Alex the next morning, which he didn't usually do on Saturdays, but he wanted to give her time to get ready and get used to the idea.

"Your mom's in town," he told her after she was fully awake.

"Here? Now?" Alex looked like he had said it was Christmas.

"She's on her way to New York. She's coming to see you after breakfast." Alex grinned broadly and bounded out of bed.

"I want to wear my new dress," she said, diving into her closet and emerging with a soft pink velvet dress and black patent leather shoes she'd bought on a shopping trip with Pattie. She brushed her long dark hair until it shone, washed her face, and put on the new dress and shoes. She was ready by nine in the morning, too excited to eat breakfast, and sat in the living room, waiting for her mother. She never moved from the spot, and Carmen showed up at noon, prettier than ever in jeans, a tight tee shirt, a black leather jacket, and high heels. Eric opened the door to her, and saw that there was a man standing behind her. He looked seedy and nervous and told Carmen he'd wait for her in the car. He seemed uncomfortable as soon as he saw Eric, and never met his eyes. He appeared to be about twenty-five years old, at most. And Eric felt like their grandfather as he ushered Carmen inside. He didn't say that Alex had been waiting for her for two hours, but he was annoyed that she wasn't on time.

Alex jumped to her feet the moment she heard her, barreled through the living room, threw her arms around her mother, and gazed up into Carmen's face, expecting to find everything there that she had felt herself for the past year. Carmen was as uncomfortable as her boyfriend had been, and out of place in the formal living room that had been her home for eight years. She looked almost like a lost teenager now.

"Wow! You've gotten so tall!" she said, as Alex held her tight around her waist, and Carmen slowly put her arms around her, as though she were a stranger and not her child. "Let me see you," she said, as she pulled away. "You're still beautiful," she said, smiling at her daughter.

"So are you," Alex said with awe. She had forgotten how striking her mother was, and how young.

Eric offered food and drink, and Carmen declined. "I just had breakfast, and we have to get on the road soon. Vince has to be in New York by six o'clock."

"Who's Vince?" Alex asked, as her face fell at the news that her mother was leaving soon, after so long. It was a five-hour drive to New York. Eric knew from what she said that they couldn't stay for more than an hour. Alex seemed crushed.

"He's my boyfriend. He's an actor and a dancer. We're going to California together. He has connections there," all of which meant nothing to Alex, but told Eric that she was still chasing rainbows and as rootless as ever.

"What are you going to do in California?" Alex asked, her huge eyes drinking her in, so she could remember every detail after she left.

"Maybe I'll be in a movie." Carmen grinned at her. "Then you can see me on the screen."

"I'd rather see you in real life," Alex said sadly, and there was silence in the room. Eric left them alone, but was nearby in the kitchen, in case Alex needed him. "I missed you," Alex added, and Carmen didn't say anything for a minute.

"I missed you too. But Vegas was a lot of fun." It was everything Alex didn't care about or want to hear. She wanted to know that her mother had thought of her all the time, which was clearly not the case.

"Are you doing well in school?" Carmen didn't know what to say, and didn't notice the new dress and shoes, or that Alex had dressed up for her.

The visit went by awkwardly, and before the hour was over, Carmen stood up and said she had to go and that it was nice seeing her, as though they were old friends. When Eric heard the front door open, he emerged from the kitchen to say goodbye. And all he could see was his daughter's devastated face as her mother was leaving. She threw her arms around her waist one last time at the door, until Carmen squirmed free, kissed the top of her head, and said she had to go. A moment later she was gone, as Alex shouted "I love you!" after her, just before the front door closed. There was no response, and they heard the car drive away seconds later, as Alex began to sob and melted into her father's arms. He led her to the couch and they sat down, as he held her and she cried. It nearly broke his heart, and for the first time he genuinely hated his ex-wife for what she was doing to their child, inflicting wounds he couldn't heal that were bound to leave scars forever, while Carmen callously pursued her own life, with total disregard for anyone else. It would ring in Eric's ears forever that Alex had called after her "I love you!" at the front door, and Carmen didn't answer. She just waved without looking back and ran to the car where her boyfriend was waiting.

"She didn't say when she'd come back," Alex sobbed, or say that she loved her, he wanted to add but didn't.

"I don't think she ever knows her plans," he said, fumbling for words of comfort he couldn't find instead of the hatred he was feeling for Carmen. "She was happy to see you, though," he said lamely.

"Why couldn't she stay longer?" It was a sad wail.

"She had to get to New York."

It took Alex hours to calm down after the visit, and weeks to get over the pain it had caused her. Even more than when Carmen had left them, Alex felt abandoned by her mother. She was older now, more aware, and felt it more acutely. Carmen vanished into the mists again without a word. There was no phone call to say how much she had loved seeing her, nor was there a promise to return.

A month later, she sent Eric her address in L.A., for him to send her monthly checks, but Alex didn't hear from her again.

Six months later, Eric got a call at midnight from someone who said he was a friend of Vince. He said they'd been in an accident on the freeway, were hit by a drunk driver, and Carmen and Vince had both been killed. He thought Eric should know, but didn't have any more details.

Eric sat for an hour afterward, staring into space, trying to feel something for her, but he didn't. All he could think of was Alex. Her mother had been so agonizingly insufficient, and now she was dead. It brought finality to it, but Alex was too young to lose her mother at nine. In truth, she had never really had her, and Carmen had left them for good almost two years before, and Alex had only seen her once since.

He waited two days to tell Alex, on a quiet rainy weekend. He didn't want to do it at night, so he shared the bad news after breakfast and knew he would never forget the ravaged look on her face.

"It's not true! You're lying!" Alex shouted at him, then ran up the stairs to her room and slammed the door. He found her on her bed, her head beneath the pillows, sobbing, and it took her hours to calm down. They went for a walk together, and later when she was in bed, he called Vince's friend in California, and asked about funeral arrangements. Eric wanted to bring Carmen home and bury her next to his first wife, so in later years Alex would know where her mother was. He didn't want her buried in California in some un-marked grave. The friend gave him the pertinent information, and he called the funeral home the next day and made the arrange-ments. They said Vince's body was being sent to his parents in San Diego. But no one had called to claim Carmen. She had no relations that he knew of. Her mother in Havana had died after they got married.

After Eric's call, Carmen's body would be in Boston in a few days, for burial. He didn't tell Alex any of it, and the day after he'd told her of her mother's death, she handed him a poem she had written for her. It was beautiful and loving and brought tears to his eyes, to think that the woman who had done so little for her had elicited so much love from the child she'd abandoned. It was more than she deserved, and almost more than he could bear.

Chapter 4

Although Alex had always been close to her father, especially since they'd been alone, Carmen's death brought them even closer. In time, Alex seemed to recover from the shock of losing her mother. Now she no longer had any dashed hopes or expectations of seeing her again, and there was a kind of unspoken closure.

She was reading more than ever. She had graduated to slightly more adult books recently, after finishing the entire Nancy Drew series several months before. Her father had given her some of the gentler "cozy" mysteries, like Agatha Christie, and now Alex was hooked on them. She loved Miss Marple and Hercule Poirot, who solved the mysteries, while she tried to figure them out before they did.

She had also been doing a lot of writing. Her fourth grade teacher said she had real talent for writing poetry and haikus. And in fifth grade, she won an English prize for a short story she'd written. It was a very poignant story about a little girl whose mother had been killed. And in sixth grade, two years after her mother's death, her English teacher, Mr. Farber, called Eric at his office and asked him to come to a meeting at school the next day. The teacher sounded grave, as though Alex had done something terrible, which was hard for her father to imagine since she had never been in trouble at school. He didn't want to say anything to her about it that evening, until he heard the full story from the teacher.

He went to the meeting with trepidation, and with a somber face, the teacher handed him six pages to read, covered in Alex's laborious eleven-year-old handwriting.

"I felt that it was important for you to see this, Mr. Winslow. My colleagues and I find it very disturbing." Eric wondered if Alex had written something shockingly inappropriate, possibly even a hate letter to one of her teachers, or a diatribe about her motherless home life. He was frightened as he began reading after seeing the expression on her teacher's face. He couldn't imagine what Alex had written that upset her teacher to that degree. But as he read, he found himself absorbed into a story. She had written it with surprising skill given her age, and a very distinct style all her own.

The first page laid out the characters and initial premise of the story. And by the second page, he was hooked, and wanted to know more. All appeared to be going well by the end of the second page, and on page three she described a gory and terrifying murder, which was pure crime thriller. On the following page, she introduced an intriguing police detective, with a visible sense of humor, despite the horrifying crime. She unveiled several unforeseeable surprises on the fifth page, and on the final page she tied it all together, exposed the murderer, whom one would never have suspected—even Eric didn't—and sent everyone to jail. It was a brilliant piece of writing and construction for anyone, let alone a child her age, and Eric was grinning proudly as he handed it back to the teacher, thinking he had brought Eric in to congratulate him on his daughter's writing talent. Their frequent conversations about the crime thrillers he loved to read had obviously paid off and inspired the story.

"Do you realize how shocking it is for a girl of eleven to write something like that?" Mr. Farber said sternly in an accusing tone. "How she can even imagine violence of that nature is something for a psychologist to analyze. Were you aware that she has such morbid thoughts?" he asked Eric reproachfully, who looked stunned for a moment.

"Well, actually, no, I wasn't aware, but I'm very impressed." Eric was delighted, and Alex's English teacher was appalled.

"This is no laughing matter, Mr. Winslow. This story indicates to me that your daughter is a very disturbed young girl." As he heard it, Eric became severely annoyed.

"It indicates to me that she's a hell of a writer. The story is flawlessly constructed and even surprised me at the end. I read a lot of crime thrillers, you might say they're my hobby, and Alex and I discuss them frequently. She appears to pay more attention than I thought."

"Do you realize how unhealthy and unsuitable it is for a child her age to think about things like this, and have a knowledge of sinister events of this kind? The story reads as though it was written by an adult."

"I think that's quite a compliment for her, to have written a short story that can scare the pants off us."

"You need to take this seriously, Mr. Winslow," the teacher almost shouted at him.

"I do. She told me several years ago that she wants to write crime thrillers when she grows up. Apparently she was more serious about it than I believed at the time, and this is evidence that with some creative writing classes, she might have the talent to do it." He refused to believe that her story was the product of a sick mind, but rather the first signs that she might have real ability as a writer, which Eric found exciting. "I am very proud of her," he said as he stood up. "May I have a copy of the story? I'd like to discuss it with her tonight." The teacher looked even more outraged, and handed the original to Eric, who folded it and put it in his pocket, and then shook hands with the teacher, who watched him leave his office in disgust.

"You are going to cause her untold psychological damage if you encourage this kind of thing," were his final words to Eric, and Eric intended to do just that, encourage her. He couldn't wait to tell her how great her story was.

He brought it up to her that night, at dinner, over enchiladas and Spanish rice that Elena had left them, with a salad Eric had added to the meal.

"I saw your English teacher at school today," he said casually, as they dug into the cheese and chicken enchiladas that were their favorite, with homemade tortillas.

"Mr. Farber?" She looked surprised. "Why?" She had no idea of the furor her innocent short story had caused. And her father laughed in answer.

"Because they think I'm fostering some kind of dangerous atmosphere in our home, if you can write about a murder like that. That's one hell of a fantastic story, Al. How did you come up with it?" She was beaming at his praise, and her father was bursting with pride.

"I used the book you told me about last week as inspiration, but I made up all the details, threw in all the gore I could think of about the murder, but tried to make it as real as possible. I tried to keep it very short and surprise you at the end."

"Well, it's dynamite. You had me hooked right from the beginning, and you did surprise me. I think you have real talent." There was nothing soft or namby-pamby about it. And it wasn't a "cozy" detective story by any means. "If you work at it, I think you're going to be one hell of a terrific writer one day. I am *so* impressed!" They talked about it for the rest of the meal, and she told her father about another idea she had.

"I think you ought to keep those stories at home from now on. Don't waste them on your English classes. Let's talk about them here. And write gentler things for Mr. Farber before he has me put in jail." He was laughing as he said it, so she wasn't worried. She was still surprised that her teacher had dragged her father to school. But she was thrilled that her father loved her story.

With Eric's encouragement, Alex tried to write at home every day, and she turned out some very interesting, powerful short stories. Her father would critique them, and she would rework them until she thought she had them just right. Her father saved them in a folder, and when the folder was full, he put them in a binder. At the end of a year, they had more than fifty of them. Some were better than others, but all of them had a remarkably adult and distinctive style, with surprise endings that most of the time even Eric couldn't guess. She had a definite knack. He began to steer her reading to the crime thrillers and detective stories he liked to read, so she could learn from the style of famous writers such as Dashiell Hammett, David Morrell, Michael Crichton, and even Georges Simenon translations. Alex started spending weekends reading adult mystery books, and then creating her own work.

And on her twelfth birthday, Eric came home with a special gift for her. It was a Smith Corona portable typewriter, in perfect condition, and he taught her how to use it. She was typing with all ten fingers within two weeks and she loved the machine.

"A lot of famous mystery writers use old typewriters. It's part of the mystique," he told her. She considered the gift from her father a rare prize, and when she had a friend over from school one day, she showed it to her. Her friend Becky thought it was weird.

"What do you do with that?"

"I play around with it on the weekends," she said offhandedly.

"It looks like an antique," Becky said dismissively. Alex didn't tell her she wrote her stories on it, the more complicated the better, and that her father helped her do it. It was their secret, and she thought some of them were pretty good. And they were so much fun to write.

They had three binders of them by her thirteenth birthday, and her father took her to a mystery writers' conference called Boucher-con as a surprise. It was a meeting that happened every year in a different city, attended by mystery writers of all genres. Alex listened raptly to several lectures, and wrote a brilliant story afterward. Her father was so proud of what she'd written that he wanted to get the stories published in a mystery writers' magazine, and they were discussing which ones to submit when her father looked at her strangely, and for just the flicker of an instant, he acted as though he didn't recognize her.

"Who are you anyway?" he said in a loud voice that didn't sound like his own. "Are you one of the neighbors' children? What are you doing in my house?" She stared at him in amazement, and a moment later he seemed normal again, and looked around the room as though he had just returned from somewhere else.

"Are you okay, Dad?" He had frightened her for a moment, and he brushed it off and laughed.

"I'm fine. I was just trying to scare you. You can put that in a story," he said and went to get a drink of water.

"Don't scare me like that again. It was creepy."

It happened again a few weeks later when they went to a baseball game. The Red Sox were playing the Yankees, the score was six to three, and it was an unusually hot day. Eric turned to Alex halfway through the game with a blank look and asked her who was playing. "The Yankees and the Orioles?"

"Are you kidding? It's the Red Sox and the Yankees." A moment later he was back again, but his mind had gone blank for a minute, and this time she had seen it clearly. He acted like it was nothing and when she asked him about it later, he said it was the heat.

Then it happened at work. He came out of his office with a vague look and asked his secretary what she was doing there on the weekend. She didn't know what to say. Afterward when she saw him in his office, she decided it was a joke. He was fine.

It occurred half a dozen times over the next few months, and when he asked Elena who she was and what she was doing there one day when he came home from work, he realized that something terrifying was happening to him. He made an appointment with his doctor, explained the symptoms to him, that for several minutes his mind would go blank and he wouldn't remember where he was, who the people were around him, and sometimes even his own name. It was as though he couldn't think for a few minutes, and the power lines were down in his brain. He was afraid he had a brain tumor, and his physician was concerned, and referred him to a neurologist, who sent him for brain scans and tests.

Eric said nothing to Alex about it as he waited for the results. The neurologist called him in to discuss their findings a week later, and in the elevator on the way to the doctor's office, he got confused again. He rode the elevator alone for nearly ten minutes, up and down, unable to remember where he was going and why he was there, and then it came back to him again, and he pressed the button for the right floor, and arrived at the doctor's office looking shaken. He told him he had just had another episode. The doctor looked serious as Eric sat across his desk. It was occurring once a week now, and sometimes more frequently than that, only for a few minutes, but long enough for him to realize that something frightening was going on in his brain.

"Do I have a brain tumor, Doctor?" he asked, desperate to know the truth and if it was something that could be fixed. Maybe it was stress. Things had not been going well at work, business was down, and he was afraid they would blame him. They had lost several important bids recently, for no reason he could explain. He had made the presentations, and they hadn't gone well.

"No, you don't have a brain tumor," the doctor answered his question. "But I'm afraid I don't have good news. We took images of your brain, and there are some abnormalities."

"Did I have a stroke and not know it?" The doctor shook his head.

"From the exams we did on you, there are indications that you have early-onset Alzheimer's or dementia. There are medications we can give you to slow it down, but we can't stop it and the damage can't be reversed. It's difficult to say how severe it will get or how long it will take to incapacitate you, but it's a progressive disease."

"My father had dementia at a young age, in his early sixties. But I'm sixty-four years old, and I'm a widower with a thirteen-year-old child. Are you telling me I'm becoming senile? Who's going to take care of her?" Eric asked as tears filled his eyes.

"It's something you need to think about, Mr. Winslow," the doctor said gently. "I'm sorry for this bad news. Things may remain as they are for a while, even quite some time, but if our assessment is correct, ultimately we can't reverse the disease." He gave Eric a prescription for the medication and told him he wanted to see him in a month, unless things got markedly worse before that. Eric left the doctor's office feeling as though a bomb had hit him. He had been planning to go back to work, it was only two-fifteen, but he was so upset that he called in sick and went home instead. Elena was in the kitchen when he got there, and for several minutes he didn't know who she was and couldn't remember her name.

"You okay, Mr. Winslow?" she asked him, worried about him, and he said he was fine, but had a touch of the flu, and went to his room to lie down. His mind was racing as he lay there, and he had no idea what to do about Alex. He had no family to leave her to, no one to take care of her. He had provided for her responsibly with his savings and a life insurance policy, but she couldn't be on her own for the next five years. He made an appointment with his lawyer for the next day.

When Alex came home from school, Elena told her that her father had the flu. She thought he was sleeping, but he was lying on his bed in tears, with his door locked so Alex wouldn't see him cry.

When Eric went to see Bill Buchanan, his lawyer, the next day, he explained the situation to him, and Bill was devastated to hear it. They weren't close, but had known each other professionally for thirty years. They went over his financial arrangements for Alex, and she would have enough money to live carefully for several years and get an education, but the big question was where she would live if something happened to him. Earlier he had designated Bill as her trustee, but the arrangements he had made were more of a cautionary formality, and he had expected to live another twenty or thirty years, if he was lucky. Even if he lived that long now, it would be without full cognizance or all his faculties. And he might need his savings for his own care, and how would he care for her? It was a frightening situation, and they discussed alternate options for Alex, but none of them were what Eric wanted for her.

The lawyer suggested boarding school, and she could go home with friends for the holidays, if something happened to him. She couldn't continue to live in their house alone with a housekeeper with no relative or parental supervision as a teenager, but Eric knew she would hate being locked away in a boarding school, and he didn't want to do that to her. And she couldn't spend every school holiday with strangers. She was more accustomed to the company of adults, with him, than to kids her own age. But there was no one he could rely on to take care of her. They had no family other than each other. Even Carmen was dead. And Eric didn't want to tell Alex what was happening to him. It was too frightening for him to face, let alone for her at her age.

The lawyer couldn't think of any solution for her, other than boarding school. She attended the best private school in Boston, and would be going to high school the following year. She was an outstanding student, and deserved the kind of education Eric was able to provide for her. But she needed more than a school. If Eric died or were incapacitated, she needed a responsible caretaker.

"There may be no place to put her other than boarding school," the lawyer said sensibly. And he was even more concerned about Eric once dementia took over his brain, which was no longer an "if" but a "when." He hoped it wouldn't be soon. Bill Buchanan had agreed to become Alex's trustee, so he could help make decisions for her, as well as be executor of Eric's estate, but neither of them had come up with a satisfactory place for her to live once he was gone.

The medication seemed to slow the episodes down a little, but he was aware of them, even for a few instants, almost every day. It was getting harder and harder to work at the office, and two months after his diagnosis, the CEO called him in and told him he was no longer on top of his game. Eric assured him he would get things back in control, he said he'd had a slump recently, but the CEO reminded him that he would reach retirement age in a year, and felt he was ready for it now.

"Why not enjoy the good life?" He tried to make it sound like a positive experience, but he made it clear they wanted him to leave. It felt like the beginning of the end.

They gave him a wonderful retirement party and a bronze plaque a few weeks later, but after he stopped working, Eric found himself at home all day with nothing to do. He went on long walks, and at times forgot where he lived. It would come back to him while he was walking, but late one afternoon, he couldn't remember his address or his name. A kind young woman saw how lost he looked, and drove him around the neighborhood searching for his home. He remembered then, and he was surprised to realize how far he'd walked. Alex was already at home when he got in, after thanking the young woman for getting him safely back to his address.

"Who was that who dropped you off, Dad?" She was a very attractive young woman, and Alex wondered if he was dating someone he hadn't told her about. She knew how bored he was now that he'd retired. And he wasn't reading the crime books he loved as much as he used to.

"No one, just a friend from work I ran into this afternoon." He couldn't tell Alex that she was a stranger who had picked him up and brought him home like a lost child. More and more he felt infantile and not the adult he used to be. The realization of it filled him with rage. He was short-tempered with Alex now, which was the last thing he wanted to be. And she looked hurt when he shouted at her. He didn't seem to be enjoying his retirement as he had said he would when he announced it to her, and she had no idea it had been forced on him. No one at his old office knew he was suffering from Alzheimer's either. Only his attorney and his physician did, although increasingly Alex could see that he was confused.

He still bought the newest crime novels by his favorite authors, but he never seemed to finish them, and left three or four of them open, lying around the house.

"Are you feeling okay, Dad?" She worried about him.

"Of course." He smiled at her. But he noticed that the medication was working less well than it had in the beginning, which the doctor had warned him would happen.

They spent three weeks in Maine on vacation before she had to start high school in September, and he got lost in the woods on their third day there. The hotel they stayed at had to send out a search party for him. They found him easily, wandering around, and Eric was mortally embarrassed when they got back to the hotel. He said his compass was broken, and he'd gotten confused. The rest of their stay was uneventful, but he forgot her name several times, which shocked her. He had never done that before.

She had written a lot of stories over the summer and put them in the binder, but he never read or commented on any of them. And he didn't offer to drive her to school on the first day. There were lots of subtle changes in his behavior, and Alex noticed all of them. She wondered if he was depressed or worried. He seemed distracted all the time, disoriented when they went out, and he was wandering around the living room in his boxers one day when she got home from school. He had never done that before either. And Elena said he'd been sleeping all day.

By her second month of high school, it was obvious to Alex that there was something seriously wrong with her father. He was confused most of the time now, and even Alex could see that dementia had set in. She called their doctor one morning when he refused to get out of bed, didn't seem to know where he was, and couldn't remember her name. The doctor came to the house and spoke to her, and told her what was happening. He found her amazingly mature for a fourteen-year-old. He told her that eventually they would have to put her father in a residential facility, and she said she wouldn't allow it, and they would keep him at home and care for him there.

The doctor helped her find a male nurse to drive her father and keep an eye on him, and she insisted that on weekends she could care for him herself. All he wanted to do now was sleep anyway. She read to him from the familiar books he loved, although he usually fell asleep or seemed not to be listening to her. She spoke to him as though he still understood everything she said, and treated him with the dignity and respect he deserved, although it broke her heart to see him so confused. The disease was advancing by leaps and bounds, and by Christmas, he recognized no one except her. They added a second nurse. She could no longer manage him on her own. He had wandered down the street in his pajamas, and took his clothes off in the kitchen while Elena stood there and cried, watching him, and then ran screaming from the room. There was no hiding from the reality anymore. Less than a year after the first signs, his mind was severely impaired.

Alex was trying to keep up with her homework, hadn't written a story in months, and worried about him all the time, even when she was at school. Over Christmas vacation, he stopped eating and wouldn't get out of bed. After a week of IVs, they transferred him to a hospital and fed him from a nasogastric tube. Pattie and Elena stood with Alex when they took her father away in an ambulance. And then Pattie held her while she cried.

Alex spent the rest of her vacation at his bedside at the hospital, and by New Year's Day, he stopped recognizing her too. His mind was a blank now, and he returned to an infant state. He slept and cried, laughed for no reason, refused all food, and pulled out his nasogastric tube and had to be restrained.

The week before she went back to school, Alex was with him every night at the hospital, sleeping on a cot next to his bed, even though he didn't know who she was. And on the first day of school after vacation, she left for class from the hospital, and came back that afternoon. His bed was empty when she got there, and she was startled to realize he had been moved. She wondered if they were doing tests on him again, and the head nurse came to see her while she was looking lost in the room, trying to guess where he was. She knew the minute she saw the nurse's face. The nurses had grown fond of her during her father's stay. Alex was very mature for her age, and always polite and respectful to them. And she was obviously devoted to her father. She took care of him like an adoring mother and never left him for a minute.

"I have bad news for you, Alex," the nurse said gently, and put her arms around her, as Alex went stiff as a board, and knew she shouldn't have gone to school that day. She hadn't even had a chance to say goodbye to him, but there was no one left to say goodbye to. The father she knew and loved had been gone for months by then. The nurse told her that he had died peacefully in his sleep right after she left for school.

They called Elena for her, who came to pick her up. Bill Buchanan handled everything with Alex, and helped make the funeral ar-rangements. The church was full, with all the people who had worked with him, and known and admired him. And at the cemetery, she was shocked to see her mother's grave. Her father had never told her that he'd had Carmen buried there, but now they were together, with her father's first wife. She went home from the cemetery with Elena, and a few close friends came to visit her, but with Alex alone, most people didn't want to intrude, and there was no gathering afterward. Alex sat in his room all that night in his favorite chair, feeling him with her.

Bill Buchanan came to see her the next day, and said the court would confirm his trusteeship as a formality, according to her father's will. He also explained to her that her father had been unable to decide where Alex should live. He told her that her father had appointed him her trustee, but he had no solutions either.

"Can't I just live here with Elena?" she asked in a quavering voice. She had hoped that would be possible and if not, what was going to happen to her? Bill had told her that her father had provided for her financially, for her education and to help her afterward, within reason, but where she would live was still unresolved. And she was too young to live alone. Eric had wanted the house kept for Alex for when she was older, and had suggested to Bill that they rent it out in the meantime, which Bill thought was a good idea. It would provide some income and preserve the house for her until she could use it.

"I don't want to go to boarding school," she said, reading the lawyer's mind. But there were no relatives to send her to, and she couldn't live with the neighbors for the next four years until she turned eighteen, nor at the house, with Elena, who went home at night.

"Let's both think about it," the lawyer said reasonably. "And for now you can stay here." But boarding school was the only solution he could think of. Elena had agreed to stay at the house with Alex until they came up with a solution.

He was so upset about the dilemma of where Alex should live that he talked to his wife about it that night.

"Her father didn't want her in a boarding school either. He knew she wouldn't want that. But what am I going to do?" He felt like an ogre sending her away, but she was a fourteen-year-old girl with no living relatives. What else could he do? As her trustee, he had an obligation to solve the problem but had no idea how, other than a residential school. But even vacations would be a problem with nowhere for her to go.

"Let me make a call. I have a crazy idea," Jane Buchanan said, and got up from the dinner table to call her cousin, who was the mother superior of a busy Dominican convent in a Boston suburb. It wasn't an orphanage or a home for young girls. It was a residence for teaching and nursing nuns, all of them with jobs outside the convent, and most of whom no longer wore the habit. It always reminded Jane of a college dorm for adult women whenever she went to visit her cousin, who was a lively, very intelligent woman who was engaged with the world. They ran seminars and taught evening classes to women in the neighborhood, and maybe she'd have a suggestion or creative idea. Jane's cousin, Mother Mary Margaret, was the only one she could think of who might help. Her nickname in the family was MaryMeg. She had waited until she was thirty to join a religious order, and was a nurse practitioner by profession. And as usual, when Jane called, it took her forever to come to the phone.

"Sorry, I was taking a Pilates class. We just started it here, and I love it." She was in her late fifties, and she had taken cooking classes and photography lessons too. She loved taking advantage of the classes they offered, staying current with the world, and meeting the women who came to the convent from the community they served. Their adult classes were her personal and clever way to draw people back to the church. They were heavily attended, although the diocese reminded her occasionally that she was not running an entertainment center, but she insisted it was all in the interest of health and education, and somehow she got away with it. "What's up?"

"I need your advice. Bill has a problem relating to a client who just died."

"I don't do funerals, and I'm not a lawyer. I'm a nurse."

"And my smartest relative." She explained Alex's plight to her, orphaned at fourteen, with nowhere to live.

"And I assume there's money if her father was Bill's client," Mother MaryMeg said practically.

"A respectable amount, apparently. He wasn't crazy rich. But they have a house, and he had savings and a sizable insurance policy. The problem is no relatives, and no one to live with."

"Poor kid." Mother Mary Margaret felt sorry for her, but didn't see what she could do. "What about boarding school?"

"She doesn't want to go. Bill says she's an unusually bright kid. She's lived alone with her father for years. Her mother abandoned them, and then died when she was nine. Bill says she's exceptional, and she thinks boarding school would be like prison. I'm not sure how great she is with other kids. He says she's shy and introverted, and was very close to her father. She may be better with adults than her peers. Her life was pretty different."

"Where does she go to school now?" Mother MaryMeg asked her cousin, and was impressed by the answer. "It's too bad to pull her out of there, but you're right, she can't live alone. We don't take kids, or I'd take her here, and you can't put her in state foster care. That would be a lot worse than boarding school. What do you want from me?"

"Any bright ideas you have. You're the best problem solver I know. I thought maybe you could think of a place for her. She's not really a child at fourteen."

"Nor an adult. Our nuns aren't babysitters. They all have jobs, and they're busy with our classes at night." The mother superior sounded pensive for a minute. "On the other hand, it's a crazy idea but I wonder if we *could* keep her here. The diocese would probably have a fit. Maybe I could get special dispensation, and we could try it for a while. If she doesn't want to go to boarding school, she might not be thrilled with a convent either."

"She doesn't have much choice."

"Let me think about it, and I'll ask the others. We have a pretty full house. I've got twenty-six nuns here at the moment. But I've got an empty room upstairs. Wouldn't it be odd for her to live with a bunch of nuns, though?"

"Maybe you could get her to enlist early," Jane teased her.

"We don't do that anymore. Half the women who come in are in their forties, or just over thirty at the youngest. We don't recruit teenagers." She laughed at the thought. "If we did, that would probably drive me out of the order. Have you met her? What's she like?"

"Bill says she's a lovely kid."

"I'll call you tomorrow, let me talk to the sisters." She ran the convent democratically, although the final say was hers, with the permission of the archdiocese for anything unusual, of course.

"Thanks. I didn't know who else to call."

Mother MaryMeg thought about it that night, and prayed about it, and brought it up to the other nuns at breakfast the next day, after six o'clock mass. Most of them had to be at work by eight, and the convent was almost deserted during the day, between the teachers and the nurses. There were two older retired nuns who ran the front office while the others were at work.

"So what do you think, sisters?" she asked, as they handed around a plate of toast. They took turns in the kitchen, and the food was basic.

"Do we really want to be responsible for a fourteen-year-old?" Sister Thomas, one of the older nuns, looked skeptical. She had six children herself and had come into the order when her youngest turned twenty-one, after her husband died. "That's an awful age," she said with a grimace, and the others laughed.

"You would know."

"It's all sex, drugs, and rock and roll at that age. And a lot of back-talk. Even my two girls were awful at that age."

"She's got nowhere else to go," Mother MaryMeg reminded them. She had already made up her mind at mass, but she wanted the others to come to it on their own. She didn't want to drag them to it, or force them, or it wouldn't work. "What if we try it for a while, with the understanding that if we can't manage it, or if she's too difficult, she goes to boarding school, like it or not?"

"Where would she go to school here?" Sister Regina asked. She was their youngest nun at twenty-seven, and had had a vocation since she was fifteen, which Mother MaryMeg thought was much too young, but she had done her novitiate in Chicago, and come to them after she'd taken her vows. Mother MaryMeg would have encouraged her to do so later.

"She'd have to attend the parish school," Mother MaryMeg said. "We can't drive her into town to her current school. But she'll get a decent education in the parish. She'll manage if she's as bright as my cousin says. Why don't we meet her? She might not like us anyway.

It was my cousin's idea." They all agreed to that, and then left for work hastily after taking their plates to the kitchen, rinsing them, and putting them in the dishwasher. It was a busy house. After breakfast, Mother MaryMeg checked her messages, ordered whole-sale groceries and supplies to save money, and then called Jane. "The consensus is we'd like to meet her, which I think is a good idea. She might not want to live in a convent full of nuns either. Boarding school may sound great to her in comparison."

"And if you and the sisters like her?" Jane was hopeful.

"We'll try it for a few months and see how it works out."

"I'll tell Bill. You're a saint," she told her cousin, and Mother MaryMeg laughed.

"Not likely. I had too much fun before I got here. But it would be nice if we could help her out. Do you think he can get her here to-night?"

"I'll try."

"We have classes here tomorrow night, and it's chaos on the weekends. Tonight would be better."

"I'll tell Bill."

"We could meet her right before dinner at six o'clock."

"He can leave me a message if I'm out." Jane and MaryMeg had grown up almost as sisters, and they were still very close.

After they hung up, Jane called Bill at the office and told him to have Alex at the convent at six to meet the sisters, if the idea ap-pealed to her at all.

He met Alex at the house after school and explained the situation to her. It was the only alternative plan he could come up with.

"In a convent? With nuns?" She and her father had gone to church occasionally, but they weren't deeply religious. "Will they expect me to become a nun?" She looked shocked at the idea.

He smiled at the question, although it was reasonable for her to ask. "Not if I know my wife's cousin. If they do this, it would be to help you out. They're the busiest bunch of women I've ever met. They all work as teachers and nurses, and have classes there at night. I think they'd expect you to go to school, get good grades, and pitch in to help. You would go to their parish school."

Whatever she did, she would have to leave the school she was in. Her whole life had been turned upside down by her father's death, and after Bill left, she sat in her father's room and looked at the bookcase full of books he had loved and they had shared. They were going to put everything in storage now, until she was older and came back to this house or had a home of her own. All that she had known and that was familiar to her was going to be boxed up and put away. Everything was about to change. And now she was going to meet a bunch of nuns, and maybe live in a convent. It was either that or boarding school, and she couldn't decide which sounded worse. There were tears rolling down her cheeks as she walked out of her father's bedroom, and Elena was crying in the kitchen when she walked in. The two women clung to each other and cried, and Alex didn't know if she was crying for her father or herself.

Chapter 5

Bill Buchanan left his office earlier than usual to pick Alex up and get her to St. Dominic's convent by six o'clock. She was waiting for him in a plain black dress and flat shoes when he arrived. When she got in the car, she looked like she'd been crying, which he could well understand. He couldn't blame her father for not resolving her living situation before his death. Even he was having a hard time figuring out what was best for Alex. And in the last months of Eric's life, her father had been incapable of making any decisions, let alone one as complex as where his daughter would live. Before that, in his early sixties, it didn't dawn on him that time was running short.

Alex was silent as Bill drove her to the convent. She sat staring out the window as depressing images wended through her head of a dark, dreary convent, ancient nuns, and then of her father in his final days.

"Are you okay, Alex?" Bill asked her, and she nodded. "I think you'll like my wife's cousin. She's a character even if she's a nun. She's got a great sense of humor, and she's a nice person." Alex had trouble making the connection between humor and the mother superior of a convent. It didn't make sense to her. She just nodded and sat stone-faced when they arrived, and didn't move for a minute. Boarding school was beginning to seem like the less unpleasant plan.

The convent was a big, sprawling building that had been a good investment when they bought it. It was behind the church on a large lot, with trees and a garden, and a maze of small rooms on the top floor for the nuns, with large rooms downstairs where classes were held. It was Mother Mary Margaret who had introduced all their after-school and evening activities for children, young people, and their parents, which had been a great success and integrated them into the neighborhood, rather than cloistering themselves and setting the nuns apart.

Alex got out of the car slowly, almost dragging her feet, and followed Bill up the stairs. As they walked in, they were jostled by a flock of children being picked up by their parents. They were carrying clay objects, drawings, and paintings from an art class given by several of the nuns. The children were shouting and excited, and the mothers talking and laughing, and inside, a group of teenage boys were leaving the large meeting room that doubled as a gym. It was where their new Pilates classes were being held, which were a big success, but that was later in the evening, preceded by an exercise class for pregnant women. They also had an evening class for first-time parents on how to care for their newborns, which was given by two of the nuns who were nurses. And they were planning to offer art classes for older people in the community too.

Bill hadn't been to see the convent in several years, and was stunned by how many of the locals were congregating in the halls. Mother Mary Margaret had turned it into a booming community center, and Alex was looking around with awe as children ran by her, women chatted, and teenagers came and went. It wasn't the dark, dreary, silent place she had expected, or anything like what she'd thought. Bill inquired at a reception desk, and a woman in jeans and a tee shirt, who was actually a nun, directed them to an office at the end of a long hall, past the gym. And when they walked in, a woman in jeans and a red sweatshirt was standing on top of a ladder changing a lightbulb in a ceiling fixture. She glanced down at both of them in dismay, saw Bill in his suit and tie, and Alex in her little black dress, and looked embarrassed. She had gray hair in a ponytail, and a pretty face that always reminded Bill of his wife's. They were first cousins and the daughters of twin sisters.

"I guess I should have worn my habit. I'm sorry, I didn't have time to change." She smiled down at them, finished changing the lightbulb, clambered down the ladder, folded it, and leaned it against the wall. "We lost our handyman last month, and I've been sitting here in the dark for three days." She kissed Bill on the cheek and held a hand out to shake Alex's, who stared up at her in surprise. She was a tall, robust-looking woman, and the sweatshirt said Stanford, where she had gone to college more than thirty years before. "I'm Mother Mary Margaret," she introduced herself to Alex. "You can call me Mother MaryMeg. I'm glad you came to visit. It's pretty crazy here every day. We give lots of classes and seminars for people in the neighborhood, mostly at night since we all work."

She indicated two threadbare chairs for them and sat down at her desk. Alex found it hard to believe that she was a nun. She seemed more like a schoolteacher, or a principal, or someone's mother. "We've never had someone come to live with us, and we're not really set up for it," she said to both of them honestly, "but it could work, as long as you don't mind living in a busy place, and are willing to pitch in with us. We all take a turn in the kitchen every month. The sisters pray a lot when it's my turn. I'm better with a hammer and a power drill than at the stove." Bill knew she had many other skills and had majored in psychology in college, had a master's in theology, and had been studying toward a doctorate in psychology while working as a nurse practitioner. "How do you feel about staying here, Alex?" she asked her very directly.

"I don't know. It looks a lot different than I thought," she said in a soft, hesitant voice.

"I'm sorry about your father. I know this is a big change for you. Bill tells me you don't want to go to boarding school. Why not? That might be more fun with kids your age."

"I don't do a lot of after-school activities," she said cautiously. "I read a lot, and I like to write. My father and I did a lot of things together. I think I'd feel trapped living at school, and be forced into a lot of things I don't like to do. I've been with grown-ups, or my dad, all my life. My mom . . . left . . . when I was seven, and she died when I was nine. It's been just me and my dad all my life." Her eyes filled with tears as she said it, but she struggled not to cry, as the mother superior nodded.

"What do you like to write?" she asked gently, assuming short stories or poetry.

"Crime stories," Alex said with a small smile. "My teachers think they're weird, so I don't write them for school anymore. My dad thought they were pretty good."

"Maybe you'll be a writer one day," Mother MaryMeg said in a warm tone. "You'd have to be fairly independent here. The nuns can't chase you around if you're not home on time, or don't tell us where you are. We'd have to be able to rely on you to go to school, keep up with your work, and follow our rules about the house. That's a lot to expect of you at your age, but it won't work otherwise. How do you feel about it?" She looked Alex in the eye and spoke to her as an adult, as though she were a young nun coming to live there, not a fourteen-year-old girl, a freshman in high school, about to turn fifteen.

"I think I could do it," Alex said in barely more than a whisper. Bill Buchanan had made it clear to the mother superior that Alex had been provided for by her father, and would be no financial burden on them. The estate could even pay the convent an amount for her monthly room and board, which Mother MaryMeg had already said could be given in the form of a small contribution to the convent. "How much can she eat, after all?" she had said in a lighthearted spirit. This was not about money. It was about taking responsibility for her, and her willingness to cooperate with them. But looking at Alex and talking to her, the older nun was confident about it. She looked like a good girl, and seemed mature for her age. And her father had had no problems with her that Bill knew of. She was an excellent student, sensible, and well behaved, and the nuns taking her in would be a godsend for her if they would do it.

"What if we give it a try?" Mother MaryMeg suggested after a few minutes. Alex had impressed her very favorably, just as Bill had said she would. "Let's see how it works out. Would you like to have dinner with us tonight? I could introduce you to the others." If she came to live with them, she would have twenty-six surrogate mothers, after having none at all for the past seven years. It was going to be a big change for her, and living in community was always an adjustment for everyone, the nuns too. Some nuns lived on their own or in small groups in apartments now. Big bustling convents like St. Dominic's were rare in the modern church. It was an atmosphere that the nuns there loved, especially with Mother Mary Margaret running it.

"I'd like that," Alex said in response to the dinner invitation, and looked a little dazed at the prospect of moving into a convent, with a group of women she'd never met.

"Good." The mother superior stood up and smiled at both of them. "You can leave her with us if you want, Bill. One of the nuns can show her around after dinner and drive her home. You don't need to stick around." It was six-thirty by then and the dinner bell had sounded ten minutes earlier.

Bill left them in the hallway and promised to call Alex the next day. Mother MaryMeg led Alex down to the basement to the dining hall. You could hear the nuns' chatter from the stairs. It wasn't a silent order, and they sounded like any other large group of women, laughing and talking and catching up on the day's activities. They stood up respectfully when the superior came into the room, but went on talking and called out greetings to her. Several of them noticed Alex standing beside her, looking shy. Mother MaryMeg walked her over to a table of younger nuns who were chatting animatedly and stood up again when the superior approached, and several of them smiled warmly at Alex and said hello. They slid over on the bench where they were seated and made room for her when told she was staying for dinner, and Alex sat down cautiously with them. She was next to Sister Regina, who beamed at her and handed her a platter of roast chicken a few minutes later. "We have pizza on Tuesdays," she whispered. "Sister Sofia is Italian. She makes great pasta too. I'm a terrible cook," she admitted and the others at the table agreed, as Alex smiled at them. It was overwhelming meeting so many of them all at once. A few of the nuns around the room were still in their habits from work, most of them nurses from the Catholic hospital nearby, but the others were wearing street clothes, in most cases jeans, which Alex found reassuring.

They were modern and informal, and were a variety of ages, but many of them looked young to Alex, and nothing like what she'd expected. As she helped herself to chicken, spinach, and French fries, all of the nuns at her table asked her questions about school. A number of them had heard about her visit and wondered if she would come to live with them. They told her about all the activities they engaged in, what their daytime jobs were, and the classes they taught at night. Sister Regina said she was the instructor in the new Pilates class, and two of the others taught the art classes for young children in the neighborhood. They made it sound like fun to live and work there.

"Do you have a boyfriend?" one of them asked her, and she thought it was a trick question as she shook her head. She hadn't been out with any boys yet. There were one or two boys she liked at school, but the subject of dating had never come up, and her father had wanted her to put that off as long as possible, and she still agreed. "I had two at your age," the nun who had asked admitted, and the others teased her about it, and she said one of them had since become a priest. He still sent her Christmas cards, and was a missionary in Africa.

All the nuns in the group made her feel welcome, and Mother MaryMeg had Sister Regina show her what could be her room if she came to stay with them. It was tiny, and barely big enough for the bed, desk, and dresser that were in it, which were fairly battered and had been donated to the convent. There was nothing charming about the room, and she wondered where she would put all her things, but at least she could put her typewriter on the desk.

"We might be able to squeeze a small bookcase in here for your schoolbooks," Sister Regina said thoughtfully. Alex didn't say it, but she wanted to bring some of her father's books with her too, especially the ones they had loved reading together. It was going to be a tight fit in the small room. "We don't spend much time in our rooms," she explained, as they walked downstairs and ran into the mother superior in the hall.

"Would you drive Alex home for me?" Mother MaryMeg asked Sister Regina, who went to get the car keys. Then the nun in the sweatshirt turned to Alex and she could see that Alex was on overload from all she'd seen. Her whole life had changed in the blink of an eye, and where to live, and with whom, was a big decision for a girl her age. "What do you think, Alex?"

"I'd like to come and live here," she said politely. "Everyone was really nice to me at dinner." There were tears in her eyes again as she said it. She missed her father, and she didn't want to leave their home and Elena, but if she had to, at least the nuns seemed friendly and kind and appealed to her more than boarding school. And she might have time to write here, in the tiny room, more so than in a dormitory she'd share with other kids at a residential school. That colored some of her decision, and how welcoming they'd been to her during the visit.

"Why don't you move in this weekend? There will be plenty of us around to help you. Just let us know when, and I'll work out the details with Bill," Mother MaryMeg said warmly, as Sister Regina appeared with the car keys to one of their four station wagons that were in constant use. Alex followed her outside, got into the front seat, and put on her seatbelt, and Sister Regina chatted easily on the drive back to Alex's home.

"I'm excited that you're coming to live with us," the young nun said, smiling at her, when they reached the house Alex had shared with her father. Alex said they were going to rent it out, and keep it so she could live there one day. "I'm sure you'll miss it, but we'll take good care of you in the meantime," she promised, and Alex nodded and thanked her. Sister Regina watched her walk inside after she opened the door with her key, and she saw Elena greet her and peer out at the car that had brought her home, and then the front door closed and Sister Regina drove back to the convent, while Alex sat on her bed and looked around her familiar room.

There was space for almost none of her things in the small cell she'd been assigned, but she was going to take as many boxes of books as she could anyway. She could store them under the bed and stack them in the corners. Her books were all important to her, and were so much a part of her life with her father, and had meant so much to him, that she couldn't let them all go into storage. She combed his bookshelves for hours that night, pulling out the ones she wanted to take with her. She decided to take her favorite Nancy Drews since they had been her first mystery books, and were symbolic of her early life with him. And taking his favorites was like taking him with her. She was up long after midnight making stacks of their most beloved books, some of them first editions he had treasured. She treated them all with reverence, and the following night packed them all in boxes Elena had gotten her.

She wasn't sad about leaving her school, since she had just started recently and had no close friends there yet. It was the house that would be hard to leave. She had lived there all her life, and her father had been in it for twenty years before that. It was like leaving the womb, to go out in an unfamiliar world, full of strangers, and a way of life in the convent that was totally new to her. She had no idea how it would work out, or what would happen to her if it didn't. With her grades, she could have gotten into any boarding school, but they all seemed cold and too big to her. In an odd way, the convent seemed friendlier, and she was used to living with adults.

Bill had promised to drive her over on Sunday with all her things.

And their house would be put up for rent the following week after all their belongings were cleared out. Elena had been told to give her father's clothes away, and the moving men would pack the rest and keep it in storage at the moving company until the day Alex would be old enough to go through it, and maybe move back into their home again. But that day was a long way off, after college. Eight years away, after high school and university, or when she turned twenty-one. She had a long road to travel until then. And the next chapter of her life would begin on Sunday at St. Dominic's. She had no idea what it would be like living there, or how long she'd stay. Maybe a few months or a year or two, and after that the fates would decide what would happen to her.

Alex was waiting in the living room with Elena when Bill came to pick her up on Sunday morning. She had six suitcases of clothes, twelve boxes of books, her typewriter, and the lamp from her bedroom with blue lambs on it that she'd had since she was a little girl. Her father had always told her that the lambs were blue because they thought she'd be a boy, but as it turned out, they'd gotten lucky when she turned out to be a girl. She had fallen asleep looking at that lamp every night, so she took it with her. And she had her father's favorite crime books with her, the Nancy Drews she had loved most, some other mystery books that had inspired her, and the binders with her stories in them. And she had packed a sweater of her father's that still smelled like him, and her pillow from her bed. Everything else would be stored.

Elena started crying long before Bill arrived, and she had promised to visit Alex at the convent whenever she could. She had to look for a new job, after more than fifteen years with the Winslows, and she was dreading finding a new employer, and heartbroken that Alex couldn't stay in the house with her. Alex clung to her and sobbed before she left, and Elena pressed a little religious medal into her hand for good luck. It was agony walking out of the house for the last time, and just watching her do it, Bill had tears in his eyes when he started the car, an SUV crammed full of Alex's belongings. It was the saddest thing he'd ever seen. She sat in the front seat, crying and holding her childhood lamp, and neither of them spoke on the way to St. Dominic's. There was nothing left to say except how terrible he felt that she had lost her father and her home, and the housekeeper she loved. Pattie and her children had come to say goodbye to her the night before, and they had all cried too. It was a tough situation, but out of everyone's control, and Pattie said she hoped that Alex would be well cared for at the convent. She had talked to her husband about letting Alex stay with them, but they had no room, were already jammed to the rafters with their own four children, and didn't want the responsibility of another child.

Bill had filled out the paperwork on Friday authorizing Alex's transfer to the parochial school near St. Dominic's, and her transcript would be sent there. And he and Mother MaryMeg had agreed that a small amount would be deposited to the convent's account every month to pay for her room and board, which the archdiocese had approved.

When they reached the convent, the nuns were coming out of the church next door. Many of them had worn their habits to attend mass, but the younger ones hadn't, and rarely wore them anymore. Mother MaryMeg spotted them when they drove up, and she asked the nuns to help them unload the car and take Alex's things upstairs. She had given considerable thought to Alex living with them, and had assigned three of the nuns to supervise her, although everyone would help if necessary. Sister Regina had volunteered immediately and had bonded with Alex over dinner and when she showed her the room. She looked barely older than Alex on Sunday morning with her blond hair in a braid, in white pants and a pink tee shirt. She was unnervingly pretty for a nun, which had concerned Mother MaryMeg from the first, but her vocation appeared sound. She had also assigned Sister Thomas, who was the nun with children of her own. She had groaned and laughed when the mother superior discussed it with her. "Not again! That's why I came here, to get away from teenagers forever." But she was good humored about it, and willing to give it a try. And Sister Xavier Francis was in her early thirties and a teacher, had a great knack with kids, and could help with her homework if need be, particularly Latin and math. All three of them were waiting for her on Sunday, and several of the others carried her heavy bags and boxes up the stairs to the third-floor room. No one could move an inch once they set her suitcases down, and her boxes of books were piled high on the bed. Alex set down her lamp and typewriter on the desk, and Sister Xavier looked at the old Smith Corona with awe.

"What a beautiful machine!"

"I use it to write mystery stories," Alex said cautiously, not sure how they'd feel about that. "Crime stories, actually." And the young nun's eyes lit up at the words.

"I *love* crime stories!"

"That's what's in the boxes." Alex grinned. "They're my father's favorite books."

"Who are your favorites?" She reeled off a list of her own, including Dashiell Hammett, Agatha Christie, Eric Ambler, Frederick Forsyth, Robin Cook, and a long list of books that Alex and her father had read, and some Alex hadn't.

"I've read a lot of them." Alex smiled. "I used to love Agatha Christie when I was younger." She had recently read *The Silence of the Lambs* and loved it. "My father didn't like women writers. He said women can't write crime, only a man. I've read a lot of male writers."

"I'm not sure I agree. But I like mysteries that are softer and less violent. I like Dorothy Sayers. And I like themed mysteries too, especially about dogs." Alex smiled at what Sister Xavier said, and recognized them as "cozies." She didn't want to be disrespectful and say she'd outgrown them and had graduated to hard-boiled mysteries and crime thrillers, which were more violent and much tougher, and often written by men, as her father said.

Alex had put some of the boxes of books under the narrow bed by then, and stacked others in the corners, and Sister Regina was helping her unpack her clothes. They barely managed to squeeze them into the closet. And Alex set up three photographs of her father on the desk and one of her mother with her when she was two.

"Your mother was really beautiful," Sister Regina said, looking at her picture. "And your father was very handsome too." Alex stared at the photographs for a minute and nodded. She still couldn't believe that he was gone. The last tragic months with him were already fading from memory, they had been so unlike him. What remained were the warm images of the years before, the adventures they shared, the baseball games they went to, the books they'd both enjoyed, the long nights talking about what they'd read and what they did and didn't like about it, the fact that he was always there, and tucked her into bed every night. The memories of her mother were dim and had been for years. But those of her father stood out more sharply than ever.

The nuns came by and helped her put everything away, and

Sister Thomas came to check on them with a motherly air. She hadn't admitted it, but there was something comforting and familiar about being responsible for a child again, even one Alex's age.

"Everything going smoothly here?" she asked with a smile. She had kitchen duty that day, so had been busy making lunch. But she came upstairs to see how Alex was settling in, and she saw that she looked sad as she glanced around the room. It was a big change from home, even if everyone was friendly here. It wasn't the house she grew up in, and the father she adored was gone. Alex had said goodbye to Bill before he left, and thanked him for everything he'd done, and he had promised to stay in touch, and told her to call him if she had any problems. He encouraged Mother MaryMeg to do the same, but she was sure that everything would be fine, and had told him Alex seemed like a sweet kid.

"I know this can't be easy for you, Alex, but we're glad that you're here," Sister Thomas said kindly. "God works things out strangely sometimes, better than you expect. I hope you'll be happy with us. It's different than what you've been used to, but we have fun here too. There's something very warm and friendly about living with a lot of nice people, and sharing your life with them." Alex was curious about her and nodded as she listened.

"Do you miss your children?" she asked her cautiously, wondering why she had become a nun after being married and having kids. Mother MaryMeg had told her about Sister Thomas's six children, and Alex was stunned.

"I miss them like crazy," Sister Thomas said honestly. "But I'd miss them if I were home. They're all grown up, and live all over the place. They come to visit me, and I'd be a lot sadder home alone. This gives my life meaning, and I'm useful. I always wanted to be a nun before I got married." She had gotten pregnant at eighteen and had to get married, which she didn't tell Alex. "And now I can. I've had the best of both worlds."

"I don't want to be a nun when I grow up," Alex said quietly with a firm look in her eye, and Sister Thomas understood.

"No one expects you to. We just want to give you a home, and help you get to the next stage of your life. You'll be out of high school before you know it, and off to college. And then you'll have a job, and get married and have kids one day, and then you can come back and visit us." She made it sound very simple and nonthreatening to Alex.

"It's nice of the nuns to have me here," she said gratefully. "I didn't want to go away to school. And I want to be a writer one day."

"Then I'm sure you will, if you work hard at it. Is that your typewriter?" she asked with interest, and approached to look at it with admiration. "Where did you ever find it?" It was in perfect condition, and a vintage piece.

"My dad gave it to me to write my stories."

"I'd like to read them sometime," the nun said gently, suddenly pleased that Mother MaryMeg had assigned her to help care for Alex. She reminded her of her own children not so long ago. It seemed warm and touching now to have her there, even though she had resisted it at first, but Alex seemed like a sensible, well-brought-up girl. She had good manners, and appeared to be considerate and intelligent, although inevitably at fourteen, there would be some bumps and battles ahead in the next few years. But Sister Thomas had lived through it before and knew she could again, and this time she would have twenty-five partners to help her, not just one who thought the kids were her job and never his. She had loved her husband, but her marriage had not been easy. "Lunch is in a few minutes," she reminded Alex before she went back to the kitchen, and Sister Regina came to get her when it was time.

"Do you want to help me buy groceries today?" she asked as they walked downstairs, both of them in jeans and tee shirts, like two kids. "I'm on shopping duty. We buy out the supermarket once a week. They give us a discount."

"Sure, that would be fun," Alex said as she followed her into the dining hall in the basement and sat down next to her. Sister Xavier Francis was at the other end of the table, and Sister Thomas was sitting with the mother superior as she often did, but waved when she saw Alex come in, and Alex waved back. Overnight, she had twenty-six new friends, or adopted aunts and godmothers. It was totally different from anything she could ever have imagined, and she and Sister Regina chatted all through lunch, about movies and books and the Pilates class Sister Regina taught. She invited Alex to try it and she said she would. They wanted to add a yoga class too.

They went grocery shopping together afterward, and Alex helped her with an art class for mothers and children after that, and she peeked in at the babies in the parenting class, with young panicked-looking couples. The hours flew by, and after dinner, she went up to her room and lay down on her bed and thought about the day. She wanted to do some writing, but she was too tired, and still feeling overwhelmed by all she'd seen and done that day. It was all so new to her, and so were the nuns. She was starting her new school the next day.

She was surprised when no one came to tell her when to go to bed or turn off the light. They treated her like an adult, as her father had, and they seemed to assume she could regulate herself. She liked that. They respected her, and expected her to live up to it.

She got undressed, brushed her teeth, said good night to the photo of her father, and turned off her lamp with the little blue lambs. The bed was hard, but the pillow she'd brought with her was familiar, and she slept with her father's sweater next to her, so she could feel him near her, and smell his cologne. It was a brave new world, but not a bad one, just very different.

And as she fell asleep, she had an idea for a story that she wanted to write the next day. It would be the first one she had written in months, since her father started failing dramatically, and the fact that she had an idea for a new story seemed like a good sign. As odd as it was to be here, she was home, and she drifted off, feeling peaceful and safe.

Chapter 6

Alex's new school was much bigger than what she was used to. The classes had more students, conditions were crowded, and the kids were rougher. They had to go to mass before their first class every day. The teachers were both secular and nuns, but since none of the nuns wore habits, it was hard to tell which was which. And she was shocked by how little homework they were given. It was a good school, but much less demanding than her exclusive private school. But here she knew she would get even better grades. When she got back to the convent at the end of the day, she went straight to her room and finished her homework in less than an hour, and then got to work on the story she had thought of the night before. It was particularly violent, and the crime itself even more disturbing than usual, and the surprise ending she conjured up even surprised her. She sat back looking pleased when she took the last page out of the typewriter, and was smiling to herself when Sister Xavier knocked and walked in.

"Need any help with homework?" She noticed that Alex was smiling, and hoped she'd had a good first day at her new school. "How was it?"

"It was okay, and the homework was easy. I just finished a story. I think it's really good." She grinned and Sister Xavier smiled.

"Can I read it?" Alex nodded and handed the ten pages to Sister Xavier, who sat down on the bed, and looked up several times with a startled expression as she read. She was dazed when she finished and glanced back at Alex.

"What do you think?" Alex asked her, anxious for her opinion, since she liked mysteries and had read a lot of them.

"Do you always write like this?" She wondered if she was even more disturbed by her father's death than they thought, and was reacting with violence.

"Yeah. Sometimes they're bloodier than that, but this is about right."

"You write some brutal stuff!" she commented, but she had to admit that it was seamless, the pace relentless, the characters haunting, and the story very tight. She wrote like an adult, and she had talent. But definitely a quirky mind, or a lot of experience reading crime thrillers. She had written a detective into it inspired by some of the thrillers she'd read, she told Sister Xavier, and she was pleased. It struck the nun that her story was much tougher than anything she normally read, and she would have guessed it was written by a man, and surely not a fourteen-year-old girl. The writing was brilliant. "I like it," Sister Xavier said once she recovered from the shocking crime and surprise ending. "I just didn't expect you to write something like that. Have you ever tried publishing your stories?" she asked with interest.

"My father was going to do it for me, but then he got sick, and he never got around to it. I've got three binders full of my stories, I brought them with me." They were under her bed with his books.

"You should try publishing them," she encouraged her. And then she laughed. "I can see why you don't read Agatha Christie anymore and loved *Silence of the Lambs,* given what you write. I couldn't sleep after a story like that." Alex laughed too, pleased with the effect on her new friend.

"I'll give you some of the other stories in my binder," Alex promised. She loved having someone to show her stories to, although Sister Xavier readily admitted she preferred a different type of mystery.

"Not at bedtime, please," Sister Xavier said, and mentioned the story to the superior later. She was still worried about it, even if it was flawlessly written, and Mother MaryMeg looked intrigued.

"It's shocking for a child that age to have thoughts like that," Sister Xavier whispered to her. She liked crime fiction herself, but Alex's story had been extreme.

"Is it lewd or inappropriately sexual?" the mother superior asked, mildly concerned.

"Not at all, but it's the most violent thing I've ever read. Brilliant, though. There's everything from murder to dismemberment to cannibalism in it, and the crime is committed by the man's wife. The story is complicated, and she kept me turning the pages, but it was still very upsetting, all in all. I thought about it for hours afterward, it haunted me."

"Maybe that's a skill, and not an aberration. Apparently her father encouraged her and shared his favorite books with her. According to my cousin's husband, who knew him, her father thought she had real talent."

"She does, unquestionably," Sister Xavier agreed. "It's just disturbing to think that comes out of her head. She looks so innocent."

"Are you afraid she'll kill us all in our sleep, and chop us up and eat us?" Mother MaryMeg teased her.

"No . . . but it's very scary stuff, if that's what's on her mind."

"I'll have a look," the mother superior reassured her, and said to Alex later that Sister Xavier had been impressed by her story, and she'd love to read one.

Alex looked serious at the mention of it. "I think I upset her. I've been working on that kind of story for a long time. I was inspired by some of the writers my father liked. He always passed his books on to me after he read them." She gave the story to Mother MaryMeg to read after dinner, and the older nun was stunned. It was even more powerful than Sister Xavier had said, and the mother superior thought it was brilliant. She had an incredible way of telling the story. Her timing was flawless, and her character descriptions and development showed great insight into the criminal mind. Mother MaryMeg handed it back to Alex with a look of profound respect.

"You are a very, very talented writer, Alex. That's a gift. Don't waste it." Alex thought that she was going to tell her to write gentler stories about saner people, but Mother MaryMeg seemed to approve wholeheartedly. "I'm sure you'd win an award with it, if you publish it one day. Keep working at it, to develop your gift." She walked away duly impressed and saw Sister Xavier again later. "I think we're living with one of the future great writers of the era. She really has an extraordinary mind."

"You don't think it's a little twisted?" The younger nun looked surprised. She had read high school essays for years and had never seen one like that.

"Of course I do. That's the whole point. It's supposed to be, and she works hard at it. She certainly doesn't leave anything to the imagination. We should encourage her, not hold her back," Mother MaryMeg admonished, and Sister Xavier walked away after saying that Agatha Christie, Miss Marple, and Hercule Poirot were more her cup of tea. But definitely not Alex's, or not in many years. Her writing was razor sharp and wielded like a scalpel. Both nuns thought about her again that night. The elder of the two was in awe of her ability, and the younger shaken by the horrors she created in her mind. But both of them were haunted by the story.

Alex went to bed with another idea for a story that night. She just wished she could show them to her father, who understood her style and knew how to comment on where it needed work to improve it. His editing had been a big help to her. She didn't feel her writing was as strong without him, and it made her miss him even more. But it pleased her that the mother superior had liked her story, and that Sister Xavier was terrified by it. It made Alex smile as she thought of it and fell asleep.

Alex's first month at St. Dominic's flew by. They celebrated her fifteenth birthday three weeks after she moved in, and baked her a cake. It was her first birthday without her father, but they helped her get through it. She found her new school unexciting and uneventful. She made a few friends between classes, but no one she wanted to spend time with. She didn't want to have to explain to them why she was living at the convent. Elena came to visit her on her birthday and cried the whole time, but Alex told her that she was fine and the nuns were good to her. She had told Bill Buchanan the same when he called. Mother MaryMeg had corroborated that she was doing well.

Alex was pleased that she could be alone in her room to work on her writing, but she was also helpful to the nuns when they needed her to be. She was no trouble at all. She was closest to Sister Regina, and despite the thirteen-year difference in their ages, they had become friends, and they confided in each other. Alex was very fond of Sister Xavier too, who had helped her prepare for a math test, on which she got an A. She was getting perfect grades in school.

At the end of the semester, the teachers handed out slips at school for the students' parents to sign up for parent-teacher conferences, and Alex didn't know what to do with hers so she threw them away. She had no parents to attend. Two of her teachers kept her after class to remind her that her parents hadn't signed up yet. They didn't know her story or where she lived, as her records were confidential. Only the principal knew that she was living at the convent.

She told Mother MaryMeg about the problem that night. "Can't they just skip it? Why does someone have to go to their dumb conferences? My grades are fine." Mother MaryMeg thought about it for a minute. She didn't want to put the spotlight on Alex as different.

"What about if Sister Xavier goes for you, or Sister Thomas? Or both of them if you want. How does that sound to you?" She was trying to be creative, so the school didn't feel that Alex's family was disinterested in her, or disrespectful of her teachers or the school. Faculty didn't respond well to that.

"Okay, I guess. My father hated those conferences too, and he didn't always go. I never had a problem at school, my grades were good, and he didn't think it was necessary. And once my English teacher called him in to complain about my stories." Mother MaryMeg had read several more and that didn't surprise her at all. She could clearly see Alex's gift, and also why a teacher would find it disturbing, just as Sister Xavier had at first, although she was used to Alex's stories now.

"I'll see if Sister Xavier can make time to go, or Sister Tommy," which was their nickname for Sister Thomas. When she asked them, they both said they wanted to go, since they had grown attached to their young ward. Alex got new slips for them, and they signed up and went together. They were very satisfied with what they heard, except that all of her teachers found her introverted and withdrawn and said that she needed to socialize more with her peers. But the nuns she lived with knew another side of her now, since they saw more of her, and at times they found her gregarious and funny, and she loved to tease and play tricks on them. But outside of her home environment, which the convent was now, she was quiet and shy, and she seemed to have trouble making friends with young people her age. Both nuns mentioned it to her when they told her about the teacher conferences. At school, one of her teachers said she had met her aunts and Alex wondered if that was who they had said they were. But another teacher said she had met her mother and aunt. No one seemed to be clear about who the two nuns were, nor cared, which was fine with her. She didn't correct them either, and didn't want anyone feeling sorry for her that both of her parents were dead. It would have made her seem like a freak to the other students, and in her own eyes.

Mother MaryMeg was satisfied with their reports. She arranged to send Alex to a Catholic camp that summer in New Hampshire, where she would be an assistant counselor. And although Alex complained bitterly about going, she actually enjoyed it, and came back healthy and tan after swimming and sailing and taking care of younger kids for two months. But she couldn't wait to get into her writing again as soon as she returned. Her stories were becoming more intricate and longer, and the nuns who read them could see progress and growth. Sister Xavier said they were more disturbing than ever, which Alex took as a compliment, and she was particularly pleased when Sister Xavier said she had had nightmares for two days after reading the latest one.

"Yes!" Alex said, and did a little victory dance around her. "And wait till you read the next one. You won't sleep for a week!" she promised, and Sister Xavier rolled her eyes. But they had missed her when she was away, and were happy to hear her tales of the camp, the other counselors, and the campers, whom she had loved. It had been a great summer, and she had played baseball on the counselors' team against the older kids. It reminded her of playing baseball with her dad.

She went to work on the school newspaper in sophomore year. She had totally settled into her life at the convent by then, and made a few friends at school, but always met them outside, and didn't want them to know where she lived. She was invited to a few parties, and she commented to Sister Regina that she had nothing to wear, and Sister Regina organized a shopping trip to a mall with her. Sister Xavier came along, and the three women enjoyed it, and came back with four new dresses for Alex to wear when she went out with her friends, and her first pair of high heels.

"Can you walk in those?" Sister Xavier asked with an incredulous look, and Alex demonstrated that she could, and then Regina tried them on just for fun. She looked terrific in them. They were high-heeled black suede sandals with gold studs. And Sister Regina was shocked at the miniskirts Alex tried on, but that time Sister Xavier was the indulgent one.

"Oh, why not? She looks cute in them." Neither of them had ever owned a skirt that short, but Alex looked so innocent with her perfect face and straight black hair that they thought she could get away with the short skirts, and all the other girls her age were wearing them. They got her some new jeans too, and sweaters for school. They came home with bags full of pretty new clothes that were the first she'd had in a long time. And she had loved shopping with them.

Before, she had gone shopping with her dad, who spent as little time as possible in any store, and rushed to leave. Suddenly she had women to shop with, which she'd never had. And instead of the mother she'd always longed for, she now had two or three, or twenty-six. And Sister Tommy insisted on checking what they'd bought to make sure they hadn't gone too wild. She raised an eyebrow at the miniskirts and high heels, but gave her approval in the end, and threatened to come along the next time, just to enjoy the outing with them. It brought back happy memories for her. They giggled like three friends when Sister Regina and Sister Xavier helped Alex put her new clothes away. And then Alex wrote a story that night about a murder in a department store.

"You have a very sick mind if you can turn a nice day like that into a crime like this," Sister Xavier said when she read it, but she had to admit it was good, and Alex laughed at her as the nun walked away shaking her head. They had come to love her in the year that she'd been with them, and she was growing up before their eyes. She was maturing into a lovely young woman, and was always a willing participant helping in the classes they gave at night.

At the end of sophomore year, she won an award for her work on the school newspaper, and she finally got up the courage to send two of her stories to a crime magazine. They published both, written by A. Winslow, and paid her a hundred dollars for each, and sent her a letter praising her work and encouraging her to continue writing. She showed the letter and the check to everyone, and it was the buzz around the convent for days that Alex had sold two stories to a magazine, and they bought two more when she got back from summer camp again. She was sixteen years old, and she had to start thinking about what colleges she would apply to the following year, and visit them. Both Sister Xavier and Sister Tommy looked at lists and brochures with her to help her decide where to go. She wanted to stay in the Boston area so she'd be close to them, but Mother MaryMeg encouraged her strongly to live in the dorms when she went to college. She could come home to the convent whenever she wanted, but she thought it was time for her to enter the world of her peers, and fully experience college wherever she went.

She visited half a dozen colleges in the Boston area, as well as Middlebury in Vermont, Brown in Rhode Island, and Yale in Connecticut, and she went to New York for a day with Sister Regina to visit NYU and Columbia, but the school she liked best in the end was Boston College. There were ten she was going to apply to, but BC was her first choice.

Sister Xavier and Sister Tommy helped her with her applications the first term of senior year, and they urged her to write tamer essays than her usual fare, which she did. She had been selling stories to detective magazines for over a year by then, but since she wrote under a pseudonym, she didn't put it on her application. But she did enough extracurricular activities at St. Dominic's, had been a counselor at summer camp for three years, and had won two awards for her work on the school newspaper, so she had enough to beef up her application. And her teachers, school advisor, and the mother superior wrote glowing recommendations for her. The nuns were sure she'd get in everywhere, and when the letters came back in the spring, she had been accepted by Yale, Brown, Boston University, Middlebury, and Boston College, and was wait-listed at the others, but she decided on Boston College immediately, which was still her first choice.

"And I'll be nearby and can come home on weekends, if I want," she said, beaming at Mother MaryMeg. It touched her that Alex considered the convent home now after four years. The arrangement had worked out better than any of them had hoped. She was the child most of them had never had, and a fresh breeze of youth in their life. When she had her first date for the junior prom, a dozen of them had watched her get ready and seen her off in a pretty little black dress that set off her figure but was appropriate. Her date was wearing a tux when he picked her up and had to live through twenty-six nuns taking photographs of them and watching them pull away in the limo with his friends. Alex had told him where she lived, but he hadn't fully understood till he saw it when he picked her up. They had become friends, and didn't date again, so it didn't matter to her what he thought of it. Alex was in no hurry to start dating. She spent all her spare time writing, which was her passion. She continued to publish stories regularly in crime magazines under the name "A. Winslow." They paid very little, but it was gratifying to see them in print.

Word spread around the convent like wildfire that Alex had gotten in to Boston College, and there was celebrating in the dining hall that night. Mother MaryMeg managed to pull strings and got twenty-nine seats at Alex's graduation, so all the nuns could be there, and the Buchanans. Alex invited Elena, but she had taken a job in New York and said she couldn't come, and Pattie and her family had faded from Alex's life by then and lost touch. Her family and the center of her universe now were the nuns of St. Dominic's.

When she walked across the stage in her cap and gown to receive her diploma, Alex was beaming and the nuns sent up an embarrassing cheer in unison. They were all thrilled and so proud of her, and Sister Tommy said she felt as though her seventh child was graduating. Sister Xavier was crying, Mother MaryMeg looked on proudly, and Sister Regina gave Alex an enormous hug when they joined her after the ceremony. It was hard to believe that she'd been with them for four years and they'd watched her grow up from a young girl to a beautiful young woman, and she was off to college now.

Mother MaryMeg had convinced her to live in the dorms, although Alex was nervous about it, but she'd agreed. Five of the nuns went to settle her in her new room at the end of August. It reminded them all of the day she'd moved into the convent, but this was an exciting, happy event. She had two roommates, and the nuns unpacked for her, made her bed with the sheets and bedspread she'd bought, and helped her put up posters on her side of the room. One of her roommates asked if they were her aunts, and she didn't answer. She set out a photograph of her father on her desk. She had brought her typewriter with her, and a laptop for her schoolwork, and had bought her books a few days before. She was all set, and all of the nuns who'd come with her had damp eyes when they left her in the dorm with her new roommates, and they cried openly in the car on the way back to the convent, already missing her.

"I feel as though my baby just left home," Sister Xavier said, blowing her nose in a tissue, as Sister Tommy wiped the tears off her cheeks and agreed. Sister Regina was quiet, and was going to miss Alex acutely. And although she was thirty-one, and Alex eighteen now, their friendship had deepened, and she had confessed to Alex a few weeks before that she was having doubts about her vocation for the first time in sixteen years, and she was no longer sure she had made the right decision. Alex was shocked to hear it, and had promised not to tell anyone.

"What are you going to do about it?" Alex had asked her, as they whispered in her room late at night, while Alex was starting to pack for school.

"Nothing for now. I can't leave. I don't want to. But I'm not sure I can stay either. All of a sudden I can't imagine never having children, and not being married. I don't know what's happening to me. And what if I regret it forever if I leave . . . or if I don't?" She was seriously confused and going through a personal crisis, and Alex had urged her to think about it and not do anything hasty, which was wise advice. Her words were still ringing in Sister Regina's ears as they drove back to the convent, and she felt intensely lonely without Alex in her little room right down the hall from her own, clacking away on her typewriter in every spare moment. Her stories had matured and were more complicated, but just as violent, and Sister Xavier said she couldn't read them anymore, but the magazines loved them and couldn't get enough.

Dinner at the convent was a mournful event that night, without Alex. Mother MaryMeg began the meal with a prayer for her that she would find joy and growth, knowledge, and wonderful friends in her new life, and there were tears in many of the sisters' eyes as they prayed for her. And a few miles away at Boston College, Alex was getting to know her roommates.

They all went out for pizza, and met boys from the neighboring dorm. There were a dozen young people at dinner together, boys checking her out, girls chattering around her, pitchers of beer passed around, and for a moment Alex missed the sisters at St. Dominic's, and then started talking in earnest to her roommates. There was no stopping it now. A new time in her life was beginning. She had grown up, and she felt as though she was spreading her wings and taking flight, awkwardly at first, and then she could feel herself soaring. It was exciting and exhilarating, and terrifying all at once. Here she was, starting college. She just sat there for a minute, watching all of them, and as she did, she had an idea for a story about a murder in a college dorm. She could hardly wait to write it that night. And when the others went out after dinner to explore the campus, Alex rushed back to her room to write.

Chapter 7

Alex had taken on a heavy load of six classes for her first semester. She wanted to get her required classes out of the way as quickly as possible, so she could take more that she would enjoy. But she found that she liked the ones she had signed up for, including an eighteenth-century English literature class, which required writing. She knew it was good for her to write more than crime stories and mysteries. She took history and a math class, and a women's studies class. She had a lot of reading to do at night, and loved being challenged by the work. Most of her high school classes had been easy for her, and it was exciting to be taking more challenging courses, taught by professors she admired. She noticed that one of her roommates studied as much as she did and they went to the library together. She was from Hong Kong and a physics major. She'd wanted to go to MIT and didn't get in, but was hoping to try again and transfer for sophomore year. They never saw their other roommate, who was out all the time and had met a boy she was crazy about the first week.

At the end of her first month, Alex went home to the convent, delighted to see the nuns and have a weekend with them, although she had brought home a lot of reading to do, and had a paper to write for her English lit class. She hadn't had time to write any of her own stories for a month, and was frustrated about it.

Sister Regina came to her room after dinner on her first night back, and they talked late into the night. Regina was as troubled as ever about her vocation qualms, and she was debating about talking to Mother MaryMeg about it. She had seen other nuns leave over the years, and told Alex she didn't want to be one of them, but staying in the life she had chosen was becoming harder and harder. She had been depressed for months thinking about it, and Alex was worried about her.

"You should talk to Mother MaryMeg," Alex encouraged her. She didn't know what else to advise, and the choice that women made who wanted to be nuns was still a mystery to Alex, even after living with them for four years. She believed in God, but her religious convictions were not strong enough to make her want to give up the world. She had never been in love and had dated only a few times, for proms, or gone to the movies in groups, but the idea of never marrying and never having kids still seemed strange to her, and an unnatural choice, so she sympathized with Sister Regina's confusion. Regina had started writing, inspired by Alex, but it was more of a distraction, or an outlet of some kind, not a burning desire like what drove Alex, who was compelled to write. But she thought that Regina's short stories were good.

"What kind of work would you do if you left?" Alex asked her.

"Teach, like I do here." But leaving the convent would be like leaving the womb, and the thought of it frightened her enough to keep her there for the time being. But she wasn't happy, and Alex could see it. She didn't know what the right answer was for her, and didn't feel she had the experience to advise her.

Alex came home to the convent again for Thanksgiving, and for the Christmas holiday and semester break, and she had a chance to write then. She had an idea for a novel, but decided to wait until the summer when she had more time.

Her classes were keeping her busy. But in spare moments between assignments, she worked on the outline for the book, which was gnawing at her loudly by spring. She knew she had a story in her, and had to get it out. She couldn't wait for her classes to end in May to start the book. She vacated her room at the dorm, since she would get a new room in a different dorm in the fall, and moved back to the convent. Her first night back, she started work on the novel, which had been developing in her head for months. She worked day and night for the first three weeks and hardly left her room, and she had several chapters written before she began a summer job in a bookshop that specialized in rare books and first editions. Her father had bought books there frequently, and they were impressed by her knowledge, and offered her the job for two months.

She came home from work and wrote every night, and in the last week of August she finished the first draft of her book. It was perfect timing, since she was going back to school the following week. Alex sat staring at four hundred pages of manuscript in her hands the night she finished. She was nineteen years old and had just written her first book. She was so excited she could hardly breathe, and couldn't sleep all night, thinking about it.

She saw Mother MaryMeg at breakfast the next day, who commented that she looked like she'd had a rough night. To her knowledge, Alex still had no social life. She preferred to spend every moment on her book, and was more interested in writing than dating.

"I finished the book last night, the first draft," she said, looking awestruck. She felt as though someone else had done it, channeling through her. Her father maybe. Another writer. Someone. She couldn't believe she'd done it, and felt a little lost without the book to work on. The final weeks had been intense, and she'd worked until three or four A.M. every night, and until dawn occasionally, and then showered and dressed for work. She'd finished her job at the bookshop a few days before, and now the book.

The mother superior smiled at her, impressed by her dedication. There was no question that Alex was a writer. It was in her bones and her blood, a force she couldn't stop and didn't want to. "Would you read it for me?" Alex asked in a low voice. "I don't know if it's any good or not, or if I should just throw it away." She'd had her doubts about it several times, and needed someone to read it objectively now. She knew that her work upset Sister Xavier, and mysteries didn't interest Sister Regina, but Mother MaryMeg was always curious about her work.

"I'm sure it's very good, Alex. I'd love to read it." Twenty minutes later, Alex was in her office with the ragged manuscript in her hands. She had made many corrections and changes, and the pages were a mess. She handed it to the superior, who took it from her and set it on her desk. "I'll start it tonight," she promised. Alex would have been relieved to see her light on until three in the morning. Alex slept like a baby that night, free at last of the story that had pounded through her and tormented her for months.

She noticed that the superior looked tired the next day, but didn't dare ask what she thought of it so far. She was sure that she would hate it, or tell Alex she had gone too far this time. It was a strong book, with a terrifying story and multiple mysteries to solve, and had been difficult to write, like riding five horses at once in a circus act and not losing control.

Two days later, Alex was talking to Regina quietly after breakfast when the superior walked by and asked Alex to come and see her in her office. Alex and Regina exchanged glances. Regina looked panicked, afraid that Mother MaryMeg had guessed that she was having doubts about her vows. The mother superior always knew everything as though she had a sixth sense. Alex was subdued when she walked into her office a few minutes later.

"I should be angry at you," Mother MaryMeg said seriously, as Alex sat down across from her. "I haven't slept in three days, thanks to your book." As she said it, Alex started to look relieved, but not entirely yet. She wanted to know what she'd thought of it. "It's extraordinary, Alex. One of the best books I've ever read. It's bound to get published, and will certainly get your career going as a writer. You have to get it to a publisher." Alex looked stunned by what she was saying.

"You liked it?" Her voice was an anxious whisper as the mother superior smiled broadly.

"I loved it. Or I was mesmerized by it and totally in its grip. I'm not sure 'love' is the right word for a book with such heinous people in it, but your plot is brilliant, and the way you control it is masterful. I don't know where you get the stories from, but it's remarkable. You need to get it to a publisher. It's a very, very powerful book."

"I can't get it to a publisher without an agent," she said miserably, "and I don't know how to find one. I've been thinking about it a lot. A publisher won't take it seriously unless it comes through an agent. They might not even read it without one."

That sounded harsh to Mother MaryMeg, but she took Alex at her word, and wondered how she could find one.

"And an agent will know who would want to publish a book like mine."

"Let me think about it, and try to figure out who I know, or someone else does. Somebody must know a literary agent." She handed the book back to Alex, congratulated her again, and told her she'd see what she could find out.

Alex walked upstairs to her room, dazed by what Mother MaryMeg had said about the book. Regina stuck her head out as soon as Alex walked past her door. "Did she say anything about me? Was it that?" she whispered nervously.

"No, she liked the book. She said I should get it to a publisher, but I don't know how." Sister Regina looked instantly relieved, and apologized for leaping at her.

"I'm just so afraid she knows what I'm thinking. She always knows everything that's going on." They attributed magical powers to her, but this time Regina was wrong. It was only about her book.

Two days later, Mother MaryMeg came to see Alex in her room. "I've talked to everyone I know who might know an agent or a publisher, and this is the best I could do," she said, handing a piece of paper to Alex, with her firm handwriting on it. It was a woman's name, a phone number, and an address in New York. "One of the sisters had a brother-in-law in publishing. He's retired, but he said he'd ask around about agents for you. He just called me back. He said he's never met this woman, but she has a good reputation. She represents a number of successful authors, and she might not see you. But if not, she may recommend someone who would. Her name is Rose Porter. Why don't you call and see if you can get an appointment with her?" Alex held on to the piece of paper like the Holy

Grail, and thanked her, and Mother MaryMeg went back to her office. She was a miracle worker after all. Alex tried to compose herself, and called from the phone downstairs a few minutes later. Her hands were shaking when she did.

A young female voice answered crisply. "Porter, Stein, and Giannini," she said, and Alex almost hung up she was so terrified. She asked to speak to Rose Porter, and they put her on hold for what seemed like forever, as she clung to the receiver with a damp hand. And then the voice came back and told her to hold again while they connected her. She had given her name as Alex Winslow, which would mean nothing to Rose Porter. And they hadn't asked what the call was about, which seemed strange. Alex couldn't know that the girl answering was a summer temp, and was putting calls through left and right, luckily for her. A moment later a female voice came on the line that sounded serious and impressive, and slightly impatient.

"What's this about?" she asked in a clipped tone.

"I wrote a crime thriller, it's four hundred and twelve pages long. I've sold stories to mystery magazines. This is my first book, and I need an agent." The person at the other end laughed.

Rose Porter guessed easily that the caller was young and scared to death. Normally she would have her mail the book, and she'd have someone else read it. But there was something compelling about the voice, it was so intense. It had obviously taken every ounce of courage she had to make the call. Alex remembered then to say who had recommended her, although the agent probably didn't know him.

"What makes you think you can write a crime thriller?" Rose Porter asked, curious about her.

"I've been reading them since I was ten years old. They're my passion, and so is writing."

"How did you get your hands on them at ten?"

"My father gave them to me. They were his passion too."

"Young women don't usually write crime thrillers," she said bluntly.

"I know, my father told me that too. I publish my stories in magazines just using an initial and my last name. I could use a pseudonym for the book." The woman at the other end laughed again. Alex had been thinking a lot about whether or not to use a man's name, remembering her father's advice.

"Maybe I should read it first, before we start worrying about pseudonyms." She hesitated for what seemed like a long time, while she thought about it. "I'd like to meet you. Why don't you bring it in?" Alex held her breath for a minute and thought she might faint.

"When?"

"Does tomorrow at three work for you?"

Alex couldn't believe it. "Yes, of course, I'll be there." She would have walked to New York on bleeding feet if she had to.

"Tell me your name again," the agent said, sounding distracted.

"Alexandra Winslow."

"Right, Miss Alexandra Winslow. See you tomorrow at three."

Alex thanked her profusely and hung up, and ran into Mother MaryMeg's office to tell her. She was nearly hysterical. "I'm going to New York tomorrow . . . to see her . . . to meet her . . . and give her the book . . . Can I use the copy machine?" The mother superior said she could, and Alex spent the next hour copying the manuscript on their old machine, so she could keep a safety copy for herself.

She didn't tell anyone else she was going, and the next morning she took the train to New York and arrived at Penn Station at two P.M. She was wearing a simple black dress and flat shoes and it was a blisteringly hot New York day. Alex took a cab to the agent's office on Fifth Avenue, near Rockefeller Center, and arrived for the appointment ten minutes early, clutching her manuscript to her chest. She gave the receptionist her name. It was the same girl she'd spoken to the day before.

She had a fifteen-minute wait and then a small, impeccably dressed woman appeared, in a navy blue Chanel suit, with high heels, a short, stylish haircut, and large glasses. She looked Alex over intently, and guessed instantly who she was, and smiled.

"Why don't you come to my office, Alexandra," she said formally, and Alex followed her down a long carpeted hall with expensive art on the walls to a corner office with an impressive view and an enormous desk. Rose Porter looked tiny behind her desk, but she had a huge presence, and Alex was terrified.

"That's the book?" She pointed to the manuscript pressed to her chest, as Alex nodded. Rose Porter held a hand out, and Alex passed it to her, feeling as though she were giving up her first child. The agent thumbed through it for a minute and then smiled at her again. "I can tell you worked hard on it," she commented, noticing all the corrections and added pages.

"I did." It had been a long time since Rose Porter had seen a manuscript as battered. You could tell it was Alex's first book.

"I like the title." She had called it *Blue Steel*. "How old are you, Alexandra?" There was something very touching about her as she sat there, scared stiff. Rose had been known to frighten people intentionally, but she felt sorry for this intense young woman who was so obviously desperate to publish her book.

"Nineteen," she said, looking Rose in the eye, and the agent winced.

"I figured maybe twenty-four or twenty-five, although you look about fourteen." She'd assumed she had to be considerably older than she appeared. "We won't tell a publisher your age, if we get one."

"Or my name," Alex said firmly. "I want to publish under a male pseudonym." Alex had made the decision. Rose looked surprised.

"That gets complicated, particularly if the book does well, or you write others after this. Are you sure you want to do that?"

"Yes. Readers won't take me seriously if they think I'm a girl. My father told me that."

"I don't agree. But why don't I read the book first, and then we'll talk about it. You live in the city?"

Alex shook her head. "In Boston."

"And you came down to meet me?" She was stunned at that.

Alex nodded.

"I'm very grateful that you agreed to see me," she said in a rush, and Rose found it refreshing to talk to someone so grateful and undemanding. She had a roster full of difficult writers who thought the world of themselves and expected the moon of their publishers and agents. Alex was a breath of fresh air.

"Where can I get in touch with you?"

Alex wrote down her name, phone number, and address. "I go to Boston College." But she had given her the convent number for messages.

"You may not hear from me for a while. I have several trips planned, and I don't usually read new authors, but I'll try to read this one when I have time." Something told her that Alex was special and different, and she didn't want to rely on someone else's judgment about her book. Once in a while someone like her came in off the street, out of nowhere, with a fantastic book. She wanted to be sure that she didn't miss it. She had an odd, inexplicable feeling about Alex. Sometimes exceptional writers were compelled to write at her age. Maybe she was one of them, and the type of book she had chosen was definitely unusual for a woman.

Rose Porter stood up then, with Alex's book between them on her desk. She saw the way Alex looked at it, and she smiled at her. "I'll take good care of it, I promise. I assume you made a copy." She didn't want the responsibility of keeping the only existing copy of the book.

"Yes, I did." Alex thanked Rose again for seeing her, and a moment later, she left the office, went down in the elevator, and wanted to scream when she reached the street, she was so excited. She walked back to Penn Station in the deadly heat and felt like she was walking on air. Whatever happened now, she knew she had done her best. She had written the book and gotten it in the hands of an agent. After this, as Mother MaryMeg would say, it was up to God.

Chapter 8

Alex started her sophomore year at Boston College the week after her trip to New York to see the agent. She hadn't heard anything from her by then, and didn't expect to. Rose Porter was an important, busy woman, and Alex knew it would take a while for her to read the book and get back to her. Halfway through September, she had an idea for another book, and started working on an outline one weekend when her roommate was away. She had homework to do, but couldn't stop herself, and the words just rolled onto the page. She had figured out the plot by the end of the weekend, and was happy with it, and she'd written a few pages of the first chapter. She had the opening scene nailed and it was a knockout. The title of the book would be *Darkness*.

She had finished four chapters of her book, according to her outline, when she heard from Rose Porter two weeks later in October. Mother MaryMeg called her at school to tell her that the agent had left a message for her. Alex didn't know if that was good or bad news—maybe she called to deliver rejections too. She returned the call with trembling hands again from the phone in the dorm lobby, and got through to her very quickly.

Rose cut to the chase, sounding busy. "I read *Blue Steel.*"

"Thank you," Alex said, holding her breath.

"It's terrific. I'd like to represent you. It needs some editing, we can talk about that later. I think I can sell your book. I'm going to have it retyped and send it out next week. I'll mail you the agency agreement, and if it meets with your approval, sign it and send me back one copy, and keep the other for yourself. You can have an attorney look at it for you, if you have one."

"I do," Alex said, stunned by everything she had just said.

"And what name are you going to publish under, if we sell it? Are you still determined to publish under a male pseudonym?"

"Yes. Alexander Green," she said, off the top of her head.

"Why 'Green'?" Rose assumed it was her mother's maiden name or something similar, which was usually the case with pseudonyms.

"It's my favorite color," Alex said, smiling, and her new literary agent groaned.

"Oh God, you are thirteen years old. You'd better like the name, because you could be stuck with it for a long time, and I hope you will be. It's a very, very good book, and I'm happy to represent you," Rose said kindly. She liked her, even though it was obvious that Alex had no idea what she was doing, or about the publishing business, but she was one hell of a great writer. One of the best Rose had read in a long time. She had been an extraordinarily lucky find. It was kismet for both of them.

"Thank you," Alex said politely. "I'm working on a new one. I've done four chapters so far."

"There's someone I'd like you to meet, to help you with the editing," Rose said, sounding businesslike again. "His name is Bert Kingsley, and he happens to be in Boston. He only works with writers he likes. I want you to call him, and work on *Blue Steel* with him. And he can advise you about the new one. He's a brilliant editor. I'll give him a call first. I'll pay for it. You can pay me back when we sell the book. I think it's important. He can help you tighten your writing even more than it already is. He's a little gruff at first. Officially, he's retired, but he takes on projects like this from time to time. If he likes what you write, he'll be a wonderful ally for you. Learn as much as you can from him. There are almost no editors left like him." She was very pleased to hear that Alex was working on another book. It was the sign of a true writer. She hadn't waited to hear Rose's reaction, or to see if it would sell. She had another book in her, and had to get it out. Those were the writers Rose looked for and wanted to represent. She had a true vocation, a powerful drive about her writing, and immeasurable talent.

Alex jotted down Bert Kingsley's number when Rose gave it to her, and Rose told her to keep trying until she reached him. He didn't always answer his phone or return calls. She made him sound like a cantankerous old man, and Alex was a little nervous about working with him, but she could at least meet him once and see what she thought. She trusted Rose's judgment.

The contract arrived at the convent three days later, and Alex called Bill Buchanan to tell him, and sent it to him, and he called her the following week to say that it was fine and she could sign it.

"You've written a book, Alex?" He sounded surprised and impressed. Despite all the changes she'd been through, she was still writing, a novel now, not just stories. He knew how pleased and proud her father would have been.

"Yes, and I'm working on another one."

"That's very exciting. Don't forget to have some fun too. You should be having a good time in college." She was, but mostly with her writing. She still hadn't been on any dates, and didn't really care. She had only one roommate this year, a girl from Mississippi who had just gotten engaged and was with her fiancé all the time, which gave Alex peace and quiet to write in her room. It worked well for her.

She called Bert Kingsley the following week, to give Rose Porter plenty of time to get in touch with him and send him the manuscript so he could read it. And when he answered, he seemed as though she'd woken him out of a sound sleep. She apologized profusely, and he didn't sound happy to hear from her.

"Rose Porter called me. She sent me your book." He didn't say if he'd read it or not, and Alex was afraid to ask him.

"I'm writing my second one now," she volunteered. "Rose just signed me on as a client."

"So she said." He seemed unimpressed and sounded like a cranky old man. Rose had called him a curmudgeon, which seemed about right.

"Rose thought you could help me edit," Alex said cautiously.

"I'm retired," he growled at her. "Editing young writers is a lot of work," he complained. There was a long silence then while Alex didn't know what to say to him. "Why don't you come over on Saturday? I'll have finished reading your manuscript by then," he said grudgingly. He told her he lived in Cambridge, near the Harvard campus where he used to teach. She wasn't looking forward to meeting him, he sounded disagreeable, but she didn't want Rose to be angry at her either for not trying to meet him, so she bicycled over to his address on Saturday at the appointed time. He had told her to come at noon. And when she got there, he took forever to answer the bell. She was just about to leave when he opened the door. He was startled when he saw her, as though he'd forgotten she was coming, and then he nodded and stepped aside when she reminded him who she was. He didn't say it, but he was stunned by how pretty she was and even younger than he'd expected.

She followed him upstairs to a large living room that would have been lovely if he tidied it once in a while. There were stacks of books everywhere, a pile of newspapers, a mountain of manuscripts on the desk, half-eaten food from the night before, and an empty bottle of red wine on the coffee table. He obviously lived alone and needed a housekeeper desperately. He was as disheveled as his living room. He had a long, unkempt beard, a mane of wild white hair that made him look like Albert Einstein, and was wearing jeans, a sweater with holes in it, and tennis shoes. It was hard to figure out his age, but he seemed to be about seventy, although Rose told her later that he was only sixty. But to Alex, he looked ancient. And she had a feeling he was hungover from the empty wine bottle sitting on the coffee table.

He pushed some papers aside and made room for her on the couch, and then sat in a big overstuffed chair with sagging springs across from her.

"I read your book." He stared at her for a long time while she waited for him to tell her it was garbage and throw her out. She fully expected him to do that. "You need to simplify the beginning. And you need to slow down the last two chapters. You rushed them," he said critically in a sharp tone, but she had suspected that herself.

"You get too complicated in the second chapter, that slows it down. You can tell them most of that later. Don't interrupt the pace for your reader." He picked up her manuscript and showed her several places where he thought she should move sections to later in the book, and as she read it with him, after his comments, she could see that he was right. They were simple changes, but they made a difference in the smooth flow of the book. He got right down to business with her, and had obviously read *Blue Steel* several times and made detailed notes.

She spent two hours with him. All the suggestions he made were valid, and he had a way of spotting the problems and telling her how to correct them and where to make changes that all seemed reasonable and helpful to her. What he said wasn't complicated, but it was brilliant.

"Come back next Saturday, after you've worked on it. And I like your book, by the way." It was high praise coming from him, and she was stunned. He hadn't even offered her a glass of water while she was there. He only cared about the book. "Rose said you're good. She's right," he said simply. "Otherwise, I wouldn't have seen you. She's got an amazing eye for talent. See you next week, same time, and bring the outline for the new one," he closed the door behind her. He seemed in a hurry to get rid of her, and had wasted no time on small talk. But she could tell that the work they'd done that afternoon would make the book much better. It was like giving her book a good cleaning so it shone, and a tune-up. Rose was right to make the suggestion that they work together. Bert was a great editor, and she was flattered that he liked her work. She was curious about him, but he had volunteered nothing about himself, nor asked about her. He was interested only in the book.

She made the corrections he suggested before they met again on the following Saturday, and she brought the new outline with her and a copy of the first chapter to leave with him. He read the changes she'd made to *Blue Steel* and said he liked them. And then he poured himself a glass of wine, didn't offer one to her, and made another date for a week later, which was her cue to leave. And as weird as he was, she liked working with him. He really improved her book. She smiled at him, and couldn't help wondering how he had gotten so rumpled and his house such a mess. He looked like he'd been shipwrecked for years.

Alex couldn't resist saying something to Rose Porter about him when she called her on Monday to tell her that they had spent two Saturdays together and it had gone well. Alex told her she was sending her a copy of the changes to *Blue Steel*. Rose was pleased. Bert was the most talented editor she'd ever known and would help Alex hone her skills.

"How was he?" Rose asked, with a faint tone of concern, and Alex wasn't sure what she meant at first.

"Gruff, cranky, like you said," Alex said honestly. "But what he said about the book was terrific. All his suggestions made it better, even when they were really simple."

"That's why he's the best editor in the business. Simple is almost always better. It's about timing and balance and where to put something. His eye for that is uncanny."

Alex agreed.

"Was he okay otherwise?"

Alex hesitated and then answered her question. "His house looks like a bomb hit it and so does he. But he likes the book and was fine with me. He wasn't friendly, but he's not mean or rude. And he's very focused."

"Did he get drunk?" Rose asked her bluntly, which startled Alex a little.

"No. He poured himself a glass of wine as I was leaving, but he didn't drink while we worked, and he was sober." Alex felt sorry for him when Rose asked the question, and she could easily imagine him getting drunk after she left. "Does he have a problem?"

Rose sighed before she answered. She felt strangely close to this exceptional young woman she had taken under her wing. "He used to, for a while. I think he has it under control now. He had some tough things happen that he never got over. He was one of those confirmed bachelors who never wanted to marry. He was a great editor, and always did some teaching on the side. About twenty years ago, when he was forty, he fell madly in love with one of his students. She was a fantastic writer, a poet, and she wrote historical novels, not at all your kind of thing, but very elegantly done. She was a very talented young woman and they were very happy. But she had a dark side, some writers do. You could see it in her writing. I think there were some family problems, her sister died of cancer or something, and Faye committed suicide. She was twenty-six years old, and it was a terrible waste of a nice woman and a great talent. It always is. It almost killed Bert. I think he stayed drunk for a year. He went back to teaching eventually, but he's never been the same. He's still a fantastic editor, but part of him died with her. That was fifteen years ago. He retired a few years back. He's pretty much been a recluse since she died. Faye was the only woman he ever loved. It's a sad story, and even if he's difficult at times, I love him dearly. I'm glad you two got along. He'll be great to help you edit your books."

Alex was bowled over by the story and didn't know what to say at first. "How terrible for him," she said softly, suddenly more compassionate about how he lived and looked, and how gruff he was. They talked for a few more minutes. Rose said she liked the new outline too, and then they hung up.

*   *   *

Alex did her "homework" for Bert again that week, remembering the story Rose had told her about him. And she forgave him easily now when he was cranky with her. He always looked hungover when they met, but he never drank more than a single glass of wine, if any, with her when they were working, although once or twice she saw him pour himself a straight scotch right before she left. And the work they did together was extraordinary with great results. He guided her in the writing of her second novel all through the fall. They had a strong professional relationship but never discussed their personal lives, only her books. He had become her mentor and teacher, and improved her writing immeasurably.

She put the finishing touches on *Darkness,* her second book, during the Christmas holidays, and on January 2, with Bert's approval, she sent it to Rose Porter as a finished novel for her to sell to publishers. And she already had an idea for a third. She was becoming a book machine. He teased her about it, but he was proud of her, and so was Rose.

Although Bert didn't agree with her and said it was a waste of time, she signed up for a creative writing class at school for second semester. She thought it would teach her something to try more varied fiction assignments, but it was a disappointment. There was an arrogant student in the class who criticized her work constantly, and had no talent himself. The teaching assistant was lazy, and the famous writer supposed to teach the class was never there.

She worked on her third book, *Hear No Evil,* as soon as she finished her second one, during sophomore year, with Bert's help. Writing-wise, things were going well, although she felt like a loser socially.

She hadn't joined any clubs or sports teams, and when she got lonely, she went home to the convent for a night or weekend. There was no room for anything but writing in her spare time, so she totally neglected her social life. She said as much to Mother MaryMeg when she'd asked if she was dating, and was surprised she wasn't. Alex had grown even more beautiful than she had been as a child and young teenager.

"I haven't met anyone I really like."

"Do you give yourself a chance to meet anyone, or are you always writing the way you are here?" Alex smiled at her sheepishly, knowing it was true. She worked constantly and loved what she did. Her first two books hadn't sold yet, but Rose was sure they would. She had only represented her since September. "Have you thought about what's going to happen when you get successful?" Mother MaryMeg asked her, seeing that possibility not so far down the road.

"I can buy cuter clothes." Alex laughed, sounding her age for a minute.

"Aside from that, people will be jealous of you. That may be why the pompous student in your writing class made nasty comments. I'm sure he was jealous of your talent. Envy is a very ugly thing and very dangerous. You have to protect yourself from it every day."

"That's why I'm going to publish under a pseudonym," Alex said innocently. "Then no one will know it's me. Except you, my editor, and my agent."

"And what will you tell people you do for a living?" Mother MaryMeg was intrigued.

"I can say I'm an editor, or I write articles or something," she said vaguely.

"You can't hide your light under a bushel forever," the mother superior warned her gently.

Bert said pretty much the same thing when she told him she was going to write under a pseudonym. "Don't be afraid to be who you are. No one can take that away from you, and they shouldn't," he said firmly. He had grown very fond of her in their months of working together, and sometimes treated her more like a daughter than a pupil.

"Women aren't supposed to write crime," Alex said stubbornly, still adopting her father's prejudice as her own. "If I write under my own name, men won't want to read them." She had heard it from her father and believed it. She trusted his word and judgment completely. He hadn't liked female crime writers, and would only buy a thriller written by a man.

"It's still a men's club, but not entirely," Bert conceded. "The problem is that your books are more 'evil' than most women write. What name are you going to publish under?" he asked her, curious.

"Alexander Green," she said proudly. If they wouldn't let her into the clubhouse as a woman, she could sneak in the window as a man.

"That sounds good," he said, approvingly. "In some ways you do write like a man, Alex, but whatever you write is going to piss off some people because you're so damn good at what you do. And male readers will want you to be a man. Maybe you're right. It may just be easier for you to write under a man's name."

"That's what my dad always told me."

"I hate to give in to that kind of limited thinking," Bert said, and then smiled at her. "But Alexander Green it is." They went on editing then, and corrected a few problems she hadn't been able to solve herself. He always had the right fixes, and knew just where to insert something, what to cut, and how to move things around. It was still her writing, but he made it better, just as a good editor was supposed to do. He never inserted his own words and ideas, but he used her own to improve it, in ways she hadn't thought of and didn't see.

They finished *Hear No Evil* in March. She had three books to sell now. She was a prolific author as well as a talented one.

Alex got a call from her agent in April.

"I've got good news, Alex. We've had an offer for *Blue Steel*." She hadn't shown the other two yet, and wanted to wait till they sold the first one. Alex had to establish herself with one published book first before a publisher would buy more, which Rose had explained to her. And now they had their first sale, to a very reputable publisher offering a standard amount for a first book. They would publish it the next spring, a year from now. And they had accepted that she would do no publicity for it. She couldn't, and preserve the secret of her identity as a woman crime writer. "I expect to have a contract on my desk by next week."

Alex couldn't believe it. She thanked Rose profusely and called Bert to tell him as soon as they hung up. And then she went to St. Dominic's the next day to tell the nuns in person. She was beaming as she came through the door and told Mother MaryMeg the minute she saw her.

"I sold my book!" she shouted with glee. The mother superior gave her a hug, and Alex ran upstairs to tell the others. She stopped in her room for a few minutes to glance at the photographs of her father. He would have been so proud of her.

She found Sister Regina in her room. She had lost weight in the last few months and looked troubled. She was going to mass frequently and trying to spend more time praying. But so far nothing helped, as she wrestled with the agonizing decision of what to do with the rest of her life. The mother superior was aware of it, and had suggested counseling. She had told her that at some point in most lives dedicated to the church, there came a crisis of some kind, and either a renewal of one's faith or a change of direction. Sister Regina was still at the crossroads and felt paralyzed, but she was happy for her friend, and her good news about the book. Her career as a writer was beginning.

Alex signed the contract after Bill Buchanan checked it out. They had created a plausible biography for "Alexander Green" by then, and Rose and Alex had fun doing it. He was thirty-six years old, born in the States but had grown up and been educated in England. He was reclusive and lived in Scotland part of the year, and Montana when he came to the States. He preferred the rugged outdoors to cities, was unmarried and had no children, and under no circumstances would he agree to do publicity for the book. There were to be no photographs of him, and the publisher was so excited about the work that they agreed to all of her conditions. They had assigned her an editor, Amanda Smith, with whom Alex would communicate by email, so she didn't have to see her. And all the real editing had been done by Bert.

As soon as school ended, she moved back into the convent and wrote every day. She was working on a plot outline for another book.

"Are you still writing thrillers that will scare your readers half to death?" Sister Xavier teased her after she missed lunch one day, and she brought Alex a sandwich at her desk and some fresh peaches from the kitchen. It was hot in Alex's room, as she pounded away on her typewriter, but she didn't care. She had never been happier.

"I'm trying to." Alex smiled at her. She had more confidence in herself since selling the first book. Her only frustration was having to wait another ten months before they could sell her second and third books. It seemed like a long wait. She joined them in the dining room that night to take a break from her writing. She told them that she was going to New Hampshire for a week in August, to attend a summer camp for writers she'd read about. There were going to be several well-known guest speakers, and the writers at the camp were mostly unpublished. She thought it would be interesting, but Bert said she'd be wasting her time and her money when she told him. She felt a little more extravagant at the moment, having received the advance for her first book. Rose had explained to her how the advance worked. The publisher estimated what she would make on royalties for a certain number of books. If she sold more, they would pay her the difference. If less, she still got to keep the advance. It sounded good to her.

"What do you need with a writers' camp, for God's sake? Stay here and work on your outline," Bert told her. "They're going to be a lot of bored wannabes who are never going to write a book, and has-been hacks telling them how to do it." Bert didn't believe in creative writing workshops for amateurs. And she was a pro now.

But in spite of his dire warnings, she left for the camp in August. They promised campfires at night, and the simple life in tents, and lectures and workshops all day long to help campers hone their writing skills. The draw for her had been an important mystery writer who was supposed to be there, and she thought meeting him might be interesting and helpful.

But when she got there, the accommodations were incredibly uncomfortable, raccoons wandered through the tents at night, the mosquitoes attacked them constantly and devoured them, and teachers and would-be writers alike spent most of their time having sex or drinking too much, or both. The lectures were incredibly boring, and the well-known mystery writer never showed up, and was replaced by a very good-looking writer in his late thirties who had written two pornographic crime books that no one had ever heard of, and it was later revealed he self-published. He spent most of his time trying to seduce the housewives from Connecticut who had come to the camp to learn about more than just writing and went swimming naked at night in the nearby lake after drinking too many mojitos.

The writer's name was Josh West, and he noticed Alex immediately. She felt out of place the moment she got there, and spent most of her time hiking in the hills surrounding the camp, and avoiding the others. She was startled and a little unnerved when he followed her on one of her walks one day. He approached her when he walked into a clearing as she was sitting on a rock, gazing at the view and trying to decide if she should leave the workshop early.

"You look very serious," he said. "Am I interrupting a literary meditation?" he asked as he sat down next to her, a little too close for her liking. "It's good fun being here, isn't it?" He had a movie star smile and perfect teeth, he had the appearance of someone who worked out a lot, and he had taken his shirt off so she could admire his muscles.

"It's not exactly what I expected," she said, although it was precisely as Bert had predicted, much to her dismay.

"What did you expect then?" Josh seemed surprised. Most people loved it there.

"More writing, and a little less 'fun.'" She could hear the others having sex in the tents at night, after they sat around the campfire drinking too much and passing joints around, playing strip poker, or they came back to the camp naked after a swim. It was Sodom and Gomorrah for would-be writers.

"It's good to let your hair down. What kind of writing do you do?" He hadn't talked to her yet, and she had been avoiding him, once she observed him trying to seduce the other women indiscriminately. She was the youngest person in the camp. The only other person close to her age was a Dartmouth dropout who said he was writing a book about whales and smoked weed all the time. So far, he was incoherent every day by dinnertime, and she could smell the marijuana wafting from his tent at all hours of the day and night.

She wasn't sure how to answer Josh about her writing, and didn't want to tell him the truth. She said the first thing that popped into her head. "Young adult novels, for girls." She felt ridiculous saying it, because it was so far afield from what she did write, but her answer suited her image better than the truth.

"No sex in those, I guess," he said, looking bored, and then put a hand on her thigh and smiled at her, as she wondered in terror if he was going to rape her. "Maybe you need to do a little research so you can move on to adult novels, although the big money is in YA these days, so you're smart to aim for those, just don't live them." It was a slimy thing to say, and she stood up to get his hand off her leg. He made her feel dirty just sitting next to him.

"I think I'll go back to camp," she said as she started to walk away and he followed her. She was by far the most attractive woman in the camp—he just hadn't gotten around to her yet. He assumed that every woman there would be pleased to go to bed with him, but he was wrong about Alex, who made it clear that she wouldn't. He reminded her of a snake as he slithered along beside her.

"How about a swim in the river on the way? And since we didn't bring our bathing suits . . ." He smiled lasciviously at her, and she wanted to throw up. She sped up her pace, which only enticed him more, and just before they reached the camp, he grabbed her, pulled her into his arms, and pressed his body against her. She could feel his erection bulging in his hiking shorts, and knew exactly what it was, although she'd never been in that situation before. She was still an innocent at twenty. By pure reflex, she did the only thing she could think of to get him off her and raised her knee sharply into his groin. And as he doubled over, she ran the rest of the way back to camp, and went to pack her bags. The week at writers' camp had been expensive, but she didn't care. She was packed by the time he got back to camp, limping slightly and livid. He stopped at her tent and looked at her with eyes blazing with pain and fury.

"What are you? A lesbian?" he spat at her, while two women stopped to listen and wondered what had happened.

"No, a writer. I must be the only one here. What is this? A sex camp for bored housewives and people like you pretending to be writers?"

"Who are you? Heidi? What did you expect here?"

"A lot more than this. Have a great week," she said as she brushed past him and went to check out at the main tent. She was in her rented car five minutes later, and offered no explanation for her early departure. She drove home slowly through New England and got back to the convent four hours later, where everyone was surprised to see her. She told them about it at dinner, and they were relieved she had left. And when she saw Bert a week later, she told him he had been right about the writers' camp.

"I told you, it's just a lot of wannabes looking to get drunk or high and laid."

"You forgot to tell me that part," she said, looking embarrassed.

"You don't belong in a place like that. You're the real deal, Alex. There's nothing you can learn from them." She had discovered that herself, and she still felt sick when she thought of Josh West. She told Bert about that too. "What's a porno crime novel?" he said, laughing after she told him she had kneed him in the groin.

"I didn't want to ask. But when he gave a workshop on self-publishing, which he recommends, I realized that that's how he published his porno crime series."

"What did you tell him you write?"

"Young adult books for girls," she said, and started to laugh too. "I couldn't think of anything else."

"That's what you look like. They should know you write the scariest damn crime scenes I've ever read." And she did it with art, skill, and precision. The victims in her books so far were evildoers whose deaths were no loss to anyone. There were no crimes against women or children. The key to her books was not the violent deaths she depicted, but the intricate twists and turns in the plot to solve the crimes. They were acts of pure genius that kept the reader guessing till the end. There was nothing seamy or sordid about them, which wasn't easy to pull off and yet somehow she did. They were smart books for intelligent people—a Rubik's Cube of crime that she took apart and put back together, and presented the simple answer no one had thought of in the end. Reading her books was like watching a magic trick, even he couldn't figure out how she did it, which he loved about her work. There was no sex in the books, and the reader didn't even miss it. She had created a style all her own, distilled from all the crime books she had read, detective stories, and thrillers. And he thought her latest one was even stronger than the first two, and it involved multiple murders.

"No more writers' camps for you, young lady," he chided her. "Now get back to work," he said sternly, and then chuckled to himself as he walked to his kitchen to get a glass of wine. He loved working with her. It was the most fun he'd had in years, and he was learning from her too. It was a good exchange. He was grateful to Rose for bringing them together, and so was Alex.

He sat down in his favorite chair and read the new pages she'd brought him. She'd completed the outline and was starting to work on the book.

"This is terrible," he said, frowning at her after he read for a few minutes.

"It is? I thought it was good. I thought it was a lot tighter." She looked disappointed.

"You're right. It's terrible because there isn't a damn thing I can do to improve this. You're getting too good for me, Alex. Slow down a little. You learn too fast. Give an old man a chance." She smiled at what he said and was pleased.

"Don't worry. I just had a good run this week. I'll make a mess of it again next time." But he doubted it. She was learning quickly. And one day she wouldn't need him anymore, but the time hadn't come yet. He still had a few tricks to teach her, and she was an avid student.

He sent her home early, back to work on the book, and after she left, he poured himself another glass of wine, and thought that if he'd had children, all he could have wanted was a daughter like her. But he knew he would never have been that lucky. He was just happy to be her mentor and her friend. She had added immeasurably to his life. And he hoped it would never end. It made up for some of what he'd been missing for fifteen years.

Chapter 9

When Alex went back to college in September for her junior year, she was finally able to enroll in more of the electives she wanted to take for her major in literature and her minor in creative writing, which seemed less crucial now, with a book sold to a publisher. But she was looking forward to taking classes which were of more specific interest to her. She worked hard in school and kept up her grades. She was writing her fourth book when she went back to school, and she continued to spend Saturdays with Bert Kingsley. He always had useful comments about what she wrote.

Alex took a heavy course load again. Her advisor felt she could handle it, since she always maintained her grades. And all through the fall, she had the fun of approving the book jacket, ads, and flap copy of her upcoming book. She carefully read the galleys and made corrections. Everything was sent to her through her agent, and Rose forwarded it to the convent since Mr. Green was supposed to be in Scotland.

Alex loved the cover of the book. It was a shimmering steel blue, with a knife blade as the main graphic. She could hardly wait for it to come out in April. And for spring semester she signed up for a fiction class, despite the fact that her career was taking off. The professor was a well-known female novelist whose books Alex had enjoyed. They were entertaining and fun and totally different from her own. Scott Williams, the teaching assistant, was an unpublished writer so far, but he told the students he was working on a novel, and took over for the professor for a month, while she went on a seven-city publicity tour for her latest book.

Scott was lively and intelligent, and told Alex he liked her writing style, although he criticized her plot twists and said they were weak, which surprised her. She handed in her assignments on time, and was particularly proud of the one which he gave her a C– on, and told her that her characters were unappealing, not believable, and didn't move him. Then she realized that he was competitive with her, and judging her work harshly, whenever she felt she had written the piece well. She finally took some of the stories to Bert for his opinion.

"Is this as bad as he says?" she asked about the story she'd been shocked to receive a C– on. He read it and looked up at her with a grin.

"You must be kidding. I like your crime stuff better, but this is great. What's wrong with this guy?"

"I'm not sure. He's very nice to me, but he doesn't like what I write, and he keeps giving me lousy grades."

"It's the green-eyed monster again, my dear."

"Meaning?"

"He's jealous as hell. Have you seen anything he's written?"

"No. He's not published. He's writing the great American novel, and has been working on it for six years."

"You can write circles around him, even in a different genre from what you're best at. You're a hell of a writer, Alex. My guess is that this guy can't write for shit, and recognizes you for what you are, a real writer. I'd love to see what he's written."

"So what do I do now? I don't want grades like this on my transcript. I could drop out, but I hate to quit and waste the time and effort I've put into it, and get an incomplete in the class. I was taking his assignments seriously till now, but that last grade made me think something wasn't right. I can argue with him about the grade. But he's tougher on me than he is on everyone else."

"Has he seen your crime stories?"

"Of course not. I have you for that," she said glumly. "I don't need him to teach me how to write thrillers. Besides, I already know how to do that. I wanted to learn to write other kinds of stories."

"So you can switch to romance novels?"

"No. I just thought I might pick up some pointers and it would be interesting to write something else." But Scott was taking the fun out of it for her, and was overly critical of everything she wrote for the class.

She tried discussing it with Scott at the next opportunity, and he suggested they go to dinner and talk about it, and she accepted. She liked him, except for the bad grades.

They agreed to meet at the Washington Square Tavern, a few blocks from the campus, and she rode up on her bike on a freezing cold night. Her cheeks were pink and her dark hair gleamed when she got there. He was waiting for her at the bar. His eyes lit up when he saw her. And he managed to avoid the subject of her grades and assignments for most of dinner, and only got around to it over dessert. They had eaten burgers and ordered ice cream afterward. Hers melted while she listened to him explain everything that was wrong with her writing and why it didn't work. And none of it made sense.

He contradicted himself several times about her plots and her characters and said there was no depth to her work. He was actually quite insulting, and she would have been crushed if she didn't have a book contract under her belt and Bert to reassure her. But what she couldn't figure out was why he was so hostile about her writing. He said it politely, and smiled at her while he did, but when she thought about it afterward, she realized that he had been incredibly mean.

She got a C from him on the next short story assignment. When he asked her out again, she accepted his invitation, wanting to solve the mystery of his attitude about her. He was even more critical the second time, although he was charming and funny over dinner, and kissed her on the lips when he drove her home. But all she could think of were the things he had said about her work, which canceled out everything else.

"Maybe you just don't like my writing," she said when he walked her to the door of her dorm, and she didn't ask him up. She said her roommate was in that night, which wasn't true, but she had no intention of sleeping with him, even if he was obviously smitten with her, which was flattering. But he was anything but smitten with her writing.

"It's not personal," he explained to her. "Your work just isn't strong, compared to the others in the course. In fact, it's very weak, Alex. I think you can do a lot better than that." And oddly, instead of dismissing his comments, she wanted to try harder to convince him she could write and knew what she was doing. It was like a challenge to win him over, which made no sense even to her. She was going to be a published author very shortly, and she had no idea if he could write. But he had been a teaching assistant for four years, so she assumed he knew more than she did about the stories she was writing, and how they should read. She was obviously falling short, and believed him.

He took her to a football game after that, and the movies, and kissed her again. And no matter how hard she tried, her grades didn't improve. But she was dating at least, which made her feel like everyone else, and he was a great-looking guy. Her roommate saw them together and declared him a hunk. So it was official. But all the while they were out together, he slipped in unnerving comments about how inadequate her writing was, which made her feel awful, and then he would tell her how fabulous she was in other ways, and the most beautiful woman he'd ever seen. He made her feel good and bad alternately, and had the power to make her insecure about what she wrote. The only time she felt good about herself was when she was working on her latest book with Bert, or writing alone in her room on weekends. She turned down Scott's invitations because she had to work, and told him she had papers due for her other classes, or had too much reading to do. He invited her skiing during spring break, which she declined too, because she wanted to spend it at St. Dominic's and was hoping to finish her book.

She forgot about his cutting comments when she stood outside a bookstore in April and grinned from ear to ear when she saw her book. There it was. *Blue Steel* by Alexander Green. It was dedicated to her father, and she almost cried when she saw it in the store, it was so beautiful and real. She had given all her free copies to the nuns, who were thrilled for her. She walked past the same store again, two days later, when she was with Scott, and it was still in the window. They stopped to look at what was on display, and Scott pointed at her book.

"I'm reading that now. The guy is incredible. You wouldn't like it, it's too rough, but he has an amazing mind. It's his first book, he lives in Scotland and Montana, grew up in England. He's a man's man. It's beautifully written, with the best lurid crime scenes I've ever read. He makes murder sound like an art." Her heart flew as he said it. So he didn't hate her writing after all, just her assignments for class. She felt better after that. She had him tell her the story, just to see what he'd say, and he hadn't even finished it yet. There were unimaginable surprises in store at the end.

"I hear the ending is great," she said as they walked away.

"The whole book is great," he said, and she beamed.

The professor had returned from her book tour by then, and Alex got two A's in a row, and an A+ on her final assignment, which made her decide to meet with the professor in her office on the last day of class. Scott's grades in the professor's absence were going to pull down her overall grade for the class severely. Alex explained the situation to her, and asked if she would look at the assignments Scott had graded to see if she agreed. The professor said that she usually didn't do that, but she would this time, because the grades seemed surprising to her too, given the caliber of Alex's work.

She got her answer two weeks later. The professor said that there had obviously been a mistake, she thought Alex's stories were outstanding, and she gave her an A+ in the class. Alex was relieved to see it, but more than that, it told her something about Scott. He had been jealous and had abused his position to put her down and make her feel terrible about herself. She felt betrayed, justifiably, and when he called her that night to see her, she said she was busy and couldn't make it. She didn't care anymore about what he'd said about her writing, but she was irate about what he had tried to do to her, to crush her and shake her confidence in herself. He was passive-aggressive to an extreme degree, and it felt like abuse. It had worked for a while, but the professor's grades restored her faith in herself. It was a sad lesson to her.

As it turned out, Bert and others were right. People would be jealous of her writing, and maybe one day her success. She was treading on a minefield when she showed them her work, and Scott had hated her talent and tried to undermine and destroy it. She felt as though he had tried to steal something from her. She didn't answer his calls after that, but he showed up at her dorm the last day of school. She had just sent her latest book to her agent, and was feeling happy and free.

"Why are you avoiding me?" He confronted her in the lobby of her dorm. He had been waiting for two hours, and seemed angry when she walked in. "And what right did you have to sweet-talk the professor into raising your grades?"

"The same right as any student," she said, looking him in the eye. "That was personal, Scott. The work was better than you said."

"Not in my opinion," he answered, turning vicious immediately. "I thought it stank. I could have failed you in the course, but I didn't, because I thought you were cute. But not so cute if you sneak behind my back to complain about the grades I give." The professor had questioned him about it, and wasn't pleased.

"I asked her to judge the work for herself, and I guess she disagreed with you."

"All you care about are the grades. You don't give a damn about the quality of the writing. You won't get anywhere that way. All you'll ever write is junk. You're pathetic," he said with a look that told her how little he thought of her, or how jealous he was, or both. It was shocking to realize that he hated her for the way she wrote, which was a gift.

"By the way, how did that book turn out?"

"Which one?" He was puzzled for an instant.

"*Blue Steel,* by that new guy, Alexander Green."

"It was superb. That's writing of a caliber you'll never reach, not like the crap you write." He wanted to hurt her one last time since she'd dismissed him, for reasons he would never understand or admit to. She was on to him now. And he wasn't throwing bombs at her anymore. He was throwing praise at Alexander Green, whose work he thought was "superb."

"I'll have to buy the book," she said with an evil grin.

"Don't bother. You won't learn anything from it. You're a kiss-ass, Alex, that's the only reason she gave you the grades. You make me sick."

"Maybe you should read Green's last chapter again. It might help you finish your book. See ya." She waved and darted up the stairs, as he stood staring after her. No one had ever treated him like that before, and surely no girl. He had no idea what she meant about his reading the last chapter again. He wondered if she had read the book. It sounded as though she had, which startled him. Otherwise, how would she know about the last chapter, where a struggling young writer steals someone else's book, and murders him for it?

She told Bert about the encounter with Scott the next time they had lunch, since they weren't working on anything for the moment. She was taking a break after finishing the last book. The reviews of her first book had been excellent, and the publisher said that sales for the first month had been better than expected. She was waiting to hear from Rose, who had sent *Darkness* and *Hear No Evil* to her publisher to make a two-book deal for her.

"Beware of writers, my friend," Bert said to her as they finished lunch. "They're a jealous lot, particularly men. They usually don't want women stealing their thunder or their turf. You're a hell of a woman and a hell of a writer. There are going to be a lot of angry men in your life," he predicted. At least she had seen this one coming and had caught on to him quickly, before he did any real damage to her soul or her heart.

"I hope you're wrong about that," she said quietly, remembering what her father had said too. It struck her as sad suddenly that she had to publish her books pretending to be a man. Even her publisher didn't know the truth, only her closest friends and her agent.

"I don't think I am," Bert said wisely. "You're too good a writer for most men to be able to tolerate it, not another writer anyway. Go out with a doctor or lawyer, or a policeman. Stay away from other writers, Alex, they'll punish you every time."

"I don't want that to be true," she said sadly.

"But it is, my dear," he said as he poured himself another glass of wine. They both knew he drank too much, but it never affected his work. "If you go out with writers, and worse, if you fall in love with them, they'll try to steal your magic. But what you have to remember, always, is that they can't. It's your magic and it only works for you, on command."

She thought about it after he said it, and all the way back to the dorm. That's what Scott had tried to do, steal her magic, and maybe Bert was right. It couldn't be stolen or borrowed, or tarnished, or used by someone else. It only worked for her. The magic was hers. The others had to find their own.

Chapter 10

Two things happened to Alex in the summer before her senior year at Boston College. Rose Porter sold her second and third books to the same publisher for twice the money for each book as Alex got for the first one. Alex was thrilled with the deal. The reviews on her first book had been excellent, sales better than projected, and the publisher was rushing to publish *Darkness,* her second book, in time for Christmas that year. And the third one, *Hear No Evil,* would be published the following summer. Rose hadn't offered them her recently finished fourth book, since Alex and Bert wanted to polish it a little more. And Rose wanted to see how the next one did. If it was as successful as she hoped, she was going to ask for a lot more money on the next contract.

And the second thing that happened that summer was that totally by accident, through the creative writing professor who had raised her grade, she got a summer job in New York working for a major publisher for two months.

The professor called her and asked if she'd be interested, and Alex wanted the job. It was a different publisher than her own, and she wanted to learn more about the business. She discussed it with

Mother MaryMeg that night, who encouraged her to do it, and she accepted the next day. It was an internship so the pay was minimal, but she had the money from her book deal, and still more than enough of what her father had left her, and she found a summer sublet in the East Village, a walk-up, to share with four other girls, and it was dirt cheap. It was going to be an exciting summer for her. She was between books at the moment, so she didn't feel guilty taking the time away from her writing. Bert growled about it, and thought she should work on the outline for the next book, but finally agreed that it was a good idea, and it would be fun for her.

She left for New York on June 28 to settle into the apartment, and on July 1, she appeared at Weldon and Small in a navy blue suit she had bought for work, and high heels, with her straight dark hair pulled back, and she felt very grown up. She was assigned to work for Penelope Robertson, who was the senior editor of their very lucrative romance department. She had wild curly red hair, swore like a sailor, drank coffee all day, which Alex had to bring her at a dead run, and smoked in her office although it was forbidden. The tension around her was palpable, everything was an emergency and a crisis, and Alex felt like she was working in a war zone, but she loved it. Her boss had a good sense of humor and treated Alex like she knew what she was doing, which she didn't. She didn't have a clue, but it made her feel competent and important that her boss trusted her to figure things out and threw her into the deep end of the pool, instead of making her just pour her coffee. And there was a flock of other interns there that summer, from a variety of schools all over the country. Alex liked her roommates, three of whom were students at NYU, and one, Pascale, was an exchange student from Paris. They all had summer jobs, and were in and out with their various friends during the evening.

Alex loved being in New York and learning more about publishing, and a completely different kind of book than she wrote. She had lunch with Rose Porter to talk about her recent book sale and the fan base she was building with her first book and its terrific reviews.

"You know, sooner or later, your publisher is going to want to meet you, Alex. I'm not sure we're going to be able to keep them in the dark about you forever. I want to take you to the next level with your next contract, and for bigger money, they're going to want to see who they're buying. They tried to insist this time, and I wouldn't let them. But I doubt we can refuse again," Rose warned her. And Alex liked her editor, Amanda Smith, a lot, via email. Rose had taken her to lunch at Le Bernardin, which made Alex feel very important. It was one of the best restaurants in New York.

"Why do they have to see me? They have the books, they don't need to see me too." She was living in a bubble, and she liked it.

"There's more to it than that. They're starting to invest real money in you," decidedly so with the last contract, "and I want them to invest more. They realize now that there's a future here. It's natural that they want to meet you."

"I don't know." It was working for her and she didn't want it to change. More and more, she realized how important it was for her readers, the public, and even her publishers to believe she was a man. And if she told the truth now about being a woman, her readers would feel betrayed. She was gathering momentum and an ever stronger readership, and she didn't want to jeopardize that now, or ever. And she wanted the next two books to be even bigger successes than *Blue Steel.*

"Your publishers could get seriously pissed about it one day if you refuse to meet them. And there's no way you can do publicity for the books if we're hiding the fact that you're a woman. And one day, you may need that to boost sales."

"We'll have to find another way to do it. Alexander Green writes the books, and that's the way it's going to stay."

"I'll see what I can do, but we may not be able to hold your publishers at bay forever. You're on to a great thing here, with your own style and a powerful voice. It would come as a huge shock to everyone to discover that you're a woman." Not only that, she didn't say, but a very young girl. "So how is New York treating you?" she asked with a smile. Alex looked adorable in her little navy suit, crisp white shirt, and long straight hair.

"I love it here." She beamed at her. "It's so exciting."

"Yes, it is." Rose smiled at her, feeling like her grandmother or a wise old aunt as much as her agent. She really liked Alex. She was a profoundly decent young girl, with good values, and her success wasn't turning her head. She was very modest about her abilities, and Rose had suspected for a while that she would be enormously successful one day. She was willing to work hard, was amenable to editing, and had tremendous skill and dedication. The potential was all there.

"Would you ever want to live here?"

"I don't know," Alex said thoughtfully. "I don't know if it's too much for me. I love Boston, and living at the convent." She had never expected it to be a long-term solution, but she had been there for almost seven years by then, it had become home to her, and the nuns like a houseful of mothers. "I haven't figured out what I want to do when I graduate, except write, of course."

"Eventually you'll want more freedom and independence than you have at the convent."

Alex nodded, but also knew she wasn't ready for it yet. She felt safe at St. Dominic's, although staying in the apartment in New York was an exciting adventure. "You should consider moving to New York after graduation." It was still a year away and she had time to think about it.

"Maybe I'd be lonely here," she said honestly.

"Not once you make friends, and you can always go home to Boston for the weekend."

Alex had met several young men at the publishing house who had asked her out. There were boys in the internship program too, and her roommates had introduced her to their friends. She went out mostly in groups, with no official dates. The others were all looking for a summer romance, but Alex wasn't. All she could think about were ideas for her next book. She talked to Rose about some of them, over dessert, and her agent liked them all, and thought she was heading in an interesting direction. She wanted to continue the character of the detective from her last book into the next one. She wasn't ready to start on it yet, but she had made copious notes to show Bert when she got back to Boston. He was taking the summer off, and had called her once to say he missed her, and she told him she missed him too.

Alex was invited to New England for a weekend by some of her new friends, the Berkshires by one of her roommates, and to Greenwich, Connecticut, by a girl she met at work who went to Princeton. And she was invited by several people to go to the Hamptons, where young people she met had rented houses to share with a dozen friends, and took turns going out for weekends. She went away every week. She did no writing, just made notes for the next book.

And at the end of August, her boss was sorry to see her leave.

"You've been great, Alex," she said as she hugged her. "Stay in touch. If you're interested, I'm sure we can find you a spot for next year, after graduation," and she would strongly recommend it. Alex had been an ideal intern. Her employer had no idea that she was a writer. "You'll make a great assistant," she said, and Alex thanked her. She had written to the professor who had suggested her for the internship program, and told her how much fun it had been, and how much she'd enjoyed it, and how grateful she was for the opportunity.

She was sad to see her time in New York end. She hitched a ride with Jack, a boy who was going back to BU and dated one of her roommates. They chatted all the way back. He'd been in the art department for two months, and was a fine-arts student. He wanted to paint portraits one day, but figured he'd have to get a job in advertising first to support himself. He said he had already sent his CV and portfolio to several large ad agencies in New York and Boston. He was hoping to graduate early, in January.

"What about you?" Jack asked her. "What are you going to do?"

"I don't know yet," she said vaguely. "I want to write."

"Maybe you should look into advertising too. There are some great agencies in Boston. You could be a copywriter." It was the last thing she wanted to do, and she was planning to start her next book as soon as she got back.

"I really liked my boss," she told him, as they drove north to Boston and had plenty of time to talk. "She was pretty crazy, but nice to work for. She's an editor of romance novels."

"My mom and my grandmother love them." He smiled at her. "They eat them up."

"My dad and I used to read detective stories," Alex said wistfully, thinking of him. She still missed him, particularly at special times.

"Have you read that new guy, Andrew Green or something? I

forget what he wrote, but I hear he's pretty good. My dad gave me a copy."

"Alexander Green," she corrected him. "Did you read it?" she asked, suddenly paying closer attention to him. It was a chance to ask someone her age what he liked about it or didn't. Her very own market research, one to one.

"No, I didn't have time all summer. They kept me pretty busy," and he had met a girl he really liked, and spent all his nights with her. He had been dating Pascale, the French girl Alex roomed with, which was how Alex had met him, and he wanted to go to Paris to visit her over Christmas, if he could afford it. Maybe with his graduation money from his parents. Alex was disappointed he hadn't had time to read her book so he couldn't give her any feedback.

When they got to Boston, she directed him to St. Dominic's, where he had promised to drop her off. He started to be impressed by the size of her house, and then realized it was a convent from the name over the door, and he looked shocked.

"Are you studying to be a nun?" She shook her head and smiled in answer.

"No, my dad died when I was fourteen, my mother died five years before that, so they let me live here. And now they're my family." He was intrigued by what she said and how at ease she seemed about it.

"Is it like an orphanage?" He felt sorry for her.

"No, just a convent where the nuns live. They've been really good to me for all this time." It sounded weird to him, but she was a terrific girl, and he helped her carry her bags up the stairs and set them down in the main hall. Three of the nuns rushed over to welcome her home as soon as they saw her. Alex introduced Jack to them, and he disappeared a minute later. He liked her, and would have wanted to see her again if he hadn't met Pascale in New York and fallen head over heels in love with her. But he wanted to be faithful to her now, and was hoping to get to Paris in the next few months.

The nuns were thrilled to have Alex home, and everyone stopped to talk with her during dinner that night. They wanted to know all about the job, the people she had met, her roommates, and if she liked New York and wanted to move there. She told them she didn't want to go anywhere and was happy to be home, but it was easy to see she'd had a great summer, and had matured a lot. Mother MaryMeg thought it had done her good to get away from them for a while. Alex always returned from the dorm at Boston College like a homing pigeon, and they loved having her there with them, but one day she would need her own life, away from the nuns, and MaryMeg knew that day was coming. Alex didn't want to think about it, nor did the sisters who loved her. Sister Tommy said over and over she had become her seventh child.

Alex met with Bert the first Saturday she was back in Boston. She showed him all the notes for her next book, and told him the direction she wanted to go in. He suggested a few changes, but not many, and she explained that she wanted it to be deeper, more psychological, and even more complicated than her previous books. The plot she had outlined so far was ambitious, but Bert thought she could handle it. He was happy to see her, the summer had seemed endless without her. He missed their conversations and Saturday lunches where he drank too much wine after they worked, and she scolded him about it. She knew him well enough now to do so and worried about him.

She started school two days later and was busy going to all her classes, meeting the professors, and organizing her work and assignments. She didn't get a chance to work on the book until two weeks later, but she had set up a schedule that would allow her to do her schoolwork and write by staying up late and getting up early. It involved very little sleep, but she thought it was worth it. And it left no time whatsoever for a social life. She explained her schedule to Bert the next time they met, and he was concerned.

"Do you think that's sensible? You're only young once, you know. You need to leave some time for fun in there. This is your last year of college and your last chance to be a kid and kick up your heels and get away with it. You don't have to be in such a hurry to get the book done." It was her fifth book, a major accomplishment.

"But I want to," she said seriously. The writing was what she loved most, and the work for school was her duty. Writing her book was all the fun she needed. She was singularly devoted with a burning desire to put words on the page and create a world of her own making.

"What if you meet a cute boy this year? Your whole schedule will go to hell in a handbasket," he teased her.

"No, it won't," she said firmly, with a will of iron in her eyes. He had seen it before and been impressed by it. She knew what she wanted, and was willing to pay the price. Most people weren't. Only real writers were willing to sacrifice everything for it, and he had met only a few of those in his lifetime. Alex was the most determined writer he had ever met. "The writing comes first, then school, and boys after. And too bad if they don't understand that. And I haven't met any cute boys anyway." She still felt cheated by her experience with Scott, the teaching assistant who had been so jealous of her the year before. She didn't want to run into another guy like him, although she'd be wiser now, and more alert to passive-aggressive behavior and manipulations. He had been her baptism by fire into the world of jealous male writers. And if he'd known about the book she'd published, he would have been infinitely worse. Bert was sure of that, and had warned her of it. But Alex had no intention of telling anyone about the books she wrote under the name of Alexander Green. She was determined that no one except her agent, Bert, and the nuns would ever know about them. They were her deep secret, the hidden life that fulfilled her.

Despite Bert's misgivings, Alex managed her Herculean schedule for all of the first semester, and was getting great grades and making good headway on the book, even faster than the last one. Bert kept telling her not to rush it and to take her time, but she had a writing style that wanted to lunge forward with the story and was hard to put the reins on. She pulled the reader along with her at breakneck pace, as she whipped them through the story and surprised and confused them again and again. Her fans and the critics loved it.

She had just turned in her last paper before Christmas break when her second book, *Darkness,* came out, just in time for holiday sales, which Alex and her publisher hoped would help the book. She was packing some things to take to the convent with her when someone came to tell her that she had a call on the phone in the lobby of the dorm, and she rushed down a flight of stairs to get it. It was Rose calling from New York and she sounded breathless.

"I have a Christmas gift for you, Alex. *Darkness* is on the *Times* list a week from Sunday." She knew because the list was released to the trade ten days early. "Number ten, but you're on it. Merry Christmas!"

Alex's face was wreathed in smiles as she tried to contain herself and could barely keep from screaming. At times of great excitement or elation, she turned into a kid again, and she could hardly wait to tell the nuns.

"Something important seems to be happening with this one," Rose reported to her, "and I don't think it's just due to Christmas sales. The critics are all crazy about it. *Publishers Weekly* called it the best new read of the decade, and your publisher says sales are going through the roof."

Alex was beaming.

"Let's see where it goes after this, although you've got some stiff competition on the list. Everyone wants their new book out this time of year for holiday sales." Every big bestselling fiction writer was on it.

She told the nuns when she went home the next day, and word of her book being on the *New York Times* bestseller list spread through the convent like a tidal wave. Several of them had already read it when she gave them advance copies, and the nuns who liked crime thrillers had loved it. The others just read it because she wrote it, and they were so proud of her and wanted to support her.

The following week when Rose called her at the convent, the book had climbed from number ten to number four on the list. And her final Christmas gift after that was one more notch to number three, where it sat for two weeks, into January. The book had been the surprise hit of the season, despite its gory subject, and the fact that mostly men would read it. She didn't have a heavy female readership, and no man would buy it for a woman for Christmas, with rare exceptions. They bought it for themselves, or the women in their lives bought it for them.

Bert had called her immediately to congratulate her, and Amanda, her editor at the publisher, had sent her emails every week, announcing her ranking on the list, and telling her how thrilled they were.

"Your publisher is very excited about this, Alex," Rose told her on the phone. "This is a very important step in your career." At twenty-one. It was hard to believe, and her publisher had no idea how young she was, since all their dealings with her, even contractually, went through her agent. She was a mystery to them, except for the bio that she and Rose had created for the mythical Alexander Green.

It was difficult for Alex to absorb or even remotely understand what this could mean for her in the future. More money than the last deal probably, hopefully more readers, and the bestseller list again. But she couldn't see beyond that, and didn't need to. It meant she could support herself by writing, for now anyway, if people didn't get tired of her books. She didn't want to count on this yet, and was afraid the bubble would burst one day, and it might. It took years to develop a John le Carré, Stephen King, Georges Simenon, Frederick Forsyth, or an Agatha Christie. She wasn't there yet and didn't expect to be, maybe ever. But it felt fabulous knowing that her book had done so well, and there had been a steady build from the last one. She walked into local bookstores just for the pleasure of seeing her books stacked high on the bestseller table. She grinned from ear to ear each time she saw it, and the nuns took pictures at every bookstore where they went.

Despite the astonishing success of her book, she went back to school after Christmas vacation, for her last semester at Boston College. She had only a few easy classes left to take for graduation. She'd done all the hard ones much earlier and had gotten the required courses out of the way.

She finished her fifth novel during spring break, got Bert's blessing on it, and sent it to Rose, expecting a warm reception for it. A week later, her agent called her and sounded worried.

"The moment of truth has come, Alex. We want a new contract for your last two books. And we want a much bigger one this time, after the success of *Darkness*." She still had another book, her third one, due out in the summer. But they had two more complete now to sell. "They just told me they won't give you a contract now until they meet you. I've been arguing with them about it for three days."

"Tell them I'm in Europe and I broke both my legs." She was only half teasing, but Rose wasn't.

"They say they don't care how long they have to wait. They want to meet the phenomenon who is creating these books. Maybe they want to be sure it's just one person, and not a committee of some kind, which is happening more and more these days, where a writer does the outline but has half a dozen minions to write it for him. Whatever the reason, they say no new contract until they meet you. They won't even let me deliver the last two books to them until they do."

"That's ridiculous. After the success of the last one, they should be willing to buy the new ones even if I were a gnome with three heads."

"That's beside the point," Rose insisted. "They *want* to meet you, and they're not going to relent until they do. They're just as stubborn as you are," she said, sounding tense. Alex's future was on the line here, even if she didn't understand that. She could be a willful child at times.

"They could blow everything if they let the cat out of the bag that I'm a woman," Alex said, genuinely afraid of that. "It could really make people mad now. They might not even believe I wrote them," more because of her age than her sex.

"We could have some ironclad confidentiality agreement drawn up by an attorney, giving you a huge amount of damages if they talk. That's not unheard-of. They have to have a stake in it too, and we could put some real teeth in it. But you're not going to get out of meeting them. You're a big investment for them now, and in the future."

Alex worried that Rose may have asked for too much money for them to buy the books and they were angry, but Rose assured her that wasn't the problem.

"How much did you ask for?" Alex frowned as she asked her.

"I asked for the appropriate amount," Rose said firmly, "based on sales of the last book, and the first one. This would have happened anyway. They were already antsy the last time. You can't hide in the shadows forever."

"I have to. I'm not a man, and they and everyone else think I am," Alex told her with determination. "And I know you don't believe me, but a lot of men won't buy crime thrillers by women. My father said so." Alex had believed him all her life. And this was no time to test the theory.

Rose didn't want to risk the publisher's ire by Alex refusing to meet them. And she and Rose wanted a new contract, which wasn't going to happen unless they met. There was a real danger that if readers knew the Green books were written by a twenty-one-year-old college girl, and that she'd started writing them at nineteen, readers would feel duped. In a way, she was a genius, but Rose didn't want to have to explain that to the public, nor to her publisher. "Let me talk to a lawyer and see what kind of agreement we can draw up, where they have real money at stake if they expose you. But they might not be willing to sign it," Rose warned her.

It took a week for Rose's attorney to come up with language they both liked. They were asking for a $10 million penalty for losses into the future if the publisher exposed her. Although she could start all over again under another pseudonym, her style was too distinct and recognizable now.

With Alex's permission, Rose sent the confidentiality agreement over to the publisher, and waited to see what they would say. Alex was reassured and liked the fact that they would have $10 million at stake. She didn't think that she was worth it, and couldn't imagine making that kind of money, but it would certainly force them to be discreet, and be a strong incentive to keep her identity secret.

Much to Rose's surprise, she got a call from the president of the publishing house two days later.

"Who the hell is this guy? The president of the United States? And why is his identity worth ten million dollars?"

"No, it's not the president," Rose said calmly. "But you could injure his career severely if you expose him." She wasn't going to let on that the author of the Green books, as they called them, was a woman until they signed the agreement.

"Is he a criminal of some kind? Will his identity embarrass us?" The president was obviously worried, and with good reason for that kind of money. Any kind of slip could cost them a fortune, but it would damage Alex's career irreparably. You couldn't unring a bell once word was out, nor gauge reader reaction beforehand.

"Not at all," Rose reassured him. "It's the author who is at risk here, not you."

"Like hell, with ten million on the line if someone talks." He sounded frustrated. "I'll get back to you in a day or two. We need to think about it."

"That's fine," she said smoothly. She reported back to Alex that night. All they could do now was wait and see if the publisher came around. She thought they would. There was too much money to be made in the future for them not to.

It took longer than she thought, and he called her back in a week. He didn't sound happy about it, but an entire committee had agreed they had no choice. But they were very worried now about who the author was, if he was a gangster of some kind, or someone whose work they wouldn't want to publish if they knew the truth, although Rose had assured him that was not the case. And she was still concerned about the meeting, even with the agreement. She wasn't as afraid they'd talk afterward—in fact, she was certain they wouldn't—but she had no idea how they'd feel to learn that their star writer, big moneymaker, and latest discovery was a girl barely out of her teens. They knew that Bert Kingsley was editing Green, which they liked, since they had worked with him many times before, and they knew how superb his editing was. But they had no idea who the author was, which was why they wanted to meet him before they bought another book, let alone two, at a stiff price. It wasn't unreasonable, just very delicate and dicey.

The meeting was set for a Friday, in Rose's office, at three o'clock. The president, CEO, and CFO were coming, the editor in chief, and Amanda Smith, Alex's contact at her publishers, whom she corresponded with by email regularly and liked. Rose knew all the men coming to the meeting, but not Amanda. Each of them had signed a separate confidentiality agreement with the company, internally, accepting liability if they talked.

Alex took the train down from Boston on the appointed day. She wore a new navy blue dress and matching coat she had bought to wear to her graduation dinner in six weeks. And in case she was late and had to run through the station to make it in time, she had worn little flat black suede shoes, and she looked more than ever like a schoolgirl with her shining dark straight hair down her back, when she arrived at Rose's office at two-thirty. She was very nervous and her eyes were huge, as she sat anxiously at the edge of a chair across from Rose's desk.

"It's going to be fine. Don't worry." Rose tried to calm her down. "They're going to love you," she believed it, after they got over the initial shock, which would be enormous. Alex did not look for a minute like someone who could write intricate, brilliant, violent books like the Green books. They were far too complex for anyone her age to write, and yet she did, even though she had spent the last six and a half years in a convent, and was still in college, though not for much longer, with graduation looming.

The group from the publishers arrived on the dot of three. They were quiet and expectant, and were shown to Rose's corner office by an assistant who led the way. Rose had thought to put bottles of water with a bottle of scotch, one of bourbon, another of gin, and a bottle of champagne in an ice bucket on the coffee table in her office, surrounded by a leather couch and four chairs for important meetings. She thought they might need the booze after reality hit them, either to celebrate, or revive them. In either case, it would calm their nerves.

Instinctively Alex stood up and went to stand next to Rose before they walked in, as though she felt she needed protection from the publishing contingent. She had taken her coat off, which made her seem younger and slighter than ever. She looked like Snow White, or a dark-haired Alice in Wonderland, with terrified eyes when the four men and one woman walked into Rose's office with stern faces. Rose was afraid that Alex might faint, as Rose shook hands with all of them and invited them to sit down, and thanked them for coming. They noticed the alcohol on the table and said nothing. All five of them were tense, and they paid no attention to Alex, who was nearly shrinking behind her agent, trying to disappear, and Rose suspected correctly that they had mistaken her for Rose's assistant, although she didn't look old enough to be that either, with her long hair and flat shoes, and no makeup.

"Where is he?" John Rawlings, the CEO, asked tersely. "Is he late or in another room, waiting to make an entrance?" He was fiercely unhappy with the confidentiality agreement that they'd signed, but the president had convinced him they had no choice.

"He's here," Rose said, drawing out the suspense a moment longer, and enjoying it, as the five representatives of the publishing house stared at her expectantly. "Right here, in fact." Rose stepped aside quietly, leaving Alex exposed behind her, as Alex looked as though she would burst into tears at any moment. "I would like to introduce you to my client, Alexandra Winslow . . . otherwise known as Alexander Green." There was dead silence in the room as the five publishing executives stared at her, some literally with their mouths open. Rose put a gentle hand on her shoulder, and Alex spoke in barely more than a whisper, staring at them too.

"Hello."

"You're not serious," the CEO said, looking livid. "Is this some kind of joke? What kind of game are you playing?" he accused the agent, ignoring Alex again as Hugh Stern, the president, watched her closely. There was something very interesting in her eyes that was very different from her juvenile appearance. She had the razor-sharp, determined focus of a genius, and he could almost see her mind racing as she took them all in, even if she appeared terrified of them.

"This is not a joke," Rose said quietly. "Alexandra came to me two and a half years ago, at nineteen, through a mutual connection. She came down from Boston where she lives, and left her manuscript *Blue Steel* with me. I was bowled over by it, just as you were. And the only condition she made was that no one ever know that she's a woman, or just a girl then, really. She believes that men don't buy crime thrillers written by women, and even if I disagree, Alex's father told her that and she believed him. And I'm not at all sure that we would have had the success we did with the last book if the public knew it was written by a twenty-one-year-old girl. Alex has considerable experience with the genre, although she has diversified from it and created her own, which appears to be working. She's been reading crime books, thrillers, and detective stories with her father since she was seven years old. And I can honestly say I think she's read them all. I brought Bert Kingsley in to help her edit her work with her first book, and he's been working with her ever since. You know his work. And Alex's. What you didn't know until today is her name, how old she is, and that she's a young woman, and now you do. You can see why we have done everything possible to keep her identity secret, so as not to hurt the books, and scare off their male audience. And I suspect now you'll be just as anxious as we are to do the same."

Alex was starting to feel more comfortable, and the five publishers in their chairs looked like they were in shock, except for Amanda Smith, who was smiling broadly, and Alex shyly smiled back. Amanda Smith had a daughter the same age, and she thought everything she'd heard was great, and she loved the fact that the hardcore, hard-edged, hard-hitting, brilliant Alexander Green that everyone was in love with had turned out to be a young woman.

The CEO leaned back in his chair with his hand over his eyes and looked like he was about to have a heart attack. "Oh my God," was all he could say, and the CFO was grim-faced. The editor in chief clearly didn't know what to say. And then all of a sudden the president started to laugh. He looked at Rose and at Alex, and he patted the CEO on the arm.

"I have to say, ladies, you really had one on us. Never in a million years would I have ever guessed the Green books were written by a woman, and even less that they were the creation of a girl her age. Alex, you have a very, very twisted mind." He said it as a compliment and she grinned.

"Thank you," she said, taking it as it was meant. Rose sat down in one of the chairs then, and signaled to Alex to do the same.

"Now you understand why we don't want anyone to talk. It would only hurt the books."

"But how long can we keep it quiet?" The CEO took his hand off his eyes and chimed in, as Rose poured champagne and handed the glasses around. No one declined, and the CEO was looking at the bottle of Johnnie Walker longingly, so Rose poured him a stiff one on the rocks, which he grabbed like a life vest for a drowning man.

"Hopefully forever," Rose said. "Or for many, many years, until the brand is secure. We've created a persona for the author of the books. He's said to be a recluse. And given the nature of the books, it works, or has so far. No one is begging to see him, or complaining that they can't. They're devouring the books, and that's all we care about, all of us. Much more important, Alex is an extremely hard worker, and very dedicated to the books. She hasn't stopped working since I met her, and given her age, I think you'll get a long run out of this, gentlemen."

The president was smiling again. He thought the whole thing was incredible, and they all exploded into animated chatter at once, Amanda with Alex, as the others talked to each other and Rose. Amanda was congratulating Alex on her success. They all sat there for two hours talking about the risks and possibilities, the way to capitalize on the author's mysterious image, and how great the books were, drinking heavily while they discussed it all. Rose had opened a third bottle of champagne by then, and the CEO had had four scotches on the rocks, and needed them all to get over the shock.

It was six o'clock when they left Rose's office, and no one was entirely sober. Alex had had a glass of champagne, and Rose had had Johnnie Walker on the rocks herself with a splash of water, but only one. And the president gave Alex a hug on the way out. Before they left, Rose reminded them that you discovered talent where you found it, no matter how unlikely the source, and you never refused it or turned it away.

"Thank God you didn't in this case," the president said with feeling, endorsing what the agent said. He was in full agreement with her. And what a lucky find for all of them and the house Alex had been. "I'll get the contract for the new books over to you on Monday," he assured Rose as they left, and she nodded. Everything was moving forward again.

Rose collapsed in one of the chairs and looked up at Alex when they were alone again. "Well, Mr. Green, what do you think?" Rose was extremely pleased with how it had gone. It couldn't have been better.

"I was scared to death," Alex admitted, as she sipped what was left of her champagne. She hadn't dared drink too much.

"I thought John Rawlings was going to have a heart attack in my office," she said of the CEO and they both laughed. "I will never forget the look on their faces, but Hugh Stern is really a good guy." He had been the first to come around when he started to laugh and broke the ice.

"I'm glad I met Amanda. She's really nice and always so helpful," Alex added.

"And a good editor, but not as good as Bert."

They dissected the meeting for another half hour, and then Alex had to catch her train. She was going to take a cab to the station.

"I was very proud of you, Alex," Rose said as she hugged her before she left.

"I thought you were wonderful," Alex said softly. "Do you think they'll keep the secret?"

"They don't want to blow ten million dollars, so yes, they will keep the secret. They are now our partners in crime, to keep your identity safe."

Alex left to go back to Boston then, and Rose helped herself to another drink. It had been tense for a moment at first, but it had all gone better than she hoped.

On Monday, Hugh Stern, the president, was true to his word. He sent back the signed contract for Alex's next two books, and met Rose's demand. She smiled when she saw it. They were in the big leagues now. Alex's publisher had paid her two million dollars for her two new books, a million dollars each. The deal was done. And Alexander Green was safe, hopefully forever.

Chapter 11

Mother Mary Margaret had rented two stretch airporter vans for the day of Alex's graduation. All of the nuns were going and they were very excited as they climbed into the vans, with Sister Tommy driving one, and one of the older nuns the other. They had their tickets, and would occupy a full row in the auditorium. Alex was dressing in the dorm, and they wouldn't see her until the procession. They were so proud of her. It was one of the most thrilling days of Alex's life, and the Buchanans were coming too. Elena was still working for a family in New York, and her contact with Alex had dwindled to a Christmas card every year to stay in touch. Alex hadn't seen her in many years. When she had tried to see her the summer she worked in New York, Elena was in Martha's Vineyard with her employers, which was disappointing.

It was a beautiful day as the family and friends of the graduates took their seats in the Robsham Theater at the College of Arts and Sciences. The nuns could hardly sit still as they chatted, waiting for the procession to start. And then they saw her coming down the long aisle, with her classmates, in pairs, to take their seats and claim their diplomas. The nuns cheered even louder than they had at her high school graduation, and the graduates let out a whoop and a roar as they threw their mortarboards in the air after the ceremony. It was a very special day.

The Buchanans invited all of them to the Chart House, with harbor views in the city's oldest dock building, for lunch afterward. Alex was beaming, and each of the nuns hugged her and had a photograph taken with her. In the end, she had grown up with twenty-six mothers instead of one, and it had served her well. She was a happy, balanced person, and even though she still missed her father, she had been loved and well taken care of for more than seven years. She was twenty-two years old, and Bill congratulated her and was stunned by how much she was paid for the advance for her last books. It was a major achievement, and added to what her father had left her, she would be safe for a long time.

Alex had invited Bert to come to the ceremony too, but he said he didn't want to put on a suit, and would drink a glass of wine, or possibly rum, to her health and future success at the appointed time. She would have liked to have him there, but he said ceremonies made him uncomfortable.

By the time they got back to the convent late that afternoon after lunch, Alex was exhausted. She had thanked the Buchanans for everything, kissed and hugged all the nuns, returned her rented gown, kept the tassel from her hat as a souvenir, and set her diploma in its leather case down on her desk. It was a landmark in her life. She had graduated. And her dream now was to travel around Europe, in France and Italy. The nuns were nervous about it, but Mother MaryMeg had discussed it at length with Sister Tommy, who had convinced her to let Alex go. She had to try her wings. And she wasn't short of money, so she could stay in decent hotels in good neighborhoods. Both women thought she could take care of herself and would be safe. She was sensible and not given to high-risk behavior. She was leaving for Rome in a week, and she could hardly wait.

She was lying on her bed, thinking about the day, when there was a soft knock on the door, and Sister Regina slipped into the room. She had been looking better lately. She'd gained back a little weight and seemed more serene. She came and sat down on the foot of Alex's bed and smiled at her.

"We were so proud of you today." They always were, and Alex smiled back at her.

"It was great." It had been everything she had always dreamed of and more. And the only one missing was her father.

"There's something I have to tell you," Sister Regina began cautiously. Mother Mary Margaret had asked her to wait to tell Alex, so it wouldn't distract her from graduation. She didn't want anything to spoil it for her, in case Alex was upset by the news. But this time, Alex guessed before she said it.

"You're leaving?" Her longtime friend nodded, with tears in her eyes, but they were tears of emotion, and not regret. She had taken years to decide and mull it over, and she knew she was doing the right thing. Alex wasn't surprised and knew how hard the decision had been for her.

"I have to. If I don't, I'll always regret it, and life will pass me by. Mother MaryMeg says I can come back if I want to. I'm not being banished or anything, or excommunicated. I just need to try life outside for a while, and see if it's for me. Maybe I'll come back with my tail between my legs, but if I don't do it, I'll feel cheated forever. It's as if you had never tried to write a book. You need that to be who you are, and I want to try to have a regular life with a husband

and kids, if God decides that's what I should have." It made sense to Alex, and she thought it was the best decision, and she hoped Regina found what she was looking for out in the world. If she wanted kids, she should have them.

"Where will you live?"

"I got an apartment, with a roommate, it's very small. And I have a job, teaching at a public school in South Boston. I start at the end of August. I'll stay here till July, and then I'll move out and get settled." Regina felt like this was her last chance to have the life she had dreamed of.

"Do the others know?"

"Not yet. You're the first one I've told. We decided a month ago. Mother has been very kind." And then she looked at Alex sadly. "Will you stay in touch?" They had been friends for seven and a half years, and Regina had watched Alex grow up from a young teenager to a woman, and had seen her develop her talent. Regina wanted to write a book too, a novel, about a nun leaving the convent, although she knew she didn't have Alex's gift, but she had a story to tell, even if she only wrote one book. "But hopefully no one gets murdered in mine."

They both laughed and hugged each other, and Alex promised she'd write to her from Europe.

"How long will you be gone?"

"I don't know," Alex said. "I have nothing to rush back for. I want to travel for a couple of months. I'll be back in the fall. I want to start a new book then. But I can write while I'm away too."

"Well, come and see me when you get back."

Both of them were excited when they talked about their respective plans that afternoon, and sat on Alex's bed until dinnertime.

They went down to dinner together and the mother superior

could tell that Sister Regina had shared her secret with Alex, and she didn't mind. She knew how close they were. And Regina wasn't leaving St. Dominic's in disgrace, she was going to find herself, with their blessing. Mother MaryMeg knew full well that the religious life was not for everyone, and the vocation Regina had been so sure of as a teenager twenty years before no longer felt right to her as a thirty-five-year-old woman.

Alex left a week later, after saying goodbye to Bert and promising to write to him too, or call from time to time. He told her to take some time off from writing for the next two months, it would do her good, and give her a chance to fill the well again, as he put it. She had written five books in a relatively short time. And he thought Europe would give her fresh ideas. There were so many places she wanted to visit: Paris, Rome, Florence, Pisa, Provence. She had a long list of cities and locations she had read about and only imagined for years, and all of them would make fantastic settings for a book.

Sister Regina, Sister Xavier, and Sister Tommy drove Alex to the airport, and she had only taken two bags. One of them was very heavy because she had her Smith Corona in it. She had brought her laptop in her carry-on bag and two of her father's favorite books. She had packed comfortable clothes and a few dresses, and some notepads in case she wanted to write longhand. She had hugged Mother MaryMeg before she left and thanked her for everything. How did you thank someone for a third of your life, being your family and giving you a home? She couldn't, and they just held each other tight, and the mother superior gave her a blessing, and told her to be careful and call from time to time. Alex promised she would, and it was a tearful scene at the airport with the three other nuns she had been closest to, who had been a trio of mothers to her for all the years she'd been there. They hugged and kissed a dozen times, and waved as she went through security, until they couldn't see her anymore, and then they drove back to the convent, alternately crying and laughing, remembering things she had done when she was younger. And by the time they got to the convent, Alex was on the plane, thinking of them. She was a little nervous about traveling alone, but if it didn't work out, she knew she didn't have to stay, she could come home.

But the trip exceeded her wildest expectations. She thought Rome was the most beautiful place she'd ever seen, with the Colosseum, St. Peter's, the Vatican, and the countless small beautiful churches. She spent a week there and walked everywhere. She went to Florence and spent days in the Uffizi, and four days in Venice, visiting every church and monument on her list. Being in Venice sparked an idea for a new book, and she started taking notes. She thought the canals and the palazzi, particularly at night, were a perfect location for a sinister crime, with Interpol involved, and she created an Italian detective. She went to Milan briefly, and then flew to Paris and spent two weeks there. It was mid-July by then, and she had called the convent several times to check in, so they didn't worry about her. She rented a car, and drove to the châteaux of the Loire Valley, and fell in love with Provence when she went there. She made a detour to Ireland, and loved it despite terrible weather, and then flew to London and spent two full weeks exploring the city. She had been in Europe for more than two months, she still had no desire to go home, and her notebook was full of jotted notes for a new book.

She found a small hotel in Bloomsbury, and thought about what to do next. When she called Rose to check in, the agent made an interesting suggestion.

"Your publisher has an office in London. Maybe they could bend the rules and give you a job for a while, just to get a feeling for life there. Since it's an American company, they'll know how to get around your needing a work permit and can probably pay you from the States, or set it up as an internship of some kind." Alex liked the idea and thought it might give her an excuse to stay, since she wasn't ready to come home. She couldn't tell them that she was Alexander Green, but she could use her internship in New York as a reference to get one here. She thought that Rose's suggestion was a good one, and she walked into the publisher a few days later and inquired if they had any openings for an internship as an editorial assistant, and they said they might. One of their junior editors had gotten married recently and moved back to the States, and the current assistant who had taken her place was getting a promotion. They agreed to interview Alex the next day, and treat the junior editor's job as an internship until they found a proper replacement with a work permit.

She wore the only nice dress she had brought with her, and at the end of two hours, after she met several people, they hired her. The pay was low, but she had her own money. She was doing it for the experience, not what she'd earn, which was an enviable position to be in, unlike her friend Regina, who was about to become Brigid O'Brien again, and was worried about how to make ends meet with her teaching job. Alex had the freedom to do whatever she wanted, and stay as long as she chose. And she liked the idea of working in London. She called Mother Mary Margaret and told her about her decision, and said she was sure she wouldn't stay for more than a few months, and they'd probably have a permanent replacement for the job by then anyway.

"That's what you're there for," the mother superior encouraged her, "to discover the world. It will be good for your books."

Alex went to a real estate broker to find a furnished apartment rental, and located a small but very nice one in Knightsbridge that suited her, and rented it for three months. It seemed more sensible than staying at a hotel. So she had a job, and an apartment, and she was going to live in a new city for a while. She felt very adventuresome as she walked to work the next day and found the person she was supposed to report to, Margaret Wiseman, an older editor whose specialty was historical novels. She was chilly to Alex and told her which desk she could use, but she made no particular effort to welcome her, and handed her a stack of work to do. They were menial tasks, like filing, but it kept her busy until lunchtime, and Fiona, one of the young assistants, came to say hello and ask her to join them for lunch, and she accepted. She was three years older than Alex, and everyone was friendly as they sat at a sandwich shop, talking about people she didn't know. They thought it very interesting that Alex had come from Boston for a job there, as a junior editor on an internship. She explained that she had just graduated from college in June, and had been traveling around Europe ever since.

"Good on you!" one of the girls said admiringly, and they all walked back to the office together, and got into the elevator with an attractive man in a black shirt, black jeans, and motorcycle boots, with tousled black hair, and he looked as though he hadn't shaved in a week, which Alex assumed was intentional. She laughed, thinking that he reminded her of one of the characters in her books.

He spoke to her as they left the elevator together, the lift, as the girls had called it, and he headed in the same direction as Alex.

"New girl in town?" he asked, raising an eyebrow, and she smiled and nodded. She was wearing jeans and a sweater because she'd been told that casual dress was allowed, within reason. No flip-flops, no shorts, no halter tops, but jeans were fine.

"Yes," she said simply, as he fell into step with her.

"Ah, American?"

"Boston."

"Intriguing." He smiled as she went to her desk. She wondered what he did there, since the whole floor seemed to be mostly editorial people. He disappeared down another hall, and she didn't see him again until they met leaving the building at the end of the day.

"How was school?" he asked and she laughed.

"Not bad for a first day." The work seemed to be fairly simple so far, at least what they were giving her. She had done a lot of filing, but it was exciting to be in another country, and to have a new city to discover. And London was easy because of the language.

"Where are you staying, with friends?" He was very bold about asking her questions, as she tried to figure out what bus to get on outside the building. She had a map but was embarrassed to take it out and look like a tourist.

"No, I was lucky. I found an apartment, furnished."

"Want a lift?" He pointed to a small, battered Fiat parked at the curb, with the steering wheel on the European side, not the British. She hesitated and then nodded. She knew where he worked, so he wasn't a total stranger to her.

"Okay, thanks."

"Where do you live?" She told him the address and his eyebrow shot up again. "Very posh. Knightsbridge. I live in Notting Hill." And on the way to her apartment, he suggested dinner. It all seemed a little hasty to Alex, she wasn't sure if he was just being friendly or was putting a move on her. It was hard to tell. "There's actually a pub quite near you that I like. Want to rough it with a beer and a burger?"

"Sounds familiar." She smiled at him. "Sure, thanks."

They ordered dinner and wine when they got there, and the pub was cozy and dark. She realized she didn't know his name then, and introduced herself.

"Ivan White," he supplied. "And what do you want to be when you grow up?" he asked, as they waited for the food. "Not an editor, surely."

"Probably not. You?"

"I edit nonfiction right now. I have a novel in me somewhere. I'm waiting for it to come out." She almost groaned when he said it. Not another writer, although he was just being collegial and this wasn't romance. But he had homed in on her pretty quickly. "And you're not a writer?" He seemed surprised.

"Not really. I wrote a little in college," she said vaguely. "Mostly for school. And some short stories in high school."

"And you don't want to write women's fiction?"

"Not at all," she said empathically, and at least that was true.

"How refreshing. Most of the women I meet want to write novels. Very tedious, I assure you." She wondered why it was okay for him to want to write a novel, but not the women he went out with, but she didn't ask him.

"Why don't you like women writers?"

"They take themselves too seriously, and it's all too emotional and gushingly dramatic, or romantic. Erghk." He made a face.

"And what kind of novel would you write?" Now she was curious about him and what made him tick. He seemed very sure of himself and was undeniably handsome, and knew it. Even the five-day beard stubble looked somewhat affected, but it suited him. She still liked the look of him for a villain in a book, and maybe he was.

"I think my style is more like Tom Wolfe," he said blithely, as their burgers came.

"That's impressive."

"It's what I'm drawn to, and I think when I actually sit down and write it, it will be pretty similar." He seemed confident about it and she was amused.

"I enjoy crime books, I've been reading them all my life," she said to change the subject a little.

"Like whom?"

She reeled off some names and he was unimpressed, and then she decided to play with him a little. "Have you read Alexander Green?"

He nodded. "He's pretty good, very formulaic, though, don't you think?" It was a major put-down, that she wrote by a formula, rather than having the books be different each time.

"How many have you read?"

"Two, I think. Odd that you've read them. They're really brutal."

"I used to read some pretty gory crime thrillers with my father."

"You're a strange sort of girl, aren't you?" he mused, looking at her. "You jaunt off around the world, stop in London and get a job, find an apartment, like men's books. You must have been a tomboy as a kid. What are your parents like?"

"They died when I was very young. My father worked for a construction company, and my mother was an actress and model."

"Sounds like an ill-fated match," he said as they ate.

"It was. She left when I was seven. I lived alone with him after that, till I was fourteen."

"And then?"

"It's a long story." She didn't want to tell him about the convent. She didn't know him well enough and had told him more than she'd intended.

"It's either a very sad story, or an extremely happy one," he guessed.

"Pretty happy. It worked out well."

"You married and had three children."

"No, definitely not that!" She laughed.

"How old are you, by the way?" He had been curious about it since he first saw her that morning. He was moving quickly and wanted to know a lot about her.

"Twenty-two. I just finished college in June."

"And you're on a junket around Europe," he added. "Rich parents. Poor people can't do that. Did yours leave you a lot of money?"

"That's a little blunt, isn't it?"

"It never hurts to ask. If they did, you can pay for dinner. If they didn't, I will." He was only half teasing.

"Let's split it." She didn't want to be indebted to him anyway. And she wanted to start on the right foot so they could be friends. But in the end he didn't let her pay for dinner and said he'd only been joking. He drove her back to her apartment after dinner and told her he'd had a fun evening with her.

"So did I," she said easily. She had no friends here and was starting with a clean slate. And she wanted to have time to write, once she settled in.

"I think you're lying to me, though," he accused her.

"About what?" It was a surprising comment for him to make.

"I think you're a writer in the closet."

"What makes you think that?" She wondered why he would say that.

"Because you're a keen observer of people. I see you watching me, and everyone around the room. I'll bet you could describe everyone in the restaurant tonight, couldn't you?"

"Of course not." But he was absolutely right, which made him the keen observer as much as Alex.

"You look at people like a writer, checking out their reactions and emotions, and saving them for later."

"You make me sound like a spider or a snake ready to eat them."

"Perhaps you are, and I just don't know it yet." In truth, they knew nothing about each other. And he had told her nothing about himself in exchange for what he'd asked her, and for the little bits she'd said about her parents. It had been a one-way conversation.

"And where did you grow up?" she asked him.

"In London. With my grandmother. My parents were actors, perennially on tour. I hardly ever saw them. So our lives were not so dissimilar as children. Maybe that's why we were drawn to each other." He was presuming a lot. They had just met and had dinner. She had not been "drawn" to him yet, she was just inquisitive, and very cautious, after Scott. "I think people with dysfunctional families always seek each other out, instinctively, don't you? All of my girlfriends came from divorced parents."

Her parents had been divorced, but her father had been anything but dysfunctional. He was a very stable person, except for his one colossal mistake marrying her mother.

"I'm not sure that theory holds," she said skeptically.

"I can promise you it does. And there's a lot you haven't told me yet."

"And maybe never will," she teased him. He was very pushy for a first evening. When they got to her address, she got out of the car and thanked him for dinner.

"Let's do it again," he said as though it was his decision, and then he drove off with a wave, and she let herself into her building, and her flat. She still had a bag to unpack and clothes to put away, and she thought about Ivan White as she did. He was a would-be writer. And he was a little too aggressive for her taste, and too nosy. He seemed like a good person to keep at a distance. She put him out of her mind as she unpacked her father's photograph and his two favorite books she had brought with her.

Ivan's persistence over the next several weeks was startling. She told him she was busy every time he invited her to dinner. And he wanted to know why and with whom, and if she had a boyfriend in London. She said she didn't.

"Don't you want one?"

"Not necessarily. I want to get my bearings, figure out my job, explore London, make some friends, do some work I brought with me, and if a man I like turns up in all that, that would be nice, but I'm not shopping for a boyfriend."

"Are you afraid of men?" he pressed her.

"No. I'm afraid of making a mistake and being unhappy."

"Then you end it, and start again."

"That sounds exhausting. I'd rather be careful in the beginning."

"That's ridiculous. You have to experience life. How can you do that if you never make mistakes?" He was always trying to convince her of something. She didn't have dinner with him again for a month, but he kept badgering her and she finally gave in. She knew by then that he was twenty-seven years old, and he had recently broken up with a girlfriend who had left him for someone else. The girls in the office thought he was hot, but said he looked like a cheater. She wondered how they knew that. They said it was just a feeling, when Alex had lunch with them. She particularly liked Fiona, an assistant editor from Dublin. She edited picture books for children aged three to six, and she seemed to like it.

Alex's job had turned out to be not at all challenging. Her boss never gave her anything interesting to do, and a lot of filing. The assumption was that she wouldn't stay long as an intern. She seemed to resent Alex, and was unfriendly to her. It made for boring days and very little satisfaction. She was writing on weekends, which gave her something to do. She was working on the outline for her next book.

And Ivan's work as a "nonfiction editor" seemed to consist mostly of checking text proofs for errors before they went to print. Neither of them had interesting jobs, but Alex loved the idea of working in London. That gave her all the satisfaction she needed. She was getting very close to starting her next book, and had had several phone conversations with Bert about it. He liked her ideas for it a lot, and thought her publisher would too.

Ivan liked spending time with her, supposedly as friends, and he talked a lot about the novel he was going to write, which made her nervous. If he ever figured out that she was a writer and had published, he could be consumed with jealousy, as Scott had been, and take it out on her in some way, and she didn't want to go through that again. It made her very cautious about everything she said.

He was hanging around her apartment one day, waiting to go out with her to the contemporary wing of the Victoria and Albert Museum, and saw an envelope from her agent on her desk, with a note in it about pub dates and a royalty check for fifty thousand dollars for her first book, but fortunately there was no mention of Alexander Green on any of the paperwork, nor the title of the book, just the date of publication. She saw him glance at it, and then peek into it as she walked back into the room, and he moved away from the desk immediately. He looked startled when he turned to her. He had recognized the name of the agency, which was well known in publishing, even in England.

"What do you need a literary agent for?" He made it sound like an accusation, as though she had taken something that belonged to him.

"I don't. I worked for them one summer," she said, trying to be creative, but she didn't sound convincing, even to her own ears. "They send me letters sometimes, and they owed me some money from a tax refund." She said it in case he had seen that there was a check in the envelope, but she was annoyed at him for looking into her mail, which seemed incredibly rude to her.

"They must have paid you a fortune," he commented drily, with an edge to his voice.

"They didn't. Why? What makes you say that? Why would you assume that?"

"Because they sent you a fifty-thousand-dollar tax refund."

She cringed as he said it. "That's none of your business, Ivan," she said, shutting down the subject.

"No, it isn't, and it was presumptuous of me to look, but I was curious why they were writing to you."

"You should have asked me. Don't snoop through my mail."

"There's something you're not telling me, isn't there?" he accused her. And she knew it was a story that would have stunned him, but fortunately there had been nothing in the envelope that would expose her as the writer of the Green books. The publisher was very careful about that, so even their accounting staff didn't know. All payments went to Rose Porter's agency, and were then paid out to Alex, and the books were only referred to as Book 1, Book 2, and so on, with no titles and no author's name. But the check was a big one, and why would a literary agency be sending her that kind of money?

"There's nothing I'm not telling you, or that you need to know."

"Have you ever written a book?" he asked her, looking her straight in the eye. Previously she had said she hadn't, and had no interest in writing, which was a total lie, and he sensed that she was hiding something from him.

"I play around with short stories sometimes, but not in a long time."

"That's a lot of play money, Alex."

"I did some ghostwriting for one of their celebrity clients while I worked there." She was thinking on her feet, and that sounded more plausible to him. He was almost convinced, but not quite.

"Why didn't you tell me that before?"

"Because I signed a confidentiality agreement with the celebrity, so I couldn't, and I still can't." She looked prim as she said it.

"Some people have all the luck," he said, looking annoyed. "I'd love to do some ghostwriting for that kind of money. Who was it?"

"I told you, I'm not at liberty to tell you, or I'd be in breach of contract."

"A man or a woman?" he persisted.

"A man." She was inventing it as she went along.

"That's stupid. Why would they use a woman to write for a man? You can always tell a woman's voice when she writes something. There isn't a woman alive who can write like a man." There had been a number of them in history, but she didn't press the point. He had the same limited view and prejudices as many others, which was why she wrote under a man's name.

"I was the only one willing to do it. He was a very difficult person."

"Well, you were damn lucky to make that kind of money. So I guess you didn't have a rich father after all, just a lucky job one summer. You won't make that kind of money here," he said, and she nodded, hoping he'd calm down and forget about it. She put the envelope in her desk drawer and they left for the museum a few minutes later, but he was out of sorts for the rest of the day, and sullen when they went to dinner, and he started talking about his future novel again. She dreaded the subject with him. And if he knew the truth, and how much she'd been paid for her last two novels, he would have hated her and she knew it. She felt as though she could never get away from jealous would-be writers who would begrudge her her success if they knew she was always hiding, and pretending to be someone else. She was becoming the fictional person, not Alexander Green.

"Why don't you just do it," she snapped at him when he talked about it over dinner, "instead of talking about it? If you want to write a novel, put your ass in the chair and write it."

"When am I supposed to do that? I work all day and I'm tired when I get home." So was she, and she had been in college for four years, and she had gotten up at four o'clock in the morning sometimes to write before her classes, or stayed up all night after she finished her assignments and then worked on the book. That was the kind of dedication it took.

"You could work on the weekends," she pointed out.

"I have other things to do," he said in a plaintive tone. "And you need time to be inspired, you can't just sit down and write like an accountant with a calculator."

"Sometimes you just have to do it," she said with conviction. She had the kind of drive that was required, Ivan didn't. He wanted to write at his leisure when he was in the mood. He wasn't serious about it, and she knew he'd never write the novel. He would just talk about it. If he was compelled to do it, he'd have written his novel by then. All he wanted to do was complain, and resent others who had the grit and guts to do it. Writing wasn't an easy business, in fact, it was damn hard. She'd given up sleep and fun and parties to do it, and dates and romance, relationships she could have had. To Alex, her life was the writing, not everything else, and the reward was finishing the last page and knowing you had stuck it out till the end. She sensed that he would never know the joy of that, because he wasn't willing to sacrifice himself.

"What makes you think you know so much about writing," he said angrily, "just because you did some ghostwriting for some fat cat who wrote you a big check?" She didn't like his tone or what he said.

"I know what it takes. You have to give up a lot to write a book. But what you get back is so much better."

"Yeah, the money," he said bitterly.

"No, the pride in your work," she said with a light in her eyes he'd never seen before. "The money is nice, but it really has nothing to do with it."

"I hate my job," he said then, and she felt sorry for him.

"Maybe you should do something else."

"Like what?"

"I don't know. What do you want to do, other than write a book?" She wasn't convinced he really wanted to write either, just say he did. "The beauty about writing is that you're competing with yourself, not someone else."

"Bullshit. Every writer wants to be on the bestseller list." He spoke with the lofty tone of someone who knew all about it, and as if she didn't.

"Of course they do, but while they're writing, they're on their own, crawling their way up Everest." He looked at her blankly, as though her words had no meaning and he didn't believe her.

"You'll never write a book, Alex," he told her with conviction. "You don't know what it's all about."

"I guess not," she agreed with him, and finally got him to talk of other things, like the exhibit they'd seen that day. But she was shocked by how little he knew about the business they were in, and what the writers went through to produce a book. She had enormous respect for other writers. They were all lonely travelers, rock climbing to the top, fighting for their lives and the lives of their characters along the way. It was like trying to carve a statue out of marble, breathing life into it, and giving it the warmth of human flesh. They gave birth to their characters with each book. Ivan was missing the best part, by focusing on the money, when the words and story and characters they created were so much more valuable and interesting, although the money was nice too. But no one did it just for the money, because they had to pay with blood, sweat, and tears for the end result.

They talked about a variety of other subjects during dinner, and he was in better spirits by the end of the meal. He enjoyed her company, and thought there was something mysterious about her. And when he was charming and fun to be with, she liked him, and when he was angry and jealous, she wanted to run away from him. There was a bitter layer of envy under his skin. But also times when he was very seductive. She was confused about her feelings for him, and whether she wanted to be friends with him or something more. One thing was certain, she could never confess to him about her work. She would have loved to take someone into her confidence about the books she wrote, but she knew it would never be him.

Their friendship continued erratically, and sometimes she liked going out with him, but when she started her book a few weeks later, she no longer had as much time for him, or the girls from the office who invited her out too. She spent a lot of time on the phone with Bert in Boston, to talk about the book and get direction from him. He was like the conductor and she was the orchestra, playing all the instruments as he directed her. She had enormous respect for him, and trusted what he told her to do. He loved the subtleties of her new plot, with the psychological element she'd added. Her writing was maturing, and the book was going to be better than anything she had written when she finished. She didn't go out with Ivan for several weeks while she worked on it. He questioned her about her absence when she had dinner at the pub near the office with him again.

"Are you seeing someone else?" he asked her, looking suspicious. She thought about telling him she was ghostwriting again, but she didn't dare. Who would she say she was doing it for here? She knew no one in England, except him, her boss, and the girls at work. And she hadn't had time to make other friends, now that she had started writing again. He saw the Smith Corona on her desk, but she had put all the pages of the manuscript away in a locked drawer.

"No, I'm not," she said innocently. Except the characters in her book, who were fully alive to her.

He acted like a boyfriend at times, and a friend at others. And she was both attracted to him, and afraid of him and his competitive, jealous nature once you scratched the surface. He didn't seem like the right man to her. She didn't think Ivan was it. But he was sexy, and he kissed her one night when they came back to her place after dinner, and the kiss was searing. He'd drunk most of a bottle of wine by himself, and she responded to the kiss with more fervor than she wanted to. He ran hot and cold and criticized her so much that sometimes he turned her off totally. But when he kissed her, she felt as though her whole body was on fire. He knew all the right things to do to arouse her, and she was an innocent in his expert hands. He used sex as a means to get women to do what he wanted, and it always worked for him. She had thought she could invite him to come in, but she realized she'd been mistaken.

"No," she said softly, but without conviction, when he unzipped her jeans, as they sat on the couch together. "I shouldn't . . . I don't want to." He laughed at what she said, and slipped his hand into the small lacy underwear she was wearing, and she was startled by the tidal wave of sensations he created. It was more powerful than anything she had imagined until then. She had written about sex, but never done it.

"Which is it?" he whispered between kisses, as one expert hand started working her breast. He was coming at her from all directions, her mouth, her nipple, and between her legs, and she could hardly breathe. "You shouldn't . . . or you don't want to? And why shouldn't you, Alex?" She couldn't remember the right answer to the question. She had had a few glasses of wine herself, and shouldn't have done that either, she knew, if she wanted to keep a clear head. But she could no longer remember why that mattered . . . why did she need a clear head with all the incredible things he was doing to her, and then he slowly peeled off her jeans, and all she knew was that she wanted him to, and it all seemed right. Suddenly she wanted him as she never had before. "I want you, Alex . . . I need you," he said passionately, and she needed him too. He spread her legs wide and entered her, ripped off her blouse, and bent to kiss her nipples as she moaned. His hands were everywhere and his mouth, and she was murmuring his name as he moved rhythmically, and then suddenly she gave a sharp cry of pain as he thrust deeper and he paid no attention to it. She dug her nails into his back and was torn between wanting him to stop and wanting it to go on forever, and he gave a loud shuddering cry and so did she. It had been pain and pleasure all at once, and he looked down at her in surprise, as he lay on top of her and realized what had happened.

"Were you a virgin?"

She nodded, as two tears rolled down her cheeks. She had wanted the first time to be with someone she loved passionately, not because desire had overwhelmed her after too much wine. She was ashamed of what she'd done, but she had wanted him so much. He rolled slowly off her and went to get towels to get the blood off her legs, and then he held her tight against him. She wanted him to say he loved her, but he didn't, and she didn't love him either. She wasn't even sure she liked him sometimes, but she had loved what he had done to her, some of the time at least. And she clung to him, feeling lost and confused and guilty, but when he touched her, all she wanted was for him to do it again.

Chapter 12

Their relationship was confusing to Alex. Sometimes Ivan acted as though he hated her, other times as though he loved her, and she wasn't sure what she felt for him either. She hated his caustic words and resentment, and the chip on his shoulder about anyone who had more than he did or had achieved something he thought should be his. And at other times, he was gentle and loving, and he brought her to heights in bed that bonded her to him in ways that frightened her too. It was not the relationship she had dreamed of or imagined, and yet at times she thought they were best friends.

She never took him into her confidence about her writing, and knew she couldn't. And he sensed that there were parts of her she would never expose, allow him into, or give away. Alex was a woman with a secret, and he could never figure out the code. And she was adamant about needing time to herself, when she wanted to write. But she never explained her absences to him, or the distance she created between them when the book was on her mind. He still wondered at times if it was another man, but he found that hard to believe. Their sex life was astounding, and yet at times, she totally shut down and wouldn't let him near her. She allowed nothing to interfere with the book he didn't know about. As always, her writing came first. And she felt guilty for keeping part of herself separate.

She was debating about whether to go home to Boston for the holidays, when Fiona invited her to come to Ireland with her to spend them with her family. And Alex loved the idea. Ivan said he hated Christmas, and went somewhere on his own every year where he didn't have to hear stories about Father Christmas and see people carrying presents or dragging their Christmas trees home. He said he was going to Morocco and invited Alex to come with him, but she either wanted to go home to the nuns, go home with Fiona, or stay in London, and enjoy a British Christmas. She wasn't going to go to Marrakesh with him, ignoring the holiday entirely. She put up a tree before he left. In the end, Fiona's invitation had the most appeal. Fiona was going to Ireland for a week and coming back to London on New Year's Eve, to spend it with friends. Ivan was planning to spend two weeks in Marrakesh, so she'd be alone for New Year's. She was annoyed at him for leaving, and said that their relationship shouldn't just be about sex. She wanted to spend the holidays with him, but he was nonnegotiable about it.

"I don't do holidays. They were rotten when I was a kid. And I don't like sharing them with anyone now," he said coldly. There were a lot of things about the relationship she didn't like, the way he treated her when he was moody, the things he said to demean her, the fact that sex was all-important to him and he never told her he loved her, and then at other times he was tender with her and seemed to care about her, and the sex was extraordinary, and for him that replaced love. She wondered sometimes if he hated women, or if he was just a very unhappy person and hated himself. He was hard to read at times, and he was in such a foul mood as the holidays began that it was a relief when he left.

Alex had had a letter from Brigid, the ex–Sister Regina. She loved her teaching job in Boston, and was dating the math teacher at the school. She was going to meet his family over Christmas. She said that he was thirty-eight years old, had never been married either, and wanted children. And Brigid sounded very excited about him. Alex was happy for her. Rose Porter had sent her a white cashmere scarf with mittens to match to keep warm. She missed all of them at times, but for now her life was here, and she wanted to see it through.

She called Mother Mary Margaret to say she wasn't coming for Christmas, but she would be going to Ireland with her friend.

"As long as you're with a family over Christmas," the superior said generously, "then I won't worry about you. We'll catch up when you get back." But Alex didn't know when that would be. She didn't want to leave Ivan, or her job. She had no idea how long the relationship would last with Ivan, his feelings for her seemed to wax and wane day by day. He was impossible to predict.

"Do you love him?" Fiona asked her when they boarded the train to Heathrow to fly to Ireland.

"I don't know," Alex said honestly. "I'm not sure."

"Sex confuses everything, doesn't it?" Fiona said wistfully. There had been a boy she had loved in Ireland and wanted to marry, and then she had gone to London, gotten involved with someone else, and everything went wrong. Fiona seemed much more worldly and experienced after living in London for four years. Alex's home had been the convent and a college dorm until six months before, although now everything had changed. And Fiona was right, Alex decided, sex made everything so confusing. She no longer knew what she felt or where she belonged. At times she just wanted to go back to Boston, but she wasn't ready to give up on Ivan yet. Maybe his rough edges and bitterness would smooth down in time. He expected the world to give him what he wanted, like a successful novel, but he wasn't willing to strive and sacrifice for it. Alex didn't hear from him once he left for Marrakesh. He'd been there before, and he said it was cheap, sunny, and fun, which was all he wanted for two weeks.

But the week that Alex spent with Fiona's family was warm and wonderful. She had a hundred-and-two-year-old great-grandmother who lived with them. And Fiona's family were very kind to her while she was there. They made her feel welcome, and Alex called the nuns before they left for midnight mass on Christmas Eve, which was only seven in the evening in Boston. They were about to have Christmas Eve dinner. And she talked to everyone. They said they missed her terribly, but thought working in London was a wonderful experience for her. She was sad when she hung up. Fiona could see that she was homesick. Alex prayed for the nuns that night in church.

The next morning she and Fiona went to the kitchen and made breakfast together, and an hour later, the whole family was crammed into the kitchen, even Fiona's great-grandmother in her wheelchair. Fiona had four younger brothers and two sisters, and Alex was glad she'd come, and grateful that they'd included her. She and Fiona were sad to leave on the morning of New Year's Eve, but Fiona had plans in London that night with a hot date. The interlude in Dublin with Fiona's family had done Alex good. It was nice being with a normal family. And she and Fiona had slept in the same room with her sisters on bunk beds. It made Alex feel like a kid again. But she was hungry to work on her book when she got home to her apartment in London.

And as soon as she got back, Alex got to work in earnest. She was even beginning to think that she should give up her internship and work on the book full-time. It was difficult doing both. But she wasn't quite ready to quit the job yet. And she knew that Ivan would be upset if she did. In some ways, it was nice working in the same place as he was.

She hadn't told the nuns about him, but Mother MaryMeg suspected that she had a beau, and didn't want to ask. And Alex was old enough now to choose the right man, or so she hoped.

She had made good headway on the manuscript by the time Ivan returned from Marrakesh.

"Did you miss me?" he asked when he showed up at her apartment without calling first. She locked up the pages of the manuscript she'd been working on while he bounded up the stairs. He pulled her into his arms, nearly tore her clothes off, and made love to her on the living room floor. They never reached the bed. He made her feel like some kind of sex object at times, and not a woman he loved. It had been flattering and exciting at first, but now it depressed her when he made it all about sex and never about love. She wanted more, and she wasn't sure he had it to give. He didn't ask how her week in Dublin had been over Christmas, and didn't apologize for not calling. He was like a wild stallion that had returned to the barn to mount his mare. They made love three times that night, and then he went home. He said he had to unpack and get ready for work the next day. She took her manuscript out as soon as he left. Working on it always centered her and calmed her. She put a sex scene in the book that night after he left. She wondered what Bert would say. She hadn't mentioned it to him on the phone. She didn't want him to guess what was going on, or that her life had changed. She was still just as dedicated to her work. Nothing interfered with that.

Things seemed to calm down between them for a few months after his trip to Morocco, and they put the holidays behind them. But in March she was working hard on the book, and spent less time with him, and he got nasty with her again. They had been dating for almost six months. She was sending chapters back and forth to Bert, and he was thinking about coming to London in May to work on everything she'd done so far. And she was excited to have him come. She said something to Ivan about it one night at dinner, and he had a fit.

"Who is this guy and why is he coming here? Is he your boy-friend?"

"Of course not. I was a virgin, remember? And he's old enough to be my grandfather. He's just a very good friend." She couldn't say he was her editor or why he was coming, and Ivan didn't suspect, but he was annoyed and complained about it for a week. He said there were too many mysteries in her life. "He helped me with my school projects when I was in college, kind of like a tutor." It seemed the best way to explain it.

"You're not in school here. Tell him not to come."

"He's my friend. He's like my family, my mentor."

It became a raging battle between them, and the symbol of everything about her that Ivan sensed but didn't understand. And three weeks later, Alex was having dinner with Fiona on a night that Ivan was busy, and Alex could see that she looked pained. "Is something wrong? Problems at work?"

Fiona shook her head, and wasn't sure what to say or where to start.

"I heard some rumors," she said, staring at her plate and finally up at her friend. She wasn't sure of the right thing to do, but she didn't want Alex to get hurt.

"What kind of rumors?"

"About Ivan. There's a new intern in publicity. Someone said that Ivan's been spending time with her. I don't know if it's true, but I thought you should know. The person who told me saw them having dinner at a restaurant last week." Alex remembered instantly that she had worked on the book and hadn't seen him very often the week before. But she couldn't help it, she had promised a chapter to Bert by the end of the week, so he could edit it during the weekend. She had work to do after all. But Ivan had no idea. She wondered if he was using the time to cheat on her.

"Do you think they're having an affair?" she asked Fiona.

"I honestly don't know," Fiona said unhappily. He had done things like it before. Fiona had warned her of it in the beginning. "Maybe you should ask him."

The following night she did, and Ivan laughed in her face. "What difference would it make to you, if I were? You're busy all the time yourself."

"I had some work I had to do," she said obliquely.

"For whom?"

She debated for a long time before she answered, wanting to come clean. It might be simpler, after six months together, as long as she didn't tell him what she was writing and under what name.

"I'm working on a book," she said, barely audibly.

"I don't believe you. You haven't got what it takes."

"How do you know? You've never read a word I've written. That's why my friend is coming over next month. He's my editor."

"For what?"

"I'm ghostwriting again." She didn't know what else to say.

"For whom?"

"I can't tell you that," she said, looking uncomfortable. The web of lies she was spinning was strangling her.

"And what do I care anyway? You're not a writer, Alex. You're a file clerk, for God's sake. Ghostwriting for some celebrity isn't like writing a novel. And what makes you think you can write?" She couldn't tell him that either. She felt like an idiot trying to explain it to him. "What are you trying to do? Make me feel bad? Show me up? I told you I wanted to write a book, so you're writing one? How pathetic is that? What is this, a contest?" He had managed to deflect her from the key question she had asked him, and she brought him back to it again.

"Are you cheating on me, and having an affair?" she said calmly.

He hesitated for a long time, and then shrugged as he sat back in the chair, defying her to stop him or do something about it. "Maybe I am. We're not married. I never said I wouldn't sleep with other women. Don't be so archaic. She's a cute girl, maybe the three of us could have some fun one night." She stared at him in amazement, unable to believe what she was hearing. It showed a total lack of respect for her, and even the other girl. She knew that people did things like that, but she didn't intend to be one of them. He had no morals, or decency. He was spoiled and lazy, felt entitled, and did whatever he wanted. It was finally clear to her. He didn't love her. They were having sex. And the charade of hiding her books from him was just too difficult, and he didn't respect that either, and assumed she couldn't write.

"You need to go," she said to him and stood up. "I can't do this anymore. I never should have in the first place. And you're angry all the time, Ivan. Don't be mad at me because I'm writing. You can write a novel, if you want to, even if you're tired after work or you don't want to stay up late or get up in the morning to write. Other people do it, so can you. And don't punish me because I want to write. And no, I'm not going to have 'fun' with you and some girl. That's disgusting. You don't respect anything, you don't care about anyone except yourself. I don't want to live like this anymore, worrying about what makes you angry, afraid that you'll be jealous or pissed about something I do. You have a chip on your shoulder the size of your head. And if you're cheating on me on top of it, I quit. I'm done. I have work to do. Go home."

"Oh, give me a break. What kind of work? Are you going to write a story? What makes you think you can? A romance novel?"

"It doesn't matter what I write. At least I do it. What have you ever done except have sex and sit around and complain, and be mad at what other people do or have? You're a nasty person, and a cheat apparently. I'm finished. Go home." She stood there waiting for him to leave, and he finally unwound his long frame from the chair where he was sitting and walked to the door. He didn't look sorry to go.

"She's better looking than you are anyway, and she has bigger tits," he said, walking out and slamming the door behind him. She felt sick after he left, that he would even say something like that and cared so little for her. He had never loved her. He wasn't capable of loving anyone. Only himself.

She slept fitfully that night, and went to work the next morning. She saw him in the hall, and he ignored her and didn't even try to talk to her. And she saw him with the little blonde from publicity that afternoon. He was kissing her in the back hall. When she saw them together, she woke up. She was crazy. She was spending her days filing so she could say she had a job in London and justify staying there. She didn't need justification. She could be in London if she wanted to. And she had a book to write. Bert was coming in a month, and she had to get ready for him. She knew she had kept the job only so she could see Ivan in the daytime. It was insane. She had lost her mind for a while because she had sex with him. And even that wasn't fun anymore. He was an empty shell. She had been dazzled by him in the beginning but there was no one there. And nothing had gotten better—it had all gotten worse. And now he was cheating on her, to add insult to injury. She cringed, thinking of the abuse she had taken for almost seven months. But it would never happen again, she promised herself.

She handed in her resignation that afternoon, and gave them two weeks' notice, which they said they wouldn't hold her to, since she was only an intern. She could leave right away if she wanted. She didn't see Ivan before she left, and hoped she never would again. She had a book to write, and he was a distraction she could no longer afford. She had to have the manuscript finished for Bert. And that was precisely what she was going to do now.

She told Fiona she was leaving, and they promised to have dinner soon. Fiona felt guilty for causing the breakup with what she'd told her, but she hated Ivan making a fool of Alex. And amazingly, Alex seemed calm.

She went back to her apartment, which she had extended at Christmas until June. And she had gotten a visa a month ago to extend her stay in the UK. She hadn't told them about the internship, and now she didn't have one anyway. She set her typewriter on the desk, took her manuscript out of the drawer, and sat down to get to work. The fun and games were over. Alexander Green had a crime thriller to write, and the book she was working on was going to surprise and shock even the most loyal Alexander Green fans.

She wasn't even sad to lose Ivan to the other woman. There was nothing to lose. He was just as empty and bitter as he had been when they started, and she no longer cared. He had been a terrible mistake, and all she wanted to do now was forget him and get back to work on what really mattered to her.

Chapter 13

Without Ivan and a job to distract her, Alex plunged into her work. She wrote constantly, as many hours a day as she was able, and it was a relief to lose herself in the book. She thought of him sometimes late at night when she finished, and compared it to the relationship she'd had with Scott. He had been jealous of her writing and tried to belittle her by tearing her down, in order to aggrandize himself. But with Ivan, it wasn't her writing, since he had never read anything she'd written. It was everything, her dedication, her perseverance, her single-mindedness about life, her refusal to be swayed from the path toward what she wanted to achieve.

She kept her eye on the goal, which infuriated him, because he had none. He only said he did, like the book he claimed he wanted to write but never would. He was too lazy to do it. He was sloppy about everything he did, and angry at those who weren't. And even though he knew nothing of her secret career and association with the Alexander Green books, he sensed that she would go far one day, and hated her for it. He wanted all the prizes and praise for himself, but not to work for them. She wondered how many people like him there were in the world, jealous of others for what they had and couldn't be bothered to do themselves. He was never happy for her, just angry. She felt as though a thousand-pound weight had been lifted from her when she told him to leave. He was always angry at her about something, it was exhausting to deal with, and have to constantly try to make it up to him for what he didn't have, wouldn't work for, and thought he deserved.

And with her many hours of hard labor, Alex had finished the first draft of the book when Bert arrived in London in May. She had taken a room for him at a small hotel near her, and he was planning to stay for a week of intense collaboration. He was going to read and correct one section at a time. She would then make the changes he suggested, if she agreed with him—and she almost always did—and then they would move on to the next section. And while she was writing, he would have time to walk around and enjoy the city. He said he hadn't been to London in years. And when he rang her doorbell, it was like a family reunion for her. She threw her arms around him and he hugged her and spoke to her gruffly as he walked in. He was wearing jeans and an old tweed jacket and hiking boots, and his beard and hair were as big a mess as ever. It was wonderful to see him. She had left Boston eleven months before and missed him.

He sat down in a big, well-worn leather chair and she handed him a glass of red wine, which he accepted with pleasure, and told her she had gotten prettier in the last year, and thinner.

"Are you eating?" he asked after the first sip of wine. "You don't look it."

"I've been working really hard for the past month, so I'd be ready for you when you got here."

"Am I going to meet the boyfriend?" He was curious about him, and didn't like what she had told him, but he didn't want to scare her. He didn't think it would come to a good end, for her. The boy she described had everything to gain from the relationship, and he couldn't see what she'd get out of it, except a headache, and maybe great sex, which he didn't ask. He had known she was a virgin when she left, but suspected she wasn't now, not after seven months of dating a twenty-seven-year-old man. Even Alex wasn't that saintly, and she was human and twenty-three years old, after all.

She shook her head in answer to Bert's question. "We broke up," she said simply. "It wasn't right."

"What does that mean?" Bert asked as he studied her intently. He didn't think she seemed unhappy, just tired, and he knew she'd been writing diligently. "Did he dump you, or did you dump him?" He hoped the latter, from what he'd heard before. "Should I kick his ass? I will if he broke your heart. It's fine with me, if you broke his. He probably deserved it." She laughed at her mentor's loyalty.

"I ended it. He was angry all the time and jealous of everything I did, and he didn't even know about the books. I never told him."

"I hope not." Bert was relieved. "I told you to stay away from writers."

"He wasn't. He claimed he wants to write a book one day, but he's too lazy to even try. He just wants the glory and the money. He's an editor, theoretically, but he doesn't know the meaning of the word. Basically, he's just a low-level assistant."

"Jesus, he would have really hated you if he knew about the Green books."

"I told him I did ghostwriting on the side. He saw a check once on my desk, and I had to tell him something to explain the money. I'm not sure he believed me. It didn't help that I was lying to him and he sensed it. But anyway, he cheated on me, so that did it. I should have ended it sooner, or not started with him at all."

"I'm sorry, Alex," Bert said with feeling. That was two relationships that had gone awry, and this one had obviously been more serious, more involved, and lasted longer. "Are you heartbroken?" He hoped not, she didn't look it.

"It's kind of a relief," she said sheepishly. "He was interfering with my work, and I hate that. I need a boyfriend who doesn't want all my time and isn't jealous of everything I do or accomplish."

"That would be nice." He smiled at her, happy to see her again. He had missed her fiercely, even though they spoke on the phone a lot and had continued working together for the past eleven months, but it was different than being in the same room, face-to-face, and talking out a change or a problem. It would be much easier working now in London for the next week. "So where's our book?"

She picked the manuscript up from the desk and handed it to him. He set down his glass of wine, put on his glasses, and started glancing through the pages. He glanced up at her a couple of times and smiled, then alternately nodded and frowned while he was reading, and looked up at her once in surprise.

"A sex scene?" She blushed as he nodded. "My, my." But he didn't object to it, and then he looked up and told her to go play while he got down to work and read it carefully. He'd liked the glimpses he'd had so far in the pages she'd sent him, and she had tightened it a lot since. Her style was stronger than ever, her voice clear, the language beautifully handled with skillful turns of phrase, and he already knew the plot and liked it.

She cleaned up the kitchen, put some clothes away, and read some papers on her desk while Bert read, and she put the bottle of red wine next to him. But he was totally sober when he put the first few chapters down after three and a half hours. He made a few notations in pencil on the manuscript, but very few so far. She was nervous when she sat down across from him after he called her back into the living room.

"What do you think?"

"I think it's your best book so far. And the sex is nicely handled. It's just masculine enough not to blow your cover, but actually quite elegantly done. And the plot development is dynamite. You already have me confused and I know the story." She looked at where he was and nodded.

"The murder is in the next chapter. But there are two of them, there's another one later on. I added it. It makes the book more exciting."

"Same murderer?" he inquired.

"Of course not. That would be boring." He laughed at her comment, and went on reading after a short break. He had been reading for seven hours when he stopped and said his eyes were tired and he needed more wine. He had finished the bottle, but showed no sign of being drunk.

She had bought dinner for them while he was reading, shepherd's pie, and she warmed it in the microwave while they talked about the changes he thought she should make, but there weren't many. It sounded like an easy fix for now.

They went over the plot again during dinner, and two new characters he thought she should add, and one he felt served no purpose and preferred that she eliminate, or make bigger and more important to give him a raison d'être in the story. His suggestions always improved the books, and she knew they would this time too.

He went back to his hotel after dinner, and she got to work, executing the changes he had outlined to her, and she stopped work at two A.M., pleased with the results.

She fell into bed, and he was back at nine the next morning, with a bag of scones and croissants, and she set out jam on the table and clotted cream for the scones, which was very British but she'd grown used to it. And she made coffee for both of them, and showed him what she'd done the night before.

"I like it," he said, nodding approval, with croissant crumbs in his beard. He looked more like Einstein than ever, with his wild, unruly mane of white hair.

They worked diligently for the entire week, and by the end of it, Bert had come up with more changes, which sparked more ideas for Alex and inspired her, and they were both delighted with the end result.

"I stand by what I said when I got here. It's your best book yet."

"I hope the publisher thinks so," she said, always nervous about it. She drove herself hard, and never assumed anything. She was afraid each time that they wouldn't like it, which kept her on her toes, and it was one of those things that Bert loved about her, and that she was willing to work hard.

They went to the Rib Room for dinner to celebrate on the last night. The editing had gone well, the changes had been made. She had scanned and emailed the manuscript to Rose Porter to hand in to the publisher. Alex was as regular as clockwork, and her most recent published work was currently climbing bestseller lists at a rapid rate. She had become a regular feature on it by then, but was never blasé about it. It thrilled her every time when she got emails from Amanda congratulating her and telling her that one of her books was on the list week after week. This was another big best-seller. She was hitting one out of the park every time, and the Alexander Green books had developed a cult following among the elite cognoscenti of crime thrillers.

Her publishers were still astounded that they were written by a young woman, and her identity was the best-kept secret in the business. The publicity department occasionally planted an item about the author, that he was hunting in Scotland, or researching a new book somewhere, or had just returned to his ranch in Montana to start work on a new thriller. It had taken on a life of its own, and at times Alex almost believed he was real, like some form of alter ego. She always thought it was funny when they sent her a clipping about the elusive Alexander Green, or an alleged sighting of him somewhere unlikely, like Berlin.

After Bert left, at the end of a very satisfying visit, Alex had to look for a new apartment, since the second lease on hers was expiring in June, and the owner was returning from a lengthy stay in Australia and wanted it back.

This time it took her two weeks to find one, in Kensington. It was slightly smaller than the one she'd had, another furnished rental, which suited her, and she hoped to stay in London until later in the year, and then go back to Boston. She wasn't ready to yet. An eighteen-month stay abroad still seemed reasonable. She hadn't become an expatriate, it felt more like an extended student year abroad. She liked having her own place to live, although she missed the nuns and the warmth of being among them. She was happy too to move to an apartment where she hadn't been with Ivan. She wanted to put the memories of him behind her. She had heard nothing from him for two months, and didn't expect to ever hear from him again, and hoped she wouldn't.

The new apartment was bright and sunny, when there was sun in London. It belonged to a young woman, and Alex felt at home there, in the well-decorated one-bedroom flat, which had a feminine touch. It made her wonder if she should get her own place when she went back to the States, although she hated to move out of St. Dominic's, which was home to her now.

And Bill Buchanan had presented her with a big decision a few weeks before. She still owned the home that she had lived in with her father, which had been left to her as part of his estate. It wasn't fancy, or overly large, but it represented a solid investment for her, along with his savings and the insurance policy, much of which she'd used to pay for her education. Their old house had been rented for nine years, since her father's death, and their belongings were still in storage for a small monthly fee, which Bill paid automatically for her. There had been two tenants in the house for the last nine years. The most recent one had been there for five, and wanted to make an offer on the house if she was willing to sell it, and she didn't know if she was. She hated to give it up, out of sentiment, and the rent was a steady income for her, which was nice to have, but she couldn't see herself living there again, even years from now when she was married and had children. It would make her too sad. But giving it up forever was painful too, and severing a tie with her father and her past. She had told Bill she would think about it and hadn't made a decision yet. He contacted her again in July, and said that her tenants wanted to know, because if she didn't want to sell, they had an opportunity to buy another house, so she had to make up her mind.

The decision was harder than she thought it would be, and after many sleepless nights, remembering her time there with her father, she decided to sell it, and called Bill to tell him. He said he thought it was the right decision, and would contact the tenants and get back to her with their offer, which he did a week later. It was a decent offer that took into account the new roof it needed, and some updates and repairs, and they wanted to put in air conditioning, which she and her father didn't have. She accepted the offer without negotiating, and they were delighted. She agreed to a thirty-day closing, and in September, the house would no longer be hers. The thought of it was bittersweet, but it seemed right.

The day after she accepted the offer, she got a letter from Brigid with startling news. She was getting married at the end of August to the math teacher she had been dating for six months. His name was Patrick Dylan, and Brigid said she had never been happier in her life. Alex was thrilled for her, and Brigid said that Mother MaryMeg and the sisters were coming to the wedding. The archdiocese had released her from her vows.

She invited Alex to the wedding, which was going to be very small and intimate, at their parish church, with the reception afterward at the home of Patrick's parents in a suburb of Boston, and his sisters were cooking the wedding lunch. But she said she understood if Alex couldn't be there. It was short notice and a long way to come for a wedding, from London, and Alex had no plans to go home for now. She thought about it all day. She didn't want to go back to Boston yet, but there was no way she could miss Brigid's wedding. It was four weeks away, and she could go home for a week and catch up with everyone there, and then come back to Europe for a while.

Alex sent Brigid an email to tell her she was coming, and then called Mother MaryMeg. She had been sure Alex would come home for the wedding since Brigid was her closest friend. Alex told her she would be in Boston for a week and all the nuns were thrilled when they heard. They were all going to Brigid's wedding.

*   *   *

Alex flew into Boston five days before the wedding so she'd have time to visit with everyone. The nuns were almost as excited to see her as they were about the wedding, and they had a big celebratory dinner for Alex the night she came home. She was ecstatic to see them and it made her realize how much she'd missed them and how long she'd been gone. But she liked her life in London too, and she wasn't ready to move back. She had her apartment in Kensington till December if she wanted it, and Sister Xavier and Sister Tommy were disappointed to hear that she was going back so soon.

She managed to have lunch with Bert before she got busy helping Brigid with the wedding. And she dressed her friend on the big day. Brigid had found a beautiful vintage gown in a secondhand shop and it fit her perfectly. She looked at Alex with such peace and joy, she was glowing, and she was exquisite as Alex helped her put her veil on, and all the nuns and Alex cried as they watched her walk down the aisle in the small church. It had been a long, arduous journey for her, and Alex was happy she'd come to be there with her. Brigid had no family of her own, except the nuns and Patrick's big boisterous family. And Alex suspected they would be having babies soon. At thirty-six and thirty-eight, they didn't have time to waste.

The reception was noisy and fun. One of Patrick's brothers played in a band and they came. Everyone danced, the food was plentiful and good, the nuns were thrilled for her, and Patrick and Brigid looked like the two happiest people on earth, and Alex was ecstatic for them. She went back to the convent with the nuns after the bridal couple left for a two-day honeymoon at an inn on Long Island owned by someone they knew.

Alex stayed for three days after the wedding and then, sad to leave the nuns again, she flew back to London. She was thinking of returning to Boston for good in time for Christmas, but Mother MaryMeg told her not to come home sooner than she wanted to. She was young and free and this time would never come again. As the plane touched down at Heathrow, she was glad she had gone to Brigid's wedding. It gave one hope to see two people so much in love.

The weather was terrible in London when Alex went back. It was gray, rainy, and gloomy, and Alex decided to go to Italy for a week, to Portofino, Sorrento, and all the way south to Capri. She had the money and the time. She asked Fiona to join her, but she couldn't get the time off work, so Alex went alone. She was away for ten days, and had a good time. It felt odd to be in romantic places on her own, and lonely at times. But she visited all the touristic places, had brought a stack of books to read, and swam and slept a lot. And then she went back to London, to start working on an outline for a new book.

She spent the fall holed up in her apartment working on it, and had dinner with Fiona from time to time, but otherwise she saw no one and never went out. Fiona told her Ivan was dating two girls at work, and lying to both of them, and there would be a major explosion soon, since one of them had a fiery temper and was a bitch, according to Fiona.

"Am I glad I got out of that," Alex said with a grin.

"No regrets? He was hot. He still is."

"None," Alex answered without hesitating for an instant.

"Anyone else?"

"I haven't been out of the house, except to see you," Alex said honestly.

"That's not healthy," Fiona scolded her. "What do you do here all the time?"

"I read . . . write letters . . ." She didn't know how to explain why she stayed home for weeks on end, and couldn't tell Fiona her secret either.

"You're too young to be a recluse." She wasn't. She was a writer, which was different. But no one knew. She had a whole hidden life, which filled her nights and days, to the exclusion of all else. "You'll never meet a man if you stay home all the time," Fiona said. But she had a suggestion. She and half a dozen other women she knew were going on a ski trip to France over Christmas. It was organized by a social club for singles that they belonged to, the fees were low, and outsiders were welcome. "Do you want to come?"

"I'm not much of a skier." She had gone twice in college, but hadn't had spare time then either, to pursue sports, hobbies, or men. She was always writing. She had given up a lot, to write five books, three of them bestsellers, by the age of twenty-three. But the trip sounded like fun to her, and she liked Fiona. She had broken up with another boyfriend recently, and was looking to meet someone new. Men never lasted long with her, but the supply appeared to be plentiful, she always managed to come up with new dates.

"None of us are good skiers either," Fiona reassured her. "The trip is about more than snow and slopes. There are hot guys in that club and they bring friends. Maybe you'll meet someone. And not a loser like Ivan." His reputation at work had gotten worse with his recent escapades. He hadn't seemed as bad a year before, and had had a certain mystique. Now he was just an obvious cheater. "He's a sleaze," Fiona dismissed him with a sour expression, and Alex didn't disagree. She felt stupid for having dated him, and even more so for having lost her virginity to him. Their relationship had been all about sex and not love, despite her illusions at the time about what it might turn into. It never did. He didn't have it in him.

"So will you come?" Fiona pressed her about the ski trip. "They fill up pretty fast." It was ten days in the French Alps, over Christmas and New Year, at bargain rates. It was hard to beat, except that she had said she might be back in Boston by Christmas and didn't want to disappoint the nuns.

"Okay," Alex said with a grin, and a pang of guilt.

"Thank God. If you don't get out soon, your only date will be Father Christmas when he comes down your chimney, and he's too old for you." Alex laughed at her, and was excited about the trip.

She hated to tell the nuns that she wasn't going home for the holidays again, but she called and explained why, and they were sad but said they understood. The ski trip sounded great to them too.

She renewed her apartment lease for another six months when it was offered to her, and extended her visa. She was hoping to stay in London until June. By then it would be two years since she left Boston. The time just seemed to slip by, and she had peace and quiet to write here.

She shipped all her presents to the nuns in early December, and rented ski equipment for her trip.

The new book she had started was going well, but she had promised herself she would put it aside and leave it for ten days when she went skiing. She had a hard time doing that. Sometimes she even got up in the middle of the night to go back to work. There was no one to object and tell her not to, which was the best part of being single and not dating. She could do whatever she wanted. She couldn't imagine how she would give that up one day, if she met a man she cared about. Her freedom was so important to her now, to pursue her writing however and whenever she wanted to. She had total control over her own time, and she loved it. And writing was still the love of her life, more than any man.

Alex left with Fiona and her friends on the trip to the Trois Vallées region in the French Alps, near Courchevel, on the twenty-second of December, and the group was as lively and fun-loving as Fiona had promised. There was a lot of drinking involved, flirting, and random sex, but it was all easygoing and no one felt compelled to do what they didn't want. A number of the men were attracted to Alex at first, but picked up on a vibe that said she wasn't interested, and Fiona was disappointed. She wanted Alex to meet a great guy, as much as she wanted one for herself, but Alex didn't cooperate. She went to bed early almost every night, except New Year's Eve, and she scribbled for hours in a notebook in her room. She was incorrigible, and she knew it.

But on the bus on the way back, she told Fiona she had had a great time, and meant it. And Fiona had met a man she really liked on the trip. Clive was an accountant and worked for a solicitor's firm. He had a good job, he was great looking and a good skier, and he appeared to be crazy about her. She had slept with him on New Year's Eve, and he wanted to take her out as soon as they got back to London. He seemed promising, and Alex was happy for her.

When she got home, she had had a letter from Brigid that was so excited it was almost incoherent. She was three months pregnant and the baby was due in June. It had happened even faster than they'd hoped, not even a month after their wedding, without even trying. She had been married for four months by then. Fast work. She would be thirty-seven when the baby was born. And she said they were hoping for a boy, or Patrick's father would be bitterly disappointed. Alex was thrilled for her friends. Brigid was married and having a baby. All her dreams had come true. Fiona had met a new man. And she had her books. Alex didn't feel cheated at all not to have a man in her life. She had what she wanted, the writing career she had dreamed of, beyond her wildest dreams. It seemed like a perfect way to start the new year.

Chapter 14

Alex finished her new book at the beginning of April, and sent it off to Bert to edit. And then she decided to take a trip to visit some cities she hadn't gotten to yet and wanted to see before she went home in June.

She went to Madrid and Barcelona, Munich and Berlin, and Prague because she had heard the city was so beautiful, and she wasn't disappointed. She had become an expert at traveling alone by then. She stayed in good hotels because she could afford them with the money she was making from her writing. She ate early in respectable, moderate restaurants where she felt safe, or ordered room service, and in each city, she saw all the museums, churches, and tourist attractions she had planned to. And her last stop was Paris, because she wanted to go back one more time before she left Europe.

She spent May packing and buying small gifts for the nuns, and had dinner with Fiona several times, with her new boyfriend. She was still seeing Clive, the accountant she had met on the ski trip, and it was starting to look serious. They were both twenty-seven and he couldn't do enough for her. She was in love, they both were.

Alex was boxing up some of her papers one night when Rose called her. It was three in the afternoon in New York, and eight at night in London, and Alex was feeling a little wistful about leaving. And although she hadn't met the man of her dreams, which hadn't been high on her agenda anyway, she was sad to be leaving London, and her travels around Europe. Her last trip had been the best one so far.

"We've had a very interesting offer today," she said to Alex on the phone, "from a very important production company in L.A. They want to buy *Darkness* for a movie." It was her second book and first big bestseller, and one of her most popular titles. "They already have a screenwriter, and they have a number of stars in mind that they're negotiating with. The director is a big name. This could be a fabulous opportunity for you, and some nice money. And it never hurts the books. There's only one hitch, but I think we can work it out."

"What's that?" Alex was shocked as she listened. She hadn't thought a lot about movies of her work, she was too busy writing the books.

"They want Alexander Green on set, to correct the scripts and work with the screenwriter and keep the movie true to the book, or as close as possible."

"Well, that's the end of that. I can't do that," Alex said, disappointed for a minute.

"I've been thinking about it all day. Green is a famous recluse by now. We could set you up as his assistant, say he's in a house somewhere in L.A., and you could go back and forth with the scripts, make the corrections at night, and bring them back fresh from the pen of the famously invisible author in the morning. It's convoluted but it could work, if you're willing to sit in L.A. on a movie set for four or five months. It's all going to be shot in a studio and on locations in L.A."

"Even the African scenes?" There were several jungle scenes in the book.

"Apparently. They don't want to spend the money to go on location in Africa, and have their stars getting eaten by a boa constrictor." She laughed as Alex listened. "What do you think? Should I pursue it or turn them down?"

"I don't know. I don't want to get found out and blow everything else. We've put too much into keeping it secret. I don't want to risk someone discovering the truth."

"Let me talk to the producer and get a feel for it. If they're too pushy, we can turn them down. If they want Alexander Green badly enough, they'll cooperate with us on our terms. I won't risk exposing you, Alex, I promise." Rose had been Alex's strongest ally, and Alex loved and admired her. She was a fantastic woman, and had become a great friend. She had handled the publishers flawlessly when they told them about her, so she trusted her to deal with the movie people as well. "I'll keep you posted. When are you coming back?"

"In ten days."

"I probably won't know anything by then, but we should hear pretty soon after that. They've already got the money for it in the bank, are close to signing the actors, and they want to start shooting in September, if they get the stars they want. So we'll probably know in June, or beginning of July at the latest." Alex thanked her and they hung up, and she spent the next few days in a daze, wondering if she should do it, and if it would work out. It sounded dangerous to her, in terms of keeping her identity secret, but very exciting. And she hadn't heard from Rose by the time she left.

She had dinner with Fiona on her last night. Her bags were packed, her briefcase was crammed full, and she had a tote bag with proofs to read on the plane. And she was carrying her latest manuscript too. The apartment was neat, and she was sadder than ever to be leaving London.

She had a nice dinner with Fiona and Clive at the Shed at Notting Hill Gate, and the two young women cried when they left each other, promising to write and stay in touch. Fiona told her to go back to Boston and find a boyfriend before she turned into an old maid, which made Alex laugh through her tears. She didn't say anything to her about the possible movie deal because she couldn't. She could tell Brigid about it when she saw her, and the nuns, and Bert of course, but no one else. Her real life was totally unknown to Fiona, who thought that she lived on the modest inheritance her father had left her, didn't have to work, and was a very lucky girl. That night at dinner, Clive hinted that they might be getting married, and Alex would have to come back for the wedding. He thought Alex was a great girl, even if she was a little quiet, and shy, but pretty and bright and a nice person. Fiona had told him what she knew of her story, and he said that probably living with nuns in a convent for seven years had made her act like one, and all she needed was for the right man to come along. Fiona thought so too.

Alex checked her bags at Heathrow the next day, carried her overstuffed hand luggage, and boarded the plane to Boston, feeling like she was leaving home again, but excited to see the nuns too. The two years in Europe after college had been the beginning of her adult life, although she hadn't changed physically. She still looked years younger than she was and could have passed for a teenager in ballet flats and jeans at twenty-four.

She didn't expect it, but Sister Xavier and Sister Tommy were at the airport to meet her, as a surprise when she came through customs. They held her tight when they hugged her and both nuns cried and so did Alex. She'd seen them at Brigid's wedding ten months earlier, but that was a long time too.

"Thank God you're home now!" Sister Xavier said with fervor, as they headed for the garage to get the car. Both nuns had ascertained immediately that she looked happy and well, and she seemed to have more self-assurance after living on her own for two years. She had grown up. They thought she was even more beautiful than ever. "We got our girl back," she said to Sister Thomas with a sigh of relief as she started the car.

She told them all about her recent trip around Europe on the drive from the airport.

"I've always wanted to go to Madrid," Sister Xavier said dreamily, as they drove along the freeway.

"I went to a bullfight with my husband once," Sister Tommy said. "It was awful. He loved it. The poor bull. I almost threw up." All three of them laughed, and they were at St. Dominic's an hour later, and all of the nuns were waiting for her. It was a true homecoming. She hugged Mother MaryMeg first and lingered in her arms for a long moment.

"We were going to come over to kidnap you if you didn't come back this time," the superior teased her. "Welcome home, Alex."

"Thank you, Mother," she said, feeling at peace, and then went upstairs to her room, which had been kept intact for her. It was hers, and had been waiting, with her little blue lamb lamp from her childhood on the desk.

"How's Brigid . . . Regina?" she asked Sister Xavier before she left her.

"Ready to pop." She laughed. "She dropped by to see us a month ago. The poor thing can hardly walk, but she looks great and so happy." They didn't know what sex the baby was and were waiting to see at the birth, but were hoping for a boy. "She promised to call the minute it's born." Alex already knew that her husband and one of his sisters were going to be at the delivery, which all sounded scary to Alex. It was a subject she knew nothing about, and didn't want to. Until she had to, one day, if she ever did. Sometimes she thought she'd stay single forever, and just be a writer and nothing else, neither a mother nor a wife. She wouldn't have minded. And she thought Brigid was very brave.

She settled into her room that night, unpacked her bags, and put her papers on her desk, and in a way it was very odd. It was as though she had never left. She went downstairs for breakfast with the nuns the next morning, and she told Mother Mary Margaret about the possible movie offer after the others left.

"I haven't heard back from Rose about it, so maybe it will never happen. I think movie deals are like that, they fall apart more than they get made."

"How could you be on the set, though, and not have them figure out who you are?"

"I don't know. I'm worried about it too, but Rose thinks we could make it work, with me pretending to be Mr. Green's assistant. It's a little crazy." But so was her life, writing bestsellers under a pseudonym and pretending to be a man. It didn't get crazier than that.

"That's very exciting, Alex," she said proudly. Her career just kept growing. "So you'd be leaving us again," she added wistfully.

"Only for a few months." She wanted to go back to London one day. She had liked it, the people, the city, the culture, the history, the British humor and manners.

Mother MaryMeg rushed off to her office then, and Alex called Brigid, as she had promised. Brigid invited her to their apartment for lunch. She said she was too fat to move or go anywhere. Her due date was two days away, and she had taught her classes right till the end. School was out now and she was on maternity leave till January.

Alex couldn't believe the size of her when she saw her. "Oh my God, you're huge," she said, grinning, and Brigid looked down in dismay at the enormous lump the size of a beach ball.

"I think it's mostly chocolate cake," she confessed, "and cheesecake . . . maybe pecan pie and cupcakes . . ." she said after she hugged Alex, thrilled to see her. "I missed you so much!"

"Me too," Alex said, feeling as though she had reclaimed a sister. She had brought a little white knit outfit from Paris for the baby, with embroidered white rosebuds on it, which Brigid held up in delight. It was the prettiest thing she'd ever seen. Her face had gotten fuller too, but she looked blissful, and they talked all afternoon about what Alex had done in London for the past year since the wedding, her trips, Fiona, and a modified, less racy version of her relationship with Ivan, even though Brigid was married now. Alex thought she didn't need to know all of it, but Brigid could guess. When Alex left, Brigid waddled out to the car Alex had borrowed from the convent.

"I'll call from the hospital when I go in," she promised, and thanked her again for the little French outfit for the baby. "I hope it's soon. Like tonight." She laughed. "I can't even eat anymore. I can hardly breathe, and I have heartburn all night." It sounded awful to Alex, but Brigid had her fondest wish and looked ecstatic. Alex reported the visit to the nuns at dinner. They couldn't wait for the baby to be born, like a houseful of doting aunts. And as soon as they got up from the table, Brigid called.

"I'm in labor!" she told Mother MaryMeg victoriously. She had gotten to the hospital twenty minutes before and reported that she was two centimeters dilated, which the superior knew wasn't impressive. She had a long way to go before she'd have her baby in her arms.

"We'll all be praying for you," the superior said in a loving tone. "It'll be over before you know it. Try to get a little rest now."

"I feel great!" she said, on an adrenaline high.

"Rest anyway," she told her, and reported to the others that Sister Regina was in labor. Everyone was excited at the news.

Alex called Bert and they made a lunch date for two days later. He had editing to give her on the new book. She didn't tell him about the movie, because she was beginning to think it wouldn't happen anyway.

There was no word from Brigid at breakfast the next morning, which didn't seem to concern anyone, much to Alex's surprise. "Should we be worried?" she asked the mother superior.

"Not at all." She smiled at her gently. "She went into labor about seven o'clock last night. I'd have been amazed if it had been born by now. It'll probably be sometime late this afternoon, or maybe tonight."

"*Tonight?* How long does it take?" She had never thought about it before and didn't know. She had no female relatives and lived with a houseful of nuns, and no one she knew had ever had a baby.

"For a first baby, average would be about twenty-four or thirty-six hours. And she was in the very early stages of labor when she called us. That barely counts. I'm sure she's hard at work by now."

She had guessed accurately, and when the superior called the hospital from her office to check on her, the labor and delivery nurse at the desk told her that Brigid Dylan was in full-on labor now, and at five, which the superior, who was also a nurse, knew meant she had hours to go. Many hours. Hard ones. Especially with a baby that size.

"How's it going?" she asked with concern. Brigid was still one of hers, in her heart, even now that she was married.

"About how you'd expect, with a first baby, and a big one, at thirty-seven," the nurse told her honestly when she had identified herself. "Maybe tonight," or a C-section, they both knew, if it took too long, but she wasn't there yet, and the nurse said she wasn't even ready to push. It was going to be a while.

Alex stuck her head in the door at two o'clock to ask if there was any news, and Mother MaryMeg shook her head and smiled. "I'm sure she's fine." The nuns had made bets after breakfast and one of them had said midnight, which made Alex wince. Most of them who were nurses had guessed between eight and ten o'clock that night. Alex felt sick thinking about it for her, and wondered if Brigid had known what she was in for.

They had just finished dinner at eight o'clock when Patrick called them at Brigid's request. He called the nuns right after he called his parents. Mother MaryMeg came back to tell them. "Brigid has her baby. It's a boy. Ten pounds, two ounces, forceps delivery. He was born at seven forty-one. Mother and son are fine." The superior beamed at them, and one of the nuns at their table commented that that wasn't bad at all. Twenty-five hours for a first labor was shorter than it could have been, especially with a big baby. Alex wondered if Brigid would agree. She couldn't even imagine it. Twenty-five hours of labor. It sounded like a nightmare to her.

"I won! I won!" one of the older nuns at a back table called out, and Alex felt like she was at a bingo game. "I said seven forty-five." The other nuns cheered and Alex asked Mother MaryMeg a question.

"What's a forceps delivery?"

"Kind of like a big clamp to help get the baby out, if the baby is big. Like we use in the kitchen."

"Oh God. I'm never having children," Alex said and meant it.

"You'll be surprised. She'll forget all about it by tomorrow with the baby in her arms."

"I hope so," Alex said with feeling, while the older nun collected her winnings from the others at her table. They had each bet a quarter and she'd won more than six dollars. "When can we visit her?"

"I'd give her till tomorrow. She's going to be worn out tonight, and busy with the baby, even if it wasn't a long labor." Alex still couldn't get over the fact that twenty-five hours was considered speedy.

She went to see Brigid the next day at the hospital at lunchtime. She had dark circles under her eyes, and was sitting at an awkward angle as the nurse showed her how to nurse the baby, and she broke into a broad smile when she saw Alex. The baby was sound asleep in her arms and wasn't interested in nursing. Brigid said Patrick had just gone home to get some sleep, they'd been up all night admiring the baby. He had a face like a rosebud when Alex looked at him, and she kissed her friend. The nurse took the baby from her then, put him in a little bassinet, and wheeled him off to the nursery for a while.

"How was it?" Alex asked as she sat down in the chair next to Brigid's bed.

"Awful, worse than anything I could ever have imagined. I thought I was going to die when he came out. But worth every minute of it. I would do it again in a heartbeat."

"You're insane," Alex told her and Brigid laughed.

"Isn't he beautiful? He looks just like Pat." Alex couldn't see it and thought he looked like a baby, but he was very pretty, and very big.

"Sister Ignatius won six dollars thanks to you last night." They both laughed at that. "Six twenty-five actually. They had a pool on what time he'd be born. I was worried sick about you."

"It went fine," Brigid said, looking serene. "It was just really bad for the last four or five hours."

"I'm having my tubes tied immediately," Alex said, wincing, and they talked quietly for a while. She was happy for her friend. She had everything she wanted now.

"I guess I won't be writing for another twenty years or so," Brigid said sheepishly. "I don't have your dedication or your talent. I wanted to write a book but I guess it will never happen."

"You're a mom now, you get a pass." She kissed Brigid as they brought the baby back and put him in his mother's arms. He was crying loudly and wanted to be fed. She was trying to figure out how to do it as Alex left the room and went back to the convent, feeling happy for her.

A group of the nuns went to see her that night. They had knitted little sweaters for the baby, and booties and babies' caps, and reported that she looked great and the baby was gorgeous. Alex was still stunned by the mystery of it. But Brigid had her baby. They named him Steven Michael. And Alex and all the nuns wished him well, and his parents.

Alex had lunch with Bert the next day. They ate sandwiches she'd brought, and he showed her the editing he'd done and the changes he wanted her to make. He suggested she add details to the crime scene that would be even more vivid, and make the perpetrator of the crime even harder to guess. He was a hard taskmaster but she trusted him completely and he was usually right, so she followed his advice. She was going to start working on it that night.

She wanted to see Brigid again, but she had already gone home that day, thirty-six hours after the baby's birth, and when Alex called her it sounded like chaos in her apartment, with Pat's siblings, his parents, and their friends visiting. Brigid was exhausted and Alex didn't want to add to it. She had her hands full.

Rose had left a message for Alex that afternoon at the convent office. When she got back from Bert's, Alex called her.

"They want to buy it and they'll pay a good price. And they agreed to our conditions for Mr. Green. They'll pay to rent a house for him, and for his assistant to be the go-between. That would be you, Alex." She listed the names of the stars who would be in it, and Alex couldn't speak for a minute. "They want you and Mr. Green there on August twenty-fifth for preproduction meetings. So? What do you think?" Rose was very pleased.

"I think I'm going to faint," Alex said as she sat down in a chair in Mother MaryMeg's office. She was alone there.

"Please don't. They're sending the contracts over tomorrow. I'll email them to you. You've got a movie, Alex. This is a big deal, especially with that director and that cast." Alex was her youngest client, and one of the most successful at the moment. Rose was impressed too, and excited for her. She had never seen a career take off at lightning speed as hers had. But she worked so hard, she deserved it.

"Thank you," Alex said, and they hung up, and she was still looking shell-shocked when Mother MaryMeg walked in a minute later.

"Is something wrong?"

"I got the movie. *Darkness* is going to be a movie." She listed the cast for her. The superior was stunned too.

"Goodness." She broke into a slow smile. "Brigid has a baby, you have a movie. What's next? Things are booming around here." She gave Alex a big hug, and they announced it at dinner. She had time to do the editing on her latest book before she left, and at the end of August, she was going to Hollywood. She still couldn't believe it. She lay in her bed that night thinking about it, wondering what she had ever done to be so lucky. Bert had been thrilled too when she called him.

Alexander Green was the best thing that had ever happened to her. As far as the world knew, Alexander Green was the bestselling author, but Alex was the woman behind him in the shadows, making magic. It made her laugh to think that, in a way, she was the Wizard of Oz.

Chapter 15

As she always did, Alex turned in the editing she had to do on her book ahead of time, and it was complete before she had to leave for Hollywood, and Bert loved it. She went to say goodbye to him before she left. They wouldn't be working together for a while, because she had no time to start another book. She would have her hands full with the movie. Her publisher knew it too, but she was ahead of schedule with her work.

She went to say goodbye to Brigid too. Steven was not quite three months old, but appeared twice that, he was so huge. She had just finished nursing him when Alex arrived, and he was sound asleep and seemed drunk in his mother's arms. Brigid was loving every minute of being with him.

"He looks like he should be wearing a suit and carrying a briefcase," Alex teased her. "When is he going to get a job? He'll probably be roller-skating by the time I get back from L.A." The movie was due to wrap in January, or possibly late December, and then she had to stay for six or eight weeks of postproduction. She was expecting to be gone for about six months.

"And I'll be an elephant again by the time you see me," Brigid said happily, as Alex looked puzzled. Brigid hadn't lost much of the baby weight yet, and still seemed four or five months pregnant. But she'd had no time to exercise, taking care of a newborn, and he was colicky and cried a lot. And she wasn't dieting because nursing made her so hungry.

"Why is that?" Alex asked. "You'll lose the weight by then, Brig, don't worry."

"Not exactly." There was a long pause as Alex stared at her, waiting for an explanation. "We had a little slip a few weeks ago, I always thought nursing was effective birth control, but it turns out . . . uh . . . actually, I'm three weeks pregnant. We just found out yesterday." She looked both mortified and delighted. It was admittedly sloppy, and would stretch their budget incredibly. She and Pat were trying to figure it out.

"Are you kidding?" Alex stared at her. "You're having another one? Already? You just had him."

"Irish twins," Brigid said, faintly embarrassed. It was hard to explain to Alex, at her age, how desperately she wanted a family before it was too late, even if it meant they'd be broke and dirt poor for the next five or ten years, or longer, which was likely to be the case. But Pat wanted a family too. He was thrilled about the second baby, and didn't mind how fast it had happened. "I know it must sound crazy to you. If I were younger, I'd wait, but we're playing beat the clock here."

"How many do you want?" Alex was incredulous.

"Three or four, if we can manage it financially. His parents said they'd help us. It'll make for some lean years for a while, but it's worth it."

"You're crazy but I love you," Alex said, grinning at her. "But I guess this is why you left the convent."

"Yes, it is," Brigid said, smiling broadly.

"You're not afraid to go through it again? It sounded awful."

"It wasn't that bad, really," she said easily, as Alex shook her head.

"Mother MaryMeg said you'd say that. It must be amnesia. Twenty-five hours of labor?"

"But look what I got out of it," she said, pointing to the sleeping baby, who lay in her arms like an angel. She was more than willing to go through it again.

"And Pat's okay with it?"

"It's what we both want. I think we were careless on purpose."

"Congratulations then," Alex said, and hugged her.

"We want you to be Steven's godmother. We'll wait to christen him till you get back." Alex was touched, and they hugged warmly when she left. She still couldn't believe they were having another one so soon. She told the nuns about it at dinner, because Brigid said she could, when she had asked if it was a secret.

"That's how I had mine," Sister Tommy commented. "They were all ten and eleven months apart. Twelve months is the longest." It still seemed rough to Alex, but Brigid didn't mind at all, couldn't wait to do it again and come home with another baby. Alex could guess now that she intended to stay pregnant for the next four years.

Alex left for the airport by cab the next morning. Everyone was busy, and she said goodbye to them at the house. She wasn't going for as long this time, and they were accustomed to her leaving. She was taking one suitcase of summer clothes. She didn't need anything fancy to work on the set, and she had packed one decent dress in case she had to go anywhere.

The flight took six hours, and when she arrived at one o'clock local time, there was a limo waiting for her, with a driver holding a large card with her name on it. She had told them that Mr. Green would be flying in by private jet that night. The producer's assistant had made separate arrangements for him. Hers were made by the studio, as Mr. Green's assistant. The driver carried her bag in when they got to the house in Bel Air that had been rented for "them." It had been rented from an actor who was on location in Thailand for eight months shooting a movie. They had asked that there be no staff in the house. Mr. Green would bring his own personal staff, because Alex didn't want anyone reporting that he wasn't there. She was going to have to hire a cleaning person for herself. It was complicated creating an identity for a person who didn't exist.

The driver set Alex's bag down in the small bedroom at the back of the house where he assumed she would stay. She carried it to the master bedroom herself after he left. The house was spectacular. It was mostly made of glass with pale travertine floors. The art was beautiful, the furniture was upholstered in shades of ivory, and the pool was enormous. It had a sound system they could have used for a rock concert, and a theater-sized movie screen. She walked around grinning to herself as she checked it out. She felt like she was in a movie, not working on one. The bed looked like a football field with another wall-sized movie screen facing the bed, and you could have catered a party for three hundred in the kitchen, and they had. Alexander Green was being treated royally. Alex wished she had someone to show it to, but she didn't. Fiona and Brigid would have loved it.

The producer's assistant called her shortly after she arrived and asked if everything was to Mr. Green's satisfaction.

"He's going to love it," she assured her. "He's not here yet, he's coming in on his own plane tonight. But he's going to be very pleased. Thank you so much."

"Anything we can do for you?"

"I'm fine." There was a white Cadillac Escalade in the driveway for her use. And a white convertible Rolls in the garage for Mr. Green, which she would have loved to sneak out but didn't dare, although she might at some point.

There was food in the refrigerator of every kind, and liquor, magazines, soaps, cologne, body washes. The studio had asked for a list of all of Mr. Green's favorite brands and products, and she had had a ball filling it out, and they were all there, including some she hadn't thought of. It was luxury to a degree she had never seen before, and in a way it seemed like a shocking waste. They had money to burn, but Hollywood behaved that way and they wanted their phantom writer to be happy. She was, and would have been with a lot less. But she and Rose had to make requests suitable for the persona they had invented, and Alex thought the white Rolls they'd added as a surprise was the final touch. She went out to the garage to look at it, and then sat in it for a few minutes. It smelled wonderful, of new leather. She had to call Bert on her cellphone and tell him about it.

"You'll go to jail if they ever catch on to you," he teased her.

"No, I won't. And they won't. I'm going to be very careful."

"You'd better be or your cover will be blown forever."

"I'm not that stupid, Bert."

"Well, enjoy every minute of it, and kiss the Rolls for me."

"I will," she promised.

Alex watched two movies that night, and slept in the master bedroom. She was up at six the next morning and swam in the pool, which was heated to the perfect temperature. She was dressed and ready to leave the house at eight o'clock to be at the studio at eight-thirty. She set the GPS in the luxurious Escalade, and arrived at the studio right on time. They were expecting her at the studio gate.

They were going to be filming mostly in the studio, except the location shots. She parked outside a building and walked inside. A studio assistant was waiting to escort her to a meeting room when she said she was Mr. Green's assistant.

"Did he arrive all right last night? Was everything to his liking?" the assistant asked anxiously.

"It was perfect," she reassured her. "He came in about midnight and loves the house. He swam in the pool right away."

"Are the staff quarters working out?"

"Also perfectly." It reminded her again that she needed to find a maid for herself, or she'd be scrubbing bathtubs and toilets for six months, which she didn't want to do. She was going to call a cleaning service that afternoon. Rose had gotten the name of one for her from a friend in L.A.

The assistant ushered Alex into a room, and there were already several people sitting at a long oval conference table when she walked in, carrying her briefcase, and they introduced her. She was wearing white jeans, and they were all wearing short shorts and flip-flops.

The director introduced himself to Alex immediately. His name was Sam Jackowitz, and he introduced her to the screenwriter she would be working with, Malcolm Harris.

"Thank you for facilitating this process for us," the director said gratefully, as Malcolm looked her over and didn't say anything at first. Half a dozen production assistants filed into the room. It was their last chance to go over final details before they met with the actors the next day, to hear their notes and comments about the script.

They'd been in the meeting for an hour before Malcolm spoke to her. "You work for the greatest writer that ever lived," he said in an undertone as she stared at him for an instant, finding it hard to believe his enthusiasm.

"He'll be very flattered to hear it," she said politely.

"I've read every book he's ever written. I've learned so much from him as a writer," he said. "He must be awesome to work for."

"He is," she assured him.

"How long have you worked for him?"

"A long time. Ever since I started working. I was an intern for him in college." She was making it up as she went along, but it sounded convincing even to her, and Malcolm was eating it up.

"*Darkness* is my favorite of his books," he said in awe.

"Mine too," she agreed. "He's very pleased to have this one made into a movie."

"We're going to make an incredible picture," he promised. "What does he think of the script?"

"He hasn't seen it yet." And neither had she.

"They were supposed to give it to you yesterday." He said something to one of the production assistants and she scurried off to get two copies for Alex. "That reminds me, there's something in it I want to show you, so you can ask him how he feels about it. It's a piece of dialogue I lifted from the book, but I put into another character's scene." He opened his dog-eared copy of the script to the correct page and showed it to her. She read it and nodded.

"That should be fine," she said to him. "I like it." And he looked at her dismissively.

"I didn't ask if *you* like it. I want to know if *he* likes it." She had almost forgotten her role for a minute as the assistant with no authority to make decisions, and she apologized immediately.

"Of course. I'll ask him tonight."

"Will he take calls during the day?"

"He won't answer a cellphone," she said simply, and Malcolm nodded. He was willing to accept any quirk his idol had.

The meeting was long and wasted a lot of time. A catering group set up an enormous buffet at noon, and they were trapped in the room till six o'clock, going over meaningless details, but Alex had no choice but to sit there. She had a list of questions to ask her alleged employer, and had promised to email the answers that night. She knew the answers to all of them obviously, but had to play dumb. She was getting into the Escalade when Malcolm walked over to her. He had a swagger, and a great body, and his muscles rippled as he walked. He had thick dark hair to his shoulders, a tan, and blue eyes. He looked like a beach boy in the standard flip-flops and shorts.

"Tomorrow is going to be rough," he warned her. "The actors always come in with a list of dumb questions and complaints about the dialogue. Tell Mr. Green not to worry about it and don't take it to heart. I'll run interference for him."

"That will mean a lot to him," Alex said reverently, trying not to laugh as he lowered his voice conspiratorially.

"Look, I know what the ground rules are here, but if I swear not to tell anyone, do you think you could get me in to see him for a few minutes? It would be the best day of my life." She decided to squash his pretensions early so as not to run into problems later on, with him, or anyone else.

"I can't do that. He's my employer, and he would fire me on the spot."

"As one writer to another," he whispered, "maybe if he likes the script . . ."

"He doesn't see anyone," she said firmly. "He never makes exceptions. He's been a recluse ever since a family tragedy. I wouldn't dare cross that line with him."

"Oh my God, I didn't know . . . who died? His wife? A child?"

"I'm not at liberty to discuss it, and actually I'm not sure." She wanted to get off that hook quickly now that she had made it up. "It happened long before I came to work for him. I've only heard rumors, and I don't know if they're true."

"Well, if you see an opening, put in a word for me, will you? I want to meet him just once before we finish the film." She wanted to scream, "You have, you idiot," but she continued to look respectful and in awe of him, with no authority of her own.

"I'll email you tonight, with the answers to today's questions," she said efficiently.

"Do you know when? I have a date tonight. Should I cancel it? Will he talk to me on the phone?"

"No, he won't. Don't cancel your date. I'll be meeting with him as soon as I get back to the house. And I'll let you know right away."

"Thanks." He sauntered away again, and Alex got in the car, set the GPS, and drove home. None of the staff or crew was supposed to know the location of the house that had been rented for him, and she hoped there would be no slips, or worse, paparazzi at the gate. She was beginning to see how complicated it was going to be on the set. It was workable, but she was going to be lying through her teeth constantly.

She headed for her computer as soon as she walked in the door, to put Malcolm out of his misery. She knew all the answers he wanted, and she reeled them off in five minutes and hit send.

He responded ten minutes later.

"Wow! He's amazing. Thanks for the quick answers. Please thank him for me. This is going to be a piece of cake." But not for her.

"No problem, I'll tell him," she sent back, walked out to the patio, peeled off her clothes, and dove into the pool. It had been a long, incredibly boring day full of inane questions and people puffed up with their own self-importance who had nothing to say. The director was the only one in the room worth listening to, and Malcolm's gushing praise of Alexander Green was so excessive that it made her feel slightly sick, like eating way too much chocolate cake.

The next day was even worse. With four major stars in the room, each one was competing for attention, wanted to be heard, had problems with almost every page of the script, wasn't sure "they really felt the line in their gut" or if "it just wasn't them." Sam handled them masterfully, Malcolm just got into arguments with them, and all Alex could do was make notes about things to complain about later in the voice of her alleged employer.

There were several heated arguments, the female lead and a supporting actress hated each other, and the male lead lightly touched Alex's breast when no one was looking when he walked by and then winked at her. "Are you kidding?" she muttered after he left, and Malcolm walked over to her.

"I saw that. He does it all the time. It wasn't about you."

"Is that a compliment or an insult?" she asked him and he laughed.

"Maybe both." He complained about the female lead to her then, who he claimed was a bitch to work with. He'd been on a film with her before. But in Alex's opinion, at least she was honest and outspoken about what she didn't like. The other woman and the male lead seemed worse to her, more wheedling and passive-aggressive. And Malcolm had his hackles up over the script. So far what he'd written didn't bother Alex, although it wasn't great. But it wasn't terrible either, and she realized you had to compromise in the movies. Every word was not going to be true to the book, and she didn't expect that.

Each of the stars left earlier than they were supposed to. They had costume fittings and rehearsal the next day. And Alex's head was spinning by the time she left at eight o'clock, after wasting two hours with Malcolm, talking about himself, and then asking her again to arrange a private audience with Mr. Green, which she told him again she could not do. And Rose Porter called her that night.

"How's it going?"

"I'm not sure. A lot of temperaments and personalities, a lot of maneuvering for position, and the screenwriter thinks Alexander Green is God."

"That must be nice to hear."

"Not really. He wants me to sneak him into the house so he can kiss his feet. He treats me like a messenger, or the maid." Rose laughed at the description.

"Even when there are no secret identities, Hollywood is crazy." But the money was good, and the prestige enormous. "Did you hire the cleaning service I recommended to you?"

"I did. They're starting tomorrow. I don't need much. I'm not going to entertain or anything." She couldn't, or it would blow her cover. She couldn't have anyone to the house for the duration, nor take the risk. "It will be a long six months."

"You might enjoy it," Rose encouraged her.

"They're all so full of themselves, even the assistants. It's fun watching the stars, though." She sounded very young when she said it.

She made a salad for dinner, took a swim, went to bed early, and watched another movie. There was a fabulous library of DVDs. And the next day the fun began with one actress having a tantrum over a costume, and the other arguing with Malcolm about the script, and he stormed off the set. The director calmed both women down, and then came to sit next to Alex for a little while. He was quiet and even tempered and handled everyone with incredible sensitivity and grace. Malcolm, on the other hand, was a diva, and slunk back to the set after lunch with a scowl on his face. He acted like an angry child, despite the dazzling physique.

"I can't wait till we get to the murder scene and smear blood over both of them," he said through clenched teeth, and Alex laughed.

"I won't tell Mr. Green you said that." He looked mollified after that, and handed her a Coke as they watched the rehearsals, which were pretty rough. Sam worked with each of the actors to explain the psychology of their role, and he had nailed it perfectly, as Alex paid rapt attention. She made some notes and Malcolm asked her about them.

"Why are you taking notes?"

"Mr. Green expects me to tell him what happens on the set. I'm his eyes and ears here."

"And he listens to what you say?" Malcolm was impressed.

"Most of the time. Our relationship is based on mutual respect."

"He doesn't need advice from anyone," he said reverently. "What did he think of the script, by the way?"

"He likes it. There are a few rough spots here and there, but nothing he can't live with, or we can't fix."

"I expected him to be tougher than that."

"It's a good script," she complimented him.

"Tell him thank you," he said and disappeared again.

They worked until dinnertime again, and Malcolm surprised her by asking her if she wanted to stop for something to eat on the way home, if she had time and Mr. Green wouldn't mind.

"Sure. Why not? He'll be fine with it." Malcolm seemed like an important ally to have, and was worth getting to know for that reason.

They stopped at the Polo Lounge on the way home, and he asked her a thousand questions about her employer and none about her. But she learned that he had gone to USC film school, had worked in television before moving on to feature films, and wanted to write his own series. He was thirty-three years old, had never been married, had no kids, and had recently broken up with a rising young starlet who had left him for someone else. "I didn't really care. We'd only been dating for three months." She had the feeling, from listening to him, that Hollywood was some kind of shell game where everyone switched partners constantly in order to get ahead, and traded the last partner in for someone more important. It sounded exhausting to her, and incredibly manipulative and superficial.

"It must be complicated here."

"It is," he admitted. "Dating is all about who you want to be seen with. Like what car you drive. It's about where they can get you and how far. The person is a vehicle to the next level. Then you switch and cover the next fifty or a hundred miles up the mountain with someone else."

"Does anyone ever go out with real people?" It was an insider's view of a world she didn't want to know, where everything was false, hair, teeth, breasts, and heart.

"Not really," he answered her question honestly. "That's a waste of time."

"Does anyone here ever fall in love?" she asked, and he laughed.

"You sound like Goldilocks. Hollywood is about making movies and becoming a star. Not about love. You can go to Arkansas for that. Or Nebraska. That's where the real people are. Not here. Where are you from?"

"Boston."

"And you live in Scotland with Mr. Green?" She nodded, remembering her role, and the identity she and her agent had created for him out of whole cloth.

"I do."

"Do you go to Montana with him too?"

"Most of the time." She was nervous he would ask her questions about Montana, which she knew nothing about. "I've been in Europe with him for the last two years."

"Whereabouts?"

"Italy, Ireland, France, England, Germany, the Czech Republic, Spain," she reeled off all the places she had traveled to, and he looked vastly impressed.

"Does he have houses in all those places?"

"Some," she lied.

"He must lead such an interesting life."

"Not really. He writes all the time. He has no social life, he rarely goes out. His passion is writing." She was talking about herself, which Malcolm didn't know.

"You can tell, that's why he's so good. How did he get interested in crime?"

"I think his father got him into it as a boy." He ate it up as he listened.

They left the restaurant together, after splitting the bill for dinner, and walked outside to claim their cars from the valet. He drove a Porsche, which he said was leased.

"I only drive good cars when I'm working on a movie," he said to

her as he unlocked the door and got in. "What you drive is important here." She thought of the white Rolls they had rented for Mr.
Green. It was all about fakery here, and appearances, for the length
of the film. And then everyone turned into pumpkins and white
mice until the next one. It seemed like an odd way to live.

"Thank you for taking me to dinner," she said and smiled at him.

"It was fun. Give the man my best." She promised to do so and
they both drove off, and she thought about what he had said. She
couldn't help wondering if there were any real people there at all,
and then she laughed out loud in the car, because she wasn't real
either. She was in L.A. as a fraud too, pretending to be a man who
didn't exist.

Chapter 16

The early days of the film were arduous and the film dragged painfully, until the actors began to warm up and understand the psychology of their roles. Sam did a terrific job of explaining it to them again and again, until it became second nature, while Malcolm fought for every word of the script, which slowed them down even more. And there were daily questions for Mr. Green, which Alex answered by email, as soon as she got home. After a month of it, she was starting to miss writing, where she could move at her own pace, not be slowed down by anyone, and soar. This was lumbering and agony at times.

She was a familiar fixture on the set. The director was always pleasant to her, and Malcolm went up and down, depending on his mood, or possibly whether or not he had gotten laid the night before. She had a feeling he had a busy sex life, but he didn't talk about it, to his credit. He would stand a little too close to her at times, and she could feel him breathing on her, but he never made a pass, and she didn't expect it. In fact, she hoped he wouldn't, no matter how handsome and sexy he was. Fiona would have loved the whole scene. They were coworkers and nothing more. She was the conduit to his idol, as Sam the director called her. He didn't intend it meanly, that's what she was to them. What they didn't know was that the eyes and ears she was exercising were, in fact, her own.

And then Malcolm startled her when they'd been on the set for six weeks. They were starting to shoot the crime scenes, which made it more interesting. Alex paid close attention, to make sure they got the details right, and they had so far.

"Do you want to help me out tonight?" Malcolm asked her during a break. He was in a semi-bad mood, and as temperamental as the actors.

"How?"

"My date just bailed on me for tonight. She got a better offer. I'm going to a premiere. I tried everyone and no one's free." It wasn't the most flattering offer she'd had, but she had been home every night since she got there, and she was bored. The premiere sounded exciting and definitely more fun than watching TV on the big screen. She had no friends in L.A. to go out with.

"I'd love it." But she only had one dress with her, and wasn't sure it was the right look. It was short, black, and serious, and she had bought it in London to wear with Fiona's family in Ireland over Christmas two years before. "How dressy is it?"

"Hot. Sexy. It doesn't really matter as long as you don't show up in jeans. No one's going to look at you anyway. They don't know who you are." And neither did he. What he said would have been insulting if he were anyone else. Coming from him, it was standard fare, and how he viewed the world.

"Can I leave the set early?"

"Sure. Why? And will Mr. Green care?"

"He lets me do what I want. I want to shop for a dress for tonight. I don't want to embarrass you."

"You won't. Yeah, go whenever you want to." And then he thought of something and lowered his voice. It had never occurred to him before. "Are you his girlfriend? . . . Green, I mean." She looked at him and laughed. She would have loved to say yes, but that would have complicated things even more. Regretfully she shook her head.

"No, I'm not," she whispered back.

"Are you sure? Will he be pissed if you go out with me? The last thing I want to do is piss him off."

"Me too," she assured him. "He doesn't mind who I go out with." And then she made a suggestion that she knew Malcolm would love. "Do you want to use the Rolls? He'll let me have it if I want."

"Hell, yes!" Malcolm's face lit up like Christmas. "You're not just taking it, are you?"

"Not at all." But he was faintly suspicious of her. If Alexander Green was that free with her, there had to be something more going on between them. But that only made her more interesting to him. Suddenly she was forbidden fruit, and enhanced by association. "Where should I pick you up?" she asked him.

He gave her his address on a piece of paper. "Be there at seven." If she looked hot enough, he would take her down the red carpet for photo ops. The evening was beginning to sound better than the flop it had been moments before when his date canceled. She was going out with a hot new rapper, with whom he couldn't compete.

Alex left a little while later, and drove to Beverly Hills. She headed to Neiman Marcus, walked through the designer section, and found a short tight white satin Saint Laurent dress that looked appropriate for the occasion, with high-heeled silver and rhinestone sandals and a small silver clutch. She found big rhinestone earrings that looked like real diamonds, and a matching bracelet, put all her bags in the car, and drove back to the house, pleased with herself. She had just enough time to bathe, wash her hair, dress, and be at Malcolm's place at seven. She noticed that he lived in a seedy neighborhood in a run-down building, but the Porsche was parked outside. Apparently, L.A. was about what you drove, but not where you lived. She got out and rang the buzzer and he came downstairs a minute later in a well-cut tux, a white shirt, and no tie, and he hadn't shaved. And he was wearing expensive black patent leather loafers and no socks. It was very L.A. The combination was the right mix of hot, laissez-faire, and trendy, and gave the impression that he hadn't tried too hard, but just enough. It was a blend of messages and symbols she didn't get, but he looked good, and he whistled when he saw her.

"You clean up nicely," he complimented her. "I like the dress." It was a lot better and a whole different style than the one she'd decided not to wear, which would have made her look like an orphan or a Greek widow.

She let him take the wheel of the car and he was thrilled. "He didn't mind?" he asked, referring to "Mr. Green."

"He said to have fun." She smiled at Malcolm.

It was a long and interesting night. Pleased with her outfit, he took her down the red carpet with him, and they were liberally photographed, because they looked great. His hair was a rich brown, as dark as hers, his eyes sky blue. She had a perfect tan from sitting in the sun on her lunch breaks. The white Saint Laurent dress was fabulous on her. The premiere was fun, and all the stars were there. Malcolm saw his ex-date with the rapper and snubbed her. They had dinner at the Chateau Marmont afterward, and wound up at a nightclub, talking till two A.M. After an evening with him, she liked him better than she had so far. There was still something plastic and insincere about him, but it was the nature of the beast for men his age in the film business in L.A. Alex had thoroughly enjoyed the evening. It was all different and new to her, and good research for future books.

"I'm trying to figure out how it all works here," she said to him over a glass of champagne.

"What do you mean?"

"Like what matters and why." She thought she might use it in a book one day, about a murder in L.A. She had already figured out most of the social ground rules just by observation, but wanted verbal confirmation from him that what she was guessing was right.

"It all matters, who you know, who you're with, where you're going, where you've been, what you drive, what you wear, who does your hair." It was all superficial, there was no depth to any of it, and nothing was real, like her fake diamond bracelet and earrings.

"What about what you think, or believe in, or how you feel?"

"That's not as important." He smiled at her, vaguely curious about her for the first time. "You're awfully serious. How old are you? Twenty-seven? Twenty-eight?"

"Twenty-four," she said with an air of innocence she was unaware of.

"Wow, that's young. You have a big job for someone your age."

"Is it really all about who you know here?" She wanted to believe there was something deeper, but he dispelled her illusions about that.

"You become famous by association. *You're* important because of who you work for. I become famous if I date someone famous. I get dumped if she meets someone more important. Or I dump her for the same reason." It seemed normal to him.

"That's a cold way to deal with people," Alex commented.

"It's how it works. Those are the rules here. It's how you get to where you want to go."

"What if you make it on your own?"

"No one does. And that's a lot of hard work. The shortcuts work better."

"But the people who take the shortcuts are empty inside," she said, but most of the people in his business were.

"If you don't have a talent, that's how you have to do it. L.A. makes stars out of people who've never had a job and don't have a talent. The paparazzi follow them everywhere." He named half a dozen people and she realized he was right. "It's all cardboard and glitter, but it works. For the most part no one bothers to look behind the scenery."

"That's depressing," she said, and she was pensive on the ride back to his apartment, where she was dropping him off. When they got there, he looked at her and smiled. They hadn't had much to drink so they were both sober.

"Want to come up for some fun?"

"What kind of fun?" She could guess.

"A fun night between friends?"

"And then what?" She wanted to know what he had in mind and what it meant to him.

"We do it again if we have a good time. Or we don't. We check it out. We play for a while till something better comes along." He was brutally honest.

"This probably sounds crazy to you, Malcolm, but I want more than that. I had a great time tonight, but I don't want someone 'until something better comes along.' I'm fine alone in the meantime."

"Isn't that how it works? You make do for a while?"

"Why?" she said, confused by the rules he lived by.

"What do you want? A proposal and an engagement ring before you go to bed?"

"Not really. Just someone who knows who I am, and loves me with my flaws and rough edges, and isn't using me like a bus to get to the next stop."

"That's a harsh way to put it," he said, mulling over what she'd said.

"But it's true, isn't it? You don't know me. I don't know you. I don't want to sleep with a stranger."

"That's fair," he said, and leaned over and kissed her. "You looked great tonight. See you at work tomorrow." And then she thought of something as he stepped out of the car and she slid over to the driver's seat.

"If I didn't work for Alexander Green, would you go out with me, or want to sleep with me?" He considered the question for a minute and laughed.

"Probably not. I don't do freebies. And that's a big ticket." It was horrifying to her, but he meant it. It was all about using who you could. Never wasting an opportunity or a chance meeting. They were all scavengers on the make.

"I thought so. Thank you for being honest." He nodded. He wasn't sure why he had been that open with her, but her own honesty demanded his.

"I like you, actually. Better than I expected to. You're kind of uptight on the set."

"I'm working."

"He wouldn't have you as his assistant if you weren't smart. He knows what he's doing. The man is a genius." He had said it before, and as Malcolm waved and walked back into his building, Alex realized that he might have fallen in love with Alexander Green because of who he was, but not with her. In Malcolm's eyes, as plain old Alexandra Winslow, she didn't make the grade. And neither did he.

She and Malcolm had dinner several times during the filming. And there were a few close calls where she almost gave herself away, but she didn't. The crime scenes took forever to film, but turned out well. She checked them closely in the dailies for "Mr. Green." And Sam commented once that he wished he had an assistant like her. She had eyes like a hawk, and worked tirelessly on the set to defend Green's interests and the book.

She had Thanksgiving dinner with the crew, since she had no friends in L.A. Malcolm was sleeping with one of the young actresses in the movie by then, and was being seen around town with her. She was an up-and-coming name and very pretty. They wrapped the film two days before Christmas, and she had three weeks off before she had to come back for postproduction, so she went home to Boston. She hadn't been there for the holidays for two years. The nuns had decorated a huge tree in the front hall, had dinner together on Christmas Eve, and worked at a homeless shelter on Christmas Day, and she got to spend time with Brigid and the baby while she was in town. Brigid was already five months pregnant and big again by then, and tired from being pregnant with one baby and another in her arms. Alex went over to help her whenever she could. Brigid had taken an extended leave from the public school system to stay home with her babies, and Patrick's parents were helping them financially as best they could, as they'd promised.

"We'd be starving if they didn't," she told Alex, but she seemed happier than ever. And this time they knew that the baby was a girl, and Brigid was excited about it.

Alex went back to L.A. in mid-January, and Malcolm was dating a different starlet by then, whom he'd met at a party over Christmas. She was glad she hadn't gotten caught up in his games. There was nothing malicious about him, and it wasn't personal, but there was no depth to it either, it was all tinsel. She couldn't wait to start another book when she finished working on the movie. And she was trying to figure out where to live. Living alone in the house in L.A., and her apartments in London before that, made her realize that she didn't want to go back to live at the convent again, as much as she loved the nuns. She talked to Bert about it, and he suggested New York.

"You're ready for the big leagues, Alex. It's exciting being there. You can't hide away forever." Rose agreed. New York was electric, and she thought it would do her good to be there, at least for a while.

Alex had saved most of her writing money, and was careful with it, and she had the money from the sale of her father's house. Rose told her she should rent an apartment downtown, in one of the trendy areas where young people lived, and see how it felt.

"You can always go back to Boston if you hate it. Check it out," Rose encouraged her. Alex was still young and needed guidance, although she had grown up a lot in London and L.A.

They finished postproduction on her movie in mid-March, and everything had gone smoothly. No one had ever suspected that she was anything more than the reclusive author's assistant. She had played her part well, and she went back to Boston and talked her plans over with Mother MaryMeg, who stunned Alex by agreeing with Bert and Rose.

"You're not a nun, Alex, and you shouldn't be. That's not your life. You can't live here forever like one of us, you need to get out in the world and have some fun, meet new people, and do more than just work."

"Are you throwing me out?" she said wistfully.

"Of course not. You can have a room here forever. We love you. But go play with kids your own age," she said, smiling, and Alex laughed.

"Do I have to? What if I don't want to?" She had in London, but she was scared now. Her life with them in Boston was so safe, and it was nice being home. She was very torn about where to live.

"Yes, you do have to." Mother MaryMeg looked at her firmly. "Why don't you try New York for a while? You can always change your mind. But at least give it a chance for six months." It was almost exactly what Rose had said. Alex had lived in New York for her summer job, but that was different. She'd been a kid, she'd had roommates, and it was for a short, finite time. Moving to New York, alone in her own apartment, seemed even more daunting than being in London, although she wasn't sure why.

Alex thought about it for another two weeks after she got back from L.A., and in April, she went to see her agent, and looked at some apartments in the West Village and found one she liked. It was a big loft with a beautiful view of the Hudson River, sparingly furnished but with fine things and expensive furniture. The rent was high, but she could afford it, and there was a doorman, so it was safe. It was available for six months, so she took it and flew back to

Boston to get her things. A week later, she moved in. The nuns were sad to see her go, but Mother MaryMeg pushed her to continue moving forward. And Bert encouraged her too.

She started a new book as soon as she moved into the apartment, but Rose sent her invitations to gallery openings and other events she thought Alex would like, where she might meet people. Alex was painfully shy at first and left several art openings half an hour after she got there. She had no friends in the city and no one to go with, other than Rose, who usually sent her the invitations and didn't go herself.

She was standing alone at a gallery opening in SoHo one night, feeling foolish, when a young man in his early thirties walked over and started talking to her. They chatted for almost an hour. He had just moved to New York too, from San Francisco, and said he was raising funds for a high-tech start-up. His name was Tim Richards, and she told him she was a freelance writer, which was her latest explanation for what she did as work. And he asked to see her again as they left. She gave him her number, and didn't know if he'd call her, but she'd had a nice time with him at the art show. They both liked contemporary art. He called her the next day and invited her to lunch at the Museum of Modern Art on Saturday to see a new Jackson Pollock exhibit. It sounded appealing, and she decided to take a few hours off from her latest book and agreed to go. She didn't expect anything to come of it, but thought it might be interesting to get to know him as a friend, and she had hit a dead spot in her new book. She had talked to Bert about it, and he suggested she take a break.

It was a warm spring day on Saturday, and Alex decided to walk uptown from the West Village for the exercise, and enjoyed it. She looked relaxed and casual when she saw Tim waiting for her in the lobby of the museum. He was happy to see her, they had lunch in the cafeteria before visiting the exhibit, which had been beautifully curated, and showed an impressive amount of the artist's work, from private collections as well.

"It always amazes me how people can spend that kind of money on art and keep it in their homes," he commented on the work that had been lent to the museum by private collectors. She couldn't help thinking it was an odd thing to focus on. She had just enjoyed seeing the paintings, and hadn't thought about how much they cost. They walked to Central Park after they left the museum.

"Where did you grow up?" Tim asked her.

"In Boston." She didn't mention the convent or her parents dying when she was young, which seemed like too much information for a first date. He said he'd worked on Wall Street for two years, had gone to San Francisco for a year to join the start-up, and they'd sent him back to New York. He said the job was challenging, but he liked it.

"Raising funds has been hard to get off the ground," he admitted, but the idea seemed like a good one, when he described it, although a little technical for her. And somehow they got onto the subject of books and he mentioned Alexander Green. "He's my favorite author," he explained. "He's written some incredible books. You probably haven't read any. They are really shockingly brutal, but always surprising," he volunteered, and she couldn't resist the temptation, and surprised him by saying she had read one or two.

"They're pretty good."

"You read crime thrillers?" She nodded, as they reached the park.

"My father got me started on them when I was a kid."

"Green writes some very complicated, edgy stuff. What I love about them is that I can never figure them out. He gets me every time." She wanted to thank him when he said it, but she didn't. "They're very tight."

"He surprised me too," she said, and changed the subject, not wanting to give anything away, but it was beginning to bother her that she was never honest. She could never tell anyone "I wrote that!" She had taken on a false identity six years before, and it was a heavy burden at times. She couldn't even say truthfully what she did for a living. But at least Tim wasn't a writer in any form, so he wouldn't be jealous of that, or want to compete with her. But she felt like such a fraud at times and a liar. She told him about London then and how much she'd liked living there for almost two years.

"What did you do there?"

"I was an intern at a British publisher, but really more like a file clerk." She grinned. It was one job she could talk about, although she'd only worked there for a few months, and spent the rest of the time writing her own books.

They chatted about college and traveling in Europe. He had gone to Stanford, and had a WASPy, conservative look to him, as though he might come from money, but she didn't care. He walked her along the park to the subway to go back downtown, and told her how much he'd enjoyed spending time with her and hoped to see her again. And she said she would like that too. She had assumed that he lived in her area, because she'd met him in Soho, but he didn't. He told her he lived uptown, and left her at the subway entrance with a promise to call her soon.

And as she rode downtown, she thought of all the things she couldn't tell him, like working on her movie in L.A. for the past six months. She was like someone who'd been to prison. There were large gaps of time in her life she was unable to account for, unless she told the truth, which was taboo.

He called her again a week later, and she was back at work on the book, and didn't want to take time away from it, so she told him she was busy when he invited her to dinner. He sounded disappointed, but said he'd call her again, which he did two weeks later. She had just finished a difficult chapter, and was in a great mood. He asked her out for a movie and pizza, and she accepted. They had dinner at a little Italian restaurant in her neighborhood, and he told her he had just read that they were making a movie of Alexander Green's book *Darkness* and he wanted to see it with her when it came out, since she'd read some of the books too.

"Movies are never as good as the books, so we might be disappointed," he warned her.

"No, it's pretty true to the book. I hear he consulted on it, and had an assistant on the set the whole time," she blurted out and then wanted to cut her tongue out as soon as she said it. She knew too much about it.

"How do you know that?" He was surprised.

"I read about it somewhere. I think he keeps very close tabs on his work." Tim nodded. And they both liked the movie they saw that night, and talked about it as he walked her home afterward. She thought about inviting him upstairs for a drink, but didn't know him well enough, so she didn't, and her manuscript was all over the dining table and she didn't want him to see it. She thanked him outside her building instead. He kissed her on the cheek, and hailed a cab to go back uptown.

They had dinner two more times in the next few weeks, and he was always polite and pleasant. She asked him how his fundraising for the start-up was going and he said he was having a hard time getting investors for it, but he wasn't ready to give up yet. He looked so determined that she felt sorry for him, and he asked her what she was doing that summer.

"Working. I don't have any plans. What about you?"

"I'm sharing a house in the Hamptons with ten friends. It's a fairly big old house. We each get two weekends a month." He smiled at her, faintly embarrassed. He was thirty-two years old and obviously struggling financially, and had hinted that he was worried about his future at the start-up, if he was unsuccessful bringing in investors for it.

"That sounds like fun," she said about the Hamptons.

"Maybe you'd come with me sometime," he said cautiously, and she nodded, thinking about it. She wasn't sure if she was ready for that. She liked him, but not being honest with him was hampering them both. He asked her about it the next time they had dinner, on a warm May night, when they ate at a sidewalk café under a full moon. It was a Thursday night, and Brigid had had her baby, so Alex was going home to Boston to see her the next day. She had turned down his invitation for dinner Saturday night, and he suggested Thursday instead.

"Alex, are you seeing someone else?" he asked her hesitantly. She was surprised by the question and shook her head.

"No, I'm not."

"I don't know why, but I always get the feeling that there's a lot you're not telling me, and you're busy so much of the time." It was true and hard to explain. Her books always came first, and her assignments from Bert. She liked doing the editing as soon as possible when she got it back from him, and it was fresh in her head.

"I get too involved in my work sometimes. When I get freelance assignments, they have tight deadlines usually." He nodded and didn't seem convinced, and she felt guilty for lying to him. She was beginning to wonder if she would ever have a normal relationship with the life she led, but there was something about him that always stopped her from telling him more of the truth than she did. Maybe the fact that he was struggling and she wasn't. She felt awkward about it, and she knew he could tell just from the building where she lived. She hadn't invited him to her apartment yet either. Some strange instinct stopped her every time. But she didn't want to live in a walk-up in a bad neighborhood just to make the men she met comfortable either. She worked hard, did well, and had a nice life. But it was definitely creating distance between them.

"You've never shown me anything you've written," he mentioned. "Where do your articles get published?"

"In women's magazines mostly. You wouldn't have seen them. They're not written for men." He laughed when she said it.

"You know your audience at least. I guess that's why I like Alexander Green's books so much. You can tell they were written by a man. No woman could write that." She almost groaned when he said it. He had just proven her father right, and had the same prejudice he had about women writers.

"You never know. Some women authors might surprise you. There are some very good female crime writers around."

"Like Agatha Christie?" He laughed again.

"No, tougher than that. Patricia Cornwell or Karin Slaughter . . ." She would have liked to add herself to the list but couldn't. And feeling rude for not having done it sooner, she invited him upstairs for a drink when he took her home that night. As soon as they walked in, she knew she had done the wrong thing. It put an immediate chill on the evening. He looked tense when he sat down, and she poured him a glass of wine.

"This is quite a place," he said, as he glanced around. The loft-style living room was huge, and clearly a very expensive co-op, which impressed Tim, more than she'd expected it to.

"I'm actually apartment sitting for a friend," she said, when she saw the expression on his face. She was lying to him again.

"Or you have a rich father," he said with a snide tone. His earlier pleasantness had faded rapidly.

"My father died eleven years ago," she said quietly, sitting across from him in a vintage leather chair.

"And left you a big trust fund. How nice of him." There was something in his eyes she hadn't seen before. He had been easy-going till then. And now there was an edge to every word. It came out of nowhere.

"He left me something, but not a trust fund, and it wasn't that much. I've been working hard since I left college," Alex said calmly. Not that she owed him an explanation, but she suddenly felt as though she did.

"So have I," Tim said, sounding almost nasty, which shocked her. "I live in a studio the size of a closet. It's a walk-up. The Upper East Side address sounds good, but the building is falling apart and smells of cat piss. I don't have a doorman, and I don't live in an apartment like this. And while you're dabbling with writing recipes or whatever it is for women's magazines that keeps you so busy, I'm working my goddamn ass off trying to raise funds for a business that no one wants to invest in, and I'll probably end up getting fired!" Suddenly his pleasant, well-educated, upper-middle-class WASPy mask had slipped and he was turning out to be a very bitter, angry guy. "And my father would have left me a trust fund too, except he was a drunk and blew all our money before he blew his brains out, when I was sixteen. I've been working ever since, and put myself through Stanford with scholarships and student loans, so I don't feel sorry for you in your fancy apartment with your free-lance work." He stood up and looked down at her with ill-concealed rage, and the expression on his face terrified her, he seemed like he wanted to kill her for a minute. She felt like she was living in one of her own books. Her gut was telling her to get him out before something happened, but he was already walking toward the door.

"Sorry if this wasn't quite the right fit. At least you don't need a rich husband, or would you like to invest in the firm I work for? I guess I don't know how to play the game, or I'd have stuck around and charmed you, but you're a little too fancy for me. I guess you figured that out for yourself," he said, walking out and slamming the door behind him, and Alex didn't say a word before he left. She just wanted him to get out before he strangled her. She locked the door behind him, went to sit on the couch, and she was shaking. He had really frightened her, and it had been so unexpected. He had been so mild mannered till then. He'd obviously had a hard life, and had some bad things happen to him. But so had she. She'd been an orphan at fourteen, and abandoned by her mother at seven, but she'd had a good father, and the nuns had been loving and kind to her after that, and she had been immensely lucky with her books and she knew it, and didn't take it for granted. But she had never seen hatred like that in anyone's eyes, and she wondered if everyone was going to be jealous of her and hate her for her success for the rest of her life. The thought of it depressed her profoundly, and she was still upset about it when she took the train to Boston the next day. She went to see Bert at his apartment. He was the only man she knew and could talk to, and the only father figure she had.

She told him what had happened and he wasn't surprised.

"I told you a long time ago when you started writing that there were going to be a lot of jealous men in your life. You didn't believe me, or you didn't want to."

"But it happens to me every time. All the way back to that shit TA at BC, who was jealous of my writing and gave me rotten grades while the professor was away, and he hated me when she came back and changed them to what I deserved. Then the guy I worked with in London who hated me for writing and wanted to write a book himself but was too lazy to do it, and he cheated on me on top of it. The one in New York just now thinks I write recipes for women's magazines, he doesn't even know I'm a writer, and he loathes me because I live in a nice apartment and he thinks I have too much money and he hates me for that. And the screenwriter I worked with on the movie in L.A. thinks women are only worth going out with if they've got a name and he can use them to make connections or get in the press with them. He sees them as some kind of ticket to stardom by association. And I'm always lying to everyone about who I am, and what I do, pretending I write romance novels, or freelance for women's magazines, or ghostwriting or editing. *Nobody* knows what I do except you, Rose, and the sisters, and even not knowing who I am, these men are jealous of me."

She ran out of steam then and he looked at her seriously with an honest question.

"Do you want to come out in the open? Are you ready for that and what comes with it? You may lose some of your readership if you do, if they're pissed at you for lying to them about who you are. But if you can't live with the myth you've created, you can step forward and tell them you write the books that you do. But whatever you do, there are a lot of jealous people in the world—not just men who feel inadequate next to you, but women too. They don't feel good when other people are successful. They don't feel good about themselves. So they want to hurt you, and pull you down to their level and punish you. You're a very, very big success, Alex. Professionally you're huge. Few men are secure enough to have a woman like you in their life. I told you six years ago when we talked about it, the right man will come along at the right time, and you'll know exactly who he is when you see him, and you won't scare him. But there are a lot of shitheads out there, and you're going to meet a lot of them, even more if you come out about the Green books. Your light is so bright it blinds people. It blinds me sometimes, but I love you for it. I'm so damn proud of you I could burst. That light will attract people to you, and it will burn the bad ones and hurt their eyes, and they're going to try and hurt you for it. You need to watch out for them, learn to recognize them, and stay away from them. And you need to be patient while you wait for the right one. You don't need to look for him—he'll find you. There is nothing you can do about that light of yours. You shine like a beacon. You can't turn it down or off and you shouldn't. And that right guy is going to see the beacon, and turn up on your doorstep one of these days. In the meantime, kick the bad ones out, write your books, and stop complaining. Now go get me another bottle of wine," he said, pointing at the kitchen, and she grinned and stood up and kissed him on the cheek.

"Thank you," she said quietly, and went out to the kitchen for a bottle of wine for him. He was right. He had warned her about how jealous men would be of her. She had been just nineteen then. Now she was twenty-five. Tim had shocked her with his vicious diatribe and the rage in his eyes the night before. She hadn't seen it coming. Maybe she didn't want to. He was angry and he didn't even know how successful she was. And she didn't want to give up the secrecy surrounding her books, or her pseudonym. So she'd just have to live with it, and hope Bert was right, and the right one would come along at the right time. And she was fine alone in the meantime. Sometimes she even preferred it, so she could write.

She sat with Bert for a while longer, and then she went to see Brigid and her new baby. She was already at home, and little Steven was careening around the house. He had just learned to walk. Brigid was in bed, perched on an inflatable inner tube because she couldn't sit down yet so soon after the delivery, and the new baby was asleep in her arms. They had named her Camilla, and she was a beautiful baby and had weighed nine pounds, fourteen ounces, another big one. Brigid was made to breed, as her mother-in-law said, and she was happy with her babies and her husband. He cooked dinner for all of them and tried to keep an eye on Steven, while friends and relatives dropped by to see them. It was like visiting a firehouse after the alarm had gone off for a ten-alarm fire.

"I don't know how I could forget how bad it was the last time. I hope somebody reminds me before I do this again," Brigid said as she winced and shifted on the inner tube. "It was worse than last time, if that's possible, and she was smaller, though only by four ounces." But the baby had a sweet face, long legs, and beautiful hands with graceful fingers, and Brigid kept looking at her tiny toes with awe.

"Then you remember it before you and Patrick do it again two days from now," Alex warned her, laughing at her. She felt so much better since talking to Bert that afternoon. What she was experiencing with men went with the territory of success, hard work, and determination, which were not always appreciated in a woman. But she wasn't ready for what Brigid had either. At least not yet or not for a long time. She wanted to keep writing her books, forever if she could, and trying each time to make them better, with Bert's help, for as long as he was willing. And for now she didn't want any distractions, like a husband or children.

Alex left Brigid after half an hour. She looked exhausted and there were too many people there, as she tried to wobble around her room taking care of the baby, and calling out to Patrick in the kitchen, to ask if he was okay and if Steven had eaten dinner yet.

"How's Brigid?" Mother MaryMeg asked her when she got back to the convent.

"She can't sit down, she looks exhausted, there are a million people there, Patrick is cooking dinner, and the baby is beautiful." The superior laughed at the image.

"Sounds about right for a house with a new baby. She'll be pregnant again in no time. She loves her babies. And how are you?" She had seen Alex earlier and thought she looked troubled about something. "Everything all right in New York?"

"Couldn't be better. I love it and I'm fine." Alex gave her a hug and went upstairs to her room. It was good to be home for the weekend. And on Sunday night, she would go back, and fight her wars again.

Chapter 17

Alex was in better spirits when she went back to New York after the weekend. She slept late on Monday morning and decided to take a day off. She was just leaving the apartment to do some errands when Rose Porter called her.

"What are you up to?" she asked her. They hadn't talked in several weeks.

"I was just going to the supermarket, the hardware store, and the cleaner. I was in Boston this weekend."

"I'm glad I caught you. I just got a very interesting call from a television production company in England. They have three series on TV at the moment." She named them and Alex knew them all. They were the currently popular ones on television, and aired in the States too. "They want to turn *Hear No Evil* into a series." It was her third book, and one of her biggest sellers so far. Rose wasn't surprised. "I think they'd do a very good job with it. They have some stars in mind. Big ones. The catch, of course, is that they want you too. They want Alexander Green for script consultation on the set. I told them that wasn't possible, that he never does that, they insisted, and then I told them about the setup in L.A., and that's fine with them. They've already got a writer, and they think they could put the package together by August, and they would want you there for three months. You could be back here by late October, early November. What do you think?"

Rose also mentioned how much they wanted to pay her, it was a huge amount, and very enticing. "It worked in L.A., there's no reason why it wouldn't work in London. They wanted to put you up at Claridge's, and I said Mr. Green needs a house for himself and his staff, and that was fine with them too. Why don't you give it some thought?"

Alex didn't need to. It was three more months of pretending to be Mr. Green's assistant, but the series sounded like fun, and three months wasn't too long. She'd have to extend her apartment lease or give it up, but that could be worked out.

"I'll do it," she said simply. If she didn't do things like that now, when would she?

"That was easy," Rose said with a grin. She had thought she'd have to talk her into it, and was prepared to, because it was great exposure for her work for people who didn't read the books, and TV would pull women in too. "I'll let them know." She did, and called Alex when she got back from her errands. "They're thrilled. They said they'd find a house right away. They want you there on August first."

Alex was already thinking about going to the South of France for two weeks before that, as long as she was going to Europe. Tim was right. She led a charmed life. "It won't air till spring, to give them time to edit." It was her first TV series and sounded very exciting to her. They talked for a few minutes longer, and hung up. She fixed a light lunch for herself, and made lists about what she had to do before she went, and called her realtor to extend the lease till the end of the year, and they told her at six o'clock that the owner was amenable. So she could leave her things there, and didn't have to drag it all back to Boston. And she wanted to spend some time in New York when she got back. She hadn't had much opportunity to take advantage of the city and now she was leaving.

She spent a weekend in Boston in July to say goodbye to the nuns and Bert, and see Brigid again. She wasn't pregnant yet this time.

"You're slipping," Alex teased her and Brigid laughed.

"Give me another month."

"You're hopeless." But both her children were adorable and she was happy.

Alex flew from New York to Nice on the twelfth of July to spend two weeks at a hotel in Cap d'Antibes that she had read about and never been to. It was the height of luxury, and she wanted to be pampered and lazy before she started work in London. And the hotel lived up to all her expectations for fabulous food, a great spa, a beautiful room, and private cabanas where she could lie in the sun and read without anyone seeing or bothering her.

She arrived in London on the thirty-first of July with a honey-colored tan, looking rested and relaxed when she checked into Claridge's for one night. She was picking up the keys to the house the production company had rented for Mr. Green the next day, and they hoped it would be to his liking. There were six bedrooms for himself and his alleged entourage. She needed the house to keep up the charade that he and his staff would be there, although all she needed was the master bedroom for herself. She planned to have her own cleaning service like the one she'd had in L.A. And she called Fiona as soon as she got to her room. Alex had left London almost exactly a year before. Since then, Fiona had gotten married and was pregnant. They had agreed to have dinner that night, and Alex couldn't wait to see her.

They met at Barrafina in Soho for dinner, and Fiona told her all about married life and how happy she was with Clive, and they were over the moon about the baby.

"What are you doing back here?" She wanted to know.

"I have a job as a production assistant, working on a TV series," she said humbly. "It's a low-level job, but I thought it would be fun. It's only for three months."

"It sounds terrific." It never dawned on Fiona that they could have hired a production assistant in London, and didn't need to bring one out from New York. She was just happy to see her friend. She had changed jobs after Alex left, so she hadn't seen Ivan in over a year. She had heard that he'd gotten fired, but didn't know if it was true or not.

Fiona dropped Alex off at the hotel on her way home, and they promised to get together soon. Alex had told her the production company was paying for the hotel and she'd be moving to a house in a few days. Alex said she'd call her with the number.

The next morning, Alex reported to work on time, wearing jeans, a tee shirt, and a leather jacket. They had provided a car and driver to take her to the television studio. And they gave her an office as soon as she got there, and showed her around.

"I don't suppose Mr. Green will be coming in himself?" the head production assistant asked discreetly. "We have an office for him too, if he wants it."

"That won't be necessary, he won't come in," Alex said crisply.

"He does all his work at home, and has me bring the notes in, or email them."

"Of course." They treated her like royalty and introduced her to everyone. The screenwriter was a woman, and had a big reputation. And the director was very jovial. Alex was at her desk, trying out the computer, when the producer stuck his head in the door to meet her.

"Hello, welcome! I'm Miles McCarthy," he said with a broad smile. He looked younger than she'd expected, although she knew from his bio that he was forty-one years old. He strode across the room to shake her hand. He was tall and lanky, wearing the same outfit she was, with a baseball cap on backward that he'd gotten at a concert the night before. "Everything the way you want it?" he inquired with a smile. "Give a shout if we forgot something. My office is just down the hall. And my assistant is in the one next to mine."

"No, it's been perfect," she reassured him, and he disappeared. She went to the house they'd rented for her and "Mr. Green" after that, to meet the realtor and get the keys. It was a beautiful old house near Hyde Park, immaculately furnished and decorated, with drawings of horses and fox hunts everywhere, a formal dining room, a remarkable wood-paneled library, an elevator, and a very elegant master suite. Alex realized that, given the location, it must be costing them a fortune.

She barely had time to move her things from Claridge's and rush back to the office for a production meeting that afternoon.

There was a large group of people at the table, and the producer and director took turns discussing various aspects of the show. They introduced Alex to everyone, explaining that she would be their liaison to Mr. Green. No one seemed troubled by it, and after the meeting Miles came over to talk to her, and explained that the actors were starting rehearsals the next day. They had gotten everything on track very quickly.

"Is the house all right?" he asked with concern.

"It's fantastic. He's going to love it."

"My assistant picked it," he said, pleased. She noticed that he had sandy blond hair with gray in it, and striking blue eyes. "When is Mr. Green arriving, by the way?"

"Late tonight, by private plane, with the staff." It was the same story she'd told in L.A., and everyone believed it.

"We're so glad he agreed to do the series. It's going to be really great. And the screenwriter is excellent. I've worked with her before, on two shows. She does crime and mystery particularly well."

"I'm sure he'll be very happy," Alex reassured her.

The producer left her then, to take care of a thousand details, and she discovered that he had an assistant just to attend to the needs of the actors. It was an impeccably run operation. She went to see the soundstage then, and was impressed by that too, and then she went home to relax in the fabulous house they had rented without knowing it was for her. While she was unpacking, an enormous bouquet of flowers arrived to her attention, and a magnum of champagne for Mr. Green. She was sorry she couldn't give the magnum to Bert, and told him about it on the phone when she called him.

"Well, it won't do me any good if it's in London," he complained. She told him about the production company and the house, and he got off the phone after that. He had a leak in his kitchen, and the plumber had just arrived. And Alex went to finish her unpacking and set up everything she needed on her desk. She was all set to start work in earnest the next day, and she couldn't wait to see the script they were going to give her in the morning. They wanted Mr. Green's notes on it as soon as possible, which she had assured them she could arrange.

When Alex got to the office the next day, the place was buzzing. The actors were in their dressing rooms. Catering had set up a breakfast buffet for anyone who wanted it. Hairdressers and makeup artists were everywhere, and, as promised, one of the producer's assistants handed her two scripts, one for her and the other for her employer, and Alex went to her office to read it. It was extremely good. She made notes as she was reading, but had very few changes or comments.

"How does it look to you?" Miles stuck his head in and asked her when he saw that she was reading the script.

"It's excellent. He's going to be very pleased." She had almost no work to do.

"Why don't you come to the first reading?" he invited her. It was in a large meeting hall with many chairs set up in groups, where the actors would do their first informal run-through of the script and make comments. The readings were very good, and the actors real pros, and much less difficult than their American counterparts. Miles had Alex sit next to him, and gave her little explanations and running comments about the actors sotto voce. He was doing all he could to make her feel part of their team, and Rachel Wooster, the screenwriter, came over afterward to ask Alex to sit at her table for lunch, and the director joined them. He was Irish and very funny and had everyone laughing all through lunch. The atmosphere and collegial relationship they all had were terrific, and Alex felt totally at ease in their midst, and even though she was allegedly only Mr. Green's assistant, they treated her very well. She had status in the group.

At the end of the day, she walked out to her car and driver. Miles was leaving at the same time on a fierce-looking motorcycle, and stopped to chat with her for a minute.

"I hope you feel it went well today," he said. He had been attentive all day, and so had the entire crew.

"It couldn't be better. And I don't think Mr. Green will have any problems with the script." She had two small changes to send later, which were negligible, but she couldn't tell him that now until "Mr. Green" had officially seen it.

"I do wish he'd drop by so we can make him feel welcome," Miles said pleasantly, "but I know he doesn't do that. If he changes his mind, though, we'd love to have him."

"He'll be very grateful. But he sends me out as his emissary to the world." She smiled at him and he noticed her tan, which made her eyes look strikingly green.

"He certainly has an excellent ambassador to represent him." Miles smiled at her and she laughed.

"Thank you. I'm not sure everyone would agree with you, but I feel very fortunate to have the job. He's very easy to work for."

"So are you. You had the whole team falling in love with you today, and I'm top of that list. I'm a great fan of his, and now of yours. I read all his books. They're extraordinary."

"He'll be pleased that you think so." It was like talking about herself in the third person, which felt strange, even though she had done it in L.A. for six months and never gave herself away. And she hoped she didn't here. They seemed to pay much closer attention than the movie crew had, and the actors were less lavishly treated. Miles had been exceptionally helpful and welcoming, and was a pleasure to work with.

"I can give you a lift home on my bike, by the way, if you'd prefer it."

"I'm too big a coward," she said honestly.

"That's probably sensible," he said, waved at her, and then took off, and she went home sedately in the car they had provided her, and let herself into the house.

She sent Miles an email shortly after, with the two minor changes from "Mr. Green," and went to relax in the small, cozy den next to her bedroom. She had had a really enjoyable time on the set, and liked them all. She hadn't met anyone that she found difficult, and she was really looking forward to working with them. Even the actors were well behaved and fun to talk to, and not prima donnas despite their big names and reputations. The leaders, both director and producer, set a tone and example that put everyone in a good mood, and anxious to do their best for the team. It was a first-rate production company in every way. Even the food had been great.

She was surprised when the phone rang in the kitchen when she was opening a takeaway salad for dinner that she had picked up on the way home. Since no one had that number, she couldn't imagine who it was. It was Miles McCarthy, checking in with her that all was to Mr. Green's liking.

"He's resting right now, but I told him when I got in how well everything went today, and he was very pleased."

"Excellent," he said, and hung up a moment later, as Alex sat down to eat her salad at the kitchen table and thought about him. It had been a very, very good first day.

It took the actors a week to hit their stride with the script, and start to play well off each other and even improvise occasionally, which Alex didn't object to, and neither did "Mr. Green" when she reported his reaction and comments back to them. It took about the same amount of time for the whole team to adjust to working together, and by two weeks in, they all felt like old friends. It was a very experienced, professional cast and crew.

Alex was sitting on the soundstage, reading some changes in the script, when Miles came in and sat down in the chair next to her. She looked up and they exchanged a smile. He treated her like someone he knew well whenever they met. She knew how important and successful he was, and he was not what she had expected at all. He was much more casual and warmer than anyone she'd met on the set so far. He was a very modest person, unlike people in Hollywood, where posturing was a way of life. Malcolm had been a prime example.

"What do you think of the latest changes?" he asked her.

"I like them. They make the dialogue smoother."

"Good. I don't like playing with the master's words." He smiled at her, and he had an intelligent face.

"That's nice of you, but this works," she said, satisfied.

"I hope he agrees with you," he said cautiously, but there had been no problems so far. "I know you meet with him at night, so it's a long day for you. But would you ever want to have dinner? We can do it late, if that's better for you. I'm a bit of a night owl myself."

"I'm usually free by eight o'clock," she said easily. "He doesn't take up that much of my time. He's very considerate about it."

"That's good to know. Somehow, I could imagine that someone so intensely reclusive could be a bit of a tyrant."

"He's not a tyrant. He's just very shy." She covered for the employer who didn't exist, but everyone believed in.

"We would love to welcome him here," he said again and then turned his attention to Alex. "What kind of food do you like?"

"Anything, and casual is fine." He suggested Mon Plaisir, which she knew from when she lived there, and liked a lot.

"That would be great."

"How would tonight be? Or would tomorrow be better?"

"Tonight's fine," she said, smiling broadly. She felt pampered and spoiled.

"You're a very important person here," he said seriously.

"You certainly make me feel that way."

"I'll pick you up at eight then, in a car, not on my motorcycle." He grinned at her.

"Thank you." He went back to the others then, and she didn't see him for the rest of the day.

When she got to the house after work, she emailed her approvals from "Mr. Green," bathed and dressed, and was ready when Miles rang the doorbell at eight. She opened the door to him wearing a short denim skirt, a leather jacket, and heels, and he looked at her warmly, in black leather pants and jacket himself, and she noticed that he had shaved.

"Do you want to come in for a drink?" she offered. She could say that Mr. Green was in seclusion upstairs, without giving anything away. But he lowered his voice immediately in response.

"I don't want to disturb him. Why don't we just go."

Miles led her out to his car parked in front of the house. It was a beaten-up old Jaguar, with cracked leather upholstery and tremendous charm. Miles had his own distinctive style, and he turned to her as they drove away.

"Does he mind you going out with me? I never thought about it till after I suggested dinner." She reassured him immediately. It was the same question Malcolm had asked her in L.A.

"I'm free to do whatever I like. He doesn't monopolize my evenings or personal time. He's a very reasonable person. I'm not his girlfriend," she stated clearly. "There are no nights or weekends involved." It seemed like all he needed to know, and Miles seemed more relaxed after that. They talked easily about a variety of subjects on the way to the restaurant, and he was surprised to discover that she had lived in London for almost two years.

"So you haven't worked for him for that long? I thought your CV said you did." He was confused.

"I have, I was with him here."

"I had no idea he spent time in England too. I know he has a place in the wilds of Scotland, but no one mentioned London."

"We took a flat in Knightsbridge for two years, while he was writing here." Everything she said to him was a half-truth, and it was exhausting lying all the time and trying to avoid dangerous slips.

The restaurant was as she remembered it from the last time she'd been there, cozy and intimate, without being so dark you couldn't read the menu, or looking like a location for a tryst for married lovers. It was a perfect place to unwind with a friend after a long day, which was his purpose in bringing her here. She was surprised at how comfortable she was with him, and had been since they met. It was just his style, but the way he spoke to her was warm, and there was something very sexy about him with his rugged good looks.

They ordered dinner, and had a glass of wine, and he sighed as he smiled at her. "You're too young to have been married yet, I suppose. I just finished a bad divorce, it's a relief to focus on work. And this is such a great project." He was so enthused about it that it thrilled Alex every time he said it. He was full of energy and great ideas for the series.

"I'm sorry about your divorce. That must be rough. Do you have children?" She knew very little about him, except that his bio for publicity said he had gone to Oxford and was forty-one years old.

"I have two kids. I married very young, right after college, so they're fairly grown up, but not entirely yet. My daughter is seventeen, and my son is fifteen. Not easy ages, and they've been pulled back and forth quite a lot. Their mother wants to move to South Africa with her boyfriend, who's from there and still lives there and has his business in Johannesburg, and I don't want them that far away. I'm very close to my kids," he said with a bittersweet tone to his voice.

"Are you able to stop her from moving?" He shook his head and Alex felt sorry for him. His eyes told her how painful it was for him.

"The judge ruled against me and said I can't keep her prisoner here. We have shared custody, and the children love both of us. They don't want to leave either of us, and the court ruled that we'll have to send them back and forth as much as possible, which is hard on them. My daughter is in boarding school here, as most kids her age are, and she'll be going to university next year, but my son is moving to Johannesburg with his mother. And my schedule is crazy, so I can't always foresee how much free time I'll have when he's here. And he doesn't want to go to boarding school."

"I didn't want to either at his age."

"It's not as common in the States, but almost everyone does here. He was accepted at Eton, which is a wonderful school, where I went, and he refused to go." The school he had gone to told her he was from a good family with considerable social standing, but he had none of the snobbishness that usually went with it, and didn't put on airs. She had met some men in England who went to the best schools and were insufferable. Miles was nothing like them. "Why would you have gone to boarding school? Were you badly behaved so they wanted to send you away?" he teased her.

"No, my father died when I was fourteen, and my mother long before that, so it was a matter of necessity. I had nowhere to live, and couldn't stay alone in his house with just a housekeeper. It worked out really well in the end. I lived in a convent with a house full of loving nuns. I still stay there when I'm in Boston. I just moved to New York recently." Her history touched him. She seemed like a very unusual woman and he found her warm and intriguing. He hadn't figured her out yet, but was trying his best to. He could sense that there was a part of her she didn't let anyone know or see. She was very guarded, like a child hiding behind a tree, thinking no one could see them, although they were partially visible. Miles was watching her closely and trying to understand her better.

"So when did you meet up with the amazing Mr. Green?" He was fascinated by that too. He was such an extraordinary writer, and he was impressed that the famous writer put so much faith in such a young woman. She was clearly as capable as she had demonstrated so far to them.

"When he wrote his first book. I was nineteen and still in college."

"And where was that?" She seemed to have moved around a bit. He knew she had spent six months in L.A. working on Green's movie, and now he knew they'd been in London for two years.

"He spent some time in Boston, and we met then. I've been working for him for six years," she said quietly as their dinner arrived, and he continued questioning her, trying to piece the puzzle of her together. The stabilizing element appeared to be her work for Alexander Green, which was ironically true.

"That makes you twenty-five now," Miles commented. "I must seem like an old man to you." He laughed as he said it, and she denied it immediately.

"I forget about age, mine and other people's. It's really what's in your head that matters, and how mature you are. Some people never get there, and others arrive early. I've been responsible for a long time, and I think Mr. Green recognizes it." So did Miles. His ex-wife was exactly his age, and had been a spoiled child for all the years he knew her. There was none of that about Alex. She was a sensible woman, no matter what age she was, and he felt like he was talking to an equal as they ate their excellent dinner and explored each other's lives.

"I bought a wonderful horse farm a number of years ago in Dorset," he told her halfway through dinner to get off more painful personal subjects. "My children and I love it. I actually breed horses there, Thoroughbreds and Arabians, show horses. It's a lot of work, but very rewarding and interesting. It costs a fortune to run, but we've had a few racehorses that have done very well. I have a new one right now. You'll have to come and see the place sometime. It's about three hours from London. If we get a break in the shooting schedule, when we're further along, I'll take you there. Sometimes the actors need a few days off, if someone crucial to a scene gets sick, or they just get worn out. It's better to give them some time off than to keep pushing and screw everything up." It seemed like a reasonable solution to her, and he was obviously a practical and intelligent person, full of common sense. He was very open and direct, which she liked, and wished she could be more so with him.

"I'd love to see the farm, but I don't know anything about running a horse farm or country life. There were no horses in the convent when I was growing up." She laughed. "Although I rode with my father when I was young. I took lessons for a while."

"What did you and your father like to do?" he asked her gently.

"Read crime thrillers," she answered instantly, "and every kind of detective story we could lay hands on. He had an amazing collection, some of them first editions. I kept all of them. They've been in storage for eleven years."

"I guess that's what you have in common with your employer. That must have impressed him when he hired you, your knowledge of his kind of work." It seemed to have been a passion she and her father shared.

"Some people think that women don't read or understand crime novels, let alone write them, which really isn't true. Although my father believed that too. There are some wonderful thrillers and detective stories written by women, despite my father's personal preference for male writers—he was quite adamant about it. I realize now that his view was somewhat limited and he overlooked some very good women crime writers." It had taken her most of her life to believe it, but now she did.

"Are you an aspiring writer, Alex?" he asked her, and she shook her head. She certainly wasn't "aspiring," she was a full-on pro.

"Not really," she said blithely, wishing she could be honest with him.

"My own interests lie in an entirely different direction. I love producing quality television shows and I can put a deal together like nobody's business, but I could never write the material for a show. I can barely write a letter. I just don't have that creative gene in me, which is why I admire Alexander Green so much. I think your skills are more like mine, organizational. We can make things happen. But don't ever ask me to write a screenplay or a book. I know a good one when I see it, like great horseflesh. I leave the writing to geniuses like Mr. Green." As he had been before, Miles was humble about his own talents, but he had misjudged hers. Given all the lies she and others had told him, how could he possibly know? She just seemed like a very efficient assistant to him.

"You could probably write better than you think. You just never tried it," she said generously.

"I'll leave that to him." He smiled, totally satisfied with his life and what he did. The only thing he was unhappy about was the impact of the divorce on his kids. He had explained to her earlier in the meal that neither of them had done anything awful to each other. They had just married too young and run out of gas. He said his wife was a talented photographer, but had no desire to pursue it as a line of work. He said he had far less talent than she did, but had always been excited and ambitious about his career.

Alex told him not to sell himself short. She could tell that he was an ingenious, creative man. It was no small thing to create a successful television show, and put all the essential people together to make it work. She was more grateful than ever as the meal drew to a close that he had chosen her work for his next venture, and she was excited to be associated with him. She told him that her employer was ecstatic about what he was doing, and that pleased Miles too. He said they all hoped it would be a big success, and Alex said she did too.

"Your comments are bound to be the most sincere," he said to her over a cup of espresso after dinner, "because you have no stake in it and nothing to gain. The rest of us want to make a lot of money. You're not tainted by greed like we are," he complimented her, and she winced.

"I have my greedy moments too," she confessed, and it was truer than he knew.

"You seem like you have your feet on the ground," he praised her, and she laughed.

"I was thinking the same thing about you," she admitted.

"I'm not as sensible as I look. Breeding Thoroughbreds is an expensive venture, or raising racehorses. There is nothing reasonable about it. It's a costly passion, but I love it," he confessed.

"It sounds like fun, though."

"That it is. I can't wait for you to see my farm. The house is an old Tudor manor. It's quite historically important, and it even has a moat and its own lake, and the land is spectacular. I'm a true Englishman, I have a strong bond to the land. My family lost their property generations ago, and I've always wanted land to call my own, and pass on to my children. Now I have it, it's very important to me." She had seen a side of him that night that she wouldn't have known otherwise, and when she left the restaurant with him, she knew she had a friend. He put an arm around her shoulders as they walked back to the car, and there was a warm light in his eyes when he said good night to her, but he didn't try to kiss her. And as he watched her get through the front door safely, she waved before she closed it, and felt something she had never felt before. She wasn't sure what it was, but it seemed very direct and simple. Yet there was one complication to it. She hated the fact that she was lying to him about who she really was.

Chapter 18

The break that Miles had been hoping for so he could take her to his horse farm came a month into the filming of the show. They'd had dinner together several times by then, and had learned a lot about each other. He knew all about the nuns, her friend Brigid, and her years in college. He knew about her father and how she had never been in love. He could see how hard she worked, and how dedicated she was. He saw her vulnerable side and her strengths, and how intelligent she was. But what he didn't know, and couldn't, was that she wrote the Alexander Green books. It was the only thing she had concealed from him, and she knew she had no choice. She couldn't take him into the inner circle of her life—he didn't belong there, and if he ever misused the knowledge, he could destroy her career, and she would let no one and nothing do that. She protected her work with every ounce of her soul, even more than her heart.

Miles had shared with her his childhood in the north of England, in Yorkshire, boarding school at Eton, a year in Ireland after college, his work for the BBC when he came back, his passion for horses, love of his children, and disappointments of his marriage. He had no desire to be married again. He had dated a few women since his separation and divorce from his wife, but no one he cared about particularly or loved, or wanted to see more of.

He said he had a weakness for actresses, which didn't serve him well. "They're so incredibly narcissistic," he said, and she confessed that her nemeses were would-be writers. He asked her again if she and Alexander Green had ever been romantically involved during the years they'd worked together. It seemed logical to him that it could have happened—she was a beautiful woman—but when he asked her, she said no, and he could see in her eyes that she was telling the truth, although he still had a sense at times that there were things she wasn't telling him. He assumed they were the painful parts of her youth, like the mother who had abandoned her, and the father she had lost. It never dawned on him that it could be something else much more complicated than that.

He was incredibly drawn to Alex, but he didn't want to create a difficult situation for either of them with their work, so he held back. And he had no idea how she felt about him. He loved their evenings together, but she was demure and very shy and in some ways very young. He guessed that she had little experience, and she had admitted to him that she had gone out with only a few men. Her entire life was devoted to her work. She was just the kind of woman he would have wanted to find, if he wanted to marry again, but he didn't. He had vowed after his divorce never to make that mistake a second time. Alex wasn't the kind of woman he could take lightly, and he didn't want her to get hurt. Having a casual affair with her would have seemed like profound disrespect, even if she'd been willing, but she wasn't that kind of woman. He felt it best to remain good friends. And their friendship was deepening day by day. They enjoyed many of the same things, and had a lot in common. It became increasingly natural to spend time together when they could. It was all very wholesome and pure, which was comfortable for them both.

The male lead in the series got a terrible flu that ended in bronchitis, the female lead caught it from him, and they had to stop shooting for a few days, and it could even turn into a week. They shot around them for as long as they were able, and then they had to stop, and Miles turned up in her office grinning broadly.

"We've got it!" he whispered as he approached her desk.

"Got what?" She was looking at one of the latest scripts and was distracted.

"The time we need to go to my farm. They're sick as dogs, and the doctor just said it could turn into pneumonia if we don't let them rest. Do you think Mr. Green would give you a few days off?"

"I'll ask, but I'm sure he would. He's writing right now anyway, and he doesn't like to be bothered when he is." Her lies were getting better, and she embellished them as needed. She smiled up at Miles. She felt peaceful whenever she was with him. There was nothing heated or awkward in their relationship. It was a haven for them both. "When do you want to go?"

"Tonight?" His son had just gone back to Johannesburg, so Miles was free. "We could go when we finish this afternoon." They had to tie up a few loose ends before taking a shooting break. "We could leave by six or seven, and not get there too late. It's two and a half hours away, three at most. All you need are sweaters and jeans and some boots to muck around in if it gets wet. You could borrow a pair of my daughter's if you don't have any with you. You're about the same size." Although they looked entirely different. Both of his children were as blond as he, Alex knew from the photographs he'd shown her. She'd had dinner one night in his flat, which was a cozy, eclectic, appealing mess that put its arms around you and made you never want to leave. She had hated to go home to the elegant town-house that night and wished that things were different and she could stay with him. But thinking that was absurd, and he had never behaved as anything but a friend. "Can you call and ask Green now?" Miles asked hopefully.

"I promise, it will be fine. I'll ask him when I get home, but he won't say no. And he'd rather not have me around when he's writ-ing."

"All right, if you think so. I'll leave early, if I can, and pick you up at six." He was thrilled to be taking her to his farm. He had been wanting to show it to her for weeks and didn't see how he could. Two of the stars getting sick was providential, though unfortunate for them. Alex beamed at him as he rushed off. She left a little early too, and went home with her driver, to pack. She let him off for the next two days, and told him she'd call when she returned.

"Mr. Green won't be needing me, ma'am?" He never did, nor any of the staff the driver never saw but knew was there, or so he thought.

"No, Lambert. Thank you."

She hurried to the master suite and put some music on while she packed. There was a fabulous sound system in the house and she used it a lot to listen to Prince, the Black Eyed Peas, Santana, Michael Jackson, Stevie Wonder, and others. She packed in fifteen minutes, after calling Miles to confirm that Mr. Green had no prob-lem with her leaving. Miles called and said he was outside twenty minutes later. He didn't want to ring the bell and disturb Mr. Green while he was writing. Alex came out with a small overnight bag and a tote stuffed with everything she could think of that she might need for the weekend.

"You've got a cheek," Miles said as he took her bags from her and put them in what he called the "boot," the trunk. He sounded mildly scolding, as he would to a child.

"Why?" She had no idea what he meant, or if he was annoyed at her, and she looked worried.

"I could hear the music blaring when I called you. The poor man is trying to write, Alex. How can you put that on? I'm surprised he didn't kill you."

She laughed in response. "He was having an early dinner in the kitchen. And he's very nice about things like that. I wouldn't put it on when he's actually writing."

"What did he say? Was he really okay about your leaving?"

"Very much so. He told me to have fun."

"He sounds like a benevolent father."

"Sometimes he is," she said, glancing out the window. She hated the lies that came so easily to her now. So much so that at times she believed them herself, and she knew he did. It seemed so wrong with someone she really liked and respected. But what choice did she have? She couldn't put her life in his hands, and it would be if she ever confided in him. Instead, she had created a persona who didn't exist but seemed real to her now.

It took them three hours, going at a leisurely pace on back roads, to get to his farm in Dorset. The first hour was on highway, and the last two on old, winding country roads that were beautiful in the September light. The trees were still green, the weather not too chilly yet, but one could tell that fall was coming. They passed old farmhouses and some gated properties. There were orchards and rolling hills, cows and sheep, and horses. They talked the whole way, first about the scenes they were filming, and then about life, how they viewed things, the people they cared about, the dreams they'd had when they were younger. His children were very important to him and he missed them.

"You're so lucky you have a whole life ahead of you," he said to Alex with feeling. "You're just starting out."

"So are you," she said generously.

"No, I'm not. I'm halfway there, what's done is done. And the mistakes one makes at your age follow you forever." They were wise words. But it didn't seem as though he had made too many mistakes. He had two children he loved, and a booming career. His only mistake was one bad marriage, which didn't seem so terrible to her. And she had the books she had dedicated her life to writing for the past six years, and nothing else. She had built no relationships except the ones she grew up with. And she was almost certain she didn't want children in the future. There was too much risk involved in having them, she thought. What if something happened to her or their father? They would be alone as she had been, and maybe not as lucky to find a family of loving nuns. She didn't want to inflict those dangers on a child, and she had said as much to Miles one night at dinner, and he was surprised. He couldn't imagine his life without his children, and she couldn't imagine hers with children of her own. It terrified her.

Darkness fell about an hour before they got to the farm, and he drove between a pair of old iron gates at last. They had been left unlocked and open, and he turned the Jaguar onto a narrow rutted road that went on for a long time, and then finally she saw an enormous old-fashioned barn and a large stone house. There were wildflowers in a field, splendid old trees, and in the distance the lake he had mentioned, and a bright moon shedding light on the scene. He stopped the car and they got out, and he carried her bags across a little bridge over the moat as she followed him to the huge front door with a big brass knocker. He opened it with a key and stepped inside, and she walked in behind him into the hall, and he turned on the light.

She could see beautiful old country antiques, a long hallway, threadbare and once-handsome carpets hundreds of years old, and they walked into a living room of perfect proportions to be grand but still cozy, with a huge fireplace. There was a library, a smaller sitting room, a boot room, and an enormous country kitchen. It was what one imagined an English country estate should look like, not on a TV show or in a magazine, but in real life, and he was instantly relaxed and at home. He loved being there and came as often as he could. His children had grown up there, and he had spent much of his marriage there. The property was one of the fruits of his successful career and was one of the first things he had bought with his first hit series years before. He was deeply attached to his home, and he was happy to share it with Alex now. She felt honored to be there, in the inner sanctum of his life.

"Miles, it's just perfect." He could see instantly how much she liked it, and he was so touched by it and the warmth in her eyes that he couldn't stop himself. He walked toward her and put his arms around her and kissed her for the first time, and she didn't stop him. It was what they both wanted, and it was the perfect place for it to happen. They both felt as though they had come home.

"It means so much to me that you like it." He took her by the hand and walked her upstairs then, and showed her all the bedrooms, including the big canopied bed in his that looked like a peaceful place to hide from the world. His children's rooms were down the hall from his, each had their own suite that had been decorated for them as children, but they didn't want to change them. And there were half a dozen imposing guest bedrooms. The manor had been built for country house parties and shooting weekends. There were a dozen servants' bedrooms upstairs. And behind the barn he said there was a building where all the men who worked in the stable lived. And another that they no longer used, for additional servants that they no longer had, and hadn't during his tenure. He had thought of transforming both houses into homes for his children one day when they were grown so they could bring their families there once they were married. It was his dream home and she could see why. It was filled with love. She could feel his strong bond to it as they walked around.

"My ex-wife always wanted me to sell it. She hated it here. There's nothing much around except an ancient village, and other farms and manors. She wanted to live in the city, and buy a house in Saint-Tropez instead of this, but we never did. Maybe that would have saved my marriage, but I couldn't bring myself to part with this place, and the children love it as much as I do. This is my refuge, and a piece of my soul," he confided to her and kissed her again, and she couldn't stop kissing him. She had never felt for anyone as she did for him, and he wanted her so much he could hardly breathe. He had since the beginning and now the floodgates had opened and there was no holding back what they felt for each other. "Alex . . . I know this sounds crazy, but I love you . . . I don't want you to get hurt . . . and I don't know what will happen . . ." She would go back to New York in a few months, to her own world, and his was here, but he couldn't tear himself away from her, and he knew this was much more than lust.

"I don't care . . . I love you . . ." she answered. They walked back to his bedroom, and he paused at the door and kissed her again. He picked her up in his arms like a doll then and laid her gently on the enormous bed. It was a huge modern size, built into the original antique frame for comfort, with enormous drapes around the bed that they could close in winter when it was cold. The bed had never known love and warmth before as it did at that moment, and he gently peeled her clothes away and his own and they slipped under the covers. He lit a candle next to the bed, and the shadows flickered around them as he made love to her and she gave herself as she never had to any man, and then she fell asleep in his arms afterward, feeling safe for the first time in her life.

They woke up two hours later, at the same time, with the candle still burning, and she smiled into his eyes and then kissed him.

"Did I dream this?" he asked her, almost afraid to believe it. The strong, powerful, confident man that she had met a month before had melted in her arms, and she could have had anything she wanted from him. "How did I get so lucky? Thank God Green brought you here with him."

"I always go with him," she said softly, burrowing deeper into Miles's arms as he held her like spun glass. His lovemaking had been just strong enough to transport her, but gentle enough to drive her to heights she had never known.

"What if he had brought some awful ancient crone?" Miles whispered, and she laughed, and half an hour later they both admitted that they were starving. He'd had the house heated before they arrived, and had asked the stable master to leave food in the refrigerator. He took her hand then and they went down to the kitchen naked. They had the whole place to themselves, and Miles admired her exquisite body as they stood in the ancient kitchen. She looked like a beautiful nymph in the forest. He loved her so much he thought he could die, and wouldn't have minded dying of ecstasy in her arms. "What have you done to me?" he said to her as he pulled her into his arms again. "You have bewitched me." She smiled shyly and nestled close to him. She had never known life could be so perfect, and suddenly she remembered Bert's words to her, reiterated recently, that one day the right man would come along at the right time. He would find her, she didn't have to look for him, and then she would be happy. He was right.

She told Miles about him as they sat down to a dinner of cheese and bread, some sliced cold sausages, and a glass of wine he poured her, which was very good French wine of an important vintage.

"And whose editor is he? I'm confused." She had spoken as though he were hers and she said he was her mentor, and she corrected herself quickly.

"He's Mr. Green's, but he spends a lot of time with us, and he's very wise." Miles nodded. She led an interesting life, full of unusual people, aged sages and mentors and nuns, and her best friend was an ex-nun with two babies, and she worked for one of the most important writers in the world. It was an extraordinary existence for someone her age, and she was an extraordinary woman. He wasn't sure he deserved her, and she felt the same way about him. She was in awe of Miles, and full of admiration for him, head over heels in love with him, and couldn't believe this was happening.

They went back upstairs after dinner and made love again, and then lay in the candlelight, talking softly, and he lit a fire as she watched him. She was as mesmerized by his body as he was by hers. He felt as though they were Adam and Eve in the Garden of Eden.

They fell asleep with the fire blazing, still talking to each other, and woke up at dawn, as he looked at her and grinned. Her silky black hair was like a mysterious curtain over her face, and he ran a gentle hand along her body, and then leaned down to kiss her.

"I think I died and went to heaven last night." He knew it wasn't just the lovemaking, it was everything he felt for her. He had never known a woman like her in his entire life. It made his heart ache thinking of what he would have missed if they had never come here. But he felt destiny taking a hand in his life, and so did she.

They luxuriated in the enormous antique bathtub before they went out, and stopped in the kitchen for a piece of fruit and a cup of coffee, and then he took her for a walk in the garden. It was a beautiful sunny day. They walked past the orchards to an ancient cemetery at the rear of the property. The dates on the tombstones were as early as the 1600s, like many houses in the area. They paused at a little brook on the way back, sat down on the grass, talked for a while, and made love again. And they went to the stables so he could show her all the horses, and the impeccably kept stalls. They walked into several of them so she could see the horses more closely, and even the very modern breeding section of the barn, where other breeders brought their horses to combine with his bloodlines. They spent an hour there, and then he drove her to the village, and they had lunch at a small ancient pub, where the owner greeted him warmly and the simple fare was good, and after lunch they went back to the house.

His home was so inviting and Alex was completely under its spell and his. He pointed out some of the books in his library, which were very valuable and very old, and she told him how much her father would have loved it. And at the end of the day he made a fire in the library and they curled up, looking at the books while he kissed her. It was all so new and so perfect that they knew instinctively that this moment would never come again, while their love was being born. And they slept like peaceful children that night in each other's arms.

They went riding together early the next morning, just as the sun was coming up over the hills. He took her on hidden paths. He was an excellent rider, he had given her a gentle horse, and she was comfortable next to him. They stayed out for several hours, and then walked the horses back to the barn. She felt as though she could stay there forever, and wished they would. But they knew they had to go back the next day. He had called to check, and their stars were feeling better. They had one day left in paradise and had to resume shooting the day after.

Miles cooked eggs for her after their long ride, and they were talking quietly when he looked at her strangely, and seemed embarrassed by what he wanted to ask her.

"Can I ask you something that probably sounds crazy to you, and I could be wrong. Do you ever want to write? I know I've asked you before and you said no, but with your love of books, I just get the feeling there's a writer in there somewhere. You work for a great writer. You and your father had a passion for crime stories and mysteries. Are you never inspired to write a book too? I think I would be, in your shoes." A chill ran down her spine when he said it.

"It's not something you just decide to do," she said quietly. "It's a talent that I don't have. Just being near it doesn't make you capable of it. People always think they can decide to write a book if they want to and have the time. It doesn't work like that." He nodded and realized that what she said was true.

"I used to want to write a book, and then I realized I can't. I don't have it in me," he admitted, and she nodded, relieved to have fobbed him off, but feeling guilty about it too. And after she'd said it, she was quiet for a long moment, haunted by her own lies. He was the one person she didn't want to be untruthful with, and she just had been again. It felt so wrong to her, although what she had just said to him about writing was true, just not about her. She stared down at her plate lost in thought. Suddenly she had reached a crossroads she had never expected to come to, with this man she loved. And when she looked up at him again, there was something raw and naked in her eyes that frightened him. He couldn't tell what was on her mind, but he could see that she was upset.

"I don't want to lie to you," she said in an agonized voice.

"Have you?" He looked surprised. She seemed like an honest person. She was suddenly afraid. Telling him the truth was so high risk for her. She trusted him, but what if she was wrong?

He could sense that he had ventured onto dangerous ground, and opened a door to something she was afraid of, but he didn't know what it was. His question about writing had been benign and posed no threat to her, or so he thought. But she seemed panicked, and he had no idea why. She appeared as though she might bolt and run as he reached out and held her hand in his own. Miles kissed her then to calm her down, but there was no turning back now, for her. She realized now that she couldn't lie to him, or have an honest relationship with him as a man unless she told him the truth.

"I haven't been truthful with you," she said in a ragged voice, needing to confess it to him now. "But if I am, you could destroy me. You have to swear to me you will never tell." He couldn't even imagine what she was about to tell him, and perhaps the lie was that she was Green's mistress after all. Miles prayed it wasn't that.

"I promise you," he said, holding tightly to her hand to give her the strength to tell him whatever it was that he needed to know. "I promise you solemnly that whatever happens between us, I will not tell anyone what you tell me now." The look in her eyes said she believed him and he could see her shaking. Whatever it was, it was life-threatening to her, and that was good enough for him. He loved her. "What is it, Alex? Don't be afraid," he whispered.

"I'm not who or what you think I am." He had no idea what she meant and looked mystified, and he was in agony now too. Maybe it was worse. Maybe she was married to Green. He was almost certain now that Alex was the celebrated writer's lover, and Miles had only borrowed her, or stolen her for a few days. Clearly she wasn't free, or she wouldn't be so tortured now. And then she said it, in such a low, small voice that he barely heard her at first. "I'm Alexander Green."

He stared at her blankly, unable to absorb what she'd said, and sure he had heard her wrong. He thought she had said "I'm Alexander Green's," confirming his worst fears that he had fallen in love with another man's woman or wife, and a very important man to him now. And then she said it louder, more distinctly, seeing that he didn't understand her.

"I am Alexander Green." There was no mistaking what she said this time.

He stared at her in disbelief. "You're *what*? What do you mean? You can't be. He's a man." And that was one thing he knew for certain she was not. They had demonstrated that fully since they got there.

"I'm him. It's my pen name. He doesn't exist. I created an imaginary person, because my father told me no one would ever read crime books if they were written by a woman. I believed him, and I was nineteen when I wrote the first one and no one would have taken me seriously. So I invented the name 'Alexander Green.' I lie to everyone about it to protect it, but I don't want to lie to you," she said miserably. "I love you too much," she added, as tears rolled down her face, and he stared at her, too stunned to react at first, and then he wiped the tears from her cheeks and kissed her, while he tried to understand what she had said.

"Wait a minute. Who's at the house in London? He's there, for God's sake." For a sickening instant, he wondered if she was psychotic and trying to claim Green's identity and talent as her own. But she looked at Miles steadily, and her eyes didn't waver. If she was lying now, she was very good at it, or very sick.

"I'm at the house in London. There's no one else there. He doesn't exist." Miles observed her for a long beat and put his head down on the table and started laughing.

"Oh my God," he said, and raised his head to look at her again. "Oh my God, you are incredible. You write those amazing books that the whole world loves? A little girl like you? You scare everyone to death with the crimes, and write the most intricate plots I've ever read? You minx!" He couldn't stop laughing, and he got up and pulled her into his arms and held her, and she felt safe again. She trusted him completely, and now he could trust her too. She had told him the truth. "I swear, I will never, ever tell anyone. I thought you were going to tell me you're married to him, or his girlfriend, and you could never see me again." She smiled at what he said. She was as relieved as he was, having shed the burden of six years of lies and secrecy.

"You can't tell anyone," she reminded him again, with a look of panic.

"Of course not. And how brilliantly you created him, the famous recluse. Who else knows?"

"My agent, my editor, and the nuns. And I had to tell my publisher or they wouldn't buy any more books, after the first three. But they have to pay me ten million dollars if they talk." Miles walked around the room alternately laughing and shaking his head, so happy that he was free to love her as much as he did, and totally bowled over by the hoax she had perpetrated on the world. And she was smiling too. She was so glad that she had told him. A huge weight had been lifted from her heart. She didn't have to lie to him anymore. She could be honest with him.

"You've played the game masterfully. I never, never suspected it for a minute," he said, still grinning.

"But I lie all the time," she said unhappily.

"That's the price you have to pay for your success. And there is one, for all of us. You cannot ever tell, Alex," he said seriously. "Your readers would never forgive you for lying to them about being a man. They trust you and idolize you. They'll feel betrayed now if you tell them the truth. But I think you are absolutely the most brilliant woman I've ever met and I adore you."

"You're not mad at me for lying to you?"

"How could I be? What choice did you have? I'm honored that you trust me now. And you never slipped!"

"I almost do once in a while, but I'm pretty good at it by now. I've never told any man before, or anyone really, except Rose, Bert, and the nuns."

"I'm truly honored," he said again and meant it, and then looked at her with a broad smile. "Well, this certainly is interesting." He had huge respect for her, even more than he'd had before, and it showed.

They talked about her writing career late into the night, in the library after dinner, and then they went upstairs and made love again. She was an honest woman now, and felt as light as air. She loved sharing the secret with him, and he teased her about it and had brought out a bottle of fabulous champagne to celebrate her confession and the fact that she was not secretly Mrs. Alexander Green, which was the greatest relief of Miles's life.

He woke up in the morning smiling at her, and they went back to the city as late as possible, after riding in the hills one last time, and taking a long walk. He told her how much he loved her, and that he wanted to come back here with her as soon as they could get away.

And when he dropped her off at the house, she asked if he wanted to come in. He hesitated, not wanting to get caught, but there was no one to catch them now. She was living in the house alone.

"Are you sure Mr. Green won't mind?" he teased her.

"I'll talk to him. I handle him pretty well."

"You certainly do, you devilish little creature I adore," he said, and then followed her into the house, looking very circumspect, as though he were going to a meeting with the author himself at eleven o'clock at night. And as soon as they closed the door behind them, he kissed her, and they made love in the master suite, and then sat in the bathtub together for hours.

It was as though their two lives and hearts and souls had blended in the past three days.

"I don't know how I'm going to pretend we're just friends on the set tomorrow," she said wistfully while they were sitting in the bathtub drinking champagne.

"Are you serious? You've been leading a double life as an imaginary man for six years, you can do damn near anything . . . and you write the best fucking books in the world. And I'm going to make you the best TV series you've ever seen." He kissed her and grinned. "And then I'm going to make love to you for the rest of your life. You are the most wonderful woman I've ever known, even if you're an incredible liar." He laughed, set down his glass, and made love to her again.

Chapter 19

Miles left the house before she did the next morning, so her driver wouldn't see him, or his car, and he hoped no one else would either. They had agreed that in the future, he would put his car in the garage, particularly when he spent the night. And they were exemplary on the set, friendly, cordial, and professional. No one would ever have suspected they had spent three days together, had made love incessantly, confessed their love for each other, and he knew the deepest secret of her life. At most, they seemed like friends and nothing more.

The actors were in good form again, and the filming moved forward at a rapid pace. Too rapidly for them. They got another break in early November, and hadn't been back to his farm since the first time. There was snow on the ground, winter had come early, and they spent two heavenly days making love and trying to figure out their plans. They had made a pact that she would not tell anyone that she had shared her secret with him. It was better not to and would panic everyone. It was their secret now that he knew who Mr. Green was. And that he spent every night with her. He left every morning by seven, they worked together side by side, and he was back every night. She had never been happier in her life, and it was devastating for both of them when the filming was over. They had shot the whole first season of TV shows. It was mid-December, the nuns were expecting her in Boston for Christmas, and she had to make a decision whether to extend her lease on her apartment in New York. She hadn't been there since the summer.

Miles was going to Johannesburg to see his children for Christmas, leaving in a week, and he had another show to produce in January, which would take him several months, so he would have no time to come to New York to see her.

They spent their last days together after the show was finished, at his farm. The production company had given up the house, and allegedly Mr. Green had gone to Montana on his plane the day after the shooting ended, and she was going to move back to Claridge's, but disappeared to the farm with him instead. But this time it was not joyous, it was mournful. London was wearing all its finery for Christmas and looked festive, but they had to face that their time together was over. They couldn't be with each other every day on the set, fall asleep in each other's arms, or wake up side by side in the morning. And she was going to start a book in January in New York, while he worked on his new project in England. The thought of not seeing each other every day was agonizing for both of them, and when he left her at Heathrow for her flight to JFK, they both cried. Alex was in a daze, alternately crying and sleeping as she flew home, and when she got to her apartment, he called her the minute she walked in and they talked for an hour. He was leaving for South Africa in two days and she was taking the train to Boston after meeting with Rose for lunch. Her latest book was currently number one on the bestseller list and Rose wanted to celebrate with her, but Alex was pining for Miles.

Mother MaryMeg noticed immediately that Alex seemed serious and more grown up when she met her at the train station, although the others didn't see it. She asked if Alex was all right, and if everything had ended well in London, and Alex couldn't lie to her either.

"I fell in love with the producer," she said in a breathless voice as tears filled her eyes, and the mother superior's heart went out to her.

"And did something go wrong?" She hoped not, but Alex looked devastated.

"No, it was perfect. We love each other. But he lives there and I live in New York. We don't know what to do now."

"Is he married?" MaryMeg couldn't understand the problem.

"No, he's divorced."

"Do you think he'll ask you to marry him?" Her heart took a little leap, thinking about Alex moving to London permanently this time, but she wanted her happiness above all. And like any child, Alex had never belonged to them. She was on loan. She belonged to herself now, and possibly to Miles.

"He doesn't believe in marriage. He had a very bad divorce with his ex-wife. His kids live in South Africa with her, or his son does. And he's busy all the time. He's got a big project now after the holidays." Mother MaryMeg smiled as she listened to her.

"Well, that doesn't sound so bad. Except for the part about not believing in marriage. But that's probably just temporary after the divorce. If you love each other you'll work it out. I can't wait to meet him." Alex still had no idea when they would see each other again. Miles was frantic about it too.

She went to see Bert the next day with his Christmas present and she told him about Miles. He could see immediately how much she loved him. He remembered a love like that and envied her for a moment. But he was happy for her, if it lasted and was real.

"Beware of happiness," he warned her, as she looked at him as though he was crazy. "Misery is a wonderful thing for writers and will drive you to write your best books. But happiness will make you lazy and complacent. You'll forget about your priorities and sit around all dewy-eyed with the one you love. Happiness can destroy a career if you're not careful."

Alex decided that all the wine he drank had finally gotten to his brain. She told him all about the shooting of the TV series, which he found very interesting, except that she had fallen in love with the producer, which he assumed would be a passing thing for both of them and didn't take it seriously. She tried to tell him it was the Right Man at the Right Time, as he had promised, and he didn't want to believe her. He was in one of his cranky moods and didn't want to remember those feelings.

"You'll get over it," he told her after the usual bottle of wine, and Alex felt sorry for him, thinking that Bert went too far sometimes and was a sour old man, and he didn't understand how much they cared about each other or how fabulous Miles was. She forgot sometimes how much he had loved the young woman who had died, and that losing her had changed his life forever.

And when she visited Brigid, she found her pregnant again, with twins this time, which had come as a shock to her and they couldn't afford, but Pat's parents were still helping them. He had taken a second job, and they were going to buy a house with his parents' help. The twins were due in June, if she didn't have them early.

"You're turning into a baby machine," Alex said, laughing at her.

"I know," Brigid said proudly. She was still on extended leave and she admitted to Alex that she wasn't going back to work until the children were older. She wanted to be at home with them, and childcare would cost them more than she made at her job.

Two days after Christmas, Alex went back to New York. She had three days left to extend her lease with the owners of the apartment. They had been understanding, and she hadn't gotten around to it yet. She had no plans for New Year's Eve, and didn't want any. She was going to work, and prove Bert wrong that happiness would destroy her career. She was still annoyed at him. What a stupid thing to say, just because he'd had a terrible time and lost the woman he loved.

She was at her desk on New Year's Eve, working on an outline by hand on a big yellow pad and having trouble concentrating, when the doorman rang and told her there was a delivery. She wasn't expecting any, and wondered if Miles had sent her something. They had been talking to each other from South Africa every day, and he was as miserable as she was, and they still didn't know when he'd have time to visit her in New York, or have her come to London during a break. The project he was working on was all-consuming and ate up all his time.

She opened the door for the delivery, and found Miles in front of her with a bottle of champagne and an armload of Chinese takeout. He set it down on the table and pulled her into his arms. She screamed with delight and he spun her around.

"What are you doing here?" She beamed at him.

"I couldn't stand it anymore. Duncan wanted to be with his pals, I had nothing to do in JoBurg, and all I wanted to do was be with you." He looked at her seriously as he said it. "I have no right to ask you this, Alex, but would you move to London for me, and live with me? I'm paying my ex-wife a fortune. I had to pay her half the value of the farm and the London apartment, which wiped out my savings, and I don't want to sell the farm. I'm in no position to ask you to marry me, but I love you, and I want you with me for the rest of my life." It was all she'd wanted to hear and all she cared about.

"You don't have to have money to marry me, you know," she told him, but she wasn't pushing for marriage either, and she had her own money, mostly from her writing, and a small amount left from the sale of her father's house.

"I'm not going to marry you as a pauper," he said clearly. "And I'll have to help my kids for a long time. And I don't want you to be responsible for my debts if something happens to me, and you would be if we're married. The whole institution seems like a bad idea to me." He had made a lot of money in his life, and spent a lot of it financing his horse breeding and maintaining the farm, and then for his divorce, which was why he was so bitter about his ex-wife now—that and the fact that she had taken their son to South Africa. And she had just married her boyfriend, so she was staying, and he and his children would have to continue to fly back and forth to see each other, which was difficult and costly for him.

"I don't need to get married. I just want to be with you." She had no one to answer to but herself.

"That's all I want too. So will you move to London to be with me?" he asked again. She didn't need to think about it. She nodded. All she had to do was give up her apartment, pack her suitcases, grab her typewriter, and go. "How soon can you come?" She figured it out for a minute.

"In the next couple of weeks, sooner if I can. How long are you here for?"

"I have to go back tomorrow, we start shooting on the second." It was tight, but he had come to spend New Year's Eve with her.

They spent a magical night and saw the New Year in, and made plans for her arrival in London. She wanted to spend time at the farm, it would be a good place to write, and she could work in his apartment too, when he was working. It would be an enviable life, and she finally felt as though she had a home. Their plans were set by the time he left the next day.

When she notified the owner of her apartment that she was moving, they were sorry to hear it. She spent two days packing, and after that she went to see Rose just to touch base with her and talk about the new book.

"I smell a man," Rose said, smiling at her, and Alex nodded, and told her who it was, and Rose was pleased. He had an excellent reputation and an impressive career. He was a respectable person, and they loved each other. That was enough for her. And Alex was almost twenty-six years old. It was a reasonable age to find a good guy and settle down, even if not officially. Alex had told her they weren't getting married, and Rose said it didn't matter, and Alex agreed.

She spent the last few days in Boston, seeing everyone she loved there. She had dinner with Bert and hugged him. She spent several evenings with the nuns, and days with Brigid. And she flew to London from Boston on January 10. Miles was waiting for her at Heathrow and took her home to the apartment. Neither of them could believe how lucky they had been, how blessed to find each other, and how happy they were going to be together. Everything had worked out perfectly. More so than either of them could have dreamed.

*   *   *

She had a big bestseller that spring, a huge hit. So her work was going well and her publishers were pleased. And Miles's project went smoothly and ended in April, and he decided to take three months off so he and Alex could do some traveling and spend time on the farm. His production company believed that he had fallen in love with Alexander Green's assistant, and stolen her from him, which amused them. And they all liked Alex.

Brigid had the twins a month early, and they each weighed eight pounds, so it was a mercy she had had them early, a boy and a girl. She said she was done now. She had two boys and two girls, had just turned thirty-nine, and said she couldn't handle any more but loved the family she had. They had christened Steven without her, but one of their friends stood in for Alex as godmother.

Alex finished her new book that summer. It took her longer than usual, after spending plenty of time in bed with Miles when he came home from work. And Bert worked with her on the editing as he always did. They sent the material back and forth between Boston and London. Bert said the book was her best, and Rose agreed. And Miles loved it too. So happiness was not destroying her career after all, she reminded Bert, and he growled.

The series was on the air in the fall, and had solid ratings and was becoming popular. They had been signed for a second season, and were shooting it with the same actors. Alex was still consulting but the screenwriter was doing most of the work, with scripts being sent by fax and email to Alexander Green.

Time continued to rush by. Alex wrote more than ever, always working with Bert to learn more, write better each time, and tighten her plots. She drove herself hard, as always.

They spent time at the farm whenever they could, and luckily

Madeleine and Duncan, Miles's children, liked her, and his ex-wife calmed down once she remarried and didn't hound Miles for money all the time, which was a relief, although maintaining the farm cost a fortune. At one point Miles was considering selling it, and Alex helped him with an important amount that made it possible for them to keep it after all. He was embarrassed that she had to do it, but it was either that or sell the home that they loved.

Miles came to visit the nuns with Alex after they'd lived together for six months. They all thought him handsome and charming and Mother MaryMeg approved, although she had reminded him pointedly that they could get married in the chapel any time, and he had politely agreed, but they had no plans to marry.

He thought Bert was a character, and they liked each other and got drunk together one night without Alex. They drank tequila and rum and suffered fiercely the next day, which Alex said served them right. And she took Miles to meet Pat and Brigid, which was like going to the zoo. The kids were crying, the babies had to be nursed at the same time, Pat was looking frazzled, you couldn't hear yourself talk in their living room. It was like being inside a tornado, but Brigid looked blissful surrounded by her babies, and Miles looked shaken when they left.

"Wow, if one ever needed a reminder why having children will drive you insane, she would be it." He was glad that Alex didn't want any, and felt that his two were enough. She hadn't changed her mind about it, and he hoped she never would. She loved his children, enjoyed them when they saw them, and didn't seem to want her own.

It was hard to imagine where the years went, as Alex wrote novels and Miles produced TV shows. The series based on her book was on the air for three seasons, and then two of the main stars wanted out to do a Broadway play and a movie, and the show had to end without them, which was the fate of most shows like it. The best thing about it was that she and Miles had met and fallen in love as a result.

Miles gave Alex a thirtieth birthday party, and all their London friends came, including Fiona and Clive, who had three small children by then. Alex still had lunch with her when she was in London and Fiona had time.

The next year passed quickly, and there wasn't a single thing about their life that either of them would have changed.

Alex continued to help him with the expenses of the farm. She turned in a book a year and they were published every Christmas and went straight to number one every time. The nuns still prayed they would get married one day, but there was no sign of it. And Mother MaryMeg never entirely gave up hoping.

They had been together for six years when Alex was thirty-one, and much to their amazement, Miles was forty-seven, which seemed hard for both of them to believe.

They had a particularly busy spring. Duncan graduated from Oxford, and Madeleine announced the previous Christmas that she was getting married that summer, at twenty-three. Miles thought she was too young and Alex agreed with him, but she was engaged to someone from an important family in South Africa, and her mother was pushing hard for it. They owned diamond mines and her fiancé gave her a fifteen-carat engagement ring, which Miles disapproved of and thought was vulgar, and Madeleine's mother thought was fabulous.

Plans went ahead for the wedding, and just before they left for Johannesburg, Miles got sick. He came down with a particularly bad flu and high fever and still felt rotten afterward. He was barely well enough to travel, and Alex was worried about the long trip. She insisted he go to the doctor again and they ran some tests. His physician didn't like the results, but there was no time to do more, and they promised to come again when they got home. Miles kept saying it was ridiculous and he was fine, but he didn't look it.

He barely got through the wedding and nearly collapsed before he walked his daughter down the aisle. Alex sat with him in the rectory until she was sure he was all right, and she talked to him about it later. She was scared.

"Don't be silly. It was a very emotional moment, any father would have nearly fainted, especially when I got the bill." The wedding had cost a fortune, money Miles didn't have. He was mortally embarrassed, and Alex told him not to worry about it. She gave him a check for what he owed his ex-wife. Alex was still carrying a lot of the expenses at the farm. Miles had been low on money for a while. His production company hadn't been doing well, three of his best TV shows had folded, and he wasn't getting as much work as before. There were new faces on the scene. It was a business for young lions and wolves, younger men were putting shows on the air more aggressively, and with subjects that had shock value and were more controversial. Miles remained locked into a previous style of TV which was less popular now.

As a result, Miles's income suffered and the farm became increasingly expensive to run. Alex always shored things up for him, and she didn't mind. She made enough money for both of them, and invested quite a bit of her money, so she could afford to help him and was happy to do it. She had been luckier than most, and was willing to share the wealth with him. And it was her home now too. He was so good to her, and they loved each other so much.

They went back to the doctor when they got home to London after the wedding and he ran more tests, PET scans, MRIs and other scans, and extensive blood work. Miles insisted it was unnecessary but he did it to humor Alex. Miles didn't look well, and Alex was desperately afraid that something serious was wrong.

They went to his doctor together when his physician had the results. He asked them to come in, and neither of them expected the kind of news they got. Miles had stage 4 pancreatic cancer. It had snuck right by them, and when Alex spoke to the doctor alone the next day, he told her honestly that the prognosis wasn't good.

"He only has a few months," he said regretfully, while she felt like someone was choking her. "Six months, maybe three. You can't predict these things, it could be less, or he could surprise us and hang on for a year." Surprise us? A year? Alex wanted him to live forever, not three months to a year. She could no longer conceive of a life without him. It was unimaginable that Miles was dying. That wasn't possible. The doctors couldn't let that happen. They had to be wrong.

Miles agreed to try an aggressive program of radiation first to shrink whatever tumors there were on his pancreas, and then chemotherapy to kill the cancer cells. It was in his liver too. They started immediately and he was desperately sick. He was exhausted from the radiation, and then throwing up all the time from the chemo. His hair fell out, he lost a shocking amount of weight, and some days he couldn't get out of bed. He was doing it for Alex, hoping to get more time with her, and his children, and maybe even to cure the disease, which the doctor said would not happen. The cancer was too advanced. He lay in bed sometimes, just holding Alex's hand, too weak to say anything to her except that he loved her. They were the worst six months of his life, but he was still alive at the end of them, and they gave him a brief respite from the chemo. Then a spot appeared on his kidneys in a PET scan, and they started all over again, and gave him transfusions to improve his blood count.

Alex had told the sisters at St. Dominic's and asked them to pray for him, which they were doing ardently. When they finally told Madeleine and Duncan, they visited him as often as they could. Madeleine lived in South Africa with her new husband, but she spent two weeks in London with them. And Duncan was working in London, so he came to see Miles almost every night. There was nothing any of them could do for him except pray and love him. And Alex did a lot of both. She never left him for a moment. She stayed at the hospital on a cot in his room when he had to spend the night or was too sick to leave after a treatment. She was grateful now that she didn't have children. All her strength and force and energy and time and love went into Miles, willing him to get better. If love could extend his life, he would live forever. She loved him so much and fought so hard alongside him to make him well again.

She had been halfway through writing a book when they got the diagnosis, and she called Bert immediately to tell him that she had to put the edit on hold. She couldn't work and take care of Miles. They were ahead of schedule, so she wasn't worried. Bert was sorry to hear the bad news, and wished Miles the best. Miles was a good guy and Bert liked him. Bert had stayed with them several times at the horse farm in the past six years, when he had to do work with Alex, and he loved the place. And Bert had finally agreed that Miles was the Right Man at the Right Time. It had taken Bert years to admit it, because he saw himself as the champion and protector of Alex's career. He was aware that Miles knew the truth about her pseudonym and had for several years, and Bert trusted him. Miles had never divulged her secret or even hinted at it, and he won Bert's respect forever.

She had also warned Rose that she might be late with the book, but she had to focus on Miles, and Rose understood completely. Everyone who knew them admired Alex for what she was doing. She devoted herself selflessly and a thousand percent to her man and his recovery from the cancer. Rose notified the publisher that there was a delay, and they were understanding about it. And then as the doctors started more aggressive treatment again, Alex got sick, and suddenly they were both throwing up after his treatments. The stress had finally gotten to her. But she didn't want him to know how ill she felt, and she couldn't give in now. She had to keep on going. His doctor saw Alex at the hospital one day while Miles was getting a transfusion, and she was green and sweating profusely, with perspiration running down her face as she fought not to faint or throw up.

"How are you doing, Alex?"

"I'm fine," she said, as her eyes rolled back in her head and she fainted. Miles was at the lab and unaware of it, as his doctor took Alex into a room and examined her. Christmas had come and gone by then, and all they focused on were his treatments. Alex had no time for herself and didn't want any.

"What's going on with you?" the doctor asked her.

"I'm fine. It's just stress. It's nothing."

"You're under the worst stress that someone can be under. The man you love is dying."

"He's not dying, he's sick," she said with a steely look.

"You're going to have to face it." He wondered if that was why she was sick, because she was refusing to accept it. "May I run some blood tests on you, Alex? Even a simple blood test might tell us a lot. You're probably anemic." She was thirty-two years old, and otherwise healthy, but she looked terrible and she knew it, and she didn't sleep at night, watching him. She was afraid he would slip away or need her so she barely slept.

"You can do a blood test, but I'm fine," she said stubbornly. "And don't say anything to Miles about it." The doctor nodded, ran a blood panel on her, and had the results the next day. He called Alex into his office while Miles was being checked, and she left him with the nurses. The doctor looked at her seriously and asked her to sit down.

"I think we have a situation here, and I'm not sure how you'll feel about it. I'll do whatever I can to help you. The blood test tells me that you're anemic, but there's an underlying issue." He gazed straight at her. "You're pregnant."

"I'm what? I can't be." Knowing how sick her husband was, the doctor wondered if it was somebody else's baby. People did strange things in stressful situations, and he knew they weren't married, although he could see how much she loved him. "That's not possible," she said, looking vague.

"When was your last period?" he asked her, and she thought backward.

"I don't know, it was after the diagnosis, or right before. I don't think I've had one since. And that was four and a half months ago, but I've always been irregular."

"Were you and Miles sexually active then?"

"For the first couple of months, but not in the last three or four, he's been too sick."

"So if you're pregnant with Miles's baby, you could be four or five months pregnant. Is your abdomen enlarged?"

"I thought I was bloated from stress," she said with tears in her eyes. How could she have a baby now, if Miles was dying? How could she bring up a child without him?

"You need to see your gynecologist as soon as possible to figure out how pregnant you are. I won't say anything to Miles about it."

"Please don't, he'll worry about me." She went back to Miles then and said nothing about the test. The only questions were how pregnant she was and what she was going to do about it. She couldn't have a baby now. She'd never even wanted one before.

She called her gynecologist the next day and asked for an emergency appointment. When she went in, her doctor had no trouble feeling the pregnancy. They did a sonogram in her office and Alex cried as the doctor watched the screen.

"You are pregnant, Alex. The computer says you're four and a half months pregnant, the baby is due in late May, early June, and the heartbeat is strong." Alex could hear the rhythmic beep of the monitor, as the doctor turned the screen so she could see it. The baby looked fully formed, and she could see its heart beating. "It's too late for a normal abortion. Given your situation now, if you want one, I'll apply to the hospital board for a psychiatric justification, that you are not mentally strong enough to have the baby. I'll do that if you want." Alex thanked her as tears poured down her cheeks. "Do you want to know the baby's sex?" Before she could stop herself, Alex nodded and the doctor told her. "It's a little girl." It only made Alex cry more. If she had an abortion now, she would know she had killed a baby girl. And she didn't want Miles to know about it. He was dealing with enough, fighting to stay alive. If he were to see this baby born, he would have to live till June. Four and a half more months of agony and treatment for him. And she had nothing to give a baby now, she was giving every ounce of love and energy she had to him.

She left the doctor's office and went home to drive Miles to get another transfusion. He felt better afterward, as he sometimes did. She took him out to lunch in a wheelchair, and he picked at a salad while she ate nothing. She was feeling sick, and all he wanted to do was go back to bed. While he slept that afternoon, she thought about their baby, trying to decide whether or not to have the abortion. It was a living, moving being inside her. How could she kill it? It looked like a baby on the screen.

By sheer bad luck, Rose called her that afternoon and asked if she had any news about when she would finish the book she had been working on when Miles got sick. Alex explained to her that there was no way she could work on the book. Miles was in no condition for her to leave him for a second, she couldn't concentrate or write, and now she was having health problems herself.

"Nothing serious, I hope," Rose said, sounding concerned.

"No, just stress. This is very hard." Alex knew she wouldn't get any money if she didn't deliver the book.

"I think if this goes on much longer," Rose said regretfully, "your publisher is going to want some money back, until you have time to finish the book, and it doesn't sound like you have time for that right now."

"How much will they want?"

"A million dollars," the first payment of the advance on her last contract. The truth was that she had no idea when she could work again. Her priority was Miles. Alex had the money in the bank, but it was going to eat most of her savings. She had invested some money in the stock market, and it hadn't done well and she'd lost half of it. She still got royalties periodically, but the big money was always the advance. And the farm continued to chip away at her savings too.

"I'll pay them if they want it," Alex said nobly. She couldn't work now. There was no question of it. She wanted to take care of him.

"Let's wait till they ask," Rose said kindly. "Take care of yourself, Alex."

"I need to take care of Miles," she said firmly.

"Take care of both of you," Rose said, and Alex thought, "All three of us." There were three of them, whether Miles knew it or not.

She spent two weeks agonizing over the decision, and lay in bed awake every night after he went to sleep. She could feel the baby moving, now that she knew what it was.

Miles had a bad reaction to a treatment two days later, his heart stopped and they started it again and kept him in the hospital for three days. He rallied and they let him go home, and at some point while Alex watched them use the defibrillator on him, and when he opened his eyes and smiled at her, the decision was made. She wanted his baby. She told him about it that night. He looked panicked.

"Can you manage that right now? I don't want you to get sick. How can you be pregnant now? I can't do anything to help you." Tears of frustration and sadness ran down his cheeks, and hers.

"I want our baby. I love you," she said, sobbing.

"I love you too. You're a brave woman."

"We're brave together." She put his hand on her belly and he could feel the baby move, and he smiled through tears of joy this time, and then he kissed her.

She had no time to focus on the pregnancy, only on him, but the checkups were fine and the baby was growing. She hadn't told the sisters yet or anyone, and at Easter Miles looked at her with her big belly. He was looking haggard and was still on chemo but he was hanging in. It had been nine months since his diagnosis. He was defying the odds, but he was not getting better. And she was seven months pregnant.

"I think I have to make an honest woman of you," he said quietly, and then he pulled himself out of their bed and got down on one knee. "Alexandra Winslow, will you marry me? Do I have to propose to Alexander Green too?" he teased her, and she dragged him back into bed.

"Yes, I will marry you." She was smiling at him. "Where and when?"

"Well, you look like you're going to pop any minute, so I think there's no time like the present. Name the day and the place and I'll be there." She was touched that he'd asked her. She called Mother MaryMeg and told her and she was relieved. She told her again that they were praying for Miles every day. And then Alex told her about the baby, which made MaryMeg doubly glad that they were getting married.

They got married at the registry office, an old school friend of Miles stood up with him, and Fiona was Alex's witness as her oldest friend in London. Fiona was heartbroken to see the condition Miles was in, and shocked to realize that Alex was pregnant.

"Will you be able to manage afterward?" Fiona whispered after the ceremony.

"I'll have to, won't I?" Alex said in a strong voice. Things had been even harder recently. Her publisher had finally asked for the return of their million-dollar advance, which Alex had sent them, and she never stopped signing checks for the farm, which cost a fortune. There was always some repair or problem, especially without Miles to oversee it. Money was getting tight. He was desperately sick. She wasn't writing and hadn't in months, he had run out of money and his only asset was the farm, which Alex had sunk her savings into, and she was having a baby and had no idea when she could work again.

But they celebrated their marriage that night quietly at home in bed. He had a sip of champagne, and she lay next to him, and he ran a hand over her belly and felt the baby. All she wanted now was for him to be alive when she was born. They had already picked out a name. Desiree, which meant desired. She never wanted there to be any doubt in her daughter's mind later about whether or not they had wanted her. Desiree Erica Mila, for Alex's father and Miles. They had gotten it all in since there would never be another.

Miles slid slowly downhill in the next two months. There were no brutal changes, but many subtle ones, as he ran out of time. He slept most of the day, as Alex sat next to his bed and watched him. They diminished the dose of chemo he was getting since it wasn't helping and made him so ill. Alex never gave up and wouldn't let the doctors give up either, but Miles seemed ready to let go, and he was very peaceful. Their focus was on the baby about to be born, less than what was happening to him, and he rubbed Alex's back when she was tired. She was with him every night.

Bert had called Rose to see what was happening. He didn't want to bother Alex. Rose knew about the baby by then and told Bert.

"Do you think she'll ever go back to work?" He hated to see her waste a career like hers, and a talent.

"She'll have to eventually, but she can't focus on that now. Her husband is dying and she's about to give birth." It couldn't get much worse in his opinion, and he didn't want to call her with Miles so sick.

He knew all Alex wanted to do was be with him and share each precious moment left to them, so he sent her encouraging emails, just to touch base with her, but not intrude. And Rose did the same.

Desiree's timing was perfect. Miles was at the hospital for chemo, and Alex was with him, lying next to him on the bed, when she felt the first labor pains and her water broke a few minutes later. They wheeled her up to labor and delivery on a gurney, with Miles on his own bed wheeled along beside her, and the nurses put his bed next to hers so he could help her. He was holding Alex's hand as she pushed Desiree into the world, all six and a half pounds of her. She was tiny and exquisite. And the nurses said they had never seen such an easy delivery. Alex had barely made a sound, and she and Miles cried when they saw their baby. She was a beautiful little girl with her mother's perfect features and her father's pale blond hair. And every part of her was delicate and lovely. The nurses carefully handed her to her father so he could hold her, as Alex lay next to them and watched them.

Duncan came to see his sister that night and said she was very pretty. And Fiona came and cried when she saw her. Alex had asked Brigid and Fiona to be her godmothers, and Alex called Brigid and the nuns that night to tell them Desiree had arrived and she was beautiful. And as she held her in her arms, Alex knew she was the best thing she'd ever done, and Miles's most precious gift to her.

The three of them went home two days later to the London apartment, with a baby nurse to help them. There were nurses on duty for Miles by then too. He was very tired and slept as much as the baby, while Alex lay in bed with both of them.

Desiree was five days old on a brilliantly sunny June day. The baby nurse tucked her into her lacy white bassinet and wheeled her away to her room, while Alex held Miles in her arms. He glanced up at her and smiled, and took his last breath as she cradled him, and then he was gone. He looked so peaceful lying there, and she lay with him for a long time until one of the nurses came into the room and saw what had happened. Alex stayed with him until they took him away a little while later, and after he was gone, she held their baby. Desiree was the last gift from Miles. In seven precious years there had been so many gifts and blessings, but she was the sweetest of all.

They buried Miles in the old cemetery at the farm, and Alex and the baby stayed there afterward, while Alex decided what to do. It would be a good place for Desiree to grow up. Miles had wanted his children to have the farm forever, and Alex knew that she would see to it that she followed his wishes. She knew how much the farm meant to him and how much he loved it. And she loved it too. And after all he had done for her, keeping the farm in his memory seemed like the least she could do, whatever it took.

Chapter 20

After Miles's death, Alex gave up his London apartment, and the money helped her dwindling funds. She and the baby stayed at the farm and after the initial shock that he was finally gone, she met with her financial advisors and learned that the situation was much worse than she had expected. Her stock portfolio had shrunk to almost nothing. She had returned the million-dollar payment to her publishers for failure to deliver the last book. She was nearly a year late when she returned it. And giving them back their money had left a huge hole in her finances. She still got royalties, which helped, but there were no payments for new books, and there wouldn't be until she started writing again. The money had flowed only out and not in for the past year with Miles so sick, and she had stopped working. She had a half-finished book in her desk, but hadn't had the time or heart to touch it. And she felt even less able to now.

Miles's horse-breeding operation ate up all her cash, and every time she turned around, she had to write another check. The obvious solution was to sell the farm and the horses, get an apartment in London, and start writing again. Most of what she had saved was gone. She had been lending Miles money for years, and helping to keep the farm running. His production company had been failing, either through bad management or lack of work. He had never made the kind of money she did, and she had never begrudged him a penny of what she'd given him. She knew she could barely squeeze by with what she had left, and then she discovered that Miles had left two million dollars' worth of debts, some of them attached to his production company and some of it from the racehorses he'd bought, and the stallions he'd used for his breeding lines, all of which had cost far too much. It was why he had never wanted to marry her, so she wouldn't be saddled with his debts, but now she was anyway, and she had to figure out a way to pay them. There was no way she was going to sell the farm, she had already made that decision, and she loved it as much as he did. It was their home, and she wanted to preserve it for the children. But she had to find a way to support it, and to pay his debts, and for her and Desiree to live in the meantime.

She found a local girl, Maude, to help her with the baby, and contacted the dealers Miles had used to purchase his horses. She sold those she could privately through agents, and put the rest up for auction. She kept five of the Thoroughbreds to ride, but got rid of all the others, and she reduced the staff to two young stable hands who were knowledgeable about horses. It took six months to sell the horses, but she was amazed by how much money it brought her.

She got a mortgage on the farm, since the property was valuable, and little by little and month by month she paid off his debts. It took her two years to do it. She tried writing once or twice, but she just couldn't concentrate. All she did was go over figures and numbers, bank statements and bills. She dreamt of them at night or woke up at four A.M. to calculate it all again. And every time she tried to get back to work, her mind went blank and she sat staring at the paper, and she went back to the stack of bills again.

It was three years after Miles's death before she could see her way clear, and didn't panic every time she saw a bill come in. She had enough money in the bank to support them for a while. Desiree was a chubby three-year-old by then, running everywhere and chattering to her mother.

Alex hadn't had a book published in almost three years. There had been countless stories at first about why Alexander Green had stopped writing. Was he ill? Was he dead? Had he been killed? Was he the victim of a crime? Did he have a stroke? There were avid fans pleading for answers. And Alex offered none.

She spoke to Bert from time to time, and he begged her to start writing again.

"I can't, Bert. I don't know why. Something stops me."

"You went through too much," he said kindly. "It will come back. Just give it time." But how much time? Miles had been gone for more than three years, and it had taken that long to get a handle on his debts and right the ship again. "It will start again when you stop pushing."

"What if it never comes back and it's gone forever?" She had no ideas anymore. She couldn't concentrate. All she could do was run the farm and take care of her daughter. Alexander Green appeared to be dead. Her publishers were shocked.

"Go somewhere, take a trip, come back to Boston. Get some air," Bert suggested. But it felt overwhelming to go anywhere without Miles.

"I shouldn't really spend the money to travel," she said to him. She had to be careful, there was no money coming in except for a few remaining royalty payments on the old books that continued to sell. She was relieved to have sold the horses. Even if Miles had loved them, they needed the money more. At least she had been able to preserve the property, the land he loved so much.

She hadn't spoken to Rose Porter in a year, because she had no book to sell, and Alex hated disappointing her. She felt like a has-been. The ideas for her thrillers had stopped coming. Bert said that when it came back, the books would be better than ever, but she no longer believed him. The dry spell had gone on for too long. She no longer had a burning desire to write. She couldn't.

The joy of her life was Desi now. They went on long walks. She traded a mare for a pony and taught her how to ride, holding her in the saddle. She called Brigid from time to time late at night, and her children sounded like hellions, but at least she had stopped at four, and was enjoying them immensely. Alex talked to Fiona occasionally too, but hadn't been to London in two years, and didn't want to go. She had retreated from the world.

Miles had been gone for four years when she started having ideas again. She just had bits and pieces and snippets. She jotted it all down in notebooks, and put them away in a locked drawer. Maybe she would write again one day, although it seemed unlikely.

She called Bert and told him what she was doing, writing in her notebooks and saving them. He told her that the sleeping giant was waking up. And she would know when the time was right to start writing again. She still didn't believe him and ignored what he said.

"What makes you think I can still do it? I think I've lost it, Bert." She was sure of it.

"You can't lose it, Alex. Your talent is too big to disappear like that. It's all about timing. And it's all cooking somewhere inside.

Something will get you going again." She wanted to think it was true but she didn't. She missed the days of being able to write effortlessly, but that was long gone.

When Desiree turned five, Alex hadn't talked to Bert in a while so she called him, just to say hello. There was no answer. She called him the next day, and still got nothing. She wondered if he'd gone on a trip, but he never did. She got an odd feeling about it, and called Rose Porter the next morning. She came on the line quickly.

"I was just going to call you," she said in a subdued voice.

"Have you talked to Bert lately? I've been calling him for two days. The message machine isn't on and he's not answering." Rose was silent for a moment at her end.

She didn't know how to tell her, but she knew she had to. "I wanted to talk to you today. I was worried about him too. I don't know why, but I have his landlady's phone number. I called her yesterday. He had an accident two days ago. He slipped on the sidewalk and hit his head on the curb. It was a freak accident." Alex felt sick as she listened.

"Where is he now?" she asked, sounding panicked, but not wanting to know the end of the story. "Is he at the hospital? Is he okay? Did he have a concussion?"

"Alex," Rose said in a strong firm voice. "It's over. Bert is gone. He died instantly when his head hit the curb." There was silence at Alex's end as she tried to process what Rose had told her, but her brain didn't want to. What Rose had just said couldn't be true. He couldn't be gone. She needed him. She loved him like a father. She was thirty-eight years old and had known him for exactly half her life.

"Are you sure?" she said in a whisper.

"Yes, I'm sure . . . I'm so sorry." Alex was more than sorry, she was devastated. She couldn't imagine a world without him, any more than she could a world without Miles, and now they were both gone. They had left her alone, just like her father.

"I have to go," Alex said, unable to talk to Rose any longer. She sat in a chair in her room crying for a long time, and Desiree came to find her. She was just back from playing in the garden, and saw Alex with tears running down her face.

"Mama's crying?" her beautiful little blond child asked, and Alex nodded. There was no point hiding it from her. She couldn't. Another of the most important people in her life had disappeared.

"Mama's sad," she said, pulling the child onto her lap and holding her in her arms. Desi was all she had now. Everyone else was gone, except people who were so far away. She hadn't seen the nuns in years, or Brigid, not since Miles died, and now Bert was gone forever.

"Don't be sad, Mama," Desi said and kissed her where the tears were, and Alex smiled at her, and went to make her lunch. She thought about Bert all day, and fell asleep thinking about him, and in the middle of the night, she sat bolt upright, as though he was sitting in the room with her, and she knew what she had to write. The story came out in one piece, already finished in her head, and she hadn't even begun it.

She sent Desi out to play with Maude the next day, sat down at her desk, and pulled out her Smith Corona. The case was dusty. She hadn't touched it in years. For five years the sleeping giant in her, as Bert called it, had been in a coma, and now it was wide awake, turned into a dragon in her chest, fighting to get out, and nothing could stop it. She wondered if Bert was doing it to her, if he had willed it to happen, or if it was simply time. He had said something would get her going again. And ironically the something was him. She couldn't stop writing from the moment she sat down.

She wrote day and night for three weeks, and then she sent Rose Porter two chapters. She called Alex as soon as she read them.

"That is one fantastic story." She sounded thrilled and so was Alex. It felt like the best book she'd ever written.

"I started writing the night you told me about Bert. I think he gave me the story."

"No, you gave you the story, Alex. It's all in there, you just have to find it again."

"That's what Bert told me. I thought it was gone."

"No," Rose said firmly, "it's better than ever. It will never be gone. Keep writing."

Alex kept writing for the next four months with no one to show the book to. She couldn't send it to Bert now, or follow his directions. But she could hear him in her head, telling her what to do, when to stop and when to move ahead, when to end a chapter or write something really vivid with details of brutal murders. The story just rolled out of her head and onto the page, and she couldn't hold it back. And on the last page, with a shocking exposé at the end, she knew it was finished, she didn't need anyone to tell her. Not even Bert. And she knew he would have loved it.

She spent two more weeks polishing it and making small corrections. It was surprisingly clean, and then she scanned and emailed it to Rose Porter.

She read it the next day, in one sitting. She finished at 3 A.M. and called Alex. It was 8 A.M. in England.

"You're back!" Rose said, sounding elated, as Alex sat smiling, staring into space. She knew it too. She had found the magic again, the secret. After five years of silence, Alexander Green had come alive again, returned from the dead, stronger than ever. "I'm sending this to your publisher tomorrow. And you'll be paid three million this time."

"That would be nice," Alex said, smiling broadly. But it wasn't about the money. It was about the dragon in her that wasn't dead but only sleeping, and had roared to life again.

Rose told the publishers she wanted three million per book and a four-book contract, which made Alex nervous at first, but now she knew that she could do it, and so did her publishers. They all agreed, it really was the best book she'd ever written. She was better than ever. The shock of Bert's death had brought her back to life. The pain of losing Miles had put her to sleep, and now every fiber of her being was tingling as though there was an electric current passing through her body.

She walked out into the garden with Desi after Rose called to tell her she got the four-book contract for her asking price. After scrimping and saving, losing everything, and almost having to sell the farm, she was back with more money than she'd ever had. She had lost Miles and Bert, but now she had Desi. Life had a strange way of trading one blessing for another. It had worked out in the end, and she hadn't sold the farm. She knew Miles would have been proud of her. And now so was Bert.

Chapter 21

It took Alex two years to write the four books in her new contract. When the first book was published it was the biggest seller she'd ever had. She turned forty on the day she sent in her last book. It seemed a suitable way to celebrate her birthday. She dedicated the first one to Miles, the second to Bert, and the third to Desi, and she hadn't decided who to dedicate the last one to. She had already dedicated books to her father and the nuns over the years. But the last one in the contract wouldn't be out for eighteen months, so she had time to decide. And she already had an idea for another book, and possibly for another one after that. The ideas were flowing again, just as Bert had promised. She realized more than ever now how wise he had been. He had been gone for two years, and Miles for seven, and she was writing again. It had been a peaceful two years while she worked on the new books, in the same single-minded way she always had before. The books were deeper and stronger, as though she had learned something while her gift was dormant. And Bert had been right about something else too so long ago. The books were "cooking" even when she didn't know it and she thought the stove was off. The stove was never off, and there was always a book in her somewhere. That was the magic she hadn't lost, even when she thought she had.

The day after her birthday, she took a morning ride right after dawn. She felt free and alive and hadn't done that in years. She and Miles had always loved their rides together. It reminded her of the weekend they'd spent together so long ago, when he had brought her to the farm for the first time.

She was cantering back as the sun rose in the sky, when her horse stumbled and she slowed him to a walk, pulling him up in time. He was one of the few Thoroughbreds she had kept when she sold the others. He was a good ride, and she liked going out in the hills with him, and was sorry she hadn't done it in so long. She was walking back through the woods, giving him a rest, when she heard a horse coming toward them, and her mount shied sideways as a man came into view on a handsome stallion. The rider had dark hair like her own, and looked as surprised to see her as she was to see him. It was rare for anyone to come on their property, and she wondered who he was.

"Good morning!" he called out to her from the distance, so she would know he wasn't a poacher or a trespasser. He slowed his horse to a walk and came up beside her. "I'm sorry if I startled you." Alex's horse had calmed down again, and the rider looked slightly embarrassed. "I cut across your pasture. I do that sometimes, but I've never run into anyone." She noticed that he had a southern drawl.

"I don't ride very often anymore. I'd forgotten how nice it is this time of day." She smiled at him. And then she realized who he was. An American had bought the farm next to theirs two years before, she'd never met him.

"I hear you had some fabulous horses here a few years ago." He reined the stallion in and rode along next to her. His was an Arabian.

"We did have some nice ones. They were my husband's. I sold them seven years ago. It's been a while. He bred them."

"So I've been told." And then he decided to come clean with her. "I've been wanting to buy your south pasture since I bought my farm, but they tell me you're not interested in selling any of your land." Their horses were dancing as they stood and talked.

"That's true," she said.

"I'm Jerry Jackson. We're neighbors but we've never met. I have a stud farm in Kentucky and spend a lot of time there." She had heard that he had some of the best racehorses in the States, and had brought a number of them to England. One of his horses had won the Kentucky Derby the year before.

"Alex McCarthy," she introduced herself.

"You're American," he said with some surprise. No one had told him that.

"I've lived here most of the time for fourteen years, and before that in London for a couple of years." He thought she didn't look old enough to have lived anywhere for fourteen years as an adult. He guessed she was much younger than she was. She correctly estimated that he was in his late forties.

"This is beautiful country. I'd like to spend more time here. I've got business in London and try to get down here whenever I can," he said with an easy smile.

"My daughter and I actually moved here full-time from London seven years ago when my husband died. It's a good life." He nodded.

"How old is your daughter?" He was curious about her.

"Seven. She was five days old when her father died."

"Oh, I'm sorry." He apologized for bringing up a painful subject, and they rode on the path in silence for a few minutes. "I'd love to show you my stables sometime, if you're interested. It's a nice operation, and I've got some very fine horses here, since you know something about it."

"I don't know as much as my husband did." She turned to look at him. "You have racehorses, don't you?"

"I do, and a few I'm very proud of," he said as they reached a fork in the trail. She had to go to the right to get back to her barn. "Please come over sometime."

"Thank you," she said, and cantered off toward home.

She had breakfast with Desi after that and took her out to play in the garden, and she gave her a riding lesson that afternoon in the ring they still had in the barn. She was teaching her to jump, because Alex knew it would have pleased her father. He had taught Alex and turned her into a better rider, and she enjoyed instructing her daughter.

They had just come into the house after Desi's lesson when Jerry Jackson called her. Alex was surprised to hear from him.

"I thought I'd give you a call and see if you'd like to see the stables today."

Maude was there to bathe Desi and give her her dinner, and Alex was curious about Jerry's horses and his interest in her pasture. "I'd like that," she said. She had nothing else to do, and was taking a few days' break from her writing. She did that now, and wrote intensely once she got started, just as she always had.

"Come on over in ten minutes."

She took the road outside her property to the next farm, and turned into his driveway. It was a long drive to a stone house that was smaller than hers, but the grounds were impeccable, and the stables beautifully maintained, and she saw two grooms walking two spectacular horses.

Her host was waiting for her in the courtyard and escorted her into the stables, where she saw how meticulously they were set up. The horses in the stalls were among the best looking she'd seen, even better than those Miles had.

They looked around for half an hour, and she complimented him on the setup. He had restored the house and the outbuildings when he bought it. She and Miles had looked at the property when it was for sale, but it had been in terrible condition and would have cost a fortune to restore. Jerry had done a fabulous job.

"You did an amazing transformation." She smiled at him. "I saw what bad shape it was in before," Alex said with admiration, as they returned to the courtyard and walked slowly toward the house.

"It was a lot of work, but it was worth it. I love it here."

"So do I." She smiled and followed him through a side door directly into the library, which was a shortcut, and a moment later a man in a white shirt and black slacks brought in an enormous silver tea tray with a proper English tea, complete with perfect little watercress and egg salad sandwiches, and scones with jam and clotted cream. It looked delicious as he set it down on a table in front of them.

"I love the traditions here, it's all so civilized." Jerry smiled, and as he said it she noticed the book left open facedown on the coffee table that he'd been reading. It was one of hers, the first one from the new contract. It was the one that had broken the spell, when she first started writing again. He saw her glance at it, and laughed. "My favorite author. Alexander Green. He writes incredible crime thrillers. I'm addicted. His books are my drug of choice. I went into withdrawal when he disappeared for about six years, but now he's back, better than ever. This one is fantastic. Have you ever read him?"

"Actually," she couldn't resist tweaking him a little, "I think it's fair to say I've read them all." He looked pleased to have that in common with her.

"Aren't they fantastic?" he said, as he offered her the tray of sandwiches, and she took one and helped herself to a scone. "How did you get into reading crime thrillers?"

"My father. He started me on Nancy Drew, and kept ramping it up from there." It was a long way from Nancy Drew to Alexander Green, and he laughed.

He talked about his children then. He had three. "Two in New York, and one in L.A. They're grown up. One is still in grad school, the other two are married. They fled Kentucky when they left for college, and they're not interested in coming here. It's too quiet for them."

"I suppose I'll get to that point eventually with my daughter, but not for a while. She still likes it here, and I've really kept the property for her to enjoy one day. She'll probably hate it and head straight for London." But Alex loved it here now too. It was so full of memories of Miles and their days together. It suited her and was a great place to write, it was so peaceful. "My husband had two older children too. They both live in South Africa now, and haven't been here in two years."

"Once they fly the nest, it's all over," he said, with intimate knowledge of it. "And my ex-wife would have hated it here. She liked New York and Paris. This would have been much too quiet. And she's not fond of horses."

Alex laughed. "Well, then, she wouldn't like it here. You know, I was thinking today about your interest in my south pasture. I might be willing to sell it to you. We really don't use it anymore, now that we have fewer horses, and it borders your land. I don't think I'd miss it." She had enough land and had decided that she could give that one piece up to him. Having met him and seen his horses, she realized that it would be far more useful to him than it was to her.

"That's very good news." He looked pleased as he ate a scone himself, with jam and cream. "If you ever want to sell the whole property, I'd be interested in that too." He wanted to set up a real horse farm, like the one he had in Kentucky, and spend more time here.

"Now, don't get greedy. You'll have to settle for the south pasture," Alex said and he laughed again.

"Sorry. But I hear you have a wonderful house, with a moat and a lake."

"Why don't you come over and see it tomorrow, though not as a potential sale. It will be my daughter's one day. My stepchildren have no interest in it. And I'm afraid our tea is not as elegant as yours."

"I'd love to take a look," he said, and he was still intrigued by her knowledge of crime thrillers. She left a little while later and they set a time for him to visit her the next day. She invited him to come at four, so she could show him around. She liked him. She didn't know why, but she felt comfortable with him, as if they'd known each other before, and she was amused that he was reading one of her new books.

She was curious about Jerry Jackson. When she got home, she Googled him and sat reading about him for half an hour. Princeton undergrad, Harvard MBA, owner of several Kentucky Derby winners, his breeding farms were legendary, and their bloodlines. He had started several major corporations, was a well-known philanthropist, had an engineering degree, and had invented a laser that was used worldwide for medical procedures. He was a scientist, an engineer, and a businessman. He bred racehorses, was divorced, had three children who had attended Stanford, Yale, and Columbia, and he seemed like a pleasant, kind person. He was forty-nine years old. Reading about him was impressive and daunting. She couldn't think of anything he couldn't do.

And it was serendipity that he lived right next door and was such an interesting person *and* liked her books.

She spent her days and nights with Desi now, and never traveled anywhere to see her friends. She didn't get a chance to speak to intelligent adults, unless she called them in other cities, like Rose, Brigid and the nuns, or Fiona, living in a suburb of London. She still missed Bert acutely. And Miles beyond words.

Jerry arrived promptly at the appointed hour the next day, and said he loved her house. They walked around, looked at the moat, and wandered down to the lake, which had scared Alex when Desiree was little. She didn't want her to fall in, and she could have. But they never left her alone for a minute. They wandered through the gardens, and she had a maze. They looked in the barns briefly and he admired her horses, and then they walked into the house for tea. Hers was also set up on a silver tray—she had done it herself—but her house and lifestyle weren't as formal as his. She led a country life, and he was a man of many facets and great sophistication.

"All right," he said before he sat down to tea. "I want to see your collection of Alexander Green books."

"I don't keep them," she said breezily, and he looked shocked.

"I treasure mine forever. They'll be collectors' classics one day. He's right up there with some of the best crime writers of our time. How can you give them away?"

"So someone else can enjoy them," she said simply.

"You have a point." He hadn't thought of that before. "I'm too selfish. I want to keep them for myself, to read again." She smiled as he said it and didn't comment.

They enjoyed the tea and sandwiches she had made, and he asked her more about herself.

"Do you work?"

There wasn't much one could do far out in the country, except what she really did. She didn't want to lie to him, nor tell him the truth. "I write, or I did before my daughter was born. I took a number of years off after I had her and lost my husband, and now I'm writing again."

"I wish I had that talent," he said enviously. "Like Alexander Green. It takes an incredible mind to write thrillers like that. I can never guess the ending."

"Me neither," she said, grinning. "The murderer is never who I think it will be." She was telling him the truth. There were always surprises for her as she wrote the books too.

"It's an extraordinary gift. What kind of things do you write?" Jerry persisted.

"Mystery, crime." She didn't know what else to say, and she no longer wanted to hide what she wrote. And claiming she wrote women's fiction or romance novels would make her feel ridiculous, because it was so far from the truth.

"You'll have to let me read one." She nodded and changed the subject.

As he left, he invited her to dinner the next day. "My chef makes the best southern fried chicken ever. I brought him over from Kentucky, now he's more English than the English." They both laughed at that.

"That happens here. And thank you for the invitation. The British used to give wonderful house parties, for centuries, to make country life more interesting. Now we sit in solitary splendor and listen to the birds sing. I think they had the right idea." Alex smiled at him.

"I agree," he said. "I keep meaning to have friends here, but I never have time. I'm always too busy. And sometimes when I get here, I enjoy the peace and quiet and solitude. It's nice to have a break."

She'd had a five-year break after Miles died, and her life was still very quiet, but she didn't say it.

"What did your husband do?" He was curious about him too.

"He was a television producer, at one time for the BBC, then on his own. He produced TV series." She mentioned a few of them. Jerry knew them all, and was impressed.

"See you tomorrow," he said as he left. He was intrigued by her. There was something mysterious about her, and she didn't give much away.

She dressed carefully for dinner the next day in black slacks and a soft pink cashmere sweater. She looked very pretty, and they had a good time when she went to his house. And she agreed that the fried chicken was fabulous.

They went riding together again, and she checked out the south pasture with him. He made her a very decent offer for it, on the high side, and she accepted. He was a fair person, a nice man, and good company. And it was such a pleasure having an adult to talk to, and not just Desi or the babysitter. She loved her daughter, but missed grown-up conversations and companionship.

He asked her about her books again, one afternoon when he stopped by for coffee.

"You know, I Googled you so I could order one of your books, but I couldn't find you. Do you publish under another name?" She hesitated for a long moment, pondering the question, and then she made a decision and nodded. She was certain she could trust him. "What name is it? I'd really like to read one."

"You already have," she said with a mysterious smile.

"Have I? I don't think so." He looked puzzled.

"Alexander Green," she said simply and he laughed.

"Very funny. No, really, tell me." He was insistent. And then he saw the look in her eyes and grew serious. "Oh my God, you're Alexander Green?"

"Not exactly. He's a figment of my imagination, but I write under that pseudonym. I have since I was nineteen." He was stunned into silence as the full impact of it hit him.

"You're brilliant, Alex. Absolutely brilliant. You're my favorite author, my idol. You're a phenomenon." All his admiration was in his eyes.

"I'll give you an advance copy of my next one, if you like. But you can't tell anyone what I just told you. I only told my husband, other than the publisher, my agent, and my editor." Her heart ached for a moment when she mentioned Bert—it always did. She still missed him. "It's been a dark secret all my life. And a heavy burden at times. But I felt I couldn't write them under my own name. My age wasn't in my favor at the time, and my father suggested I write under a male pseudonym if I ever wrote a book. I followed his advice, and then I became stuck with it. I had no idea how complicated it would turn out to be. I stopped writing for about five years when my husband died. I had some dark years, and then I got back to work." She looked peaceful as she said it.

"I remember, I combed every bookstore for years, hoping you had a new book. And then you finally came out with a new one, and it's your best. You have a frightening mind," he teased her. "But also a fascinating one. I'm very flattered that you told me."

"I just wanted to be honest with you. I haven't told many people out in the world, just my husband. And the nuns I grew up with." She had told him about them on one of their walks in the garden, and he was touched by the story.

"I won't say a word, I promise. I'm truly honored. You deserve the recognition for what you've accomplished, though. It's a shame you can't have that, without jeopardizing your readership." As she listened to him, she realized that he wasn't jealous of her. He admired her. And as the thought crossed her mind, she heard Bert's words in her head, for the first time in a long time. The Right Man at the Right Time. And he would find her. Miles had. And now she had learned that she was living next door to this extremely accomplished, intelligent man. She looked at him as though seeing him for the first time. He had just thought of something too.

"I'm doing something that might be fun in a couple of months, while I'm here. I'm going to Ascot. I'm invited to sit in the royal enclosure. I have a horse running that day. Would you like to join me?" It was an extraordinary invitation, and she wanted to go with him.

"I'd love to come." Her face lit up as she said it. And she knew she'd have to go to London to get something to wear, and a fabulous hat to go with it, since everybody wore them there.

"It's a lot of fuss, but it's very entertaining." He was smiling at her warmly. He knew he'd be proud to go with her, especially with all he knew about her now. She was not just any woman. She had an amazing gift.

Alex went to London several weeks later, for the first time in years, and went shopping. She found a simple sky-blue silk dress with a matching coat, and after some searching, the hat she needed.

The night before the race, they both stayed in London at Claridge's and had dinner at Harry's Bar, where he was a member. She had let Miles's membership lapse years before, since she no longer lived in London, nor went there. It made her too sad without him. But she had a good time with Jerry.

And when they left the hotel to go to Ascot, he loved her outfit and complimented her, especially on the hat.

"You don't look like a woman who writes crime stories," he whispered as they got in the car.

His horse was a new one, and a long shot to win, the odds were ten to one, but it won. Alex had bet heavily on him and was thrilled. And so was Jerry.

Every royal was there that day, except the queen herself, who had the flu. But they got to ogle and watch and talk about them. He made her laugh and he introduced her to a great many people that he knew. It was a perfect day, and exactly right for the moment and the time in her life. Everything had its time, she thought to herself as she watched him chatting with friends and enjoying himself. He seemed like a good person, and he was very kind to her, and was proud to be with her, as she was with him. They rode back to their respective farms together, talking about the day.

And the day after Ascot, Rose called her.

"I have some big news for you," she said. "You're being given a very important award. The Mystery Writers of America want to give you a Grand Master Award." It was a very big honor, one of the highest in her field. "Who do you want to accept it for you?" Alex was startled by the question.

"I have to think about it." There weren't many people for her to choose from. Bert was gone, and Miles, whom she might have chosen. Bert probably would have refused. He didn't like formal receptions. "Would you mind accepting it for me?" she asked her agent.

"I'd be honored," Rose said, and meant it. Their association went back twenty years now, and although they weren't intimates or confidantes, they were good friends, and had accomplished great things together. Their talents and goals had complemented each other.

"Could I come too? As your guest. I'd love to see the ceremony, even though I can't pick up the award myself."

"You could, you know, accepting it for Mr. Green?"

"What if someone suspected who I was?"

"Why would they? And if you accept the award, you'd have the thrill of being part of the event. I think you should do it."

"I'll see. Let's go together, and I'll see how I feel when I'm there. When is it?" Rose told her the date. It was in New York, and a major event at the Pierre, in the Grand Ballroom. And then Alex thought of something. "Can I bring one other person?"

"Of course. I'll get three seats." She couldn't get enough seats for the nuns.

She drove over to Jerry's place after the call, and told him all about it. It was an important book award and he knew of it. He was very impressed and pleased for her.

"That's a huge deal, Alex! Congratulations!"

"Would you come?" she asked him softly. "With me, I mean. It's in New York." She told him the date, and he said he was free and had to be in New York that week anyway.

"Well, put it on your dance card." She looked shy as she said it.

"I most certainly will." She stayed for a while to talk to him, and he told her that it meant a great deal to him to go to the award ceremony with her, even if she didn't actually go onstage herself to accept the award, and someone else would. She said her agent was going to do it. But he was excited to be there with her.

"I think you should accept it yourself," he said, sounding very definite about it. "You can always pretend to be Mr. Green's assistant."

"That's what Rose said, my agent. I think it would feel odd. And it would be a shame to risk blowing my cover now, after all these years."

"It might be. But you deserve the glory of your accomplishments. You've lived in the shadows for a long time."

"I've had no choice except to live in the shadows." Alex wondered what Bert would say, or Miles, the two men whose advice she trusted most. "I'll think about it," she said to Jerry, but it didn't look like she'd do it. She had kept the secret for too long to throw caution to the wind now. Jerry insisted she could accept the award without exposing herself, as Rose had said.

Alex flew to New York two days before the ceremony so she could see Rose at her office to talk about the future books, meet with her publishers, and do some shopping. Jerry was already there, staying at the Four Seasons, and he was happy to see her. They had dinner at La Grenouille to celebrate, the night before the award ceremony.

The night of the award, Jerry met Alex in her suite at the Pierre. He was impeccably dressed in a dark blue suit, a tie, and a pale blue shirt. He looked like a banker. They walked into the event together, and no one paid any attention to her. Rose was waiting for them in a chic black dinner suit. Alex was wearing a navy Chanel cocktail dress she bought in London for the event.

The ceremony was long and impressive, as the honorees went up to receive their Edgar statues. Alex was the last one, and hers was for an extraordinary literary career and lifetime achievement.

"I feel ancient," she said to Jerry. "Listening to them, it makes me sound like I'm ninety." She was nervous and he squeezed her hand.

"And very accomplished," he added with a smile.

They called Alexander Green to the podium, and were aware he wasn't coming. Alex didn't stir as Rose stood up, ready to go, and suddenly Alex stopped her with a gentle smile, and stood up and moved forward.

Alex walked gracefully toward the stage, accepted the award, and thanked the commission on behalf of Mr. Green. A photographer took her picture holding it. It was a funny little statue depicting Edgar Allan Poe, with black hair, a blue shirt, and a black tie. She saw Rose and Jerry smiling proudly at her with tears in their eyes. And she could feel Miles and Bert and her father there with her.

They didn't announce her name when she collected the award. They didn't have to. She knew she had written the books and so did the people she loved, and now Jerry did too. It was a sign of her trust that she had told him. It would allow her to have an honest relationship with him, as she'd had with Miles.

It was a proud moment in her career. And Bert was right again. The Right Man had come along at the Right Time, twice in a lifetime, and both of them had found her. It was perfect timing.

She was beaming as she walked toward Jerry, holding the statue, and when she reached him, he kissed her.

"I love you, Mr. Green," he whispered, and they both laughed, as the entire room stood up and gave her the standing ovation she deserved. It was for Alexander Green, but it didn't matter. Alex, Rose, and Jerry knew it was for her.

TRAGEDY. DETERMINATION. TRIUMPH.

She didn't have her father or anyone else to protect her. All she had now was herself . . .

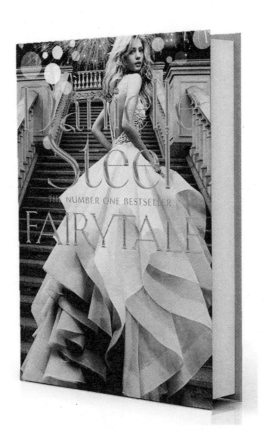